Cadderly could see the events in the room, but they were distant from him, somehow disconnected. Through a thick veil of smoky gray he saw his own body, standing very still, saw that Shayleigh, for some reason, had apparently gone down to the floor and was being pulled under the bed.

Cadderly sensed the danger back in the room, sensed that his elven companion was in trouble. He should go to her, he knew, go to the aid of his friends. He hesitated, though, and stayed clear of his corporeal form. Shayleigh was among powerful allies—Ivan and Pikel were moving, he could see, probably rushing to her side. Cadderly had to trust in them now, for he knew that if he left this realm, he would not soon find the strength to return, not in the desecrated library. He was looking for a spirit, and spirits were fleeting things. If he hoped to get Danica back, he had to find her quickly, before she took her place in the netherworld.

**Books by
R. A. Salvatore**

THE ICEWIND DALE TRILOGY
The Crystal Shard
Streams of Silver
The Halfling's Gem

THE DARK ELF TRILOGY
Homeland
Exile
Sojourn

THE CLERIC QUINTET
Canticle
In Sylvan Shadows
Night Masks
The Fallen Fortress
The Chaos Curse

**The Legacy
Starless Night
Siege of Darkness** (*August 1994*)

FANTASY ADVENTURE

The Chaos Curse

R. A. Salvatore

THE CHAOS CURSE

Random House and its affiliate companies have worldwide distribution rights in the book trade for English language products of TSR, Inc.

Distributed to the book and hobby trade in the United Kingdom by TSR Ltd.

Distributed to the toy and hobby trade by regional distributors.

Cover art by Jeff Easley.

FORGOTTEN REALMS is a registered trademark owned by TSR, Inc. The TSR logo, all TSR characters, character names, and the distinctive likenesses thereof are trademarks owned by TSR, Inc.

First Printing: June 1994
Printed in the United States of America
Library of Congress Number: 93-61469

9 8 7 6 5 4 3 2 1

ISBN: 1-56076-860-6

TSR, Inc.
P.O. Box 756
Lake Geneva, WI 53147
U.S.A.

TSR Ltd.
120 Church End, Cherry Hinton
Cambridge CB1 3LB
United Kingdom

To Ann and Bruce,
for showing me a different way
of looking at the world.

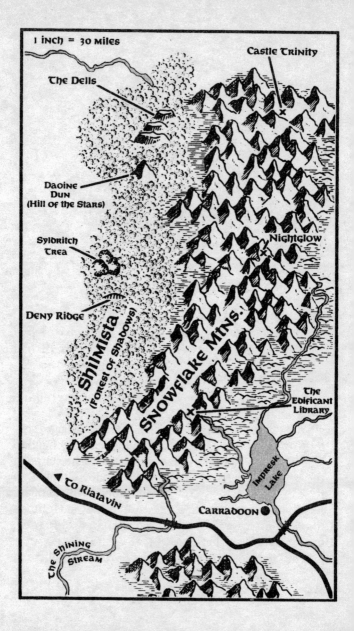

1 INCH = 30 MILES

Castle Trinity

The Dells

Daoine Dun
(Hill of the Stars)

Syldritch Trea

Deny Ridge

Shilmista
(Forest of Shadows)

Nightglow

Snowflake Mtns.

The Edificant Library

To Riatavin

Impresk Lake

Carradoon

The Shining Stream

ean Thobicus drummed his skinny fingers
on the hardwood desk before him. He had
turned his chair so that he faced the window, not the door, pointedly looking away
as a nervous and wiry man entered his
office on the library's second floor.

"You . . . you asked . . . " the man, Vicero Belago, stuttered, but Thobicus lifted a trembling leathery hand to
stop him. Belago broke into a cold sweat as he stared at
the back of the old dean's balding head. He looked to
the side, where stood Bron Turman, one of the library's
headmasters and the highest ranking of the Oghman
priests, but the large, muscular man merely shrugged,
having no answers for him.

"I did not ask," Dean Thobicus corrected Belago at

length. "I commanded you to come." Thobicus swung
about in his chair, and the nervous Belago, seeming small
and insignificant indeed, shrank back near the door. "You
do still heed my commands, do you not, dear Vicero?"

"Of course, Dean Thobicus," Belago replied. He dared
come a step closer, out of the shadows. Belago was the Edificant Library's resident alchemist, a professed follower of
both Oghma and Deneir, though he formally belonged to
neither sect. He was loyal to Dean Thobicus as both an
employee to an employer, and as a sheep to a shepherd.
"You are the dean," he said sincerely. "I am but a servant."

"Exactly!" Thobicus snarled, his voice hissing like the
warning of an angry serpent, and Bron Turman eyed the
withered old dean suspiciously. Never before had the old
man been so animated or agitated.

"I am the *dean*," Thobicus said, with emphasis on the
final word. "*I* design the duties of the library, not *Ca*—"
Thobicus bit back the rest of his words, but both Belago
and Turman caught the slip and understood the implications.

The dean spoke of Cadderly.

"Of course, Dean Thobicus," Belago said again, more
subdued. Suddenly the alchemist realized that he was in
the middle of a much larger power struggle, one in
which he might pay a price. Belago's friendship with
Cadderly was no secret. Neither was the fact that the
alchemist often worked on unsanctioned and privately
funded projects for the young priest, often for the cost of
materials alone.

"You have an inventory document for your shop?"
Thobicus asked.

Belago nodded. Of course he did, and Thobicus knew
it. Belago's shop had been destroyed less than a year
before, when the library was in the throes of the chaos

curse. The library's deep coffers had funded the repairs and the replacement ingredients, and Belago had promptly given a complete accounting.

"As do I," Thobicus remarked. Bron Turman still eyed the dean curiously, not understanding the last statement. "I know everything that belongs there," Thobicus went on imperiously. "Everything, you understand?"

Belago, finding strength in honor, straightened for the first time since he had entered the room. "Are you accusing me of thievery?" he demanded.

The dean's chuckle mocked the wiry man's firm stance. "Not yet," Thobicus answered casually, "for you are still here, and thus, anything you might wish to take would also still be here."

That set Belago back; his ample eyebrows furrowed.

"Your services are no longer required," Thobicus explained, still speaking in an awful, cold, casual tone.

"But . . . but, Dean," Belago stuttered. "I have been—"

"Leave!"

Bron Turman straightened, recognizing the inflections and the weight of magic in Thobicus's voice. The burly Oghman headmaster was not surprised when Belago stiffened suddenly and fell back out of the room. With a look to Thobicus, Turman quickly moved to close the door.

"He was a fine alchemist," Turman said quietly, turning back to the large desk. Thobicus was again staring out the window.

"I had reason to doubt his loyalty," the dean explained.

Bron Turman, pragmatic and no real ally of Cadderly, did not press the point. Thobicus was the dean, and as such, he had the authority to hire or dismiss any of the nonclerical assistants that he chose.

"Baccio has been here for more than a day," Bron Turman said to change the subject. The man he referred to, Baccio, was the commander of the Carradoon garrison, come to discuss the defense of the city and the library should Castle Trinity strike at them. "Have you spoken with him?"

"We will not need Baccio and his little army," Thobicus said with confidence. "I shall soon dismiss him."

"You have word from Cadderly?"

"No," Thobicus answered honestly. Indeed, the dean had heard nothing since Cadderly and his companions had gone into the mountains earlier that winter. But Thobicus believed that the army would not be needed, believed that Cadderly had succeeded in defeating Castle Trinity. For, as the young priest's power continued to grow, Dean Thobicus felt himself being pushed away from the light of Deneir. Once, Thobicus had commanded the most powerful clerical magic, but now even the simplest spell, like the one he had used to dispatch poor Belago, came hard to his thin lips.

He turned back to the room to see Bron Turman staring at him skeptically.

"Very well," Thobicus conceded. "Tell Baccio I will meet him this evening—but I maintain that his army should hold a defensive posture and not go traipsing through the mountains!"

Bron Turman was satisfied with that. "But you believe that Cadderly and his friends have succeeded," he said slyly.

Thobicus did not respond.

"You believe that the threat to the library is no more," Bron Turman stated. The burly Oghman headmaster smiled, a wistful look in his large gray eyes. "At least, you believe that one threat to the library is no more," he added.

Thobicus steeled his gaze, his crow's-feet coming together to form one large crease at the side of each orb. "This does not concern you," he quietly warned.

Bron Turman bowed, respecting the words. "That does not mean that I do not understand," he said. "Vicero Belago was a fine alchemist."

"Bron Turman . . ."

The headmaster held up a submissive hand. "I am no friend of Cadderly's," he said. "Neither am I a young man. I have seen the intrigue of power struggles within both our sects."

Thobicus pursed his thin lips and seemed on the verge of explosion, and Bron Turman took that as a sign that he should be leaving. He gave another quick bow and was gone from the room.

Dean Thobicus rocked back in his chair and pivoted about to face the window. He couldn't rationally call Turman on the outwardly treasonous words, for the man's reasoning was undeniably true. Thobicus had been alive for more than seven decades; Cadderly for just over two, yet, for some reason that the old bureaucrat could not understand, Cadderly had found particular favor with Deneir. But the dean had come to his power painstakingly, at great personal sacrifice and at the cost of many years of almost reclusive study. He was not about to give up his position. He would purge the library of Cadderly's open allies and strengthen his hold on the order. Headmaster Avery Schell, Cadderly's mentor and surrogate father, and Pertelope, who had been like Cadderly's mother, were both dead now, and Belago would soon be gone.

No, Thobicus would not give up his position.

Not without a fight.

One

The Promise of Salvation

Kierkan Rufo wiped the stubborn mud from his boots and breeches, and muttered quiet curses to himself, as he always did. He was an outcast, marked by an ugly blue-and-red brand of an unlit candle above a closed eye, which lay on the middle of his forehead.

"*Bene tellemara*," whispered Druzil. A bat-winged, dog-faced, scaly creature barely two feet tall, the imp packed more malicious evil into that tiny frame than the worst of humankind's tyrants.

"What did you say?" Rufo snapped. He glared down at his otherworldly companion. The two had been together for the last half of the winter, and neither much liked the other. Their enmity had begun in Shilmista Forest, west of the Snowflake Mountains, when Druzil had threat-

6

ened and coerced Rufo into serving his wicked masters, the leaders of Castle Trinity—when Druzil had precipitated Kierkan Rufo's fall from the order of Deneir.

Druzil looked curiously at the man and squinted from the flickering light of the torch Rufo held. Rufo was over six feet tall, but bone-skinny. He always stood at an angle, tilted to the side, and that made him, or the world behind him, seem strangely incongruent. Druzil, who had spent the last few months wandering through the Snowflakes, thought Rufo resembled a tree on a steep mountainside. The imp snickered, drawing another glare from the perpetually scowling Rufo.

The imp continued to stare, trying hard to view the man in a new light. With his stringy black hair matted to his head, those penetrating eyes—black dots on a pale face—and that unusual stance, Rufo could be imposing. He kept his hair parted in the middle now, not on the side as it had always been, for Rufo could not, on pain of death, cover that horrid brand, the mark that had forced him to be a recluse, the mark that made every person shun him when they saw him coming down the road.

"What are you looking at?" Rufo demanded.

"Bene tellemara," Druzil rasped again in the language of the lower planes. It was a profound insult to Rufo's intelligence. To Druzil, schooled in chaos and evil, all humans seemed fumbling things, too clouded by emotions to be effective at anything. And this one, Rufo, was more bumbling than most. However, Aballister, Druzil's wizard master, was dead now, killed by Cadderly, his son, the same priest who had branded Rufo. And Dorigen, Aballister's second, had been captured, or had gone over to Cadderly's side. That left Druzil wandering alone on the Material Plane. With his innate powers, and no wizards binding him to service, the imp might have

found his way back to the lower planes, but Druzil didn't want that—not yet. For, on this plane, in the dungeons of this very building, rested *Tuanta Quiro Miancay*, the chaos curse, among the most potent and wicked concoctions ever brewed. Druzil wanted it back, and meant to get it with the help of Rufo, his stooge.

"I know what you are saying," Rufo lied, then he mimicked *"Bene tellemara"* back at Druzil.

Druzil smirked at him, showing clearly that the imp really didn't care if Rufo knew the meaning or not.

Rufo looked back at the muddy tunnel that had gotten them under the cellar of the Edificant Library.

"Well," he said impatiently, "we have come this far. Lead on and let us be out of this wretched place."

Druzil looked at him skeptically. For all the talking the imp had done over the last few weeks, Rufo still did not understand. Be out of this place? Druzil thought. Rufo had missed the whole point. They would soon have the chaos curse in their hands; why would they then want to leave?

Druzil nodded and led on, figuring that he could do little to enlighten the stupid human. Rufo simply did not understand the power of *Tuanta Quiro Miancay*. He had once been caught in its throes—all the library had, and nearly been brought down—yet, the ignorant human still did not understand.

That was the way with humans, Druzil decided. He would have to take Rufo by the hand and lead him to power, as he had led Rufo across the fields west of Carradoon and back into the mountains. Druzil had lured Rufo back to the library, where the branded man did not want to go, with false promises that the potion locked in these dungeons would remove his brand.

They went through several long, damp chambers,

past rotting casks and crates from days long ago when the library was a much smaller place, and mostly underground, when these areas had been used for storage. Druzil hadn't been here in a while, not since before the battle for Castle Trinity, before the war in Shilmista Forest. Not since Barjin, the evil priest, had been killed . . . by Cadderly.

"*Bene tellemara!*" the imp rasped, frustrated by the thought of the powerful young cleric.

"I grow tired of your insults," Rufo began to protest.

"Shut up," Druzil snapped back at him, too consumed by thoughts of the young priest to bother with Rufo. Cadderly, young and lucky Cadderly: the bane of Druzil's ambitions, the one who always seemed to be in the way.

Druzil kept complaining, scraping and slapping his wide, clawed feet on the stone floor noisily. He pushed through a door, went down a long corridor, and pushed open another.

Then Druzil stopped, and ended, too, his muttering. They had come to a small room, the room where Barjin had fallen.

Rufo pinched his nose and turned away, for the room smelled of death and decay. Druzil took a deep breath and felt positively at home.

There could be no doubt that a fierce struggle had occurred in here. Along the wall to Rufo and Druzil's right was an overturned brazier, the remains of charcoal blocks and incense scattered among its ashes. There, too, were the burned wrappings of an undead monster, a mummy. Most of the thing had been consumed by the flames, but its wrapped skull remained, showing blackened bone with tattered pieces of rags about it.

Beyond the brazier, near the base of the wall and along the floor, was a crimson stain, all that remained as testimony to Barjin's death. Barjin had been propped against that very spot when Cadderly had accidentally hit him with an explosive dart, blasting a hole through his chest and back.

The rest of the room showed much the same carnage. Next to Barjin's bloodstain, the brick wall had been knocked open by a furious dwarf, and the crossbeam supporting the ceiling hung by a single peg perpendicular to the floor. In the middle of the room, beneath dozens of scorch marks, lay a black weapon handle, all that remained of the Screaming Maiden, Barjin's enchanted mace, and behind that were the remains of the priest's unholy altar.

Beyond that . . .

Druzil's bulbous black eyes widened when he looked past the altar to the small cabinet wrapped in white cloth emblazoned with the runes and sigils of both Deneir and Oghma, the brother gods of the library. The mere presence of the cloth told Druzil that his search was at an end.

A flap of his bat wings brought the imp to the top of the altar, and he heard Rufo shuffling to catch up. Druzil dared not approach any closer, though, knowing that the priests had warded the cabinet with powerful enchantments.

"Glyphs," Rufo agreed, recognizing Druzil's hesitation. "If we go near it, we shall be burned away!"

"No," Druzil reasoned, speaking quickly, frantically. *Tuanta Quiro Miancay* was close enough for the desperate imp to smell it, and he would not be denied. "Not you," he went on. "You are not of my weal. You were a priest of this order. Surely you can approach . . . "

"Fool!" Rufo snapped at him. It was as volatile a response as the imp had ever heard from the broken man.

"I wear the brand of Deneir! The wards on that cloth and cabinet would seek my flesh hungrily."

Druzil hopped on the altar, tried to speak, but his rasping voice came out as only indecipherable sputtering. Then the imp calmed and called on his innate magic. The imp could see and measure all magic, be it the dweomer of a wizard or a priest. If the glyphs were not so powerful, Druzil would go to the cabinet himself. Any wounds he received would heal—faster still when he clutched the precious *Tuanta Quiro Miancay* in his greedy hands. The name translated into "the Most Fatal Horror," a title that sounded delicious indeed to the beleaguered imp.

The aura emanating from the cabinet nearly overwhelmed him, and at first, Druzil's heart fell in despair. But as he continued his scan, the imp came to know the truth, and a great gout of wicked laughter burst from between his pointed teeth.

Rufo, curious, looked at him.

"Go to the cabinet," Druzil instructed.

Rufo continued to stare, and made no move.

"Go," Druzil said again. "The meager wards of the foolish priests have been overwhelmed by the chaos curse! Their magic has unraveled!"

It was only partly true. *Tuanta Quiro Miancay* was more than a simple potion; it was magic driven to destroy. *Tuanta Quiro Miancay* wanted to be found, wanted to be out of the prison the priests had wrapped about it. And to that end, the concoction's magic had attacked the glyphs, had worked against them for many months, weakening their integrity.

Rufo didn't trust Druzil (and rightly so), but he could not ignore the pull on his heart. He felt his forehead's brand keenly in this place and suffered a severe headache merely from being near a structure dedicated to

Deneir. He found himself wanting to believe Druzil's words; he moved inevitably toward the cabinet and reached for the cloth.

There came a blinding electric flash, then a second, then a tremendous burst of fire. Fortunately for Rufo, the first explosion had launched him across the room, clear over the altar and into an overturned bookcase near the door.

Druzil shrieked as the flames engulfed the cabinet, its wood flaring brightly—obviously it had been soaked with oil or enchanted by some incendiary magic. Druzil did not fear for *Tuanta Quiro Miancay*, for that concoction was everlasting, but if the flask holding it melted, the liquid would be lost!

Flames never bothered Druzil, a creature of the fiery lower planes. His bat wings sent him rushing into the conflagration, eager hands pulling the cabinet's contents free. Druzil shrieked from a sudden burst of pain, and nearly hurled the bowl across the room. He caught himself, though, and gingerly placed the item on the altar, then he backed away and rubbed his blistered hands together.

The bottle holding the chaos curse had been placed in a bowl and immersed in the clearest of waters, made holy by the plea of a dead druid and the symbol of Sylvanus, the god of nature, of natural order. Perhaps no god in the Realms evoked more anger from the perverse imp than Sylvanus.

Druzil studied the bowl and considered his dilemma. He breathed easier a moment later, when he realized that the holy water was not as pure as it should be, that the influences of *Tuanta Quiro Miancay* were acting even upon that.

Druzil moved near the bowl and chanted softly, using

one of his claws to puncture the middle finger of his left hand. Finishing his curse, he let a single drop of his blood fall into the water. There came a hissing, and the top of the bowl clouded over with vapor. Then it was gone, and gone, too, was the pure water, replaced by a blackened morass of fetid and rotting liquid.

Druzil leaped back atop the altar and plunged his hands in. A moment later, he was whimpering with joy, cradling the precious, rune-decorated bottle, itself an enchanted thing, as though it were his baby. He looked to Rufo, not really concerned if the man was alive or dead, then laughed again.

Rufo had propped himself up on his elbows. His black hair stood on end, dancing wildly; his eyes twitched and rolled of their own accord. After some time, he rolled back unsteadily to his feet and advanced in staggered steps toward the imp, thinking to throttle the creature once and for all.

Druzil's waving tail, its barbed end dripping deadly poison, brought Rufo to his senses, but did little to calm him.

"You said . . . " he began to roar.

"*Bene tellemara!*" Druzil snapped back at him, the imp's intensity more than matching Rufo's anger and startling the man to silence. "Do you not know what we have?" Smiling wickedly, Druzil handed the flask to Rufo, and the man's beady eyes widened when he took it, when he felt its inner power throb within him.

Rufo hardly heard Druzil as the imp raved about what they might accomplish with the chaos curse. The angular man stared at the swirling red liquid within the bottle and fantasized, not of power, as Druzil was spouting, but of freedom from his brand. Rufo had earned that brand, but in his twisted perception, that hardly mattered. All

Rufo understood and could accept was that Cadderly had marked him, had forced him to become an outcast.

Now, all the world was his enemy.

Druzil continued to ramble excitedly. The imp talked of controlling the priests once more, of striking against all the land, of uncorking the flask and . . .

Rufo heard that last suggestion alone among the dozens of ideas the imp spewed. He heard it and believed it with all his heart. It was as if *Tuanta Quiro Miancay* was calling him, and the chaos curse, the creation of wicked, diabolical intelligence, was indeed. This was Rufo's salvation, more than Deneir had ever been. This was his deliverance from wretched Cadderly.

This potion was for him, and for him alone.

Druzil stopped talking the moment he noticed that Rufo had uncorked the bottle, the moment he smelled the red fumes wafting up from the potion.

The imp started to ask the man what he was doing, but the words stuck in Druzil's throat as Rufo suddenly lifted the bottle to his thin lips and drank of it deeply.

Druzil stammered repeatedly, trying to find the words of protest. Rufo turned to him, the man's face screwed up curiously.

"What have you done?" Druzil asked.

Rufo started to answer, but gagged instead and clutched his throat.

"What have you done?" Druzil repeated loudly. "*Bene tellemara*! Fool!"

Rufo gagged again, clutched his throat and stomach, and vomited violently. He staggered away, coughing, wheezing, trying to get some air past the bile rising in his throat.

"What have you done?" Druzil cried after him, scuttling along the floor to keep up. The imp's tail waved ominously; if Rufo's misery ended, Druzil meant to sting and tear him, to punish him for stealing the precious and irreplaceable potion.

Rufo, his balance wavering, slammed into the door-jamb as he tried to exit the room. He stumbled along the corridor, rebounding off one wall, then the other. He vomited again, and again after that, his stomach burning with agony and swirling with nausea. Somehow he got through the rooms and corridors and half-crawled out the muddy tunnel, back into the sunlight, which knifed at his eyes and skin.

He was burning up, and yet he felt cold, deathly cold.

Druzil, wisely becoming invisible as they came into the revealing daylight, followed. Rufo stopped and vomited yet again, across the hardened remains of a late-season snowbank, and the mess showed more blood than bile. Then the angular man staggered around the building's corner, slipping and falling many times in the mud and slush. He thought to get to the door, to the priests with their curing hands.

Two young acolytes, wearing the black-and-gold vests that distinguished them as priests of Oghma, were near the door, enjoying the warmth of the late winter day, their brown cloaks opened wide to the sun. They didn't notice Rufo at first, not until the man fell heavily into the mud just a few feet away.

The two acolytes rushed to him and turned him over, then gasped and fell back when they saw the brand. Neither had been in the library long enough to know Kier-kan Rufo personally, but they had heard tales of the branded priest. They looked to each other and shrugged, then one rushed back into the library while the other began to relieve the stricken man.

Druzil watched from the corner of the building, muttering *"Bene tellemara"* over and over, lamenting that the chaos curse and Kierkan Rufo had played him a wicked joke.

* * * * *

Perched high in the branches of a tree near that door, the white squirrel, Percival, looked on with more than a passing interest. Percival had come out of his winter hibernation this very week. He had been surprised to find that Cadderly, his main source of the favored cacasa nuts, was not about, and was even more surprised to see Kierkan Rufo, a human that Percival did not care for at all.

The squirrel could see that Rufo was in great distress, could smell the foulness of Rufo's illness, even from this distance.

Percival moved near his twig nest, nestled high in the branches, and continued to watch.

Two

Different Paths Taken

The three bearded members of the company, the dwarves Pikel and Ivan Bouldershoulder and the red-haired firbolg Vander, sat off to the side of the cave entrance, rolling bones, placing bets, and laughing among themselves. Ivan won a round, for the fifteenth time in a row, and Pikel swept off a blue, wide-brimmed hat, with an orange quill on one side and the eye-above-candle holy symbol of Deneir set in its front, and whacked laughing Ivan over the head.

Cadderly, seeing the move, started to protest. It was his hat, after all, simply loaned to Pikel, and Ivan's helmet was set with the antlers of a large deer. The young priest changed his mind and held the thought silent, seeing that the hat had not been damaged and realizing that Ivan deserved the blow.

The friendship between Ivan, Pikel, and Vander had blossomed after the fall of Castle Trinity. Gigantic Vander, all twelve feet and eight hundred pounds of him, had even helped Pikel, the would-be druid, redye his hair and beard green and braid the bushy tangle down his back. The only tense moment had come when Vander tried to put some of Pikel's dye in Ivan's bright yellow hair, something the square-shouldered, more serious Bouldershoulder did not like at all.

But the exchanges were ultimately good-natured; the last few weeks had been good-natured, despite the brutal weather. The seven companions, including Cadderly, Danica, Dorigen, and Shayleigh, the elf maiden, had planned to go straight from the victory at Castle Trinity to the Edificant Library. Barely a day's hike into the mountains, though, winter had come in full force, blocking the trails so that not even Cadderly, with his priestly magic, dared to press on. Even worse, Cadderly had fallen ill, though he insisted that it was simple exhaustion. As a priest, Cadderly served as a conduit for the powers of his god, and during the battle with Castle Trinity (and the weeks of fighting before that) too much of that energy had flowed through the young priest.

Danica, who knew Cadderly better than anyone, did not doubt that he was exhausted, but she knew, too, that the young priest had taken an emotional beating as well. In Castle Trinity, Cadderly had seen his past and the truth of his heritage. He had been forced to face up to what his father, Aballister, had become.

In Castle Trinity Cadderly had killed his own father.

Danica held faith that Cadderly would overcome this trauma, confident in the depth of Cadderly's character. He was devoted to his god and to his friends, and they all were beside him.

With the trails closed and Cadderly ill, the company had gone east, out of the mountains and their foothills, to the farmlands north of Carradoon. Even the lowlands were deep with a snow that the Shining Plains had not seen in decades. The friends had found a many-chambered cave for shelter, and had turned the place into a fair home over the days, using Danica's, Vander's, and the dwarves' survival skills and Dorigen's magic. Cadderly had aided whenever he could, but his role was to rest and regain his strength. He knew, and Danica knew, that when they returned to the Edificant Library, the young priest might face his toughest challenge yet.

After several weeks, the snows had begun to recede. As brutal as the winter had been, it was ending early, and the companions could begin to think about their course. That brought mixed feelings for young Cadderly, the priest who had risen so fast through the ranks of his order. He stood at the cave entrance, staring out over the fields of white, their brightness stinging his gray eyes in the morning sunlight. He felt guilty for his own weakness, for he believed that he should have returned to the library despite the snows, despite the trials he had faced, months ago, even if that meant leaving his friends behind. Cadderly's destiny waited at that library, but even now, feeling stronger once more, hearing the song of Deneir playing in the background of his thoughts again, he wasn't sure that he had the strength to meet it.

"I am ready for you," came a call from inside the cave, above Vander and the dwarves' continuing ruckus. Cadderly turned and walked past the group, and Pikel, knowing what was to come, gave a little "Hee hee hee." The green-bearded dwarf tipped the wide-brimmed hat to Cadderly, as if saluting a warrior going to battle.

Cadderly scowled at the dwarf and walked past, moving to a small stone, which crafty Ivan had fashioned into a stool. Danica stood behind the stool, waiting for Cadderly, her beautiful daggers, one golden-hilted and sculpted into the shape of a tiger, the other a silver dragon, in hand. For any who did not know Danica, those blades, or any weapons, would have looked out of place in her deceivingly delicate hands. She was barely five feet tall—if she went two days without eating, she wouldn't top a hundred pounds—with thick locks of strawberry blond hair cascading over her shoulders and unusual almond-shaped eyes a light but rich brown. On casual glance, Danica seemed more a candidate for a southern harem, a beautiful, delicate flower.

The young priest knew better, as did any who had spent time beside Danica. Those delicate hands could break stone; that beautiful face could smash a man's nose flat. Danica was a monk, a disciplined fighter, and her studies were no less intense than Cadderly's, her worship of the wisdom of ancient masters no less than Cadderly's of his god. She was as perfect a warrior as Cadderly had ever seen; she could use any weapon, and could defeat most swordsmen with her bare hands and feet.

And she could put either of the enchanted daggers she now held into the eye of an enemy twenty paces away.

Cadderly took his seat, pointedly facing away from the boisterous gamblers, while Danica began to softly chant. Cadderly found a meditative focus; it was vital that he remain absolutely still. Suddenly, Danica broke into motion, her arms weaving intricate patterns in the air before her, her feet shifting from side to side, keeping perfect balance.

The impossibly sharp blades began to turn in her fingers.

The first one came around in a blinding flash, but Cadderly, deep in concentration, did not flinch. He barely felt the scrape as the knife's edge brushed his cheek, barely had time to smell the oiled metal as the silver dragon whipped in under his nostrils and shot down to his upper lip.

This was a ritual that the two performed every day, one that kept Cadderly clean-shaven and Danica's finely honed muscles at their peak.

It was over in a mere minute, Cadderly's stubble swept away without a nick to his tanned skin.

"I should chop this tangle away, too," Danica teased, grabbing a handful of Cadderly's thick, curly brown hair. Cadderly reached up and grabbed her wrist and pulled her around and down, over his shoulder so that their faces were close. The two were lovers, committed to each other for life, and the only reason they had not yet been married in open vows was that Cadderly did not consider the priests of the Edificant Library worthy of performing the ceremony.

Cadderly gave Danica a little kiss, and both jumped back as a blue spark flashed between them, stinging their lips. Immediately, both turned to the entrance to the chamber on the cave's left-hand wall, and were greeted by the joined laughter of Dorigen and Shayleigh.

"Such a bond," remarked Dorigen sarcastically. She had been the one to cause the spark—of course it had been the wizard. Once an enemy of the band, indeed one of the leaders of the army that had invaded Shilmista, Dorigen, by all appearances, had turned to a new way of life and was going back with the others to face judgment at the library.

"Never have I seen such a spark of love," added Shay-leigh, shaking her head so that her long, thick mane of golden hair fell back from her face. Even in the dim light streaming in through the cave's eastern door, the elf's violet eyes sparkled like polished jewels.

"Should I add this to your list of crimes?" Cadderly asked Dorigen.

"If that was the greatest of my crimes, I would not bother to return to the library beside you, young priest," the wizard replied easily.

Danica looked from Cadderly to Dorigen, recognizing the bond that had grown between them. It wasn't hard for the monk to discern the source of that attraction. With her black hair, showing lines of gray, and her wide-set eyes, Dorigen resembled Pertelope, the head-mistress at the library who had been like Cadderly's mother until her recent death. Pertelope alone seemed to understand the transformation that had come over Cadderly, the god-song that played in his thoughts and gave him access to clerical powers to rival the highest-ranking priests in all the land.

Danica could see some of the same perceptive charac-teristics in Dorigen. The wizard was a thinker, a person who weighed the situation carefully before acting, and a person not afraid to follow her heart. Dorigen had turned against Aballister in Castle Trinity, had all but gone over to Cadderly's side despite her knowledge that her crimes would not be forgotten. She had done it because her conscience had so dictated.

Danica had not grown to love, or even like, the woman over the weeks of forced hibernation, but she did respect the wizard, and did, to some extent, trust Dorigen.

"Well, you have been hinting at this for many days," Dori-gen said to Cadderly. "Is it time for us to be on the road?"

Cadderly instinctively looked back to the door and nodded. "The passes south to Carradoon should be clear enough to travel," he replied. "And many of the passes back into the mountains will be clear as well, the snow fallen from them." Cadderly paused, and the others, not understanding why the mountain passes should be of any concern, watched him carefully, looking for clues.

"Though I fear that the melt might bring some avalanches," the young priest finished.

"I do not fear avalanches," came the firbolg's voice booming from the door. "I have lived all my life in the mountains, and know well enough when a trail is safe."

"Ye're not going back to the library," piped in Ivan, eyeing his giant friend suspiciously.

"Oo," added Pikel, apparently not too happy about it.

"I have my own home, my own family," said Vander. He, Ivan, and Pikel had discussed this matter many times over the last few weeks, but not until this moment had Vander made a decision.

Ivan obviously wasn't thrilled with it. He and Vander were friends, and saying farewell was never an easy thing. But the sturdy dwarf agreed with the firbolg's decision, and he had promised, before and now again, that he would one day travel north to the Spine of the World Mountains and seek out Vander's firbolg clan.

"But why are you talking of the mountains?" Shayleigh asked Cadderly bluntly. "Except for Vander, we'll not have to go into the mountains until we pass Carradoon, and that will entail no less than a week of walking."

"We are going in sooner," Danica answered for Cadderly, thinking that she had the man's mind read. She found that she was half right.

"Not all of us," Cadderly stated. "There would be no need."

"The dragon's treasure!" Ivan roared suddenly, referring to the cave they had left behind, where old Fyrentennimar had lived. The friends had dispatched the old red in the mountains, leaving his treasure unguarded. "Ye're thinking of the dragon's treasure!" The dwarf slapped his round-shouldered brother on the back.

"An unguarded hoard," Shayleigh agreed. "But it would take all seven of us, and many more than that, to bring that great treasure out."

"We do not even know if the treasure will be found," Cadderly reminded them. "The storm that Aballister threw at Nightglow Mountain likely sealed many caves."

"So you wish to go back to see if the treasure might be recovered," Danica reasoned.

"Recovered when the weather is more agreeable," said Cadderly. "And so we need not all make the journey to the mountain."

"What do you propose?" Danica asked, and she already knew the lines that Cadderly would draw.

"I will return to the mountain," the young priest answered, "along with Ivan and Pikel, if they are agreeable. I had hoped that you would come along as well," he said to Vander.

"Part of the way," the red-bearded giant promised. "But I am anxious . . . "

Cadderly cut him short with an upraised hand. He understood the firbolg's feelings and would not ask Vander, who had been so long from home, so long tormented by the assassin, Ghost, to delay any longer. "Any step you take beside us will be welcomed," Cadderly insisted, and Vander nodded.

Cadderly turned back to the three women. "I know you must get back to Shilmista," he said to Shayleigh. "King Elbereth will need a full report on the happenings at Castle Trinity, so that he might stand down the elven guard. The fastest route for you would be south past Carradoon, then along the more traveled trails west from the library."

Shayleigh nodded.

"And I am to accompany Dorigen back," Danica reasoned.

Cadderly nodded. "You are not of either host order," he explained, "thus, Dorigen will be your prisoner and not under the jurisdiction of the headmasters."

"Whom you do not trust," Dorigen added slyly.

Cadderly didn't bother to respond. "If all goes well at Nightglow, the dwarves and I should come to the library no more than a few days after you."

"But since I came in alone, Dorigen will remain my prisoner," Danica reasoned, and she smiled despite the fact that she did not wish to miss the adventure at Nightglow, and did not want to be apart from Cadderly at all.

"Your judgment will be more fair, I am sure," Cadderly said with a wink. "And it shall be easier for me to convince the headmasters to accept that judgment than to get them to pass a fair punishment of their own."

It was a solid plan, Danica knew, one that would likely spare Dorigen from a hangman's noose.

Dorigen's smile showed that she understood the plan's merits as well. "Again you have my gratitude," she offered. "I only wish that I believed myself worthy of it."

Cadderly and Danica exchanged a knowing look, and neither was the least bit worried about splitting the party with a prisoner in tow. Dorigen was a powerful wizard, and if she had wanted to escape, she certainly could have done so by now. Over the weeks, she had not been bound in any way, and only in the first few days had she even been guarded. Never was there a more willing prisoner, and

Cadderly was confident that Dorigen would not try to escape. Even more than that, Cadderly was convinced that Dorigen would use her powers to aid Danica and Shayleigh if they got into trouble on the way to the library.

It was settled then, with no disagreements. Ivan and Pikel rubbed their hands together often and slapped each other on the back so many times that they sounded like a gallery at a fine performance. Nothing could set a dwarf to hopping like the promise of an unguarded dragon's hoard.

Danica found Cadderly alone later that morning, while the others busied themselves for the journey. The young priest hardly noticed her approach, just stood on a clear patch of stone outside the cave, staring into the towering Snowflake Mountains.

Danica moved up and hooked her arm under Cadderly's, offering him the support she thought he needed. To her thinking, Cadderly wasn't ready to return to the library. No doubt, he was still in turmoil over the last incident with Dean Thobicus, when he had forcefully bent the dean's mind to his bidding. Beyond that, with all that had happened—the deaths of Avery and Pertelope and the revelation that the evil wizard Aballister was, in truth, Cadderly's own father—the young priest's world had been turned upside down. Cadderly had questioned his faith and his home for some time, and though he had finally come to terms with his loyalty to Deneir, Danica wondered if he still had a hard time thinking of the Edificant Library as his home.

They remained silent for several minutes, Cadderly staring up into the mountains and Danica staring at Cadderly.

"Do you fear a charge of heresy?" the monk asked at length.

Cadderly turned to her, his expression curious.

"For your actions against Dean Thobicus," Danica clarified. "If he has remembered the incident and realizes what you did to him, he will not likely welcome you back."

"Thobicus will not openly oppose me," Cadderly said.

Danica did not miss the fact that he had named the man without the man's title, no small matter by the rules of the order and of the library.

"Though he most likely will have recalled much of what happened when last we talked," the young priest went on, "I expect he will solidify his alliances . . . and demote or dismiss those he suspects are loyal to me."

Despite the grim reasoning, there was little trepidation in Cadderly's tone, Danica noted, and her expression revealed her surprise.

"What allies can he make?" Cadderly asked, as though that explained everything.

"He is the head of the order," Danica replied, "and has many friends in the Oghman order as well."

Cadderly chuckled softly and scoffed at the thought. "I told you before that Thobicus is the head of a false hierarchy."

"And you will simply walk in and make that claim?"

"Yes," Cadderly answered calmly. "I have an ally that Dean Thobicus cannot resist, one who will turn the priests of my order to me."

Danica did not have to ask who that ally might be. Cadderly believed that Deneir himself was with him, that the deity had assigned him a task. Given the man's powers, Danica did not doubt the notion. Still, it bothered Danica somewhat that Cadderly had become so bold, even arrogant.

"The Oghman priests will not become involved," Cadderly went on, "for this does not concern them. The only contention I will see from them, and rightly so, will manifest itself after I unseat Thobicus as head of the Deneirian order. Bron Turman will contest me for the title of dean."

"Turman has been a leader in the library for many years," Danica said.

Cadderly nodded and seemed not at all bothered.

"His will be a powerful challenge," Danica reasoned.

"It is not important which of us ascends to the position of dean," Cadderly replied. "My first duty is to the order of Deneir. Once that is set aright, I will worry about the future of the Edificant Library."

Danica accepted that, and again the two lapsed into long minutes of silence, Cadderly staring once more at the majestic Snowflakes. Danica believed in him, and in his reasoning, but she had trouble reconciling his apparent calmness with the fact that he was out here, standing in deep contemplation, instead of at the library. Cadderly's delay revealed the true turmoil behind his cool facade.

"What are you thinking about?" she asked, and pressed her hand gently against the young priest's cheek, drawing his gaze from the mountains.

Cadderly smiled warmly, touched by her concern.

"Up there is an unguarded hoard of treasure greater than anything in all the region," Cadderly said.

"I've never known you to care much for material wealth," Danica remarked.

Again Cadderly smiled. "I was thinking of Nameless," he said, referring to a poor leper he had once met on the road outside Carradoon. "I was thinking of all the other Namelesses in Carradoon and all around Impresk Lake. The wealth of the dragon's hoard might bring great good to the land." He looked at Danica squarely. "The treasure might give all of those people names."

"It will be more complicated than that," Danica reasoned, for both of them knew well the equation of wealth and power. If Cadderly meant to share the riches with the impoverished people, he would find resistance among those "gentlefolk" of Carradoon who equated wealth with nobility and rank and used their riches to feel superior.

"Deneir is with me," Cadderly said calmly, and Danica understood at that moment that her love was indeed ready for this fight, ready for Thobicus and all the others.

* * * * *

Several priests worked furiously over Kierkan Rufo on the cold, wet ground outside the Edificant Library's front door. They wrapped him in their own cloaks, disregarding the chill wind of early spring, but they did not miss the brand on his forehead, the unlit candle above the closed eye, and even the Oghman priests understood its significance, that they could not bring the man into the library.

Rufo continued to gag and vomit. His chest heaved and his stomach convulsed, tightening into agonizing knots. Blue-black bruises erupted under the man's sweating skin.

The Oghman priests, some of them powerful clerics, enacted spells of healing, though the Deneirians did not dare evoke the powers of their god in this man's name.

None of it seemed to work.

Dean Thobicus and Bron Turman arrived together at the door, pushing through the growing crowd of onlookers. The withered dean's eyes widened considerably when he saw that it was Rufo lying outside.

"We must bring him into the warmth!" one of the attending priests shouted to the dean.

"He cannot enter the library," Bron Turman insisted, "not with such a brand. By his own actions was Kierkan Rufo banished, and the banishment holds!"

"Bring him in," Dean Thobicus said unexpectedly, and Turman nearly fell over as he registered the words. He didn't openly protest, though. Rufo was of Thobicus's order, not his own, and Thobicus, as dean, was well within his powers in allowing the man entry.

A few moments later, after Rufo was ushered through the crowd and Thobicus had gone off with the attending priests, Bron Turman came to a disturbing conclusion, an explanation of the dean's words that did not sit well with the Oghman. Kierkan Rufo was no friend of Cadderly's; in fact, Cadderly had been the one to brand the man. Had that precipitated the dean's decision to let Rufo in?

Bron Turman hoped that was not the case.

In a side room, an empty chamber normally reserved for private prayers, the priests pulled in a bench to use as a cot and continued their heroic efforts to comfort Rufo. Nothing they did seemed to help; even Thobicus tried to summon his greatest healing powers, chanting over Rufo while the others held him steady. But, whether the spell had not been granted or Rufo's ailment had simply rejected it, the dean's words fell empty.

Blood and bile poured freely from Rufo's mouth and nose, and his chest heaved desperately, trying to pull in air through the obstruction in his throat. One strong Oghman priest grabbed Rufo and yanked him over onto his belly, pounding at his back to force everything out.

Suddenly, without warning, Rufo jerked and turned so violently that the Oghman priest went flying across the room. Then Rufo settled on the bench and calmed strangely, staring up unblinkingly at Dean Thobicus. With a weak hand, he motioned for the dean to come closer, and Thobicus, after looking around nervously, bent low, putting his ear near the man's mouth.

"You . . . you invi . . . vited me," Rufo stammered, blood and bile accompanying every word.

Thobicus stood up straight, staring at the man, not understanding.

"You invited me in," Rufo said clearly with his last bit of strength. He began to laugh then, weirdly, out of control, and the laughter became a great convulsion, and then a final scream.

None in attendance remembered ever seeing a man die more horribly.

Three

The Ultimate Perversion

There ain't no durned cave!" Ivan roared, and a rumble from above, from the unsteady, piled snow, reminded the dwarf that a bit more care might be prudent.

If Ivan didn't get the point then, he got it a second later, when frantic Pikel ran up and slapped him on the back of the head, knocking his helm down over his eyes. The yellow-bearded dwarf grabbed a deer antler and adjusted the thing, then turned a scowl on his brother, but Pikel didn't relent, just stood there waggling a finger in Ivan's face.

"Quiet down, both of you!" Cadderly scolded.

"Oo," replied Pikel, and he seemed honestly wounded.

Cadderly, thoroughly flustered, didn't notice the look. He continued his scan of the ruined mountain, amazed that the opening—an opening large enough to admit a dragon with its wings spread wide—was no more.

"You are sure that it is not just snow?" Cadderly asked, to which Ivan stamped his boot, dislodging a chunk of snow from above that fell over him and Pikel.

Pikel popped up first, snow sliding off the edges of the flopping, wide-brimmed hat he had borrowed from Cadderly, and was ready with another slap when Ivan reappeared.

"If ye don't believe me, go in there yerself!" Ivan bellowed, pointing to the snow mass. "There's stone in there. Solid stone, I tell ye! That wizard sealed it good with his storm."

Cadderly put his hands on his hips and took a deep breath. He recalled the storm Aballister had sent to Nightglow, the wizard thinking that Cadderly and his friends were still there. Aballister had no way of knowing that Cadderly had enlisted the aid of a hostile dragon and was many miles closer to Castle Trinity.

Looking at the destruction, at the side of a mountain torn asunder by hurled magic, Cadderly was glad that Aballister's aim had been misplaced. That did little to comfort the young priest now, though. Inside this mountain waited an unguarded dragon hoard, a treasure that Cadderly would need to see his plans for the Edificant Library, and for all the region, realized. This had been the only major door, though, the one opening they could push carts through to extract the treasure before the next winter's snows.

"The whole opening?" Cadderly asked Ivan.

The yellow-bearded dwarf started to respond in his typically loud voice, but stopped and looked at his brother (who was readying yet another slap), and just growled instead. Ivan had bored through the wall of snow for more than an hour, pushing in blindly at several locations until the rock wall behind the snow curtain inevitably turned him away.

"We'll go around," Cadderly said, "to the hole on the mountain's south face that first got us into the place."

"It was a long walk between that hole and the dragon hoard," Ivan reminded him. "A long walk through tight tunnels, and even a long drop. I'm not for knowing how ye're planning to bring a treasure out that way!"

"Neither am I," Cadderly admitted. "All I know is that I need the treasure, and I'm going to find some way to get it!" With that, the young priest walked off along the trail, in search of a path that would lead him around Nightglow's wide base.

"He sounds like a dwarf," Ivan whispered to Pikel.

After Pikel's ensuing "Hee hee hee" brought down the next mini-avalanche, it was Ivan's turn to do the head-slapping.

The trio arrived on the south face early the next morning. Climbing proved difficult in the slippery, melting snow. Ivan got almost all the way to the hole (and was able to confirm that there was indeed a hole in this side of the mountain) before he slipped and tumbled, turning into a dwarven snowball and bowling Cadderly and Pikel down the hill with him.

"Stupid priest!" the dwarf roared at Cadderly when the three sorted themselves out far down the mountainside. "Ain't ye got some magic to get us up this stupid hill?"

Cadderly nodded reluctantly. He had been trying to conserve his energies since their departure from Castle Trinity. Every day he had to cast spells on himself and his companions to ward off the cold, but he had hoped that would be the extent of his exertion until he returned to the library. Cadderly was more tired than he had ever been. His trials, especially against Aballister and Fyrentennimar, had thoroughly drained him, had forced him to delve into magical spheres that he did not understand and, by sheer willpower, bring forth dweomers that should have been far beyond his capabilities. Now young Cadderly was paying the price for those efforts. Even the weeks of relative calm, holed up in the cave, had not rejuvenated him. He could still hear Deneir's song in his head, but whenever he tried to access the greater magic, his temples throbbed, and he felt that his head would explode.

Pertelope, dear Pertelope, who alone had understood the obstacles facing Cadderly as a chosen priest of the god of the arts, had warned Cadderly about this potential side effect, but even Pertelope had admitted that it seemed as though Cadderly had little choice in the matter, that the young priest was facing enemies beyond anything she had ever seen.

Cadderly closed his eyes and listened for the notes of Deneir's song, music taught him from the *Tome of Universal Harmony*, his most holy book. At first he felt a deep serenity, as though he were returning home after a long, difficult journey. The harmonies of Deneir's song played sweetly in his thoughts, leading him down corridors of truth and understanding. Then he purposely opened a door, turned a mental page from his recollections of the most holy book and sought a spell that would get him and his friends up the mountain.

Then his temples began to hurt.

Cadderly heard Ivan calling him, distantly, and he opened his eyes just long enough to take hold of Pikel's hand and grab hold of Ivan's beard when the confused and suspicious Ivan refused Cadderly's offered grasp.

Ivan's protests intensified into desperation as the three began to melt away, becoming insubstantial, mere shadows. The wind seemed to catch them, and it carried them unerringly up the mountainside.

Pikel was cheering loudly when Cadderly came out of his trance. Ivan stood still for a long while, then began a tactile inspection, as if testing to see if all of his tangible mass had been restored.

Cadderly slumped in the snow beside the small opening in the hill, collected his wits, and rubbed the sides of his head to try to alleviate the throbbing. It wasn't as bad as the last time he had tried a major spell. Back in the cave he had tried, and failed, to make mental contact with Dean Thobicus to ensure that no invasion force was marching north toward Castle Trinity. It wasn't so bad this time, and Cadderly was glad of that. If they could get their business done quickly, and if the weather held, the three would be back at the Edificant Library within two weeks. Cadderly suspected that there waited his greatest challenge yet, one that he would need the song of Deneir to combat.

"At least there's no stupid dragon waiting in there this time," Ivan huffed, and he moved up to the entrance. The last time Cadderly and the others had come to this spot, a fog enshrouded the area and all the snow near the hole had been melted away. The air was still warm inside the hole, but not nearly as oppressive, and ominous, as when Fyrentennimar had been alive.

Pikel tried to push Ivan aside, but the yellow-bearded dwarf held his ground stubbornly, showing that he was more intrigued by the prospects of a dragon's hoard than he let on. "I'm going in first," Ivan insisted. "Ye'll follow by twenty paces," he explained to Pikel. "So that I can call to yerself, and ye can call to Cadderly."

Pikel's head bobbed in agreement, and Ivan started for the hole. He considered it for just a moment, then removed his helmet and tossed it to Cadderly.

"Ivan," the young priest called, and when Ivan turned back, the young priest tossed him a short metallic tube.

Ivan had seen this item, one of Cadderly's many inventions, before, and he knew how to use it. He popped off the snug cap on its end, allowing a beam of light to stream forth. There was a disk inside the tube, enchanted with a powerful light-giving dweomer, and the tube was really two pieces of metal. The outer tube, near the end cap, could be turned along a corkscrew course, lengthening or shortening the tube, thus tightening or widening the beam of light.

Ivan kept the focus narrow now, since the tunnel was so constricted that the broad-shouldered dwarf had to often turn sideways to squeeze through, so narrow that Pikel reluctantly gave Cadderly back his wide-brimmed hat before entering.

Cadderly waited patiently for many minutes, his thoughts lost in the anticipated confrontation with Dean Thobicus. He was glad when Pikel reappeared in search of rope, knowing then that Ivan had made it through the tightest of the tunnels and had come to the vertical shaft that would take him to the same level as the dragon treasure.

Twenty minutes later, both dwarves came bobbing out of the hole, Ivan shaking his head.

"It's blocked," he announced. "I can get down to the big room under the shaft, but there's nowhere to go from there. I'm thinking we might be better in trying to cut through that front door."

Cadderly blew a deep sigh.

"I'll call for me kin," Ivan went on. "Of course, it'll take 'em the bulk of the next two seasons to get down from Vaasa, and then we'll have to wait for the next winter to blow over . . . "

Cadderly tuned out as the dwarf rambled on. By conventional means, it might take years to extract the dragon treasure, and the delay would bring about some unexpected obstacles. Word of Fyrentennimar's demise would spread fast throughout the land, and most of the peoples in the region, of races both good and evil, knew that the dragon resided in Nightglow Mountain. The fall of a dragon, especially one that had sat for centuries on a legendary treasure hoard, always brought scavengers.

Like me, Cadderly thought, and he chuckled aloud at the self-deprecating humor. He realized then that Ivan had stopped talking, and when he looked up, he found both dwarves staring at him intently.

"Fear not, Ivan," Cadderly said, "you'll not need to summon your kin."

"They would take a bit o' the treasure for their own," Ivan admitted. "By the gods, they'd probably set up a keep right inside the mountain, and then we'd be hard pressed to get a single copper outta them!"

Pikel started to laugh, but caught himself and turned a stern look on Ivan, realizing that his brother was serious, and probably correct.

"I'll get us into the mountain, and we'll have plenty of help from Carradoon when the time comes to take out the treasure," Cadderly assured them both. "But not now."

The young priest let it go at that, thinking that the dwarves need know no more. His next task, he knew, was to get to the library, to put things spiritually aright. Then he could concentrate on the treasure, could come back here rested and ready to clear the path magically for the foragers.

"This place is important to ye," Ivan remarked. Cadderly looked at the dwarf curiously, more for the tone Ivan had used than the specific words.

"More important than it should be," Ivan went on. "Ye always had money, particularly since ye penned that spellbook for the frantic wizard, but ye never seemed to care so much for money."

"That has not changed," Cadderly replied.

"Eh?" Pikel squeaked, echoing Ivan's sentiments exactly. If Cadderly had no care for money, then why were they up here in the middle of the dangerous mountains, freezing their stubby feet off?

"I care about what this treasure might bring for us all," Cadderly went on.

"Wealth," Ivan interrupted, eagerly rubbing his strong hands together.

Cadderly looked at him sourly. "Do you remember that model I kept in my room?" the young priest asked, more to Pikel than Ivan, for Pikel had been particularly enchanted with the thing. "The one of the high, windowed wall with the supporting buttress?"

"Oo oi!" Pikel roared happily in reply.

"Ye're thinking to rebuild the library," Ivan reasoned, and the dwarf blew a huff of spittle into the frosty air when Cadderly nodded. "If the durned thing ain't broke, then why're ye meaning to fix it?" Ivan demanded.

"I am thinking to improve it," Cadderly corrected. "You yourself have witnessed the strength of the model's design, and that with soaring windows. Soaring windows, Ivan, making the library a place of light, where books might truly be penned and read."

"Bah! Ye've never done any building," Ivan protested. "That much I know. Ye've no idea of the scope of the structure ye're planning. Humans don't live long enough for ye to see yer new . . . What was it ye once called that thing?"

"A cathedral," Cadderly answered.

"Humans won't live long enough to see yer new cathedral even half finished," Ivan went on. "It'll take a full clan of dwarves a hundred years . . . "

"That does not matter," Cadderly answered simply, stealing Ivan's bluster. "It does not matter if I see the completion, only that I begin the construction. That is the cost of, and the joy of, faith, Ivan, and you should understand that."

Ivan was back on his heels. He hadn't heard such talk from any human before, and he'd known many humans in his day. The dwarves and the elves were the ones who thought of the future, who had the foresight and the good sense to blaze the trail for their ancestors to walk. Humans, as far as most of the longer-living races were concerned, were an impatient folk, a group that had to see material gains almost immediately to maintain any momentum or desire for a chore.

"You have heard recently of Bruenor Battlehammer," Cadderly went on, "who has reclaimed Mithril Hall in the name of his father. Already, by all reports, the work has begun in earnest to expand on the halls, and in this generation, those halls are many times larger than the founders of that dwarven stronghold could ever have imagined when they first began cutting the great steps that would become the famed Undercity. Isn't that the way with all dwarven strongholds? They start as a hole in the ground, and end up among the greatest excavations in all the Realms, though many generations—dwarven generations!—might pass."

"Oo oi!" Pikel piped in, the wordless dwarf's way of saying, "Good point!"

"And so it shall be with my cathedral," Cadderly explained. "If I lay but the first stone, then I will have begun something grand, for it is the vision that serves the purpose."

Ivan looked helplessly to Pikel, who only shrugged. It was hard for either dwarf to fault Cadderly's thinking. In fact, as Ivan digested all that the young priest had said, he found that he respected Cadderly even more, that the man had risen above the usual limitations of his heritage and was actually planning to do something quite dwarf-like.

Ivan said just that, and Cadderly was gracious enough to accept the sideways compliment without a word of argument.

* * * * *

Two Oghman priests approached the square stone mausoleum butted against the cliff behind the Edificant Library.

"Let them take care of their own, I say," muttered the muscular chap nicknamed Berdole the Brutal because of his wrestling prowess and snarling demeanor. The other, Curt, nodded his agreement, for neither of them liked this detail. Kierkan Rufo had been a priest of Deneir, not Oghma, and yet, because of his brand, Dean Thobicus had determined that Oghman priests should prepare and bury the body. By custom, Rufo's body had lain in state for three days, and now it was time for the final preparations.

Berdole fumbled with his large belt ring, finally finding the long-necked key that fit the heavy door. With some effort, he opened the lock and pulled the door wide.

A damp, musty smell, tinged with the scent of decay, rolled out at the two. Except to put Rufo's body inside, this structure had not been opened since the death of Pertelope in the late fall.

Curt lit and hoisted his lantern, but motioned for Berdole to lead the way in. The muscular priest obliged, his hard boots stomping noisily on the bare stone floor.

The vault was large, perhaps thirty feet square, supported at ten-foot intervals both ways by thick columns. A single window, right of the door, allowed some sunlight to trickle in, but the glass was filthy and deeply set in the thick stone, and the illumination was meager. A series of stone slabs lined the center of the room, all but one empty.

On that slab, between the two columns farthest from the door, lay Kierkan Rufo's body beneath an unremarkable shroud.

"Let us be done quickly," said Berdole, pulling the pack from his back. His obvious nervousness did not sit well with his smaller companion, who looked to Berdole the Brutal for protection.

The two did not bother to close the door as they moved in, and neither noticed the soft rush of air as an invisible creature glided in behind them.

"Maybe he threw up enough blood so this will not take so long," Berdole said with a halfhearted chuckle.

Curt snickered at the grim humor as well, knowing that jokes might be his only defense against his abhorrence of this task.

High in a corner of the mausoleum, on the opposite wall and to the right of the door, Druzil sat and scratched his doglike head, muttering curses under his breath. The imp had tried to get into this place since Rufo's body had been put here, thinking that he might somehow recover at least a portion of the chaos curse from the corpse. Too many priests had been around then, including one of the leading members of the Oghman order, and so Druzil had waited, thinking he would just break in after the others had left. He found the door locked, though, and the window blessed, so that he did not dare enter.

The imp knew enough of the human rituals to understand what the two men now meant to do. They would drain the blood from the body and replace it with a smelly, preserving liquid. Druzil had overheard that Rufo could not be given a proper Deneirian or Oghman burial, and the imp had hoped that the priests wouldn't waste their time with this pointless embalming. Druzil thought of swooping down and stinging the men with his poison-tipped tail, or of hitting them with magical spells, burning their behinds with little bolts of energy to chase them away. It simply was too risky, so all the imp could do was sit and watch and mutter silent curses.

Every drop of blood that the priests took from Rufo's body would be a little less of *Tuanta Quiro Miancay* the imp might recover.

Berdole looked at his partner and took a deep breath, holding up the large needle for Curt to see.

"I cannot watch this," Curt admitted, and he turned away and walked past a couple of the slabs, near the other set of columns.

Berdole laughed, gaining confidence from his friend's weakness, and moved beside the slab. He pushed the shroud away just enough so that he could pull out Rufo's left arm, pushing back the black robes that Rufo had been dressed in and turning the arm so that the exposed wrist was up.

"You might feel a small pinch," the muscular priest

joked lightly to the corpse, drawing a disgusted groan from Curt.

From the far rafters, Druzil chewed his bottom lip in frustration as he watched the large needle go against Rufo's exposed wrist. He would have to steal the blood, he decided, every drop of it!

Berdole lined the needle's point up with the vein in Rufo's skinny wrist and angled the instrument for a good puncture. He took another deep breath, looked to Curt's back for support, then started to push.

The cold, pallid hand snapped around in a circular motion, catching the needle and Berdole's hand in a crushing grasp.

"What?" the muscular priest stammered.

Curt turned about to see Berdole hunched low at the slab, both his strong hands wrapped around Rufo's thin forearm, with Rufo's clawlike digits clasping tightly to his lower jaw. This was Berdole the Brutal, the strongest of the strong Oghman's. This was Berdole the Brutal, two hundred and fifty pounds of power, a man who could wrestle a black bear to a standstill!

Yet that skinny arm of Kierkan Rufo—of dead Kierkan Rufo!—jerked Berdole down to the slab as though his muscular frame were no more than a wet towel. Then, to Curt's disbelieving eyes, Rufo's hand pushed up and back. The muscles in Berdole's thick arms strained to their limits, but could not halt the push. Up and over went his chin—it sounded to Curt like the cracking of a large tree right before it tumbled to the ground—and suddenly, the surprised Berdole was staring at the world upside down and backwards.

The Oghman's strong hands let go of the skinny, pallid arm and twitched uncontrollably in the empty air. Rufo's fingers loosened, and Berdole fell backward to the floor, quite dead.

Curt hardly remembered to breathe. He looked from Berdole to the shrouded corpse, and his vision blurred with dizziness wrought of horror as Rufo slowly sat up.

The shroud fell away, and the gaunt, pale man turned his eyes, eyes that simmered red with inner fires, toward Curt.

Druzil clapped his clawed hands together and squealed in happiness, then flapped off for the door.

Curt screamed and fled with all speed, five long strides bringing him near the sunlight, near salvation.

Rufo waved a hand, and the heavy stone door swung shut, slamming with a bang that sounded like a drum of doom. The Oghman threw all his weight against the door, but he might as well have tried to move a mountain. He scratched at the stone until his fingers bled. He glanced back over his shoulder and saw that Rufo was up, walking stiffly toward him.

Curt cried out repeatedly and went for the window, but realized that he had no time. He fell beyond it, backing and watching the corpse, crying for mercy and for Oghma to be with him.

Then the side wall was against his back; he had nowhere to run. Curt caught his breath finally, and remembered who he was. He presented his holy symbol, a scroll of silver on a chain about his neck, and called to Oghma.

"Be gone!" Curt cried at Rufo. "In the name of Oghma, evil undead thing, get you back!"

Rufo didn't flinch. He was ten steps away. Nine steps away. He staggered suddenly as he crossed in front of the window, as though he had been burned on the side. But the light was meager, and the monster passed beyond it.

Curt began a frantic chant of a spell. He felt strangely disconnected from his god, though, as if Rufo's mere presence had despoiled this place. Still he chanted, summoning his powers.

He felt a sting in his lower back and jerked suddenly, his spell disrupted. He turned to see the bat-winged imp, snickering wickedly as it flew away.

"What horror is this?" Curt cried. Rufo was there then, and the terrified man swung his lantern out at the monster.

Rufo caught him by the wrist and easily held the makeshift weapon at bay. Curt punched out with his other hand, connecting solidly on Rufo's chin, knocking Rufo's head to the side.

Rufo calmly turned back to him. Curt made to punch again, but Rufo hooked his arm under the man's, brought his skinny fingers around Curt's back, and grabbed the man's hair on the opposite side of his head. With terrifying strength, Rufo pulled Curt's head to the side, pressed Curt's cheek against his own shoulder, laying bare the side of the man's neck.

Curt thought that Rufo would simply snap that neck, as he had done to Berdole, but the Oghman learned better when Rufo opened his mouth, revealing a set of canine fangs, half an inch longer than the rest of his teeth.

With a look of supreme hunger, Rufo bent over and bit down on Curt's neck, opening the jugular. Curt was screaming, but Rufo, feasting on the warm blood, heard none of it.

It was ecstacy for the monster, the satiation of a hunger more powerful than anything he had ever known in life. It was impossibly sweet. It was . . .

Rufo's mouth began to burn. The sweet blood became acidic.

With a roar of outrage, Rufo spun away and heaved the man away with the arm still hooked behind Curt's back. The poor man flew head over heels, his back striking the nearest column. He slid to the floor and lay very still. He felt nothing in his lower body, but his chest was on fire, burning with poison.

"What have you done?" Kierkan Rufo demanded, looking to the rafters and the perched imp.

A creature of the horrid lower planes, Druzil was not usually afraid of anything this world could present to him. The imp was afraid now, justifiably afraid of this thing that Kierkan Rufo had become. "I wanted to help you," Druzil explained. "He could not be allowed to escape."

"You tainted his blood!" Rufo roared. "His blood," the monster said more quietly, longingly. "I need . . . I need."

Rufo looked back to Curt, but the light of life had gone from the man's eyes.

Rufo roared again, a horrible, unearthly sound.

"There are more," Druzil promised. "There are many more, not far away!"

A strange look came over Rufo then. He looked to his bare arms, held them up in front of his face, as though he had realized for the first time that something very unusual had happened to him.

"Blood?" he asked more than stated, and he put a plaintive look Druzil's way.

Druzil's bulbous eyes seemed to come farther out of their sockets as the imp recognized the sincere confusion on the dead Rufo's face. "Do you not understand what has happened to you?" Druzil cried excitedly.

Rufo went to take a steadying breath, but then realized that he wasn't breathing at all. Again that plaintive, questioning look fell over Druzil, who seemed to have the answers.

"You drank of *Tuanta Quiro Miancay*," the imp squealed. "The Most Fatal Horror, the ultimate chaos, and thus you have become the ultimate perversion of humanity!"

Still Rufo did not seem to understand.

"The ultimate perversion!" Druzil said again, as though that should explain everything. "The antithesis of life itself!"

"What are you talking about?" asked a horrified Rufo, Curt's blood spewing from his lips.

Druzil laughed wickedly. "You are immortal," he said, and Rufo, stunned and confused, finally began to catch on. "You are a vampire."

four

Delusions

ampire. The word hung in Rufo's thoughts, a dead weight on his undead shoulders. He crawled back to the stone slab and flopped down on his back, covering his eyes with his skinny, pale hands.

"*Bene tellemara*," Druzil muttered many times as the minutes passed uneventfully. "Would you have them come out and find you?"

Rufo did not look up.

"The priests are dead," the imp rasped. "Torn. Will those who come in search of them be caught so unaware?"

Rufo moved his arm from in front of his face and looked over at the imp, but did not seem to care.

"You think you can beat them," Druzil reasoned, misunderstanding Rufo's calmness. "Fool! You think you

49

can beat them all!"

Rufo's response caught the imp off guard, made Druzil understand that despair, not confidence, was the source of the undead man's lethargy. "I do not care to try," Rufo said sincerely.

"You can beat them," the imp quickly improvised, changing his emphasis so that the statement suddenly did not seem so ridiculous. "You can beat them all!"

"I am already dead," Rufo said dryly. "I am already defeated."

"Of course, of course!" Druzil rasped happily, clapping his hands and flapping his wings to perch on the end of Rufo's slab. "Dead, yes, but that is your strength, not your weakness. You can beat them all, I say, and the library will be yours."

The last words seemed to pique Rufo's interest. He cocked his head at an angle so that he could better view the untrustworthy imp.

"You are immortal," Druzil said solemnly.

Rufo continued to stare for a long, uneasy moment. "At what price?" he asked.

"Price?" Druzil echoed.

"I am not alive!" Rufo roared at him, and Druzil spread his wings, ready to launch away if the vampire made a sudden move.

"You are more alive than you have ever been!" Druzil snapped back. "Now you have power. Now your will shall be done!"

"To what end?" Rufo wanted, needed, to know. "I am dead. My flesh is dead. What pleasures might I know? What dreams worth fancying?"

"Pleasures?" the imp asked. "Did not the priest's blood taste sweet? And did you not feel power as you approached the pitiful man? You could taste his fear, vampire, and the taste was as sweet as the blood that was to come."

Rufo continued to stare, but had no more complaints to offer. Druzil spoke the truth, it seemed. Rufo had tasted the man's fear, and that sensation of power, of inspiring such terror, felt wonderfully sweet to the man who had been so impotent in life.

Druzil waited a little while, until he was certain that Rufo was convinced to at least explore this vampiric existence. "You must be gone from this place," the imp explained, looking to the corpses.

Rufo glanced at the closed door, then nodded and swung about, dangling his legs over the side of the slab. "The catacombs," he remarked.

"You cannot cross," Druzil said as the vampire began stiffly walking toward the door. Rufo turned on him suspiciously, as if he thought the imp's words a threat.

"The sun is bright," Druzil explained. "It will burn you like fire."

Rufo's expression turned from curious to dour to sheer horror.

"You are a creature of the night now," Druzil went on firmly. "The light of day is not your ally."

It was a bitter pill for Rufo to swallow, but in light of all that had happened, the man accepted the news stoically and forced himself to straighten once more. "How am I to get out of here?" he asked, his tone filled with anger and sarcasm.

Druzil led Rufo's gaze to rows of marked stones lining the mausoleum's far wall. These were the crypts of the library's former headmasters, including those of Avery Schell and Pertelope, and not all of the stones were marked.

At first the thought of crawling into a crypt revolted

Rufo, but as he let go of those prejudices remaining from when he had been a living, breathing man, as he allowed himself to view the world as an undead thing, a creature of the night, he found the notion of cool, dark stone strangely appealing.

Rufo met Druzil by the wall, in front of an unmarked slab set waist-high. Not knowing what the imp expected, the vampire reached out with his stiff arms and clasped at the edge of the stone.

"Not like that!" Druzil scolded, and Rufo stood straight, eyeing the imp dangerously, obviously growing tired of Druzil's superior attitude.

"If you tear it away, the priests will find you," the imp explained, and under his breath he added the expected, "*Bene tellemara.*"

Rufo did not reply, but stood staring from the imp to the wall. How was he to get inside the crypt if he did not remove the stone? These were not doors that could be opened and closed; they were sealed marker blocks, removed for burials, then mortared back into place.

"There is a crack along the bottom," Druzil remarked, and when Rufo bent low, he did see a line running along the mortar at the bottom of the slab.

The vampire shrugged his shoulders, but before he could ask Druzil how that crack might help, a strange sensation, a lightness, came over him, as though he was something less than substantial. Rufo looked to Druzil, who was smiling widely, then back to the crack, which suddenly loomed much larger. The vampire, black robes and all, melted away into a cloud of green vapor and swirled through the crack in the slab.

He came back to his corporeal form inside the tight confines of the stone crypt, hemmed in by unbroken walls. For an instant, a wave of panic, a feeling of being trapped, swept over the man. How long would his air last? he wondered. He shut his mouth, fearful that he was gulping in too much of the precious commodity.

A moment later, his mouth opened once more and from it issued a howl of laughter. "Air?" Rufo asked aloud. Rufo needed no air, and he was certainly not trapped. He would slip out through that crack as easily as he had come in, or else he could simply slide down and kick the slab free of its perch. He was strong enough to do that, he knew he was.

Suddenly the limitations of a weak and living body seemed clear to the vampire. He thought of all the times when he had been persecuted—unfairly, by his reckoning—and he thought of the two Oghman priests he had so easily dispatched.

Oghman priests! Wrestlers, warriors, yet he had tossed them about without effort!

Rufo felt as though he had been freed of those living limitations, free to fly and grab at the power that was rightfully his. He would teach his persecutors. He would . . .

The vampire stopped fantasizing and reached up to feel the brand on his forehead. An image of Cadderly, of his greatest oppressor, came clear to him.

Yes, Rufo would teach them all.

But now, here in the cool, dark confines of his chosen bed, the vampire would rest. The sun, an ally of the living—an ally of the weak—was bright outside.

Rufo would wait for the dark.

*   *   *   *   *

The highest-ranking priests of the Deneirian order gathered that afternoon at Dean Thobicus's bidding.

They met in a little-used room on the library's fourth and highest floor, an obscure setting that would guarantee them their privacy.

Seclusion seemed important to the withered dean, the others realized, a point made quite clear when Thobicus shut tight the room's single door and closed the shutters over the two tiny windows.

Thobicus solemnly turned about and surveyed this most important gathering. The room was not formally set up for an audience. Some of the priests sat in chairs of various sizes; others simply stood leaning against a bare wall, or sat on the weathered carpet covering the floor. Thobicus moved near the middle of the group, near the center of the floor, and turned slowly, eyeing each of the thirty gathered priests to let them fully appreciate the gravity of this meeting. The various conversations dissipated under that scrutiny, replaced by intrigue and trepidation.

"Castle Trinity is eradicated," Thobicus said to them after more than a minute of silence.

The priests looked around at each other, stunned by the suddenness of the announcement. Then a cheer went up, quietly at first, but gaining momentum until all the gathered priests, except the dean himself, were clapping each other on the back and shaking their fists in victory.

More than one called out Cadderly's name, and Thobicus winced each time he heard it, and knew that he must proceed with caution.

As the cheering lost its momentum, Thobicus held up his hand, calling for quiet. Again the dean's intense stare fell over the priests, silencing them, filling them with curiosity.

"The word is good," remarked Fester Rumpol, the

second-ranking priest of the Deneirian order. "Yet I read no cheer in your features, my dean."

"Do you know how I learned of our enemy's fall?" Thobicus asked him.

"Cadderly?" answered one voice.

"You have spoken with a higher power, an agent of Deneir?" offered another.

Dean Thobicus shook his head to both assumptions, his gaze never leaving Rumpol's. "I could not collect the information," he explained to them all. "My attempts at communion with Deneir have been blocked. I had to go to Bron Turman of Oghma to find my answers. At my bidding, he inquired of agents of his god and learned of our enemy's defeat."

That information was easily as astonishing as the report of Castle Trinity's fall. Thobicus was the dean of the Edificant Library, the father of this sect. How could he be blocked from communion with Deneir's agents? All of these priests had survived the Time of Troubles, that most awful period for persons of faith, and all of them feared that the dean was speaking of a second advent of that terrible time.

Fester Rumpol's expression shifted from fear to suspicion. "I prayed this morning," he said, commanding the attention of all. "I asked for guidance in my search for an old parchment—and my call was answered."

Whispers began all about the room.

"That is because . . . " Thobicus said loudly, sharply, stealing back the audience. He paused to make sure they were all listening. "That is because Cadderly has not yet targeted you!"

"Cadderly?" Rumpol, and several others, said together. Throughout the Edificant Library, particularly in the Deneirian order, feelings for the young priest were strong, many positive and many negative. More than a few of the older priests thought Cadderly impetuous and irreverent, lackadaisical in the routine, necessary duties of his station. And many of the younger priests viewed Cadderly as a rival that they could not compete against. Of the thirty in this room, every man was at least five years older than Cadderly, yet Cadderly had already come to outrank more than half by the library's stated hierarchy. And the persistent rumors hinted that Cadderly was already among the very strongest of the order, in Deneir's eyes.

Dean Thobicus had apparently confirmed this theory. If Cadderly could block the dean's communion with agents of Deneir, and from all the way across the Snowflake Mountains . . . !

Conversations erupted from every corner, the priests confused as to what all of this might mean. Fester Rumpol and Dean Thobicus continued to stare at each other, with Rumpol having no answers to the dean's incredible claim.

"Cadderly has overstepped his rank," Thobicus explained. "He deems the hierarchy of the Edificant Library unfit, and thus, he desires to change it."

"Preposterous!" one priest called out.

"So thought I," Dean Thobicus replied calmly. He had prepared himself well for this meeting, with answers to every question or claim. "But now I have come to know the truth. With Avery Schell and Pertelope dead, our young Cadderly has, it would seem, run a bit out of control. He deceived me in order to go to Castle Trinity." That claim was not exactly true, but Thobicus did not want to admit that Cadderly had dominated him, had bent his mind like a willow in a strong wind. "And now he blocks my attempts at communion with our god."

As far as Thobicus knew, that second statement was correct. For him to believe otherwise would indicate that he had fallen far from Deneir's favor, and that the old dean was not ready to believe.

"What would you have us do?" Fester Rumpol asked, his tone showing more suspicion than loyalty.

"Nothing," Thobicus replied quickly, recognizing the man's doubts. "I only wish to warn you all, that we will not be taken by surprise when our young friend returns."

That answer seemed to satisfy Rumpol and many others. Thobicus abruptly adjourned the meeting then and retired to his private quarters. He had planted the seeds of doubt. His honesty would be viewed favorably when Cadderly returned and the dean and the upstart young priest faced off against each other.

And they would indeed, Thobicus knew. He had neither forgotten nor forgiven the young priest for his actions. He was the dean of the library, the head of his order, and he would not be treated like a puppet by any man.

That was Dean Thobicus's greatest shortcoming. He still could not accept that Cadderly's domination had been granted by Deneir, by the true tenets of their faith. Thobicus had been tied up in the bureaucracy of the library for so long that he had forgotten the higher purpose of the library and the order. Too many procedures had dulled the goals. The dean viewed his upcoming battle with Cadderly as a political struggle, a fight that would be decided by back room alliances and gratuitous promises.

Deep in his heart, of course, Thobicus knew the truth, knew that his struggle with Cadderly would be decided by the tenets of Deneir. But that truth, like the truth of the order itself, was so buried by false information that

Thobicus dared to believe otherwise, and fooled himself into thinking that others would follow his lead.

*   *   *   *   *

Kierkan Rufo's dreams were no longer those of a victim. He saw Cadderly, but this time it was the young Deneirian, not the branded Rufo, who cowered. This time, in this dream, Rufo, the conqueror, calmly reached down and tore Cadderly's throat out.

The vampire awoke in absolute darkness. He could feel the stone walls pressing in on him, and he welcomed their sanctuary, basking in the blackness as the minutes turned into an hour.

Then another call compelled Rufo; a great hunger swept over him. He tried to ignore it, consciously wanted nothing more than to lie in the cool black emptiness. Soon his fingers clawed at the stone and he thrashed about, overwhelmed by urges he did not understand. A low, feral growl, the call of an animal, escaped his lips.

Rufo squirmed and twisted, turning his body completely about in the crypt. At first the thrashing vampire thought to tear the blocking stone away, to shatter this barrier into a million pieces, but he kept his senses enough to realize that he might need this sanctuary again. Concentrating on the minute crack at the base of the slab, Rufo melted away into greenish vapor—it wasn't difficult—and filtered out into the mausoleum's main area.

Druzil, perched on the nearest slab, doglike chin in clawed fingers, waited for him.

Rufo hardly noticed the imp, though. When he assumed corporeal form, he felt different, less stiff and awkward. He smelled the night air—his air—about him and felt strong. Faint moonlight leaked in through the dirty window, but unlike the light of the sun, it was cool, comfortable. Rufo stretched his arms into the air, kicked off with one foot, and twirled around on the other, tasting the night and his freedom.

"They did not come," Druzil said to him.

Rufo started to ask what the imp might be talking about, but, as soon as he noticed the two corpses, he understood. "I am not surprised," the vampire answered. "The library is full of duties. Always duties. The dead priests may not be missed for several days."

"Then gather them up," Druzil ordered. "Drag them from this place."

Rufo concentrated more on the imp's tone than on the actual words.

"Do it now," Druzil went on, oblivious to the fast-mounting danger. "If we are careful . . . " Only then did Druzil look up from the nearest corpse to see Rufo's face, and the vampire's icy glare sent a shiver along the normally unshakable imp's spine.

Druzil didn't even try to continue with his reasoning, didn't even try to get words past the lump that filled his throat.

"Come to me," Rufo said quietly, calmly.

Druzil had no intention of following that command. He started to shake his head, large ears flapping noisily; he even tried to utter a derogatory comment. Those thoughts were lost in the imp's sudden realization that he was indeed moving toward Rufo, that his feet and wings were heeding the vampire's command. He was at the end of the slab, then he hopped off, flapping his bat wings to remain in the air, to continue his steady progress.

Rufo's cold hand shot out and caught the imp by the throat, breaking the trance. Druzil let out a shriek and instinctively brought his tail about, waving it menacingly in Rufo's face.

Rufo laughed and began to squeeze.

Druzil's tail snapped into Rufo's face, its barbed tip boring a small hole.

Rufo continued to laugh wickedly and squeezed tighter with his horribly powerful grasp. "Who is the master?" the confident vampire asked.

Druzil thought his head would be popped off! He couldn't begin to squirm. And that gaze! Druzil had faced some of the most powerful lords of the lower planes, but at that moment, it seemed to the imp that none was more imposing.

"Who is the master?" Rufo asked again.

Druzil's tail fell limp, and he stopped struggling. "Please, master," he whined breathlessly.

"I am hungry," the vampire announced, casually tossing Druzil aside. Rufo strode for the mausoleum door with a graceful and confident gait. As he neared the door, he reached out with his will and it swung open. As he crossed through the portal, it banged closed once more, leaving Druzil alone in the mausoleum, muttering to himself.

*　*　*　*　*

Bachtolen Mossgarden, the library's cook since Ivan Bouldershoulder had gone away, was also muttering to himself that night. Bachy, as the priests called him, was fed up with his new duties. He had been hired as a groundskeeper—that was what Bachy did best—but with winter thick about the grounds, and with the dwarf gallivanting in the mountains, the priests had changed the rules.

"Slop, slop, and more stinkin' slop!" the dirty man grumbled, overturning a bucket of leftover cabbage down a slope behind the squat library. He moved to pick his nose, but changed his mind as the finger, reeking of old cabbage, neared the nostril.

"I'm even startin' to smell like the stinkin' slop!" he whined, and he banged on the metal bucket, spilling the last of its remains onto the slick, stained snow, and spun about to leave.

Bachy noticed that it had suddenly grown much colder. And quieter, he realized a moment later. It wasn't the cold that had given him pause, but the stillness. Even the wind was no more.

The hairs on the back of Bachy's neck tingled and stood on end. Something was wrong, out of place.

"Who is it?" he asked straightforwardly, for that had always been his way. He didn't wash much, he didn't shave much, and he justified it by saying that people should like him for more than appearance.

Bachy liked to think of himself as profound.

"Who is it?" he asked again, more clearly, gaining courage in the fact that no one had answered the first time. He had almost convinced himself that he was letting his imagination get the best of him, had even taken his first step back toward the Edificant Library, the back door of the kitchen only twenty yards away, when a tall, angular figure stepped in front of him, standing perfectly still and quiet.

Bachy stuttered through a series of beginnings of questions, never completing a one. Most prominent among them was Bachy's pure wonderment at where this guy had come from. It seemed to the poor, dirty cook that the man had stepped out of thin air, or out of shadows that were not deep enough to hide him!

The figure advanced a step. Overhead, the moonlight broke through a cloud, revealing Rufo's pallid face.

Bachy wavered, seemed as if he would fall over. He wanted to cry out, but found no voice. He wanted to run, but his legs would barely support him while standing still.

Rufo tasted the fear, and his eyes lit up, horrid red flames dancing where his pupils should have been. The vampire grinned evilly, his mouth gradually opening wide, baring long fangs. Bachy mumbled something that sounded like, "By the gods," then he was kneeling in the snow, his legs having buckled underneath him.

The sensation of fear, of sweet, sweet fear, multiplied tenfold, washed over Rufo. It was the purest feeling of ecstacy the wretch had ever known. He understood and appreciated his power at that moment. This pitiful slob, this man he did not even know, couldn't begin to resist him!

Rufo moved slowly, determinedly, knowing that his victim was helpless before the spectacle of the vampire.

And then he tasted blood, like the nectar he had drawn from the foolish Oghman priest inside the mausoleum before Druzil's poison had tainted it. This blood was not tainted. Bachy was a dirty thing, but his blood was pure, warm, and sweet.

The minutes slipped past, and Rufo fed. He understood then that he should stop. Somehow he knew that if he didn't kill this wretch, the man would rise up in undeath, a lesser creature, to serve him. Instinctively the vampire realized that this one would be his slave—at least until Bachy, too, had fully followed the path to becoming a vampire.

Rufo continued to feed. He meant to stop, but no level of thought could overrule the pleasure the vampire knew. Sometime later, Bachy's husk of a corpse tumbled down the slope behind the other discarded garbage.

By the time the night began to wane, Kierkan Rufo had become comfortable with his new existence. He wandered about like a wolf scouting its domain, thinking always of the kill, of the taste of the dirty man's blood. Dried brown remnants of the macabre feast stained the vampire's face and cloak as he stood before the side wall of the Edificant Library, looking up to the gargoyles that lined its gutter system, and past the roof, to the stars of his domain.

A voice in his head (he knew it was Druzil's) told him he should return to the mausoleum, to the cool, dark crypt where he might hide from the infernal heat of the coming sun. Yet there was a danger in that plan, Rufo realized. He had taken things too far now. The revealing light of day might put the priests on their guard, and they would be formidable opponents.

They would know where to start looking.

Death had given Kierkan Rufo new insights and powers beyond anything the order of Deneir had ever promised. He could feel the chaos curse swirling within his body, which he inhabited like a partner, an adviser. Rufo could go and find a place to be safe, but *Tuanta Quiro Miancay* wanted more than safety.

Rufo was barely conscious that he had changed form, but the next thing he knew, his bat claws had found a perch on the edge of the library's roof. Bones crackled and stretched as the vampire resumed his human form, leaving Rufo sitting on the roof's edge, looking down on a window that he knew well.

He climbed headfirst down the wall, his strong undead fingers finding secure holds where in life he would have seen only smooth stone, past the third floor, to the second. To Rufo's surprise, an iron grate had been placed over this window. He reached through the bars and pushed in the glass, then thought of becoming vaporous and simply wafting into the room. For some reason, some instinctive, animalistic urge, as though it occurred to him that the grate had been put there only to hinder his progress, he grabbed an iron bar and, with one hand, tore the grate free and sent it spinning into the night.

The entire library was open to him, he believed, and the vampire had no intention of leaving.

Five

Well-placed Faith

Danica stared into the flames of the campfire, watching the orange and white dance and using its hypnotic effects to let her mind wander across the miles. Her thoughts were on Cadderly and the troubles he would face. He meant to oppose Dean Thobicus, she knew, and to rip apart all the rituals and bureaucracy that the Deneirian order had been built on through the years. The opposition would be wicked and unyielding, and, though Danica did not believe that Cadderly's life would be in danger, as it had been in Castle Trinity, she knew that his pain, if he lost, would be everlasting.

Those thoughts inevitably led Danica to Dorigen, sitting wrapped in a blanket across the fire from her. What of the wizard? she wondered. What if Thobicus, expecting what was to come from Cadderly, did not respect Danica's rights as captor and ordered Dorigen executed?

Danica shook the disturbing thoughts from her mind and berated herself for letting her imagination run wild. Dean Thobicus was not an evil man, after all, and his weakness had always been a lack of decisive action. Dorigen was not likely in danger.

"The area remains clear," said Shayleigh, pulling Danica from her thoughts. She looked up as the elf maiden entered the camp, bow in hand. Shayleigh smiled and nodded to Dorigen, who appeared fast asleep.

"The mountains haven't awakened from the winter's slumber," Danica replied.

Shayleigh nodded, but her mischievous, thoroughly elven smile showed Danica that she thought the time for the spring dance was growing near. "Rest now," Shayleigh offered. "I will take my reverie later in the evening."

Danica eyed Shayleigh for a long while before agreeing, intrigued, as always, by the elf's referral to her "reverie." The elves did not sleep, not by the human definition of the word. Their reverie was a meditative state apparently as restful as true sleep. Danica had asked Shayleigh about it on several occasions, and had seen it often during her stay with the elves in Shilmista Forest, but though the elves were not secretive about the custom, it remained strange to the monk. Danica's practice involved many hours of deep meditation, and though that was indeed restful, it did not approach the elven reverie. Someday, Danica determined, she would unlock that secret and find her rest as an elf.

"Do we need to keep a watch?" she asked.

Shayleigh looked around at the dark trees. It was their first night back in the Snowflakes, after a long trek south across the open fields north of Carradoon. "Perhaps not," the elf replied. She sat at the fire's side and took a blanket from her pack. "But sleep lightly and keep your weapons close to your side."

"My weapons are my hands," Danica reminded with a grin.

Across the fire, Dorigen peeked out from under half-closed eyelids and tried to hide her smile. For perhaps the first time in all her life, the wizard felt as if she was among friends. She had secretly gone out and placed magical wards about the encampment. No need to tell Danica and Shayleigh of them, though, for Dorigen had worded the spells so that the monk and the elf could not trigger the traps.

With those comforting thoughts in mind, Dorigen allowed herself to drift off to sleep.

* * * * *

Shayleigh came out of her reverie sometime before dawn, the woods still dark about them. The elf sensed something amiss, so she rose from her bed, shrugged off the blanket, and took up her longbow. Shayleigh's keen eyes adapted quickly to the night. Towering mountains loomed as dark silhouettes all about her, and all appeared quiet and as it should be.

Still, the tiny hairs on the back of Shayleigh's neck were tingling. One of her senses was hinting at danger, not so far away.

The elf peered hard into the shadows; she tilted her head at different angles, trying to discern an out-of-place sound. Then she sniffed the air and crinkled her nose in disgust.

Trolls. Shayleigh knew that foul odor; nearly every

adventurer in the Realms had encountered a wretched troll at least once in his or her travels.

"Danica," she called softly, not wanting to warn her enemies that she knew they were about.

The wary monk came awake immediately, but made no sudden movements.

"Trolls," Shayleigh whispered, "not far away."

Danica looked to the fire, no more than glowing embers by this time, with all the wood fully consumed. Trolls hated fire, and feared it, if they feared anything at all.

Danica called quietly to Dorigen, but the wizard did not stir. A look to Shayleigh sent the elf maiden sliding gently around the side of the fire, near enough to prod Dorigen with her bow.

Dorigen grumbled and started to come awake, then popped her eyes wide when Danica yelled out. An explosion went off to one side, one of Dorigen's wards taking down a monster in flaring blue flames. But three more trolls rushed past their burning companion without regard for its terrible fate and crashed into the clearing, eyes glowing a fierce red, their stench nearly overwhelming the companions. The monsters' long, thin frames towered over the group—one had to be nearly eleven feet tall—and, as they came into the light, their rubbery skin showed as putrid grayish green.

Shayleigh's bow was up and firing in the blink of an eye, three arrows blasting into the closest troll. The monster jerked with each hit, but came stubbornly on, its skinny arms waving its hands awkwardly in wide, arcing swipes.

Shayleigh did not gain confidence from the awkward movements; the three fingers on those hands ended in long, sharp claws that could easily tear the hide from a bear.

A fourth arrow hit the monster squarely in the chest, and Shayleigh hopped away, thinking it better to pummel this creature from a distance.

Two flashes, one silver, one gold, went past the elf as Danica led with her daggers. The monk leaped up and spun head over heels over the fire, following the shots (both solid hits on the next troll) at full speed. She barreled in, jumped, and spun, her trailing foot flying about to slam hard into the troll's midsection.

Danica winced at the sickly, squishy sound of that impact, but she didn't dare hesitate. She spun again for a second kick, then came up straight and landed a one-two punch on the lurching troll's jaw.

"Dorigen!" she screamed, seeing the third troll bearing down on the sitting wizard. To Danica's knowledge, Dorigen had no weapons, and few, if any, components for spellcasting—not even a proper spellbook that she might have studied. The monk, too engaged with this monster, and with Shayleigh still battling the first troll, thought her new companion doomed as the troll reached down at the blanketed woman.

There came a bright flash, and the troll fell back, holding the blanket and nothing more. That blanket flared suddenly with fire, scorching the monster's arms, causing it to scream out in pain.

Danica had no idea where Dorigen had come up with that spell, but she had no time to ponder the issue now. The troll swiped at her repeatedly, and she did a fair, twisting dance to keep clear of its deadly arms. She came in close, inside the monster's reach, thinking to wriggle out the backside and score a few hits before the lumbering thing turned, but the troll proved faster and more resourceful than she believed, and she nearly swooned as the monster opened its wide, horrible

mouth. The long, pointy teeth came within an inch of
Danica's face—she could smell the thing's disgusting
breath!—and the troll would have had her, except that
the incredibly agile monk snapped her foot straight up
before her, lifting it right in front of her face, though she
had only a few inches to spare between herself and the
troll.

Her kick caught the troll on its long nose and drove
the proboscis up and back with a loud crackling noise.
Danica was down in a crouch in an instant, dodging the
flailing arms, and out she slipped, under the troll's
armpit, around the back, where she exploded with fury,
launching a barrage of heavy punches.

Shayleigh continued to backpedal, firing arrow after
arrow into the pursuing troll. She knew that this would
not do, though, for the troll's initial wounds were already
on the mend. Trolls could regenerate, their rubbery
skin binding of its own accord, and could take an incredible amount of punishment before falling dead.

No, not dead, Shayleigh realized to her horror, for
even a dead troll, even a troll that had been cut into little
bits, would come back to life, whole again, unless its
wounds had been completely burned. That notion led
the elf's gaze to the fire, but the embers promised little
help. It would take some time to coax that glow back
into any sort of flame, and Shayleigh and her companions had no time at all. The elf looked to the side of the
encampment, but found that the troll that had been consumed by the explosion (which Shayleigh did not fully
understand) had fallen into the snow, and already the
fires that had destroyed the thing were nearly extin-
guished. Shayleigh muttered an elven curse.

Another arrow thudded into the troll, hitting the creature in the face. Still the stubborn thing advanced, and

Shayleigh looked down to her half-empty quiver doubtfully. She thought of running into the woods then, of leading this monster away, but one look at Danica told her that she could not, that her friend would not be able to follow.

The troll that had gone unsuccessfully after Dorigen was after the monk now, it and its gruesome companion circling fast to find an exposed flank. Danica worked hard to keep up her guard against attacks from all angles, for with their long arms the trolls could simply reach around any straightforward defense.

"Where did she go?" Danica cried to Shayleigh, obviously referring to the missing wizard.

Shayleigh sighed helplessly and fired another arrow into the pursuing troll. Where indeed had Dorigen gone? she wondered, and she suspected that the wizard had determined this was a good time to escape.

Danica's powerful punch landed heavily against the side of a bending troll's head with a sickly splatting sound. When she retracted the hand, she found a bit of the monster's skin on her knuckles, along with some strands of the thing's hair. Danica groaned in revulsion when she noticed the mess, for the troll hair was writhing of its own accord.

She turned that revulsion into anger, and as the troll came about to swipe at her again, she stepped in close and pounded it repeatedly. Then she wisely fell to her knees and rolled fast to the side as the second troll came rushing at her back. Both monsters were on her as she sprang up to her feet, and up snapped her foot, knocking a lunging hand aside.

"They heal as fast as I hurt them!" the tiring monk cried in frustration.

Danica's statement wasn't quite true, as Shayleigh

found out when her next arrow, her sixteenth shot, dropped the troll to the ground. She looked to her quiver, to the four arrows remaining, and sighed again.

Danica went left, was forced back to the right, and backpedaled frantically as both trolls suddenly rushed ahead. An angled log at her back, a dead tree that had toppled to lean against another tree, ended her running room.

"Damn!" she spat, and she leaped high, kicking out with both feet, scoring two hits on one of the trolls and knocking it back several steps. She realized that the other would hit her, though, and she twisted as she came down to protect her vital spots.

As the troll started its attack, an arrow slammed into the side of its head. The monster's momentum flew away in its surprise, and though the swinging arm did indeed hit Danica, there was little strength behind the blow.

Danica spun completely to regain her balance, then she quickly lashed out, her flying foot slamming the monster several times in succession.

"And when I'm finished with you," she called defiantly, though of course the beast could not understand what she said, "I'll hunt down a certain cowardly wizard and teach her about loyalty!"

At that moment, as if on cue, Danica noticed a small sphere of fire appear in the air over the closest troll's head. Before she could ask, the hovering sphere erupted, sending a shroud of hungry flames down over the troll's body.

The monster shrieked in agony and flailed wildly, but the flames would not let go and would not relent. Danica did well to slip away from the waving inferno. She kept her wits enough to concentrate on the second monster as it came around its burning companion (giving the flaming troll a wide berth), and she met the monstrous thing with another flying double-kick.

Danica had the devious notion of herding the troll into its flaming companion, but the cunning monster wanted no part of that. It staggered back from the kick, then came around again, pointedly putting Danica between it and the burning troll.

An arrow thudded into its side; it turned its ugly head to regard Shayleigh.

Danica flew into it again before it turned back, and the monster stumbled and toppled. Danica was up quickly, thinking to leap atop the monster, but she skidded to a stop, seeing another flaming sphere come to life in the air above the prone troll.

An instant later, that troll, too, was shrieking in agony, engulfed by the biting magical flames.

Shayleigh held her next shot, sensed movement to the side, and spun and fired—into the troll she had already dropped. The thing went down in a heap again, but stubbornly writhed and squirmed, trying to rise.

Danica was on it at once, pounding wildly. Shayleigh joined her, sword in hand, and with mighty hacks, cut off the troll's legs.

Those severed limbs began to wriggle immediately, trying to reattach to the torso, but Danica wisely kicked them away toward the glowing remnant of the campfire.

As soon as one of the legs touched the embers, it burst into flames, and Danica scooped it up by the other end, using it as a grotesque torch. She ran across the clearing and shoved the flaming limb into the face of the unburned troll, the amazing monster still thrashing against Shayleigh's repeated strikes. Soon, that troll, too, was ablaze, and the battle was ended.

Dorigen walked back into camp then, inspecting her

work on the two flame-shrouded trolls. They were little more than crumpled black balls by that time, and their regenerative process was surely defeated by the wizard's flames.

Danica could hardly bear to look at Dorigen, ashamed of her earlier doubts. "I thought you had run off," she admitted.

Dorigen smiled at her.

"I vowed to . . ." Danica began.

"To hunt me down and teach me about loyalty," Dorigen finished for her, lightly and with no accusation in her tone. "But, dear Danica, do you not know that you and your friends have already taught me about loyalty?"

Danica stared hard at the wizard, thinking that Dorigen's bravery here, and the fact that she had bothered to stay around and aid in the fight, would weigh in her favor once they returned to the library. As she thought about it, Danica realized she was not surprised by Dorigen's heroics. The wizard had been won over, heart and soul, and, though Danica agreed that Dorigen should pay a strict penance for her actions in favor of Castle Trinity, for the war she helped direct against Shayleigh's people, the monk hoped that the penance would be positive, in which Dorigen might use her considerable magical powers for the good of the region.

"You likely saved our lives," Shayleigh remarked, drawing Danica's attention. "I am grateful."

That remark seemed to please Dorigen greatly. "It is but a pittance of the debt I owe you and your people," the wizard replied.

Shayleigh nodded her agreement. "A debt that I trust you will pay in full," she said sternly, but with apparent confidence.

Danica was glad to hear it. Shayleigh had not been

cold to Dorigen in any way, but neither had the elf been friendly. Danica could appreciate the elf maiden's turmoil. Shayleigh was an intelligent and perceptive elf, one who based her judgments on an individual's actions. She, more than any of her clan, had accepted Ivan and Pikel as true friends and allies, had not allowed typically elven preconceptions concerning dwarves to cloud her judgment of them. And now she, alone among the elves of Shilmista, had seen this new side of Dorigen, had come to where she was ready to forgive, perhaps, if not to forget.

That support, as well as King Elbereth's (and Danica was confident the elf king would accept Shayleigh's judgment), might prove critical in Cadderly's forthcoming showdown with Dean Thobicus.

"It is almost dawn," Dorigen remarked. "I have no stomach for breakfast with troll stench in the air."

Danica and Shayleigh wholeheartedly agreed, so they packed up their camp and started out early. They would reach the Edificant Library in just three short days.

Six

An Invited Guest

Dean Thobicus was surprised to find a blanket draped over the lone window in his office the next morning. It ruffled as he approached, and he felt the chill morning breeze, which led his gaze to the floor, to the base of the blanket, where the window's glass lay shattered.

"What foolishness is this?" the surly dean asked as he brushed some of the glass aside with his foot. He pulled out the edge of the blanket and was surprised again, for not only was the glass broken, but the grate was gone, apparently ripped from the stonework.

Thobicus fought hard to steady his breathing, fearing that Cadderly might somehow be behind this, that the young priest had returned and used his newfound and indisputably powerful magic on the grate. The iron bars had been new, bolted in place soon after Cadderly had disappeared into the mountains. The dean had explained to the others that it was necessary to ensure that no thieves—agents of Castle Trinity, probably—broke into his office in this time of turmoil and stole off with battle plans. Actually, Thobicus had put the grate on the window not to keep anyone out, but to keep anyone from falling out. When Cadderly had mentally dominated the dean, the young priest had shown his superiority by threatening to make Thobicus leap from the window, and Thobicus knew without doubt that he would have done exactly that if Cadderly had so instructed, that he would have been powerless to ignore the command.

Seeing that window now, broken open and with no blocking grate, sent shudders along the thin dean's spine. He eased the impromptu curtain back into place and turned about slowly, as if expecting to find his nemesis standing in the middle of the office.

He found Kierkan Rufo instead.

"What are you . . . " the dean began, then his words were lost in his throat as he recalled that Rufo had just died. Yet here the man was, standing at that curious and customary angle!

"Do not!" Rufo commanded as the dean's hand went up to grasp the blanket for support. Rufo held his own bony hand out toward Thobicus, and the dean felt Rufo's will, as tangible as a wall of stone, blocking him from grasping the blanket.

"I favor the darkness," the vampire explained cryptically.

Dean Thobicus narrowed his dark eyes to study the man more closely, not understanding. "You cannot come in here," he protested. "You wear the brand."

Rufo laughed at him. "The brand?" he echoed skeptically. He reached up and ran his nails across his forehead, tearing his own skin and scraping away the
distinctive Deneirian markings.

"You cannot come in here!" Thobicus said more frantically, finally catching on that something was terribly
amiss, that Kierkan Rufo had become something much
more dangerous than a simple outcast. Such a brand as
Rufo wore was magical, and if covered or marred, it
would burn inward, tormenting then killing the outcast.
Rufo showed no pain now, though, just confidence.

"You cannot come in here," Thobicus reiterated, his
voice no more than a whisper.

"Indeed I can," Rufo countered, and he smiled wide,
showing bloodied fangs. "You invited me in."

Thobicus's mind whirled in confusion. He remembered those same words, spoken by Rufo at the moment
of the man's death.

At the moment of the man's death!

"Get out of here!" Thobicus demanded desperately.
"Be gone from this holy place!" Out came the symbol of
Deneir, hanging on a chain about the dean's neck, and
he began a chant as he presented it before him.

Rufo felt a sting in his unbeating heart, and the glare
of the pendant, seeming to flare with a life of its own,
hurt his eyes. But after the initial shock, the vampire
sensed something here, a weakness. This was Deneir's
house, and Thobicus was supposedly the leading member of the order. Thobicus above all should have been
able to drive Rufo away. Yet he could not; Rufo knew
with certainty that he could not.

The dean finished his spell and hurled a wave of magical energy at the vampire, but Rufo didn't even flinch.
He was staring directly at the presented holy symbol,

which, to his eyes, no longer flared in the least.

"There is a blackness in your heart, Dean Thobicus," Rufo reasoned.

"Be gone from here!" Thobicus countered.

"There is no conviction in your words."

"Foul beast!" Thobicus growled, and he boldly approached, hand and holy symbol extended. "Foul dead thing, you have no purpose here!"

The vampire began to laugh.

"Deneir will smite you!" Thobicus promised. "I will . . . "

He stopped and grunted in pain as Rufo snapped a strong hand up and caught him by the forearm. "You will do what?" the vampire asked. A flick of Rufo's wrist sent the holy symbol spinning from Thobicus's weak hand. "There is no conviction in your words," Rufo said again. "And there is no strength in your heart." Rufo let go of the arm and grasped the front of the dean's robes, easily lifting the thin man into the air.

"What have you done, fallen priest?" the confident vampire asked.

Those last two words echoed in the dean's thoughts like a damning curse. He wanted to scream out for the headmasters; he wanted to break free and rush to the window and tear the blanket aside, for certainly the light of day would do ill to this horrid, undead thing. But Rufo's claims, all of them, were true—Thobicus knew they were true!

Rufo carelessly tossed the man to the floor and paced to put himself between the dean and the window. Thobicus lay very still, his thoughts whirling with confusion and desperation, wallowing in self-pity. Indeed, what had he done? How had he fallen so far and so fast?

"Please," the vampire said, "do go and sit at your desk, that we might properly discuss what has come to pass."

All through the early morning, Rufo had sat in this office, thinking that he would lie in wait for Thobicus, then simply tear the man apart. It was no longer hunger that drove the vampire—he had feasted well the previous night. No, Rufo had come after Dean Thobicus purely for revenge, had decided to strike out against all the library for the torments the Deneirians had given him in his life.

Now, unwittingly guided by the designs of the chaos curse, the vampire was thinking differently. In that moment of confrontation, Rufo had seen into the heart of Dean Thobicus, and there he had found a malignant blackness.

"Have you eaten this day?" Rufo asked pleasantly, sliding to a sitting position on the edge of the oaken desk.

Thobicus, still a bit ruffled, straightened defiantly in his chair and answered simply, "No."

"I have," Rufo explained, and laughed wickedly at the irony. "In fact, I have feasted on the one who would prepare your meal."

Thobicus looked away, his expression filled with disgust.

"You should be glad of that!" Rufo snarled at him, and slammed the desk, forcing Thobicus to jump in surprise and turn back to face the monster. "If I had not already eaten, then my hunger would have overcome me by now, and you would be dead!" Rufo said fiercely, and he bared his fangs to accentuate his point.

Dean Thobicus tried to sit still, to hide the fact that his hands were working under the desktop, fingering a loaded crossbow that he had recently come to keep there. The weapon was supported by sliding brackets so that it could be swiftly and easily pulled out in times of need. The dean's shoulders sagged a bit when he thought of the weapon, when he realized that he had put the crossbow there not for any emergency against a foe such as this, but in case Cadderly had come to him again, and had tried to dominate him.

Rufo was concerned with his own thoughts and seemed to notice neither the dean's delicate movements nor the turmoil boiling within the withered man. The vampire slid off the desk and walked to the middle of the room, one skinny finger tapping thoughtfully on his lips, still red from the blood of his meal.

Thobicus realized that he should pull out the crossbow and shoot the monster. Well versed in theology, the dean recognized Rufo for what he was, knew that he had somehow become a vampire. The crossbow bolt probably wouldn't kill Rufo, but it had been blessed and dipped in holy water, so it would at least wound him, and possibly allow the dean to flee the room. The library was waking up by now; allies would not be far away.

Thobicus held his shot, and held back his words, letting the vampire make the next move.

Rufo turned back to the desk suddenly, and Thobicus inadvertently gasped. "We should not be enemies," the vampire remarked.

Thobicus eyed him incredulously.

"What would be the gain of a fight?" Rufo asked. "For either of us?"

"Ever were you a fool, Kierkan Rufo," Thobicus dared to say.

"A fool?" Rufo mocked. "You could not begin to understand, fallen priest." Rufo threw back his head and let his laughter flow out, He spun about so that his black burial robe trailed his form like a shadow. "I have found power!"

"You have found perversion!" Thobicus declared, and he clutched the crossbow tightly, thinking that his remark would send the angry monster hurtling toward him.

Rufo stopped his spin and faced the dean. "Call it what you will! But you cannot deny my power—power gained in mere hours. You have spent all of your life in wasted study, I say, praying to Deneir."

Thobicus inadvertently glanced at his holy symbol, lying on the floor by the wall.

"Deneir," Rufo said derisively. "What has your god given you? You toil for endless years, then Cadderly . . . "

Thobicus winced, and Rufo did not miss it.

"Then Cadderly," the vampire went on, seeing the weakness for what it was, "reaches out and grasps at levels of power that will forever be beyond you!"

"You lie!" Thobicus roared, coming forward in his chair. His words sounded empty, even in his own ears.

The office door swung open then, and both Thobicus and Rufo turned to see Bron Turman stride in. The Oghman priest looked from the dean to Rufo, his eyes going wide as he, too, recognized the vampire for what it was.

Rufo hissed, showing bloody fangs, and waved his hand, his magic compelling the door to slam shut behind Turman.

Bron Turman had no intention of running back out, in any case. With a determined snarl, the Oghman grabbed at a pendant and tore the chain from his neck, presenting the silver scroll replica before him. It flashed and radiated a powerful light, and to the surprise of Dean Thobicus, the vampire backed away, ducking under his robes and hissing.

Turman recited words very similar to the ones Thobicus had used, and the holy symbol flared even more, filled the room with a glow that Rufo could not bear. The vampire fell back against the wall, started for the window, then realized that he could not go out there, under the light of the infernal sun.

Turman had him, Thobicus realized, and Rufo seemed very weak to him then, even pitiful. Without even realizing it, Thobicus had the crossbow atop the desk.

Rufo began to fight back, was struggling to stand straight. A blackness rolled out from his form, filling that section of the room.

Bron Turman growled and thrust his symbol forward, its flare attacking the vampire's darkness. Rufo hissed wickedly as he clenched his bony fists in the air.

"Shoot him!" Bron Turman implored Thobicus.

The struggle between the two was a standoff that a crossbow quarrel would break.

Thobicus took up the weapon and leveled it. He meant to pull the trigger, but hesitated as a wall of doubts came up before him. Why hadn't his presented symbol so affected the vampire? he wondered. Had Deneir deserted him, or was Cadderly somehow continuing to block his efforts to bask in the light of his god?

Mountains of doubt rolled across the dean's thoughts, black thoughts made blacker by the continuing subtle intrusions of the vampire's will. Rufo was still there, compelling, prompting doubts.

Where was Deneir? The thought haunted the withered dean. In his moment of greatest need, his god had not been there. In the one instant of his life when he had consciously called on Deneir, when he had absolutely needed Deneir, the god had deserted him!

And there stood Bron Turman, straight and confident, holding the vampire at bay with the power of Oghma in his strong hand.

Thobicus snarled and hoisted the crossbow. Evil Rufo was standing tall in his new power, standing against a

man who would have easily defeated him when he had
been just a disciple of Deneir, though Rufo had spent
years of study.

Now, after three days of death, Rufo could match the
Oghman.

Thobicus shook his head, trying to clear the mounting confusion. He pushed through one web of lies, only
to find another, and to find the one he had left closing
fast behind him.

Where was Deneir? Why was Cadderly so damned
powerful? Where was justice, the rewards of his own
long years of study? So many years . . .

Thobicus came back to the present situation, focusing
his thoughts, steadying his trembling hands, and training his eye. His shot was perfect.

Bron Turman jerked from the impact and looked over
at the desk in disbelief. The Oghman's grip soon weakened, and Rufo stepped forward and casually slapped
the holy symbol from Turman's hand, then fell over him.

A minute later, the vampire, his face bright with fresh
blood, turned to the desk. "What has Deneir ever given
you?" he asked the stunned Thobicus, the old dean
standing zombielike, his wrinkled face frozen with disbelief as he stared at the dead Oghman.

"He deserted you," Rufo crooned, playing on the
man's obvious doubts. "Deneir has deserted you, but I
will not! There is so much I can give you."

Thobicus, in his stupor, realized that the vampire was
next to him. Rufo continued to whisper assurances,
promising power beyond belief and eternal life, promising salvation before death. Thobicus could not resist
him. The withered dean felt a pinch as the vampire's
fangs jabbed into his neck.

He realized only then how very far he had fallen. He

realized that Rufo had been in his mind, inciting the doubts, quietly compelling him to fire the crossbow at the powerful Oghman.

And he had complied. Doubts swirled in the air all about the dean, but no longer were they centered on the faults of Deneir. Had Deneir really deserted Thobicus when he had tried to present the holy symbol against Rufo, or had Thobicus long ago deserted Deneir? Cadderly had dominated him, and had claimed that power to be the will of Deneir.

And now Rufo . . .

Thobicus let the thought go, let the guilt go. So be it, he decided. He denied the consequences and washed in the promises of the vampire.

So be it.

Seven

Fall From Grace

Fester Rumpol watched suspiciously. He didn't understand the change that had come over Dean Thobicus. The last time he had spoken with the dean, the man was preoccupied—no, obsessed—with the notion that Cadderly was coming back to the library to tear the heart out of the Deneirian order.

Now Thobicus seemed almost jovial. He had secretly called together the four leading Deneirians, three of them headmasters, for what he termed "a most vital conference."

They were gathered in a small dining room adjacent to the main hall and kitchen, around an oaken table, bare except for huge, empty goblets set in front of the five chairs.

"Dear Banner," Thobicus chirped lightly, "do go to the cellars and fetch a particular vintage, a special red bottle on the third rack."

"A bottle of red?" Banner asked, crinkling his features. Banner favored white wines.

"A red bottle," Thobicus corrected. He turned to Rumpol and gave a wink. "Magically preserved, you know. The only way to keep Feywine."

"Feywine?" Rumpol and all the others asked together. Feywine was an elven drink, a mixture of honey and flowers and moonbeams, it was said. It was rare, even among the elves, and getting a bottle from them was nearly impossible.

"A gift from King Galladel when he ruled Shilmista," Thobicus explained. "Do go and retrieve it."

Banner looked to Rumpol, worried that the man was near an explosion. Indeed Rumpol was boiling. He feared that Thobicus had somehow learned of Cadderly's demise, and if that was the occasion of this celebration, the dean was surely out of line!

Banner waited a moment longer, then tentatively started to leave.

"Wait!" Rumpol blurted, and all the others turned to regard him.

"Your mood has brightened, Dean Thobicus," Rumpol said. "Dramatically. Might we learn what has so affected you?"

"I found communion with Deneir this morning," Thobicus lied.

"Cadderly is dead," Rumpol reasoned, and the other three Deneirians immediately turned sour looks on the dean. Even the priests who despised Cadderly and his unconventional climb through the ranks would not celebrate such a tragedy—at least not publicly.

Thobicus put on an expression of horror. "He is not," he replied vehemently. "From all that I know, the fine young priest is even now on his way back to the library."

Fine young priest? Coming from Dean Thobicus, those words rang hollow indeed to Fester Rumpol.

"Then why are we celebrating?" Banner asked bluntly.

Thobicus gave a great sigh. "I had hoped we might toast the occasion with the Feywine," he groaned. "But very well, I sympathize with your impatience. Simply put, there will be no second Time of Troubles."

That brought sighs of relief and private murmurs from the group.

"And I have learned much of Cadderly as well," Thobicus went on. "The order will survive—indeed, it will be strengthened when he returns, when he and I work together to improve the ways of the library."

"You hate each other," Rumpol remarked, and looked around somewhat nervously. He hadn't meant to openly voice that opinion.

Thobicus, however, merely chuckled and seemed to take no offense. "With Deneir as moderator, our differences seem petty indeed," the dean replied.

He looked around, his bright smile infectious. "And so we have much to celebrate!" he proclaimed, and nodded to Banner, who rushed off with sincere enthusiasm for the doorway to the wine cellar.

The conversation continued, lighthearted and hopeful, with Thobicus paying particular attention to Rumpol, the man he deemed to be potentially the most troublesome. Twenty minutes later, Banner still had not returned.

"He cannot find the bottle," Thobicus remarked to quiet any trepidation. "Dear Banner. He probably dropped his torch and is stumbling around in the dark."

"Banner has the power to summon light," Rumpol

said, an edge of suspicion still in his voice.

"Then where is he?" Thobicus asked. "The bottle is colorful, and should be easy enough to find on the fifth rack."

"You said the third rack," one of the others quickly put in.

Thobicus stared at him, then scratched his head. "Did I?" he whispered, then he dramatically dropped his face into his hand. "Of course," he mused. "The Feywine was in the third rack until the . . . incident." All the others knew that the dean was referring to the dark time of the chaos curse, the time when the evil priest Barjin had invaded the library and sought to destroy the place from within.

"There was quite a bit of trouble down in that cellar," Thobicus went on. "If I remember correctly, several of the affected priests even went down there and drank to . . . shall we say, excess."

Rumpol turned away, for he had been one of those hearty drinkers.

"Fortunately, the Feywine survived, but I do recall that it was moved to the fifth rack, that being the most stable," Thobicus finished. He motioned to one of the others. "Do go and help out dear Banner," he bade, "before the man comes back here raising Cyric himself against me!"

The priest ran off for the door, and the conversation resumed, again without much concern. Fifteen minutes later, it was Rumpol who remarked that the two wine hunters were long overdue.

"If one of the lesser priests stole that bottle, my good mood will vanish," Thobicus warned.

"There was an inventory of the wine cellar," Rumpol said.

"A list I saw, though I do not recall any record of Feywine," added the other, and he gave a jovial laugh. "And

I would have noted the presence of such a treasure well, I assure you!"

"Of course the bottle was mislabeled," Thobicus explained, then he nodded, as if something that should have been obvious had just come to him. "If dear Banner decided to test the wine before he returned, then likely we will find our two missing brothers sitting in a stupor in the cellar!" the dean roared. "Feywine, in its own subtle way, bites harder than dwarven ale!"

He rose to leave, and the other two were quick to join him. Their mood was light, any fears or suspicions quenched by the logical assumption offered by the dean. They got to the wine cellar door, and Thobicus took up and lit one of the small lamps set in a cabinet to one side, then led the way down the wooden staircase, into the darkness.

They heard no chatter, no drunken conversation, and grew a bit concerned when they saw that their lantern was apparently the only source of light in the damp, shadowy cellar.

"Banner?" Rumpol called softly. Thobicus stood by silently; the remaining priest began a quiet chant, thinking to bring a great magical light into the area.

That priest jerked suddenly, drawing the attention of his two companions.

"I fear a spider has bitten me," he remarked to Rumpol's questioning expression, and he began to jerk spasmodically, his eyes twitching, then rolling back into his head.

He fell facedown to the floor before Rumpol could get to him.

"What is this?" Rumpol cried, cradling the fallen priest's head. He began a frantic chant, beginning a spell that could counter any poison.

"Rumpol," Thobicus called, and though the priest did not interrupt his frantic spellcasting, he did look back to regard the dean.

His words fell away as he looked upon Kierkan Rufo, the vampire's face bright with fresh blood.

The vampire extended one pale hand toward Rumpol. "Come to me," he bade.

Rumpol felt the wave of compelling willpower roll over him. He rested the fallen priest's head back against the floor and rose without even being conscious of the movements.

"Come to me," the vampire said tantalizingly. "Join me, as has your dean. Come to me and see the truth."

Rumpol was inadvertently sliding his feet along the smooth floor, drifting toward the darkness that was Kierkan Rufo. Somewhere in the back of his mind he caught the image of an open eye above a lit candle, the symbol of Deneirian light, and it shook him from his trance.

"No!" he declared and pulled out his holy symbol, presenting it with all his heart against the undead monster. Rufo hissed and lifted his arm to shield himself from the spectacle. Dean Thobicus turned away in shame. The light from his lantern went with him as he walked around the next rack, but the light in the area near Rumpol did not diminish, bolstered by the power of his presented symbol, by the light that was in the sincere priest's heart.

"Fool!" the vampire proclaimed. "Do you think you can stand against me?"

Fester Rumpol wasn't shaken. He basked in the light of his god, used his sincere faith to blast away any horror-inspired doubts. "I deny you!" he proclaimed. "And by the power of Deneir . . ."

He stopped suddenly and nearly swooned. He glanced around to his back to see the dog-faced imp staring at him, waving its barbed, poison-tipped tail—the same tail that had dropped the other priest, and that Druzil had just poked into Rumpol's kidney.

Rumpol staggered for the stairway, stumbled to his knees as Druzil struck him a second time. Then he was up again, but the world was slipping away into blackness. The last image he saw was that of Kierkan Rufo, of Kierkan Rufo's fangs rushing for his throat.

When he was finished, the vampire found Thobicus standing by the fifth rack. There lay the priest Thobicus had sent after Banner, his chest torn apart, his heart on the floor beside him. Banner, though, surprisingly, was sitting against the rack, his head down, but very much alive.

"He heeded my call," Rufo casually explained to the confused dean. "And so I thought to keep him, for he is weak." Rufo presented a perfectly awful bloody smile to the dean. "Like you."

Dean Thobicus had not the strength to argue. He looked to the torn priest, and to living Banner, and he pitied Banner the most.

* * * * *

A few hours later, Druzil hopped and skipped into short flights about the library's hot attic, clapping his hands happily at every turn. The air was warm, he was at work in desecrating a holy place, and beneath him, Rufo, with the help of Dean Thobicus, continued dividing the priests into small groups and was summarily destroying them.

Life was suddenly very good for the malicious imp. Druzil flapped his wings and lifted himself up to one of the short peaks in the roof, so that he could survey his latest design. The imp knew all the runes of desecration and had just completed his favorite in the area directly over the library's main chapel (though that chapel was two floors down). Thobicus had provided a virtually unlimited supply of ink—reds, blues, blacks, and even a vial of a strange greenish-yellow (which Druzil favored) —and the imp knew that every stroke he ran across the floorboards put the foolish priests in the rooms below a bit farther from their respective gods.

At one point, Druzil paused, then moved away from the spot with an angry hiss. Someone was singing in a room below him—that wretched Chaunticleer, Druzil realized. Chaunticleer was singing to Deneir and to Oghma, lifting his voice against the encroaching blackness in notes pure and sweet.

It wounded Druzil's ears. He moved away from the spot, and the vibrations of Chaunticleer's voice were no more. With all that was happening in his favor, Druzil quickly forgot about the singing priest.

Happy again, Druzil clapped his hands rapidly, his toothy smile nearly swallowing his ears. When Rufo had come for him in the mausoleum the previous night, he hadn't known what to expect, had even considered using all of his magical abilities and knowledge to try to open a gate, that he might retreat to the lower planes, abandoning Rufo and *Tuanta Quiro Miancay* altogether.

Now, just half a day later, Druzil was thrilled that he had not chosen that course. Barjin had failed, but Rufo would not, the imp knew.

The Edificant Library would fall.

*   *   *   *   *

His tentative steps down into the wine cellar revealed Thobicus's continued fear of Kierkan Rufo, and his continued uneasiness with his own decisions. He still could not believe that he had killed Bron Turman, long a friend and ally. He still could not believe that he had flown so far from the teachings of Deneir, that he had thrown away the work of his entire life.

There was only one antidote to the guilt that threatened to destroy Dean Thobicus. Anger. And the focus of that anger was a young priest who would likely soon return to the library.

Cadderly had done this, Thobicus decided. Through his lust for undeserved power, Cadderly had brought all of this about.

Thobicus carried no lantern or torch as he stepped off the bottom step of the dark stairway. With each passing hour, the man grew more comfortable with the darkness. Now he could see the wine racks, even the individual bottles, though a week before he would not have been able to see his hand flapping an inch from his face in this lightless place. Rufo called it another benefit; the frightened dean wondered if it might be more a symptom.

He found Rufo in the far corner, behind the last of the racks, asleep in a wooden casket the vampire had recovered from the work shed behind the mausoleum. Thobicus moved toward Rufo, then stopped abruptly, eyes wide with fear and confusion.

Bron Turman walked toward him.

As he turned to flee, the confused dean found several others, including Fester Rumpol, blocking the way. They had come back to life! Somehow, these priests had been resurrected and had come back to destroy Thobicus!

The dean squealed and leaped for the wine rack. He climbed it like a spider, with agility the aged and withered man had not known for several decades. He neared the top and could have easily slipped over, but a command rang out within his head, an order compelling him to stop.

Slowly, Thobicus turned his head about to see Kierkan Rufo sitting up in his casket, his grotesque smile wide.

"You do not like my new playthings?" the vampire asked.

Thobicus did not understand. He looked closer at the nearest man, Fester Rumpol, and realized that Rumpol's throat was still ragged from Rufo's raking and tearing. The man could not possibly be breathing, Thobicus realized; the man was still dead.

Thobicus sprang from his perch, flying the ten feet to land with catlike grace on the stone floor. Bron Turman, near where he landed, reached out with a stiff arm and grasped him tightly.

"Tell him to let you go," Rufo said casually, but his patient facade went away immediately, replaced by a judgmental, even dangerous expression. "Take control of him!"

Without saying a word, Thobicus steeled his gaze and mentally ordered Turman to let go—and the dean was relieved indeed when the man released him and stepped back, standing quietly to the side.

"Zombies," Thobicus breathed, understanding that Rufo had animated the torn corpses into undead, unthinking servants, among the lowest forms in the hierarchy of the netherworld.

"Those who submit will know an intelligent existence, as you have come to know," Rufo declared in an imposing voice. "Those who choose to die in the favor of their god shall become unwitting servants, unthinking zombies, to their ultimate torment!"

As if on cue, Banner appeared from around the corner, smiling at Thobicus. Banner had submitted, had denied his god in the face of Kierkan Rufo.

"Greetings, Thobicus," the man said, and when Banner opened his mouth, Thobicus realized that he, like Rufo, sported a pair of fangs.

"You are a vampire," the dean whispered, stating the obvious.

"As are you," Banner replied.

Thobicus looked to Rufo skeptically, then, following another mental command, reached up to feel inside his own mouth, to feel his own set of fangs.

"We are both vampires," Banner continued, "and with Kierkan Rufo, we are three."

"Not quite," Rufo interjected. Both men regarded him curiously, Banner's eyes full of suspicion, Dean Thobicus too wrapped up in confusion.

"You are not yet fully in the realm of vampires," Rufo explained, and he knew that he was speaking the truth, though where he had gained such an understanding of this undead state, he did not know. It was the knowledge imparted by the chaos curse, he figured.

"You promised me that I would be a vampire," Banner said. "That was our deal."

Rufo held up a hand to calm him. "And so you shall be," he assured the man, "in time."

"You rose into full power soon after your death," Banner complained.

Rufo smiled and considered the chaos curse, swirling inside of him, the potion that had imparted such strength and understanding. But I had an advantage, fool Banner, Rufo thought. To Banner he only repeated his promise of, "In time."

Rufo turned to the confused Thobicus. "This very night you will suffer the blood thirst," he explained into the dean's wide-eyed stare. "And you will seek out one of the lesser priests and feed. I grant you this, but be warned. If ever you hold a thought against me, I will deny you your victims. There is no greater torment than denial of the blood thirst—this you will believe when the hunger comes to you."

Dean Thobicus's mind whirled at the unexpected news. He had become a vampire!

"This very night," Rufo said again, as if in answer to the dean's silent exclamation. "And be warned that the sun tomorrow and forever after will be your enemy. Seek a dark spot to sleep after you have fed, Thobicus."

The dean's breath came in short gasps, and when he realized that fact, he seriously wondered if this would be the last day he would ever draw breath.

"Have you done as I instructed?" Rufo asked him.

He looked up at the vampire, startled by the unexpected change in subject. He collected his wits quickly.

"The five Oghmans are on the road to Carradoon," Thobicus answered. "They wanted to wait until morning and complained that they would have only a short hour or two of light before they had to stop and set up camp."

"But you convinced them," Rufo reasoned.

"I sent them," Thobicus corrected, as defiant a tone as he had ever used against the vampire. "But I do not understand the value in allowing them out of the library. If Druzil is at work . . . "

A sharp pain in Thobicus's head cut the statement short, nearly knocking the dean from his feet.

"You question me?" Rufo asked.

Thobicus found he was on his knees, clutching his temples. He thought his head would explode, but then, as abruptly as it had started, the pain ceased. It took him a long moment to muster the courage to look up at Kierkan Rufo again, and when he did, he found the vampire at ease, Banner comfortably at his side.

Thobicus, for some reason he did not understand, hated Banner at that moment.

"The Oghmans might have sensed the desecration," Rufo explained. "Or might have soon recognized you for what you have become. They will understand the desecration fully when they return to the library, and they will welcome it."

Thobicus considered the words, and did not doubt Rufo's claim. There remained less than sixty living priests, Deneirian and Oghman, at the library, and but six visitors, none powerful enough to stand against the master vampire.

"Is the priestess of Sune in her room?" Rufo asked suddenly, startling Thobicus from his private musings. The dean nodded, and Rufo, looking to Banner, nodded as well.

Two hours later, when the sun had fallen behind the western horizon and the dark shadows had become complete, Kierkan Rufo walked out of the Edificant Library's front doors, his black robes sweeping behind him and the mischievous imp perched on his shoulder.

On a high branch in a nearby tree, a white squirrel crouched in fear, watching the vampire's progress with more than passing curiosity.

Eight

Campfires

W hat do you see?" Danica asked Shayleigh, moving to the camp's border,
where the elf stood quietly.

Shayleigh held out a delicate arm,
pointing far down the mountain trails
to a flickering light. Danica's heart leaped for an instant,
the monk thinking she might be catching her first
glimpse of the Edificant Library.

"A campfire," Shayleigh explained, seeing the monk's
hopeful visage. "A group of emissaries or traders from
Carradoon on their way to the library, or perhaps a band
of priests heading down to the city. The spring has
come, so the trails awaken to the sound of caravans."

"It is a spring you thought would be full of cries of
battle," Dorigen reminded Shayleigh as she moved to

join the two.

Danica eyed Dorigen curiously, wondering what the woman hoped to gain by reminding Shayleigh of the carnage in Shilmista, and of her fears that an army—an army led by Dorigen—might soon return to the wood.

"So it might," Shayleigh was quick to reply, fixing the wizard with a cool stare. "We do not know if the orc-kin we sent scrambling into the mountains will return to Shilmista once the trails are clear."

No gain, Danica decided. Dorigen was merely continuing her acceptance of guilt.

Dorigen did not back away from the accusing look. "If they do," she said, her chin held high, "I will demand that part of my penance be that I fight on the side of the elves in that conflict."

Well said, Danica thought. "If the elves would have her," the monk quickly put in, drawing Shayleigh's attention to her disarming smile before the suspicious elf could reply.

"We would be foolish to refuse," Shayleigh answered. She looked back to the quiet night and the distant flickers. "It is likely the orc-kin will enlist the aid of trolls." In her own way, the elf had, for the first time, agreed with the decision to return Dorigen to the library and argue for a positive judgment, rather than one of punishment. Shayleigh had made no moves against Dorigen since the wizard's surrender in Castle Trinity, but neither had she befriended her. Shilmista was the elf's home, after all, and Dorigen had been instrumental in bringing ruin to the forest's northern reaches.

Behind Shayleigh's back, Danica and Dorigen exchanged hopeful nods. If King Elbereth and the elves could forgive Dorigen's crimes, then the library's claims against her would seem almost trivial.

"If it was earlier, I would suggest we go down to that light," Danica remarked. "I could do with a bit of good food, and maybe a taste of wine."

"I'd settle for ale," Dorigen said, to which Shayleigh promptly spun about and gave the wizard a sour look.

"Wine," the elf agreed, and it seemed to Dorigen and Danica as if the whole atmosphere of the encampment had suddenly changed, lightened, as if Shayleigh had come to terms with Dorigen's past and was now a true ally. The two women went to their bedrolls then, taking comfort in the knowledge that the alert elf was guarding over them.

Shayleigh remained where she was, standing quietly and watching the flicker of the distant campfire. Her second guess as to its origin had been correct; a group of priests was making its way down to Carradoon—a group of Oghman priests, sent out by Dean Thobicus.

Like Danica, Shayleigh wished the night was earlier, that they might have hiked the couple of miles down to the group.

Kierkan Rufo, approaching the flickering fire from another trail, would have been pleasantly surprised if they had.

* * * * *

He dreamed of towering spires stretching three hundred feet into the air. He dreamed of all the folk of Carradoon, and all the elves of Shilmista, congregating before the cathedral, come to worship and to find inspiration in its massive windows and walls that were, in truth, works of art.

The nave dwarfed the individual. The arching ceiling soared a hundred feet from the stone floor. Graceful walls were lined by corridors housing statues of the worthy priests of both Deneir and Oghma who had gone before. Avery Schell was there, as was Pertelope, there for all time, and at the end of the high walkway was an empty pedestal, awaiting the statue that would be most fitting in this tribute to Deneir.

The statue of Cadderly.

He dreamed of conducting a service in that cathedral, of Brother Chaunticleer's *a cappella* gift to the brother gods, Oghma and Deneir, the talented tenor's voice echoing about the graceful walls like the songs of the heavens themselves.

Then Cadderly saw himself, wearing the sash of the library's dean, leading the service, with Danica sitting proudly by his side.

He was a hundred years old, withered and worn and near death.

The shocking image shook Cadderly from his slumber, and his eyes opened wide to take in the starry sky. He closed his eyes quickly and tried to recapture that last fleeting glimpse, to learn why it might be so startling. Cadderly could only hope that the new library would be constructed before he reached his hundredth year, even if construction began in full this very summer and Ivan and Pikel delivered a thousand dwarves to help with the work.

Cadderly, so filled with divine faith, certainly did not fear his death. Then why had he awakened, and why was his forehead cold with sweat?

He looked back into the dream, forced the image to linger. Even though it was clear, it took Cadderly time to discern what might be out of place.

It was he, the old dean of the library. He looked as if he had lived a century or more, but Danica, sitting beside him, seemed no older than she was now, barely in her twenties.

Cadderly let go the surreal scene and looked up at the stars, reminding himself that it had been just a dream. The Bouldershoulders' wild snoring—Ivan snorting and Pikel whistling in response—calmed him somewhat, told him that all was as it should be.

Still, many hours passed before Cadderly found his slumber again, and that image of an old, dying priest leading a service in the cathedral went into his dreams with him.

* * * * *

Two of the five Oghmans sat awake, chatting quietly and keeping a halfhearted watch on the dark trees surrounding their encampment as the darkest hours of the night passed. None in the group was really afraid of trouble this far south in the mountains. The trails between Carradoon and the Edificant Library were well traveled, and these were powerful clerics—behind Bron Turman, the most powerful of the Oghman order at the library. They had lined the perimeter of their camp with wards that would not only alert them of the presence of monsters, but would send jolts of lightning into the creatures, probably destroying them before they ever crossed into the opening.

So these two Oghmans were awake more to enjoy the night than to guard the camp, and their eyes were more often on each other, or on the fire, than on the dark and ominous trees.

Kierkan Rufo was in those trees, along with Druzil, watching the priests' movements and listening to the rhythmic snoring of the other three, fast asleep.

Rufo nodded and began his steady approach, but Druzil, still in many ways the wiser of the two, scanned the camp's perimeter, his knowing eyes looking for the revealing emanations of magic.

He kicked off the ground and flapped his wings to land hard against Rufo's shoulder. "It is guarded," he whispered into the vampire's ear. "All the way around."

Rufo nodded again, as though he had suspected that all along. He jerked suddenly, throwing Druzil from his shoulder and lifting his black robes high into the air about him. As the material descended, Rufo's corporeal form seemed to melt away. As a bat, Rufo zipped up into the treetops, Druzil following closely.

"Did they think to guard from above?" the vampire bat asked the imp in a voice so high-pitched that it hurt Druzil's ears, and though Rufo had spoken loudly, the men on the ground could not even hear the sound.

The two picked their way down the branches. Rufo noticed that Druzil had turned invisible, as was the imp's way, but the vampire was surprised—pleasantly so—to learn that he could still see the imp's vague outline. Another benefit of this undead state, Rufo decided. One of many, many benefits. A few moments later, the vampire was hanging upside down from the lowest branch over the encampment, barely fifteen feet above the heads of the two seated guards. Rufo had thought to swoop right down on them, but paused, wondering if something valuable might be gained from their conversation.

"Bron Turman's going to be surprised when we walk unannounced into Carradoon," one of them was saying.

"His own fault," answered the other. "His rank does not give him the privilege of rewriting the Oghman orders without consulting the other leaders."

Rufo was impressed at how resourceful a liar Dean Thobicus could be. With all the strange goings-on, the Oghmans had been on the alert back at the library. Only the dean's hint that something was indeed amiss, instead of simply telling them that everything was all right, had brought them out here.

"If that is what Bron Turman is doing in Carradoon," the first priest remarked, his tone full of doubt.

The other nodded in agreement.

"I am not convinced of Dean Thobicus's words," the first went on. "Not even his motives. He is frightened of Cadderly's return—in that, I agree with Bron Turman's assessment."

"Do you believe Dean Thobicus wanted all the Oghmans out of the library so we would not interfere with his plans for his own order?" the other asked, to which the first only shrugged.

Rufo nearly squealed aloud at the irony of that question. If only these two knew the truth of the "order" to which they were unintentionally referring!

The ruse had worked, of that much the vampire was now certain. Almost all of the leading Deneirians were dead or undead and under his control, and now the Oghmans were divided and off their guard.

One of the priests gave a great yawn, though a moment before he had seemed perfectly alert. The other followed suit, overcome by a sudden compulsion to lie down and sleep.

"The night grows long," the first remarked, and, without even moving toward his bedroll, he slipped down to the ground and closed his eyes.

The other Oghman thought the movement somewhat silly, until it struck him as suspiciously odd that his friend should fall so quickly into slumber. He fought against that compulsion, that little suggestion in the back of his mind that sleep would be a good thing. He opened his eyes wide and vigorously shook his head. He even reached down, hoisted a waterskin, and poured the fluid over his face.

When the man tossed his head back to wet his face a second time, he was stopped by the image of a black-robed man standing on a branch fifteen feet above him.

Rufo fell down atop him with catlike grace. The vampire grabbed the man's chin and the hair on the back of his head as he opened his mouth to scream, tugging so fiercely that the man's head turned around on his shoulders with a sickening crack of bone.

The vampire stood straight, eyeing the other four, all sleeping. He would wake them one by one and give them a chance to forsake their god, a chance to kneel before him, the personification of *Tuanta Quiro Miancay*.

Nine

The Words of Romus Scaladi

Fare well," Shayleigh offered when the three women came to a fork in the trail early the next morning. One bend went south, for the library. The other continued on generally west. "King Elbereth will be pleased to hear all that I have to tell him."

"All?" Dorigen asked, and the perceptive elf maiden knew that the wizard was referring to herself, to the fact that she was still alive and well and ready to face judgment for her crimes.

Shayleigh's smile was enough of an answer for Dorigen.

"Elbereth is not a vengeful sort," Danica added hopefully.

"*King* Elbereth," Dorigen quickly corrected. "I will

remain at the library," she said to Shayleigh, "whatever the decision of the priests, to await word from your king."

"A fair judgment I will be pleased to deliver," Shayleigh replied, and with a nod, she was gone, slipping down the western trail so gracefully and noiselessly that she seemed to the two women almost an illusion, an artist's tapestry, a perfect embodiment of nature. She was out of sight in mere seconds, her gray-green cloak shielding her form in the sylvan shadows, though Danica and Dorigen did not doubt that she could still see them.

"I am ever amazed by their movements," Dorigen remarked. "So supple and graceful, yet in battle, I have never known a race to match the elves' ferocity."

Danica did not disagree. During the war in Shilmista, the monk had found her first real experiences with elves, and it seemed to her that all her years of training in harmony and movement had made her somewhat akin to what came naturally to Shayleigh's people. Danica wished she had been born an elf, or had been raised among them. Then she would have been closer to the spirit of Grandmaster Penpahg D'Ahn's writings, she knew.

Still staring down the empty trail, she imagined she might return to Shilmista and work with Elbereth's people, bringing them the vision of Penpahg D'Ahn. She pictured an open meadow full of elves, practicing the graceful dance of the grandmaster's fighting style, and the sight made her heart skip excitedly.

Then Danica let go the image, shook it away as she recalled the demeanor of elvenkind, recalled what it meant emotionally to be an elf. They were a calm and casual people, easily distracted, and though fierce in battle, their way was playful. The grace of movement was their nature, not their practice, and that was very different from Danica's life. Following her mentor, the young monk was rarely casual, always focused. Even Shayleigh, whom Danica would wish at her side whenever danger was near, could not hold any course for very long. Through the weeks in the caves, waiting for winter's break, the elf had spent long hours, even days, just sitting and watching the snow, occasionally rising to dance, as though no one else had been in the room, as though nothing else in all the world mattered except the falling snowflakes and the movements that Shayleigh hardly seemed conscious she was making.

The elves could not follow the rigorous discipline of Penpahg D'Ahn. Danica didn't pretend to understand them, any of them, even Shayleigh, who had become so dear to her. The elf was fiercely loyal, she knew, but she could not begin to understand all of Shayleigh's motivations. Shayleigh saw the world from a perspective that Danica could not comprehend, a perspective that put friendship in a different light. While Danica did not doubt the love Shayleigh felt for her, she knew that the elf maiden would likely witness the dawn of several centuries after she, Danica, had died of old age. How many new human friends would Shayleigh come to know and love in those centuries? Would the memory of Danica withstand the test of such a long time, or would she become just a fleeting moment of Shayleigh's future reveries?

Simply put, there was no way that Danica could ever be as important in Shayleigh's eyes as Shayleigh had become in hers. She would remember the elf maiden vividly until the moment of her death.

She considered that difference between them for a

moment and decided that hers was the better way, the more passionate existence. Still, Danica found that she envied Shayleigh and all of her kind. The golden-haired elven maiden innately possessed what Danica sought: the peace and grace of true harmony.

"We will be there today?" Dorigen asked, and for the first time, Danica noted a slight tremor in the determined woman's voice.

"Today," Danica answered as she walked off down the southern trail.

Dorigen paused a moment, mustering her courage. She knew she was doing right, that she owed this, at least, to the library and the elves. Still, the wizard's first step along the final trail came hard, as did the second, the third, and all the rest.

Back a short distance down the western trail, Shayleigh watched Dorigen's every move. She didn't doubt Dorigen's sincerity, knew that the wizard honestly meant to follow through, but she knew the journey would be more difficult than Dorigen implied. It was quite possible that Dorigen might be walking to her death. Somewhere along the way, Shayleigh understood, Dorigen would have to battle her survival instinct, the most basic and powerful force in any human.

Shayleigh waited a moment longer, then slipped quietly into the underbrush alongside the southern trail. If Dorigen lost that battle, she would be ready.

For the time being, Shayleigh called Dorigen a friend, but the elf maiden could not forget the scars on Shilmista. If Dorigen could not bring herself to face the rightful judgment of the victors, then Shayleigh would enact the judgment of Shilmista . . . in the form of a single, well-placed arrow.

* * * * *

"Where is Bron Turman?" one of the younger priests asked nervously. He leaned against a low railing surrounding the altar in one of the library's first-floor chapels.

"Or Dean Thobicus?" added another.

Romus Scaladi, a short, dark-complexioned Oghman whose shoulders seemed nearly as wide as the man was tall, tried to calm his five brother priests of both orders, patting his hands in the empty air and saying, "Shh," as though the men were young children.

"And surely Cadderly will return," a third priest, kneeling before the altar, said hopefully. "Cadderly will set things right."

Two of the other young priests, the only Deneirians in the group, who had listened to Thobicus's warning concerning Cadderly, looked to each other and shrugged, sharing a common fear that Cadderly might actually be the one behind all of the strange things that were going on about them. None of the leaders—of either order— had been seen all day, and both Thobicus and Bron Turman had been missing for two full days.

It was rumored, though none of this group could confirm it, that half a dozen lesser priests had been found dead in their rooms this morning, lying peacefully— under their beds! The priest who had told the group this startling news was not the best of sources, though. He was the newest member of the Oghman order, a small, weak man who had snapped his collarbone in his very first wrestling match. It was common knowledge that this man did not wish to remain in the order, and his appeals to join the Deneirian order had not been received warmly. So when they had encountered him early in the day, his belongings in a sack slung over one shoulder and his eyes squarely on the front door, the six did not panic.

Still, there was no denying that the library was strangely quiet this day—except in one corner of the second floor, where Brother Chaunticleer was holed up in his room, singing to his gods. Not a soul stirred in the headmasters' area. It was strangely quiet and strangely dark, even for the perpetually gloomy place; barriers had been constructed over nearly every window. Normally the library housed nearly eighty priests—before the disaster of the chaos curse, well over a hundred—and at any given time, five to thirty visitors. The guest list was small now, with winter just giving way, but so was the list of priests who had gone to Carradoon, or Shilmista.

So where was everybody?

Another troubling sensation that the six priests could not ignore was the subtle but definite feeling that the Edificant Library had changed somehow, as though the gloom about them was more than a physical feature. It was as if Deneir and Oghma had moved away from this place. Even the midday ritual, in which Brother Chaunticleer sang to both the gods in the presence of all the priests, had not been performed in two days. Romus himself had gone to the singing priest's room, fearing that Chaunticleer had taken ill. He found the door locked, and only after several minutes of pounding had Chaunticleer called out, telling him to go away.

"I feel as if someone has built a ceiling above me," one of the Deneirians remarked, following the suspicions of Cadderly that Dean Thobicus had implanted. "A ceiling that separates me from Deneir."

The other Deneirian nodded his agreement, while the Oghmans looked to each other, then to Romus, who was the strongest cleric among them.

"I am certain there is a simple answer," Romus said as calmly as he could, but the other five knew that he agreed with the Deneirian priest's assessment of the gods. This library had always been among the holiest of places, where priests of any goodly faith could feel the presence of their god or goddess. Even the druids who had visited had been surprised to find an aura of Sylvanus within the walls of a man-made structure.

And for the priests of Oghma and Deneir, there was, perhaps, no holier place in all of Faerun. This was their tribute to the gods, a place of learning and art, a place of study and recital. The place of Chaunticleer's song.

"We will wrestle!" Romus Scaladi announced surprisingly. After a moment of shock, the Oghmans began to bob their heads in agreement, while the Deneirians continued to stare dumbfoundedly at the stocky Scaladi.

"Wrestle?" one of them asked.

"Tribute to our god!" Scaladi answered, pulling off his black-and-gold vest and fine white shirt, revealing a chest bulging with muscles and thick with dark hair. "We will wrestle!"

"Oooo," came a woman's purr from the back of the chapel. "I do so love to wrestle!"

The six priests swung about hopefully, every one of them thinking that Danica, the woman who not only loved to wrestle, but who could defeat any priest in the library, had at last returned.

They saw not Danica, but Histra, the alluring priestess of Sune, dressed in her customary crimson gown that was cut so low in the front that it seemed as if her navel should show, and slitted high on the thigh to show off the woman's shapely legs. Her long, lush hair, dyed so blond this week as to appear almost white, flew wildly, as usual, and her makeup was thickly applied—never had the priests seen any lips so bright red! Her perfume, also poured generously, wafted across the chapel.

Something was out of place. All six of the priests recognized that fact, though none had figured it out. Behind Histra's generous paint, her skin was deathly pale, as was the leg sticking out from under her gown. And the perfume aroma was sickly sweet, something less than alluring.

Romus Scaladi studied the woman intently. He had never much liked Histra, or her goddess, Sune, whose only tenet seemed to be the physical pleasures of love. Always, ever-hungry Histra had set the hairs on the back of Scaladi's neck to tingling, as they were now, but more than usual.

It was uncommon to see Histra on the first floor, Scaladi knew; it was uncommon for the woman to be out of her room, or out of her bed.

"Why are you here?" the wary priest started to ask, but Histra seemed not to notice.

"I do so love to wrestle," she purred again, openly lewd, and she opened her mouth and laughed wildly.

All six priests understood; all six nervous priests recognized the vampire's fangs for what they were.

Five of the six, including Scaladi and both Deneirians, went immediately for their holy symbols.

Histra continued to laugh. "Wrestle with these!" she cried, and several torn, rotting, stiff-walking men came into the room—men the priests knew.

"My dear Deneir," one of the priests muttered hopelessly.

Romus leaped forward and presented the symbol of Oghma boldly. "Be gone from this holy place, foul undead things!" he cried, and the zombies stopped their shuffling, a couple of them even turning about.

Histra hissed viciously at the monstrous group, compelling them to continue.

"I deny you!" Romus roared at Histra, and it seemed as if she nearly fell over backward. A zombie reached awkwardly for the Oghman, and he growled and punched out with his holy symbol, slamming the monster on the side of the face. Acrid smoke rose from the wound, but the monster kept on, its companions filtering around Romus to get to the others.

"I cannot turn them away!" one of the priests behind Romus cried. "Where is Deneir?"

"Where is Oghma?" cried another.

A stiff arm clubbed Romus on the shoulder. He grunted away the blow and cupped his hand under the zombie's chin, bending the head back, then slashed at the monster's throat with the edge of his holy symbol. Again came a puff of smoke from the wound, and the zombie's rotting flesh opened up easily to the strong man's blow.

But zombies needed no air, so the wound was not serious.

"Fight them!" Romus Scaladi screamed. "Beat them down!" To accentuate his point, the powerful Oghman launched a barrage of punishment on the zombie, finally lifting the corpse over his head and hurling it into a statue against the wall. The Oghman spun about to see to his friends, and found that they were not fighting, but backing away, their faces horror-stricken.

Of course, Scaladi realized. These undead monsters they now face, these men, had been their friends! "Do not look at their faces!" he ordered. "They are not of our order. They are mere tools, weapons!

"Weapons of Histra," Romus Scaladi finished, spinning about to face the vampiress. "Now you die," the outraged man promised, lifting his flaring holy symbol toward the monster. "By my hands."

Histra wanted nothing to do with Scaladi. Like Banner and Thobicus, she had not come into her full power yet. Even if she had, she might have thought twice about facing Scaladi, for she recognized that the man had was fully in his faith, that his heart could be hers, but not his soul, for he would deny any fear—and fear was perhaps the greatest of a vampire's weapons.

Histra defiantly spat at Scaladi's presented symbol, but he saw the bluff for what it was. If he could get to her, cram his god's symbol down her wretched throat, then the zombies would be leaderless and could be more easily driven away.

Unexpectedly, Histra darted up the side toward the altar, deeper into the chapel, and Scaladi suddenly found two zombies between him and the vampiress.

The other priests were fighting now. The two Deneirians had carried weapons with them into the chapel, blessed maces, and two others had rushed to the altar table, wisely breaking off legs to use as clubs.

The remaining Oghman, the one priest who had not pulled out his holy symbol when Histra revealed herself, was off to the side of the room, trapped against the wall, shaking his head in sheer terror. And how that terror heightened when Histra pushed aside the zombies near the man and let him see her toothy smile!

Scaladi was hard pressed immediately by the zombies. He knew then, in his heart, that the library was no longer a house of Oghma, or of Deneir, that this desecration was nearly complete. The day outside was overcast, but the sun peeked through enough to be their ally.

"Fight out of the room!" Scaladi ordered. "Out of the room and out of the library!" He shifted forward, putting the two zombies' backs to the wall, trying to give his friends an avenue of escape.

On came the Deneirians, their heavy maces pounding zombies aside. Suddenly the path seemed clear for them all, and the Deneirians, and then Scaladi, bolted for the door. The club-wielding Oghmans chased after them, but one, when he tried to leap the altar rail, hooked his foot and sprawled facedown on the stone floor.

Zombies swarmed over him; his companion turned back and rushed to his aid.

Scaladi was already at the chapel door when he looked back to see the disaster. His first instinct was to charge back in and die beside his comrades, and he took a step that way. But the two priests of Deneir caught him by the shoulders, and though they could not have held the powerful man back if he wanted to continue, the pause gave Scaladi a moment to see things more clearly.

"You cannot help them!" one of the Deneirians cried.

"We must survive to warn the town!" the other added.

Scaladi staggered out of the chapel.

The zombie horde tore apart the two Oghmans.

Worse still was the fate of the priest against the wall, a man who had spent many secret evenings with Histra. He was filled with too much guilt to resist the vampiress now. He shook his head in weak denial, whispered, begged, for her to go away.

She smiled and came on, and the man, despite his horror, offered her his neck.

The three fleeing priests scrambled along the corridors, meeting no resistance. The front doors were in sight, one of them open, a weak line of sun streaming into the library's foyer.

One of the Deneirians cried out and grasped at his neck, then pitched forward to the stone.

"The door!" Scaladi cried, pulling the other along. The Deneirian looked back to his brother and saw the man flailing wildly at a bat-winged imp as it hopped about his shoulder, biting at his ear and stabbing repeatedly with a poison-tipped tail.

Scaladi dived for the door—it moved away from him, seemingly of its own accord, and slammed shut with a resounding bang, and he fell headlong at its base.

"My dear Deneir," he heard his lone companion whisper. Scaladi turned himself over, to see Dean Thobicus standing in the shadows, to see Kierkan Rufo—Kierkan Rufo!—moving quietly behind the withered man.

"Deneir is gone from this place," Thobicus said calmly and unthreateningly, approaching the man with his arms open and to the side. "Come with me now, that I might show you the new way."

The young Deneirian wavered, and for a moment, Scaladi thought he would give himself over to Thobicus, who was now no more than two paces away.

The young priest exploded into action, cracking his mace across the dean's wrinkled face. Thobicus's head jerked violently to the side and he was pushed back. But only a single step—and he turned straight again, eyeing the disbelieving young Deneirian. There ensued a long pause, a long and horrible moment, the hush of a crouched predator.

Thobicus threw his arms up, fingers bent like claws, gave an unearthly roar, and sprang over the young priest, burying the man under his flailing limbs.

Scaladi scrambled about and grabbed at the door, tugging with all his considerable strength.

"It will not open," Kierkan Rufo assured him.

Scaladi tugged furiously. He heard Rufo stepping near him, right behind.

"It will not open," the confident vampire said again.

Scaladi spun about, his holy symbol thrust toward Rufo. The vampire leaned back, away from the sudden glare.

But Rufo was not Histra, was full of the swirling chaos curse and was many times more powerful. The moment of surprise passed quickly.

"Now you die!" Scaladi promised, but by the time he finished the simple statement, all conviction had flown from his voice. He felt Rufo's will inside his head, compelling him to surrender, imparting a sense of hopelessness.

Romus Scaladi had always been a fighter. He had grown up an orphan on the tough streets of Sundabar, every day a challenge. And so he fought now, with all his own will, against Rufo's intrusions.

Green bolts of searing energy burned into his hand, and his holy symbol was knocked away. Both Scaladi and Rufo looked to the side, to the smiling Druzil, still perched on the body of the Deneirian.

Scaladi looked back helplessly as Rufo grabbed his wrist and yanked him forward, the vampire's face only inches from his own.

"You are strong," Rufo said. "That is good."

Scaladi spat in his face, but Rufo did not explode with anger, as had Thobicus. The chaos curse guided this vampire, kept him focused on what was best.

"I offer you power," Rufo whispered. "I offer you immortality. You will know pleasures beyond . . . "

"You offer damnation!" Scaladi growled.

Across the foyer, the Deneirian screamed, then went silent, and Thobicus feasted.

"What do you know?" Rufo demanded. "I am alive, Romus Scaladi! I have chased Deneir and Oghma from this place!"

Scaladi held his jaw firm.

"The library is mine!" Rufo went on. He grabbed Scaladi's thick hair in one hand and with strength that horrified the Oghman, easily tugged the man's head back. "Carradoon shall be mine!"

"They are just places," Scaladi insisted, with the simple and undeniable logic that had guided the man all his life. He knew that Rufo wanted more than the conquest of places. He knew what the vampire desired.

"You can join me, Romus Scaladi," Rufo said, predictably. "You can share my strength. You like strength."

"You have no strength," Scaladi said, and his sincere calm seemed to rattle Rufo. "You have only lies and false promises."

"I can tear your heart out!" Rufo roared at him. "And hold it up, beating before your dying eyes." Histra came into the foyer then, along with a couple of her zombies.

"Would you be like them?" Rufo asked, indicating the zombies. "Either way, you will serve me!"

Scaladi looked at the wretched zombies, and to Rufo's dismay, the priest smiled. They were corporeal animations and nothing more, Scaladi knew, had to believe with all his heart. Secure in that faith, the man looked Rufo straight in the vampire's blood-red eyes, straight in the vampire's drooling, animal-like face.

"I am more than my body," Romus Scaladi proclaimed.

Rufo snapped the Oghman's head back, shattering neck bones. With one hand, the outraged vampire heaved Scaladi across the foyer, where he crashed into a wall and crumpled at its base.

Histra hissed wickedly, and Thobicus chimed in, a horrid applause as the two circled their master. Caught up in the frenzy, Rufo dismissed Scaladi's damning words and hissed and snarled with all his wicked heart.

" . . . more than my body," came a whisper from the side. The three vampires stopped their macabre dance and song and turned as one to the broken priest, propped on his elbows, his head flopping weirdly.

"You are dead!" Rufo declared, a futile denial of the priest's words.

Scaladi promptly corrected him. "I have found Oghma."

And the man died, secure in his faith.

*   *   *   *   *

Outside the library, Percival hopped excitedly from one branch to another, hearing the torment of those still alive inside. The squirrel was down to the ground, just outside the door, when Rufo slammed it shut before Scaladi.

Now Percival was high in the trees, as high as he could go, chattering frenetically and leaping from branch to branch, turning wide circles about the grove. He heard the screams, and from one window on the second floor, he heard, too, the song of Deneir, the prayer of Brother Chaunticleer.

The screams were louder.

Ten

The Nature of Evil

The trail meandered around a wide expanse of rock, but Danica was growing impatient. She went to the stone abutment instead, looked up its thirty-foot height, and carefully began picking her way up along a crack in the stone.

Dorigen came to the spot beneath her. The wizard was talking, but Danica, concentrating on hooking her strong fingers in cracks and picking rough spots where she could set her feet, wasn't listening. Soon after, the agile monk lifted her hand over the lip and felt about, finally grasping the thick base of a small bush. She tested her weight, then, convinced the bush was secure, used it to pull herself over.

From that vantage point, Danica got her first look at

the Edificant Library. It lay nestled atop a flat juncture in a climbing trail, a cliff to its northern side and a steep drop south of the place. It seemed just a squat block of unremarkable stone, not a particularly attractive piece of architecture, and from this distance Danica did not notice that the small windows (there were so few) had been covered by boards and tapestries.

All seemed quiet and calm, the way things usually were at the ancient library, and Danica, anxious to get this messy business about Dorigen's punishment over with, was relieved to see it again. She turned about on the stone, meaning to tell Dorigen that the library was very close, but was surprised to find the woman scaling the cliff, slower than Danica, of course, but making progress.

Danica fell to her belly and called out directions. She was proud of Dorigen at that moment, proud of the wizard's willingness to fight obstacles. The cliff was small and no real challenge to one of Danica's training, but she could appreciate how imposing it must seem to Dorigen, who had spent years with her face buried in books. Yet here was Dorigen, reaching for Danica's offered hand, climbing without complaint.

A hundred yards away, concealed in a copse of evergreens, Shayleigh was equally impressed. When Danica had been so obviously exposed on the cliff face, Dorigen could have taken any number of actions to ensure her freedom. But again the wizard had proven her heart, and Shayleigh, like Danica when Dorigen had aided in the troll fight, found that she was not surprised.

Suddenly the elf maiden felt foolish for her suspicions. She reached down, unstrung her long bow, and mumbled quietly that she should have gone straight to Shilmista, as she had claimed, instead of following the two nearly all the way to the library.

They would be at the building within the hour, Shayleigh knew, and she could have been well on her way to her forest home. She waited in the trees until Danica and Dorigen had moved off again, then she, too, went to the stony rise. With a natural agility that at least matched Danica's practiced skill, the elf scampered to the top. She went down to one knee and scanned the dark line of the trail ahead as it wove in and out of hollows thick with trees and around tumbles of great boulders. Finally she spotted Danica and Dorigen, walking easily some distance ahead, and, with the patience of a being that would live for centuries, Shayleigh marked their movements along the trails, all the way to the library's front doors. She was no longer looking for trouble from Dorigen, but rather, was saying farewell to her friends.

* * * * *

Percival greeted the two as they came onto the library's grounds, the white squirrel dancing wildly about the trees and squawking as if he had gone insane.

"I have never seen such a reaction," Dorigen remarked, for there was no missing the squirrel's frantic movements.

"That is Percival," Danica explained, "a friend of Cadderly's."

They watched curiously as the squirrel leaped down a dozen feet, ran to the end of the branch closest to them, and screamed at Danica so crazily that the woman wondered if he had contracted some disease.

"What is the matter?" Danica asked the rodent, and Percival kept hopping in circles and screeching as if he had been dropped into a kettle of boiling water.

"I have heard of a disease of the mind that affects such animals," Dorigen offered. "And once saw the result in a wolf. Look closely," she bade the monk. "If you discern foam at the creature's mouth, then you must kill the beast at once."

Danica turned a wary and knowing eye on Dorigen, and when the wizard noticed the look, she straightened and wondered what she might have said to evoke so strong a reaction.

"Percival is Cadderly's friend," Danica said again. "Perhaps Cadderly's closest friend. If you think the squirrel is mad, you would be overwhelmed by Cadderly's madness if ever he learned that we killed the animal."

That settled Dorigen. Danica eyed Percival squarely and told him to go back into the trees.

The two women turned for the door then, and Danica knocked loudly. Percival raced along the branches, higher into the boughs, following a course that allowed him to leap to the library's gutter system atop the lowest edge of the front roof. The white squirrel hopped along to a point just above the doors, meaning to leap down onto Danica and stop her progress, but by the time Percival got to the spot, Danica and Dorigen had grown tired of waiting for an answer to their knock and Danica had pushed open the unlocked doors and entered the foyer.

It was dark and quiet. Danica looked behind her and saw a heavy blanket stretched across the small windows above the doors.

"What is this?" Dorigen asked. She had never been in the library, but she surmised that this atmosphere was not normal for the place. Where were all the priests? she wondered. And why were the hairs standing up on the back of her neck?

"I have never seen the library like this before," Danica answered. The monk wasn't as suspicious or nervous as Dorigen, though. She had spent the last few years in the Edificant Library; the place had become home to her.

"Perhaps there is some ceremony going on," Danica reasoned, "one I do not understand."

Unsuspecting Danica could not begin to appreciate the truth of her statement.

*   *   *   *   *

"Phooey!"

Pikel scrunched up his little nose and waggled his head at the terrible stench. He turned suddenly and let fly a tremendous sneeze, showering his dour brother with spittle.

Not surprised (not after so many decades beside Pikel), Ivan didn't say a word.

"Troll stench," Cadderly remarked.

"Burned troll," Ivan replied, wiping his face.

Cadderly nodded and moved cautiously down the path. They were only three days from the library, moving easily along the same trail Danica and the others had used. The path went up a short rise, then around a bend and some gnarly bushes, and into a clearing that had been used as a campsite.

Cadderly's heart beat wildly as he came near that camp. He felt certain that Danica had been here, and, it would seem, had encountered some wretched trolls.

The smell nearly overwhelmed the young priest as he clambered around the bushes, skidding to a stop in front of the gruesome remains of the battle.

Three large forms, three lumps of blackened flesh, lay about the small clearing.

"Looks like they got 'em," Ivan remarked, coming in more confidently behind Cadderly.

Pikel started to chant "Oo oi!" but sneezed again instead, just as Ivan turned back to face him. Ivan answered by punching Pikel in the nose, to which Pikel responded by poking the end of his club between Ivan's knees, then diving to the side, tripping his brother. In a moment, the two were rolling about the ground.

Cadderly, on his hands and knees, searched around to determine exactly what had transpired, paying the two bouncing dwarves no heed. They had fought a dozen times over the last few weeks, and neither of them ever seemed to get hurt.

The young priest inspected the closest troll, quickly surmising that Shayleigh had hit this one with a barrage of arrows before flames had consumed it. The next troll he went to, lying across the way, far from where the campfire had been, showed no signs that it had been downed or even wounded before flames engulfed it. Cadderly searched carefully, even shifting the charred corpse to the side. He found no brand, though, no trace that any torch had been brought out to combat the troll.

He rose and turned back toward the stone circle that had held the campfire, hoping to discern how much of a fire had been burning when the trolls attacked.

Ivan and Pikel rolled right across the ashes and scattered the rocks, too absorbed in their wrestling to notice the young priest's movements. They crashed into the body of the third troll, and the blistered skin popped open, pouring forth the creature's melted fat.

"Yuck!" Pikel squealed, hopping to his feet.

Ivan hopped up, too. He grabbed his brother by the front of the tunic and heaved Pikel headlong into a bush, then coiled his muscled legs and sprang in after him, burying Pikel as he tried to stand once more.

Cadderly, worried for his absent friends and trying to confirm something important, fast grew impatient with the two, but still said nothing. He simply stormed over to the broken firepit and began his inspection.

He suspected that the fire could not have been high at the time of the attack, or the trolls, fearful of flame, would have lain in wait. He also knew that his friends would not have remained in this area after the fight—the stench would have been too great. And Danica, and particularly Shayleigh, who so revered nature, would not have left the camp with the fire burning.

As Cadderly expected, he found no charred logs of any significant size. The fire had been low. The young priest looked back to the consumed troll and nodded, his suspicions confirmed.

"Get yer fingers outta me neck!" Ivan bellowed, drawing Cadderly's attention to the side.

Pikel stood at the clearing's edge with his back to the young priest, facing Ivan as the yellow-bearded dwarf pulled himself free of the tangling bushes.

"Get yer fingers outta me neck!" Ivan bellowed again, though he was looking straight at Pikel, who stood with his hands out wide, one empty, the other holding nothing but the dwarf's tree-trunk club.

Ivan, finally realizing the truth of it, paused and scratched at his beard. "Well, if it ain't yerself . . . " he muttered suspiciously.

Ivan leaped and spun, expecting to find an enemy standing in the bush behind him. There was indeed an enemy grabbing at Ivan's neck, but the whole of it came around with his turn.

Cadderly swallowed hard and put a hand up to shield his eyes.

"Ick," Pikel said, and gagged.

A troll arm, severed at the elbow but still alive, held on tight to Ivan, its claws clamped tightly on the back of the dwarf's neck.

"What?" Ivan asked and started to turn back. He blanched when he saw Pikel's heavy club arcing fast for him. All he could do was close his eyes and wait to be clobbered, but Pikel's aim was perfect. The green-bearded dwarf swatted the disembodied arm free of his brother and sent it flying across the way.

It collided against a tree and fell to the ground, then scrabbled away like some five-legged spider-thing, dragging the forearm behind it.

It was Ivan's turn to gag, and he grabbed desperately at his neck.

The troll arm scrambled under a bush, and Pikel started for it. The dwarf stopped abruptly when he noticed Cadderly, though, the young priest standing grim, one arm extended, his hand clenched in a fist.

"*Fete!*" the young priest cried, and from an onyx ring, which he had taken from Dorigen, there came a line of fire. It engulfed both the bush and the troll arm immediately. In mere seconds, the bush was no more than a blackened skeleton and the charred arm beneath moved no more.

To Cadderly's surprise, though, the line of fire dissipated sooner than he expected.

"Ick," Pikel said again, considering the remains.

Ivan, too, stared at the pile, his face scrunched up with disgust. Cadderly used the distraction to turn his arm to the side, and again he commanded the ring to spew forth its fire.

Nothing happened. Cadderly understood then that the enchantment in the ring was a finite thing, and now had expired. Likely, the item would still serve as a conduit, so he could probably reempower it, or at least get Dorigen or some other wizard to do it. He wasn't too concerned, though, for he believed that his future battles would be ones of will and not physical force.

By the time he came from his contemplations and looked up to the dwarves, they were arguing again, pushing and shoving. "Can I persuade the two of you to stop your fighting and help me search?" Cadderly asked angrily.

Both dwarves stopped abruptly and bobbed their heads stupidly.

"Our friends had this camp," Cadderly explained, "and defeated the trolls."

"Got 'em good," Ivan remarked, turning to Pikel. "Smart girls to use the campfire."

"They did not," Cadderly corrected, drawing a confused look from both brothers. "The fire was low when the trolls attacked."

"Trolls look burned to me," Ivan said.

"It was Dorigen and her magic that won the day," Cadderly replied.

"Oo," Ivan and Pikel said together, and they looked at each other as they spoke.

"So ye was right," Ivan said.

Cadderly nodded. "So it would seem," he replied. "The wizard has found her heart, and it is more generous than I had dared hope." Cadderly looked to the southwest then, in the general direction of the Edificant Library. Ivan and Pikel read his thoughts in his serious expression; he was considering the nature and value of punishment.

"The ore is hid," Ivan remarked.

Cadderly, curious, looked at him.

"Dwarven saying," Ivan explained. "Ye find a lump o' stone that looks worthless, but ye can't be knowing that until ye've cracked it open. It's what's inside that counts. And it is so with Dorigen."

Cadderly smiled and nodded. "Let us be on our way," he offered, suddenly anxious to get back to the library.

To their relief, they found three sets of prints leading away from the encampment, close together.

The way friends would walk.

* * * * *

Danica and Dorigen found the first body in the small chapel to the side of the foyer. Romus Scaladi was mutilated.

"Get out," Dorigen whispered, and Danica nodded as she turned for the door, turned back toward the foyer.

The two women skidded abruptly.

Histra of Sune stood in the doorway, smiling, showing her fangs. "I am so glad you have returned," she said calmly. "There were but three women in all the library, and so many, many men. Even I could not attend to them all."

The words, and Histra's appearance—the woman was obviously dead!—brought a hundred questions to Danica's mind. She had one definite answer, though, one that concerned Histra's obvious intentions, and Danica, never one to be paralyzed by fear, was quickly in a crouch, ready to lash out. She peeked out of the corner of her eye at Dorigen, and took comfort in the mage's subtly moving lips.

Histra saw the movement, too, and opened her mouth wide in a protesting hiss, then turned as if to flee. Danica didn't want to get in the way of Dorigen's forthcoming spell, but her reactions were instinctive.

She sprang ahead, quick as a hunting cat, and landed in a spin, one foot swinging wide to connect solidly against Histra's ribs.

The vampiress flew away several feet, but did not seem hurt, and came right back at Danica, arms flailing.

Danica brought a foot straight up in front of her, between Histra's arms, to smack the monster in the face. Histra's head snapped back violently, but again, if the blow had hurt the vampiress, she did not show it.

Danica smelled the stench of Histra's breath and responded by jabbing a straightened and stiffened finger deep into one of the woman's blood-red eyes.

That made Histra back off, but at the same moment, she snapped up her own hand and caught Danica by the forearm.

Danica could not believe the strength in that grasp; it was stronger than any grip she had felt from the huge, muscled Oghman wrestlers, stronger than any human grip could ever be. She tried to twist away, hit Histra with a rapid series of kicks and punches—all in vital areas—but the vampiress held on stubbornly.

Danica felt her adversary's hot breath again, too close.

Dorigen watched the fight intently. She had been forced to dismiss her first spell, a bolt of lightning, for it would have caught Danica in its path. Now the wizard was chanting again, concentrating on a more controllable and accurate attack.

She didn't hear the slight flutter of wings behind and to the side, and her surprise was complete when the bat shifted form in midair and Kierkan Rufo caught her suddenly by the throat, jerking her head back so forcefully that Dorigen nearly lost consciousness.

Histra's lusting expression revealed her supreme confidence that this mortal woman could not really hurt her.

She twisted harder on Danica's arm, taking obvious pleasure in the woman's pained face.

"You are mine," she purred, but her expression
changed when a dagger, its hilt sculpted into the shape
of a silver dragon, ripped deep into her elbow! Histra fell
back and howled. Danica quickly retrieved her other
enchanted dagger and stood facing the vampiress, not
backing down an inch.

The monk's confidence slipped away considerably,
though, when she peeked back over her shoulder and
saw Kierkan Rufo holding Dorigen, the woman's head
angled so that the man could easily snap her neck.

Danica felt a wave of nausea roll over her as she considered the implications of Rufo in the library, Rufo and
Histra both vampires! She understood the coverings
over the windows then, and realized, to her horror, that
the place had apparently fallen fully.

"Danica," Rufo said lewdly. "My dear, dear Danica. I
cannot tell you how I have longed for your return!"

Danica's knuckles whitened as she gripped her daggers tightly. She was looking for a shot, looking to put
one of the enchanted knives over Dorigen's shoulder
into Rufo's ugly face.

As if he read her thoughts, Rufo tightened his grip on
Dorigen and jerked the mage's head back a bit more,
forcing her to grimace at the pain.

"It would be a little thing to tear her head from her
shoulders," Rufo taunted. "Would you like to see that?"

Danica's muscles relaxed slightly.

"Good," the perceptive vampire said. "There is no
need for us to be enemies in this. Dear Danica, I will
make you a queen."

"Your queen will cut your heart out," Danica replied.
She knew she shouldn't have said those words with

Dorigen so obviously in peril, but the thought of what Rufo was offering filled her throat with bile. She couldn't bear to talk to the man in life. Now . . .

"I expected as much from you, stubborn Danica," Rufo retorted sharply. "But as for you, Dorigen," he purred, turning the mage's head so that she could readily view his pallid face. "We were allies once, and so we shall be allies again! Come to me, and be a queen, and know more power than Aballister could ever give you!"

For just an instant, Danica feared that Dorigen might give in. The price of refusal was obvious. Danica reconsidered her fear immediately, though, remembering all she had learned of Dorigen during their journey to the library.

"Cadderly will destroy you," Danica warned Rufo. The tall vampire relaxed his grip and turned angry eyes toward her. Nothing could get Rufo's attention more than the mention of Cadderly.

Danica locked stares with the vampire, but not before she noticed Dorigen's lips moving again.

"He should be at the library's doors by now," Danica went on, feigning confidence. "He is strong, Rufo. He crushed Aballister and all of Castle Trinity."

"I would know if he had arrived!" the vampire roared, and his tone alone told Danica that she had rattled him. "If he had, I would be eagerly . . . "

Rufo's words turned into a jumble, all his body jerking suddenly as arcs of blue lightning shot out of Dorigen's hands and pulsed about the vampire's body. Dorigen twisted, growled, and pulled away, and the final shock of the spell sent the two flying apart, wafts of smoke from Rufo's burning flesh rising in the air between them.

Dorigen was casting again, immediately, as Rufo tried to recover his senses.

"I will torture you for eternity!" the vampire promised, and Dorigen knew she was doomed, knew that she could not complete her spell before Rufo fell over her.

A spinning metallic sliver caught Rufo's attention. He threw his arm in front of his face and shrieked as the tip of Danica's dagger bored through his forearm.

Danica smelled sulphur mixed with the scent of burned flesh. She looked to Dorigen, then back to Rufo as he yanked out her dagger and tossed it to the floor.

"Run," Danica heard Dorigen say, and when she looked back to the wizard, her heart fell. Dorigen stood calmly, too calmly, a small ball of flame dancing in the air above her uplifted palm. Danica knew enough about wizardry to understand.

"No!" Rufo roared. He threw his robes tightly about him and fell within himself, seeking the source of his newfound powers.

"Run," Dorigen said again, her voice serene.

Danica had taken two steps through the doorway before she looked ahead and realized that Histra was coming for her again. She lashed out with her remaining dagger, more to throw the vampiress off balance than to score a hit, then spun to the side and down, coming around with a circling kick that caught the dodging Histra on the back of the leg. She heard Rufo command Dorigen to stop and heard the confident wizard laugh in response.

Danica kicked off, launching Histra back toward the chapel's open door and using the momentum to propel herself farther from harm's way. She stumbled for the effort, and threw herself with the flow, falling and rolling, as Rufo's form melted, as Dorigen dropped a ball of flame on the floor between herself and where the vampire had stood.

It all seemed surreal to Danica, as if all the world had gone into slow motion. Flames rolled out the chapel door; she saw Histra's hair and arms reach forward from the force of the blast. Then there was just the fireball, reaching lazily toward Danica.

She curled up, tucked her head, and became, through years of training, like stone. The flames licked at her, swirled around her, but Danica felt only the slightest heat. When it was ended, an instant later, she was unharmed, and only the fringes of her cloak had been so much as singed.

The slow-motion effect of that horrible instant was gone, reversed, it seemed, when Danica looked upon Histra, the vampiress hurling herself about the room, slamming walls and flailing against the back of her shoulders as her flesh bubbled under the hungry flames. The oaken support beams about the room smoldered; tapestries a thousand years old were fast consumed; and acrid black smoke poured from the destroyed chapel— where Dorigen had given her life.

Danica fought back tears as she scrambled for the door. She had to link up with Cadderly and the dwarves, maybe find Shayleigh. She had to . . .

The door would not open.

Danica tugged with all her might, and the handle broke off, sending her sprawling to the floor.

A green fog rolled out of a crack in the wall beside the door, swirling into a funnel cloud, then blowing away suddenly and dissipating, leaving an angry and hardly wounded Kierkan Rufo standing before the monk.

Eleven

Danica's Fall

Danica's right hook caught Rufo on the side of the jaw and snapped his head to the side. Slowly and ominously, the vampire turned back to face the monk.

Danica hit him again with another vicious hook, then a third time, in the same place, with the same punch.

Rufo laughed as his head turned slowly back to center, not a welt or mark on his white cheek.

"You cannot hurt me," the vampire said in quiet, even tones.

In response, Danica drove her knee straight up between Rufo's legs, the force of the blow lifting the vampire up on his toes.

Rufo merely smiled.

"I should have guessed you'd have nothing there to hurt," Danica said, stinging the monster with words where her fists had failed.

Rufo's face contorted, rage bubbling through his cool demeanor. A feral snarl escaped his lips, and his arm shot forward for Danica's throat.

Danica's golden-hilted dagger, sculpted like a tiger, drove deep into Rufo's forearm. Faster than Rufo could react, the skilled monk ripped the blade along his arm, then tore it out and slashed Rufo across the face, marring the same cheek she had punched.

She went into a frenzy then, and so did Rufo, Danica slashing this way and that, Rufo's grasping hands trying futilely to catch the nasty blade. Danica scored hit after minor hit, then plunged the enchanted dagger deep into Rufo's chest, seeking his heart.

By the way Rufo suddenly froze, his hands going wide to the side and his expression shocked, she could tell she had hit the mark. Unblinking, eyeing the vampire squarely and showing not a trace of fear, Danica gave a sharp, short twist.

The side of Rufo's mouth began to twitch; Danica expected he would fall.

They held that macabre pose for a long while, small growls escaping Rufo's mouth. Why didn't he fall? Danica wondered. Why didn't he just die?

Her confidence began to waver as Rufo's hand eased toward her wrist. She gave another sharp tug, and the vampire grimaced. She turned the blade again, and though Rufo's pain was obvious on his pallid face, his hand kept its steady approach.

Suddenly, his strong fingers grabbed tight to Danica's wrist. The monk's left hand went into a flurry, slamming the vampire's throat and face.

Rufo never blinked, just watched as he gradually forced Danica to retract the blade, her muscles corded with strain, no match for the physical strength of the vampire. As soon as the dagger's tip came clear of his chest, Rufo yanked Danica's arm up high.

"Fool!" he said, his smelly breath in her face.

Danica slammed her forehead into his nose.

Rufo yanked her back, and his other hand came snapping across, smacking the dagger from her hand, sending it spinning about the foyer.

"You cannot hurt me," Rufo declared again, despite his obviously painful wounds.

This time, though, both of her enchanted weapons lost to her, Danica found she believed him. And she believed Rufo would tear her apart.

"Look at me!" came a shriek from across the foyer. Both Rufo and Danica turned to see Histra kneeling by the chapel door, looking down at her hands, held out in front of her. The flesh had bubbled from fingers and arms and hung down in grotesque flaps. Histra looked plaintively at her master, and even Rufo could not disguise his disgust at the sight, for Histra, who had spent her living years primping and powdering, seemed a caricature of her former self, a cruel joke on the order of Sune, Goddess of Love. Jowls of burned flesh hung low below her chin and, though they remained intact, there was no flesh around her eyeballs, so they seemed as if they would roll from her face. Her upper lip was gone, as was the flesh on one side of her nose. Her hair, that beautiful, silky, alluring mane, was no more than short, scraggly clumps of gray.

Rufo's disgust came out as a long, low growl, and without even thinking of the movement, he clenched his hand tighter and lowered his arm, forcing Danica to her knees. The monk thought to use Rufo's distraction for her own benefit and break away, but, though she had her free hand working on only one of Rufo's grasping fingers, she could not budge the digit. She tried to twist and squirm, but without even thinking, Rufo held her steady. Soon Danica came to accept that all her efforts would get her only a dislocated elbow.

"You are a vampire," Rufo said, to comfort Histra. "Your wounds will heal." Danica didn't hear much conviction in Rufo's voice, and she understood why. Vampires healed as did trolls, knitting tears in their skin and regenerating lost blood. Histra's garish wounds, though, had been caused by fire, and they would not repair.

A smidgeon of hope crossed Histra's destroyed features.

"Find a mirror!" Danica shouted suddenly. "See what your choice has done to you!"

Rufo turned and glared down at her; she could feel his grip tightening, and that reminded her that she was taking a dangerous chance here.

"Immortality?" Danica asked boldly. She groaned as Rufo subtly shifted her arm, bent it to the side, above the elbow. "Is that what he promised you?" the monk stubbornly went on. "Then you shall be ugly for all eternity!"

Danica knew that last statement would pain Histra more than anything else in the world. Rufo knew it, too, and the look he put over Danica promised her nothing short of an agonizing death. Rufo's free hand whipped across, slapping Danica so hard on the side of her head that she nearly passed out.

She shook off the blow and could feel warm blood rolling down from her ear when Rufo hit her again.

"Your wounds will not heal!" Danica cried through clenched teeth, trying to fend off the continuing attack with her free hand.

Rufo opened his mouth wide, fangs moving near Danica's neck.

"They are of fire!" Danica yelled, then she cried out, thinking she was about to die.

Outraged beyond rational thought, Histra barreled into Rufo, slamming him back against the wall.

Danica shifted her legs and threw all her weight to one side. She heard her elbow pop out of its joint, but had to ignore the agony, had to break free.

She did so just as Rufo hurled Histra back across the foyer, where the disfigured priestess slumped to the floor, her shoulders bobbing with sobs.

Danica was up, but Rufo was ready. "Where will you run?" the vampire casually asked. Danica looked to the library's outer doors again, but Rufo laughed at that notion.

"You are mine." The vampire took a step forward, and Danica's foot came up hard, slamming his chest and knocking him back. Danica went into a spin then, her trailing foot flying wide, and Rufo, not understanding, merely laughed and stayed back, apparently out of range.

As soon as the foot whipped past, the vampire came in hard, but Danica had hit her mark perfectly, had never been aiming at Kierkan Rufo. Her foot went up high and drove through the library's outer door, splintering the wood. Rufo stepped right into a shaft of sunlight that streamed through.

The vampire recoiled, raised his arms to block the searing beam. Danica started for the door, thinking to break it wider and make her escape into daylight, but Rufo's fist shot out and clipped her shoulder, and, though Danica was quick enough to partially brace for the blow, she found herself spinning through the air.

She caught her balance and touched down in a shock-absorbing roll, then came back to her feet many yards from the door. By then Rufo had crossed the beam of sunlight and now stood blocking her way.

"Damn," Danica muttered, a fitting curse if ever there was one, and she turned and fled for the stairway.

* * * * *

Banner spent this day in sleep, a deep sleep filled with dreams of power, basking in the pleasures Kierkan Rufo had promised him. He had forsaken his god, thrown aside all that he had learned about morality in life, in exchange for that personal gain.

There was no remorse, no guilt, interrupting his slumber. Truly Banner was a damned thing.

His dream took him to Carradoon, to a brothel he had once visited, on the eve of his acceptance into the Edificant Library. How pretty the women were! How wonderful their scent!

Banner pictured them now as his queens, faces pallid, sharing his life, washing in the warmth of blood.

The warmth.

Waves of heat rolled over the sleeping vampire, and he exalted in them, picturing them as blood, a sea of warm blood.

The warmth took on a vicious edge, began to lick painfully at Banner's sides. His eyes popped open and, to his horror, he found himself immersed in a thick gray cloud. Wafts of smoke rose from the smoldering lining of his casket, tucked under a bed on the library's second floor, right above the chapel Dorigen had fireballed.

Banner's hair burst into flame.

The vampire shrieked and punched straight up, his powerful fists breaking through the wood of the casket—and those splintered, burning boards fell back in atop him.

Banner scrambled wildly, kicking and thrashing apart his flaming prison. His robes flared in biting orange fires. The skin on one arm bubbled and blistered. He thought to turn gaseous, as he had seen Rufo do on occasion, but he was not enough into the realm of undeath, had not mastered vampirism to that degree.

Banner heaved the engulfed bed aside and staggered to his feet, away from the burning box. His room was ablaze; he couldn't see the door for the fiery light. Several zombies, including Fester Rumpol, stood calmly inside the conflagration, feeling no pain from the flames, though they were being consumed. They were unthinking things, and could not even comprehend that they must flee the fire, could feel neither the terror nor the pain.

Looking at Rumpol, Banner found that he envied the zombie.

Hot cinders swept into the vampire's eyes, stinging and blinding him, and he ran desperately, hoping for the door, but slamming hard into the unyielding stone wall instead.

He was down again, thrashing in agony, the hungry flames attacking from every angle as though they were a coordinated army. There was nowhere to run, nowhere . . .

Banner's eyes were gone by then, burned out, but for the first time since he had succumbed to Kierkan Rufo's temptations, the fallen priest could see the truth.

Where were Rufo's promises now? Where was the power, the warmth of blood?

In the last seconds of his existence, Banner understood his folly. He wanted to call out to Deneir, to beg
forgiveness, but, like everything else in the man's existence, that intent was based on personal need. There
was no charity in Banner's heart, and so he died without
hope.

Across the room, the flames consumed the zombies,
including the body of Fester Rumpol. The spirit, the
essence, of Fester Rumpol felt none of it, for he had held
true in the face of adversity, had followed his faith past
mortality.

*   *   *   *   *

She came off the landing on the second floor and ran
straight into Dean Thobicus. His hands clasped her
upper arms, holding her steady, and, for an instant, Danica thought she had found an ally, a priest who could
turn back awful Rufo.

"Fire," she stammered. "And Rufo . . . "

Danica stopped suddenly, calmed herself, and looked
carefully into Thobicus's eyes. She silently mouthed,
"No," over and over, slowly shaking her head.

She could not deny the truth, though, and if Dean
Thobicus, too, had fallen to the darkness, then the
library was doomed.

Danica took a deep, steadying breath, making no
immediate move to resist, and the vampire smiled
wickedly, revealing its fangs, only inches from Danica's
face.

Danica's foot flashed up in front of her face, slammed
Thobicus under the nose, and jerked his head back violently. The monk's arms worked in a fast circle, fists
crossing in front of her chest, then going out and down

over the dean's elbows. As strong as the vampire's grasp was, Danica's leverage pulled her free. Up came her foot a second time, again slamming the monster under the nose, doing no real damage, but buying Danica the moment she needed to break free.

She was back on the staircase and thought for a moment to go down, but Rufo was laughing, ascending the stairs behind her.

Up went Danica, to the third floor. A zombie stood silently in the stairway, but offered no resistance as Danica drove her fist into its bloated face, then heaved it down behind her to impede her pursuers.

She was free in the hallway of the third floor then, but where to go? She looked right, to the south, and then left, and found herself running north, toward Cadderly's room.

Rufo's feet made not a sound as he glided along the floor, but Danica heard his mocking laughter right behind her as she skidded into Cadderly's room and slammed the door in the vampire's face and dropped the locking bar into place. She found yet another zombie in the room, standing passively, and she hit it with a brutal barrage of kicks and punches that destroyed it in seconds. Its chest popped open as it fell to the floor, and Danica felt waves of nausea wash over her.

Those waves were stolen by fear when Rufo's heavy fist slammed the door.

"Where will you run, sweet Danica?" the vampire chided. A second slam rattled the bar, threatened to knock the door off its hinges. Purely on instinct, Danica threw her weight against the door, bracing with all her considerable strength.

The pounding stopped, but Danica did not relax.

She saw the green vapor then, Rufo's fog, wafting in

under the door, and there was no way she could stop it. She staggered across the room, mesmerized by the vampire's transformation, thinking she was doomed.

The excited chatter of a squirrel cleared her thoughts. Cadderly's room was one of the few in the library that sported a fairly large window, which the young priest often climbed through to sit on the roof and feed cacasanuts to Percival.

Danica leaped over the bed.

"Where will you run?" the vampire asked again, resuming his corporeal form. Rufo got his answer in the form of stinging sunlight as Danica cracked and tore apart the boards blocking the window.

"Impudence!" Rufo roared. Danica growled in reply and tore another board free of its mounting. She saw Percival then, through the glass, hopping about in circles on the roof—dear Percival, who had saved her life.

The light falling on Rufo was indirect, for the window faced east, to the Shining Plains, and the sun was on its way toward the western horizon. Still, the vampire would not approach, would not dare chase Danica out into the daylight.

"I'll be back for you, Rufo," Danica, remembering Dorigen, promised grimly. "I'll be back with Cadderly." She took a board and smashed out the glass.

Rufo snarled and took a step toward her, but was driven back by the light. He ripped the door's locking bar from its supports and tore open the portal, and Danica thought he meant to flee.

Dean Thobicus stood in the hall. He brought his hand up defensively as soon as the door went wide and the weak daylight reached him.

"Catch her!" Rufo screamed at him.

Thobicus took a step forward, despite his mind's

protests. He was a creature of the dark now and could not go into the light! He looked plaintively to Rufo, but there was no compromise in the master vampire's expression.

"Catch her!" Rufo growled again.

Thobicus felt himself moving forward against the pain, against his mind's protests. Rufo compelled him, as Cadderly had once compelled him. He had given himself to the dark and could not deny Rufo's will!

Thobicus knew he was a pitiful thing then. He had been dominated in life by Cadderly, and now in death by Rufo. They were one and the same, he decided. One and the same.

Only as he approached the window did Dean Thobicus realize the truth. Cadderly had been guided by morals; Cadderly would not make him jump out the window. Cadderly, Deneir, was the light.

But Thobicus had chosen the dark, and Rufo, his master, was guided by no moral code, was compelled by nothing except his own desires.

"Catch her!" the vampire's voice, the vampire's will, demanded.

Danica had not broken enough glass to go safely through, and so she spun about and smashed the board over the approaching vampire's head.

Thobicus growled at her, and there was no joy in his apparent victory, for he knew then that he was a victim, not the victor.

Danica shoved the splintered remnants of the board at Thobicus's chest, thinking to drive the makeshift stake through his heart. He got a hand up to deflect the blow, though, and the jagged wood sank deep into his stomach.

Thobicus looked at the monk, seeming almost surprised. For a long moment, they studied each other, and Danica thought the dean seemed somehow sad and remorseful.

Rufo's will shot through Thobicus's mind again, and his thoughts were not his own.

Danica and Thobicus moved together, both breaking for the window. They went through in a clinch, glass tearing at Danica's exposed arms.

Onto the roof they rolled, Thobicus clutching tightly and Danica not daring to break the momentum, knowing that if they stopped moving, she was caught and would be dragged back in to face Rufo. Over and over they went; Thobicus tried to bite Danica, and she wedged her arm in his face, holding him at bay.

For both of them the world had become a spinning blur.

Percival's chattering became a scream of protest as Danica and Thobicus plunged from the roof.

Twelve

Nowhere to Run

The vampire's fangs sought her neck, and Danica was too engaged in keeping the wild thing at bay to concentrate on landing properly. She jammed her elbow under the vampire's chin, pushing with all her strength, and twisted to put Thobicus beneath her. They flew apart under the weight of impact, to an accompanying snap that sounded like the breaking of a thick tree branch.

The vampire wasn't even dazed by the fall, but as he sprang back to his feet and rushed at Danica, compelled still by Kierkan Rufo's demands, Thobicus staggered, then looked about, as if confused.

The light of day washed over him.

Danica whimpered as she tried to stand, and found

149

that her ankle had shattered, the bone tearing out
through the skin. Pained by every movement, the stubborn monk got up on her good knee and launched herself forward, her hands grabbing tight to the vampire's
ankle.

All she had wanted was to get away, but now it was
Thobicus who wanted to flee, to get back into the dark
comfort of the library. Danica didn't want that to happen.
She could see the agony in his expression, and she knew
from legends she had heard as a child that the daylight
would peel the skin from his bones. Even in her intense
pain, in her horrifying dilemma, the monk kept her wits
enough to understand that destroying Thobicus now
would be a good thing, would make the necessary trip
back to purge the library that much easier.

Danica held on like a bulldog. Thobicus battered her
about the head, kicked and screamed. One of Danica's
eyes swelled and closed. She heard the crackle of carti-
lage as her nose shattered, and the pain in her ankle did
not relent, even intensified to the point where she had to
fight hard just to keep her senses.

Then she lay in the cold mud, in her own blood, holding nothing. Distantly she heard the retreating vampire's diminishing screams.

Thobicus ran straight for the library's front doors.
Every muscle trembled from the strain, from the burn of
the daylight, and he was a weakened and pitiful thing.
He hurled himself against the wooden barrier and was
repelled. He staggered backward and tumbled into the
dirt. He could see the hole in the door where Danica had
kicked, could see the cool dark beyond, beckoning to
him.

A patch of skin above the vampire's right eye melted
and drooped, blurring his vision. He went back for the

doors, but swayed in his path and missed, falling hard against the stone wall.

"How could you do this to me?" he cried, but his voice was no more than a whisper. "How?"

The beleaguered vampire stumbled as much as ran along the wall, to the library's edge and down the side of the building. There was a tunnel somewhere to the south, he knew, a dark, cool tunnel.

He hadn't the time to find it. Thobicus realized he was doomed, cursed by his own weaknesses and by that wretch, Rufo, who had lied to him.

The sunlight was direct around the back of the building, and the vampire stopped as he began around the corner, then fell back against the stone. Where to go? Thobicus fought hard to clear his thoughts, sublimate the pain long enough to remember the mausoleum.

Cool and dark.

To get there, though, he would have to cross the sunny side of the library grounds. The fallen dean could hardly face that prospect of pain, but he understood that to stay here meant death.

With a scream of denial, Thobicus threw himself around the corner and ran with all speed for the mausoleum. The sun's fires licked at every inch of his body, burned into his very heart and pained him more than he ever believed possible. But he got there. Somehow he fell through the mausoleum's heavy door and felt the cool shade of the stone floor under his burning cheek. He crawled on his belly to the back corner, opened the crypt of headmaster Avery, and somehow found the strength to pull the fat corpse out and crawl into Avery's place.

Trembling with agony, the vampire curled into a ball and closed his eyes. Thobicus needed to sleep, to gather strength, and to consider his folly and his fate.

Kierkan Rufo had lied to him.
He had lost the way to Deneir.

*   *   *   *   *

The shadows were long and slanted when Danica
regained consciousness. She realized immediately that
she had lost a lot of blood, and she grimaced when she
mustered the strength to look down at her injury, her foot
bloated and greenish, with the sharp edge of bone sticking out, caked with dried blood, a torn tendon hanging.

How could she hope to move, and yet, how could she
remain in this place with the shadows growing long?
Using all the concentration her years of training had
given her, all the willpower that had guided her life, the
monk managed to get up onto her good leg. Waves of
dizziness washed over her, and she feared her change in
posture would send more blood flowing from her wound.

She took a hopping step to the east, toward the main
walk leading from the library.

Then she was facedown in the dirt once more.

Breathing hard, forcing air into her lungs so she did
not pass out again—by the gods, she could not pass out
again!—Danica ripped the bottom off of her shirt and
bent over to reach her broken ankle. She found a stick
nearby and shoved it between her teeth, biting hard as
she tightly wrapped the wound, forcing the bone somewhat back into place.

She was lathered in sweat by the time she turned
back to the path, but she chanted her *einto*, her mantra,
and set off, first crawling, then hopping, faster and
faster, away from the darkness.

Whatever comfort she took in putting the library out
of sight was countered by the red sunset lining the

mountains at her back. She knew that Rufo would come after her; she was a prize that wretch had craved since the moment he had seen her.

This area was familiar to Danica, and though the going was much more difficult in the thick brush, she swerved from the main path, continuing straight to the east and knowing she could pick up the trail again later on, in the morning, perhaps, after hiding from Rufo in the deep woods through the night. She found a narrow trail through the brush, a ranger's trail or a druid's, she assumed, and the going was somewhat easier. Then, with twilight descending about her, her heart fluttered with hope as three forms made their way along the trail, heading back for the library. Danica recognized the Oghman garb and nearly shouted with joy to the priests.

Her face screwed up with curiosity as she realized that one of them was walking backward, that his head had been turned around on his shoulders. Danica's breath fell away, and her hopes as well, as the stiff gait of the three men, the three *dead* men, became apparent, and she thought then that she was doomed, for they had to have seen her.

Danica slumped against a tree trunk, knowing she could not fight them off. They were just ten feet away. Five feet away.

She lashed out pitifully and clipped one on the shoulder, but the zombie only staggered a foot to the side and continued walking, right past Danica!

Danica did not understand, and did not question her luck. She looked back only once at the retreating monsters, then started moving again, wondering if all the world had fallen under this darkness.

She was still moving after sunset, after twilight, when the dark grew thick and the night birds began to call out. She found a hollow and slumped, thinking she had to rest, hoping she would still be alive when the sun's first rays stretched across the Shining Plains. The hard remains of a snowdrift offered some relief as Danica packed the cold ice about her ankle. She scratched a **V** in the pile and secured her foot in place, then lay back, continuing her *einto*, trying to survive the night.

Sometime later, she heard music, not ominous, but gay, and she soon recognized the song as a bawdy merchant romp. After a moment of confusion, Danica remembered the season, remembered that merchants often came up from Carradoon to resupply the library after the long winter.

So all the world had not fallen, she realized, not yet, and she took hope.

Danica lay back and closed her eyes. She needed sleep.

But she could not allow herself to sleep, she understood a moment later, when she considered the larger picture. She could not remain here and let the merchant caravan roll past. She could not let these unwitting men walk into Rufo's lair, and even worse, it seemed likely to her that Rufo, in his search for her, might find the caravan this very night!

Before she was conscious of her actions, Danica was up and moving again, stumbling through the brush. She saw the campfire almost immediately and made straight for it.

She tripped before she got there and had no strength to stand up again, but crawled on, washed by dizziness and nausea.

"Here now!" cried a man at the edge of the encampment as Danica fell through the last line of brush. She saw the flash of a sword as the man leaped for her, apparently thinking her some thief, or even some wild animal.

The next thing Danica knew, she was sitting beside a canvas-topped wagon, her injured leg elevated before her and an old woman carefully tending the wound. Several men, merchants and their guards, surrounded her, all looking on worriedly, more than one biting his lip.

The old woman shifted the ankle slightly, and Danica cried out, then the woman turned to her companions and nodded her head grimly.

"You have to . . . " Danica started, fighting for the breath to speak. "You have to run."

"Easy, lass," one of the men tried to comfort. "You're safe now."

"Run," Danica said again. "Run!"

The men looked to each other, each one of them giving a confused shrug.

"To Carradoon," Danica managed to say. "Flee this—"

"Easy lass," the same man interrupted.

"A priest!" came a hopeful call from the side of the camp. "An Oghman priest!"

Hopeful smiles widened on the faces of those tending Danica, but Danica's face blanched even more.

"Run!" she screamed, and she pulled her leg free of the old woman's grasp and worked her way back along the wagon, walking her shoulders up its side until she stood once more.

The same man spoke again to comfort her.

He was the first to die, hurled clear over the high wagon to smash against the trunk of a tall tree, his neck snapped.

In a moment, the camp was in a frenzy. Two Oghman priests who had given themselves over to the dark, and a host of zombies, now had orders to kill.

The merchants fought valiantly, realizing the price of

failure, and many zombies were hacked apart. But three vampires, including the master, cut into their ranks, tearing and breaking them.

Several merchants ran off screaming into the night. Three took up defensive stances around Danica and the old woman, who would not leave the injured monk's side.

Kierkan Rufo faced these three. Half-unconscious, Danica expected a fierce battle, but for some reason, amidst all the frenzy in the encampment, this group of men stood calmly.

She realized then that Rufo was talking to them, soothing them with a web of words, intruding on their minds with his will and making them see things that were not true.

"He is lying!" Danica screamed. "Block your ears and your minds! Deny him! Oh, by the light that is your god, whatever god, see the evil for what it is!"

She never understood where that sudden power came from, where she found the strength to yell to those three doomed men, but though they soon died at the terrible hands of Kierkan Rufo, they did not succumb to the dark. They heeded Danica's words and found the strength of faith to deny the vampire.

That fight was still raging, one man scoring a vicious hit—with a silver-inlaid sword—on Rufo, when the old woman to Danica's side shrieked suddenly and fell back against the wagon.

Danica looked that way to see one of the other vampires stalking in, his fanged smile wide and his gaze set squarely on Danica.

"You leave her be!" the old woman shouted, and she produced a club from somewhere—it seemed to be the handle of a butter churn—and swatted the vampire over the head.

The monster looked at the hag with curiosity, and she raised the club a second time.

His hand shot out and caught her by the throat. Danica looked away but could not block the sound of cracking bone.

Then the vampire faced her, his expression wild and lewd.

Danica punched him in the mouth.

He seemed surprised, but hardly hurt.

Danica punched him again, her strength returning with her anger. She looked to the old woman who had helped her, lying dead on the ground, and her hands lashed out, one-two, scoring alternate hits on the vampire's throat. His windpipe collapsed under those hits, and no air would pass through.

But vampires did not draw breath.

Danica hit him a dozen more times before he finally caught hold of her and held her steady. He had her, and Rufo was still fighting, and there was nothing she could do.

A flash of white came in front of her face, and the vampire fell back suddenly, unexpectedly. It took Danica a moment to realize he was grappling with a clawing, biting squirrel.

Danica pushed off the wagon and hopped out, thinking only to go to Percival's aid.

The vampire extracted the rodent and tossed Percival aside, just as Danica leaped and crashed in, bowling him over. They rolled completely around, Danica bracing her good foot against the vampire's belly and kicking off with all her strength as they came around.

She heard a cracking sound, a tree branch snapping as the flying vampire crashed upside down.

When the world finally stopped spinning for poor Danica, she could appreciate the blind luck that had, for the moment, saved her, for the vampire was impaled on that broken branch, through the chest, kicking and thrashing wildly but to no avail.

She took heart, too, in seeing Percival scampering up that same tree, apparently unhurt.

Suddenly Danica was pulled to her feet, caught in the clutches of an angry Kierkan Rufo. She looked to his bare forearm and realized his wounds had healed, except for the reddened patch of skin that had crossed into the sunbeam before the broken door.

"You run no more," Rufo promised, and Danica shuddered. She was out of strength and out of breath. The fight was over. The remaining vampire walked up beside Rufo. He looked to the tree branch, to his limply hanging friend, and an expression of evil crossed his features.

He glowered at Danica and moved steadily toward her.

It struck Danica as odd at how easily Kierkan Rufo stopped the outraged vampire. Rufo merely held up his hand, and the vampire fell back a step, snarling, whining, helpless.

"This one is for me," Rufo reminded him.

The vampire looked to his companion again. "If I pull him from the branch, he will return to us," he reasoned suddenly, and by the legends, that statement was true.

"Leave him!" Rufo commanded as the vampire bounded for the impaled creature. The vampire looked back to his master.

"He went against my will," Rufo explained. "He would have killed Danica, or taken her for his own. Leave him to the fate he deserves."

Danica did note the skeptical, then wicked cloud that crossed the lesser vampire's pallid features. In that moment, the fallen Oghman hated Rufo with all his heart and soul, wanted nothing more than to rip out Rufo's throat. But that hatred fast melted into resignation, and the lesser vampire moved away.

"Our losses were great," he remarked, and it seemed curious to Danica that he should be the one to change the subject.

Rufo scoffed at the notion. "They were but zombies," he replied. "I will return tomorrow night and animate them once again, and animate those who defended this one as well." He gave Danica a shake, which sent pain flowing up from her ankle.

"What of Diatyne?" the vampire demanded, looking to the tree.

Rufo paused for a long moment. "He failed," Rufo decided. "His flesh is for the sun."

To the Oghman vampire, it seemed such a waste. But that was their way, he decided, that was the course he had chosen. So be it.

Rufo looked to Danica, his face now serene. "You need sleep," he whispered. Danica felt the words more than heard them, felt that falling into slumber would be a good thing indeed.

She shook her head vigorously, realizing she must fight Rufo to the last, on every point.

Rufo stared at her, wondering where that inner strength had come from.

Danica spat in his face.

Rufo hit her hard before he realized the movement, and Danica, battered and weak from loss of blood, fell limply to the ground. The angry vampire grabbed her by the hair and began dragging her, telling the lesser creature to gather the remaining zombies and follow him back to the library.

Rufo hadn't even cleared the encampment, though,

when what was left of his heart tugged at him, reminded
him of his feelings for Danica. He bent and picked her
up gently in his arms, cradling her close to him, though
his body had no warmth to offer. He saw the flash of her
white neck in the moonlight and was tempted to feed,
tempted to drink of this one's blood, and it was the
strongest act Kierkan Rufo had ever taken to deny himself that pleasure, for he knew that Danica could not
afford the act, would surely die and be lost to him forever if he took from her now.

High in the trees above the carnage, Percival watched
the unholy procession wander away. The squirrel understood their course, so he flew off, along the branches,
into the night, looking for someone who was not in
league with Kierkan Rufo.

Thirteen

To Love

The vampire looked her over, and, for the first time in the years he had known Danica, she seemed so frail. A delicate flower, she was, and a strong wind could have blown her away.

Kierkan Rufo wanted to go to her, to gently stroke her pretty neck, to kiss her, softly at first, until the urgency built and he could rightly sink his fangs, the material extensions of what he had become, into that throat, and drink of Danica's blood, feel the warmth of this woman he had desired since the first moment he had seen her.

But Kierkan Rufo could not, despite the chaos curse's urging. To feed on . . . no, to join with Danica now, would kill her prematurely. Rufo did not want Danica to die, not yet, not until he could give to her enough of himself, of

what he had become, that she might join him in this
state of vampirism. No matter the demands of the hunger
and the chaos curse, the vampire simply would not
accept and would not tolerate Danica's death.

She would be his queen, Rufo decided. This existence
he had chosen would be so much more fulfilling with
Danica at his side.

That image of his queen was sweeter still for Rufo
when he thought of how it would wound Cadderly.

As much as Kierkan Rufo desired Danica, he wanted
more to hurt Cadderly. He would flaunt Danica, his Danica, before the young priest, torturing him with the
knowledge that, in the end, it was Cadderly's life that
was a lie.

Drool slid from the vampire's half-opened mouth as
Rufo basked in the fantasy. His bottom lip trembled as
he took a sliding step forward. He almost forgot his own
reasoning and fell upon unconscious Danica then and
there.

He caught himself and straightened, seeming almost
embarrassed as he turned to Histra, poor scarred
wretch that she was, standing beside him in the room.

"You will watch her," Rufo commanded.

"I am hungry," Histra remarked, and she eyed Danica
as she spoke.

"No!" Rufo snarled, and the sheer force of his command knocked the lesser vampire back a step. "You will
not feed on this one! And if any others come in and har-
bor similar thoughts, warn them well that I shall destroy
them!"

A hiss of disbelief escaped Histra's bright red lips, and
she looked frantically, like a starving animal, from Rufo
to Danica.

"You will tend her wounds," Rufo went on. "And if she

dies, your torment will be eternal!" With that, the confident master swept from the room, heading for the wine cellar to spend the daylight hours gathering his strength.

He noted the dim outline of an invisible imp perched in a corner and nodded slightly. If anything got out of line here, Druzil would warn him telepathically.

* * * * *

Danica's trip back to consciousness was a slow and painful journey. As her mind awakened, so, too, did thoughts of the carnage at the campsite, thoughts of poor Dorigen, and the realization that the Edificant Library had fallen. Tormenting dreams carried Danica to the end of her journey, and she opened her eyes with a start.

The room was dim, but not dark, and after a moment, Danica remembered she had been taken in the deep of night, and realized that the next dawn must have come. She steadied her breathing and tried to separate reality from nightmare.

She understood then that reality had *become* a nightmare.

Danica's hands shot up suddenly—the movement sent jolts of pain along her leg—and grasped at her neck, feeling for puncture wounds. She relaxed slightly when she was convinced that the skin remained smooth.

But where was she? She struggled to get up on her elbows, but fell back at once as Histra, carrying the stench of burned skin, leaped to her side and glared down at her.

The remaining skin on the back of Histra's head had ripped apart under the strain of support, so that her face sagged, as if she were wearing a loose and pliable mask.

And those horrid eyes! They seemed as if they would fall from their destroyed sockets, land upon Danica's torso, and roll about the contours of her body.

Danica tried not to show her relief as the gruesome creature backed away. She saw then that she was in one of the bedrooms of the library, probably the private quarters of Dean Thobicus himself, for the place was handsomely furnished in dark wood. A great rolltop desk sat against the opposite wall, under a fabulous tapestry, and a leather divan was to the side of that. Even the bed showed of, and felt of, luxury. It was a huge four-posted structure with an open canopy top, and was over-stuffed so as to be pillowy soft.

"So you live," Histra said, her voice full of venom. Danica could understand the source of that rage; she and Histra had been rivals in life, when Histra had tried to use her charms, to no avail, on Cadderly. Danica, with her exotic, almond-shaped eyes the color of cinnamon and unkempt strawberry blond mane, was, by all measures, a beautiful woman. Histra, despite the tenets of her religion, did not like beautiful women, not when they were rivals—and they were always rivals.

Now Histra was an ugly thing, a caricature of her former beauty, and though she obviously held every advantage in this encounter with weak and battered Danica, that fact had her on the defensive and on the verge of exploding.

Danica used her perceptions to overcome the revulsion and the fear. She could sense danger in Histra—if Histra wanted to kill her, Danica could do little to prevent it. But Histra would not kill her, Danica believed. Rufo commanded here—Danica knew that much from their encounter in the foyer—and if Rufo wanted Danica to die, he would have killed her himself, out in the forest.

"How sweet you are," Histra remarked, talking more to herself than Danica. The abruptly change in the timbre of her voice confirmed Danica's suspicions that the vampiress was walking a very fine line. Histra put a hand on Danica's face and ran it gently over her cheek and down the side of her throat.

Histra's ugly visage shot forward suddenly, mouth opened wide, drool and hot breath spitting onto Danica's face.

Danica nearly swooned, thought in that instant that her life had come to an abrupt end. She caught her control quickly, though, and looked up to find that Histra had backed off.

"I could destroy you," the vampiress said matter-of-factly. "I could rip out your heart and eat it. I could stick my fingers through your pretty almond eyes and claw at your brain."

Danica didn't know how she should react to the threats. Should she feign horror at Histra's promises, or remain aloof to it all, calling the vampiress's bluff?

She decided to call the bluff, and took it one step further. "Kierkan Rufo would not approve," she replied calmly.

Histra's openmouthed face shot forward again, but this time, Danica did not flinch.

"He wants me," Danica said when Histra had backed off.

"I am his queen," the vampiress protested. "The master does not need you!"

"The master?" Danica whispered under her breath. It was difficult for her to associate those words with Kierkan Rufo. In life the man hadn't even mastered his own emotions. "He loves you?" she asked innocently.

"He loves me!" Histra declared.

Danica began to chuckle and acted as if she were trying hard to bite it back.

"What?" Histra demanded, and she trembled visibly. Danica realized she was taking a chance here, but she saw no other way.

"Have you looked into a mirror?" Danica asked, but caught herself as she finished the question, as though something had just occurred to her. "Of course," she added softly, condescendingly. "You can no longer look into mirrors, can you?"

Danica started to say, "Rufo loves me," but decided that would push the vampiress just a bit too far. "Rufo loves no one," she corrected Histra. "He has never learned how."

"You lie."

"Neither have you," Danica continued. "In your haste to appease the goddess Sune, you never separated lust from love."

The mention of Sune brought obvious pain to Histra's twisted features. Her hand, bones showing between blackened patches of skin, went high, as if to slam down on Danica, but the room's door swung open an instant before she punched.

"Enough," said the calm voice of Kierkan Rufo.

Histra looked back over her shoulder and gradually lowered her arm.

Rufo jerked his head to the side and waved his hand across in front of him, and Histra obediently moved to the side wall and lowered her head—and the loose skin of her face hung down to almost brush her large bosom.

"Even so obviously beaten, you find the spirit to play your games," Rufo said to Danica, his tone congratulatory. He moved beside the bed and put a calm smile on his face. "Save your strength," he whispered. "Heal your wounds, and then . . . "

Danica laughed at him, stealing the fantasies, stealing the smug smile and the calm demeanor.

"And then what?" she asked sharply. "You and I shall love for eternity?" She took note that her snicker hurt the vampire profoundly. "I was just explaining to Histra that you do not know how to love."

"You and Cadderly have gathered all of that emotion for yourselves," Rufo replied sarcastically, "as though it is some finite commodity . . ."

"No," Danica retorted, "but Cadderly and I have learned to share in that emotion. We have learned what the word means."

"I have loved you . . . " Rufo started to say, but he caught himself.

"Impossible," Danica snapped back, again before Rufo could present his argument. "Impossible. You loved Histra, too. I know you did, when you first brought her to your side." Danica looked at Histra as she continued, hoping to find some clues in the vampiress's expression to aid her improvisation.

"I did not," Rufo started to argue, meaning to explain that it was not even him who brought Histra over. Danica cut him short, though, and the hanging words carried a very different meaning to Histra's ears, seemed a denial that Rufo had ever loved her.

"You did!" Danica cried with all her strength, and she had to pause for a moment just to catch her breath and beat back the ensuing waves of pain. "You loved her," she went on, sagging deep into her pillow, "when she was pretty."

That got to Histra; Danica recognized that clearly enough. The vampiress lifted her head, her already grotesque features seeming more so as they twisted with mounting rage.

"But now she is an ugly thing," Danica said, taking care that her words conveyed her disappointment with Rufo and nothing against Histra. "And no longer appealing." Danica saw Histra take a short step forward.

"*Bene tellemara.*" Druzil, invisible and perched upon the room's desk, growled and shook his dog-faced head.

Rufo shook his head as well, wondering how this conversation had gotten so out of hand. It was difficult for him to bring things back under control while at the same time move beyond the pain that Danica's words brought him.

"If I had been scarred so," Danica pressed, "if I became ugly, as Histra has become, Cadderly would love me still. He would not seek a new queen."

Rufo's lips moved around the edges of words that did not seem sufficient. He steadied himself abruptly, straightened, and found a measure of dignity.

Then Histra barreled into him, and both flew sidelong, spinning and crashing into the wall. They bit and clawed each other, punched, kicked, anything at all to inflict pain.

Danica knew her moment of opportunity would be brief. She threw herself into a sitting position and gingerly, but as fast as she could, shifted her injured leg to the side of the bed. She stopped suddenly and went perfectly still, trying to concentrate on something minute that had caught her attention, trying to block out the continuing sounds of Rufo and Histra's struggling.

Danica's hand shot out to the side like a biting snake, fingers clenching about something she could not see, but could surely sense, an instant before the barbed tail could snap at her.

Druzil began thrashing immediately, caught fast in the woman's strong grasp. He came back to visibility, for expending the magical energy now seemed foolish; Danica obviously knew where he was.

"You are still not quick enough," Danica said coldly.

Druzil started to respond, but Danica's other hand came across furiously, pounding right between his bulbous black eyes, and suddenly, for the imp, all the room was spinning.

Druzil hit the wall hard and slumped, muttering "bene tellemara" over and over. He understood what Rufo would have done to him, or would have tried to do, if his attack on Danica had been successful; in an odd way, Danica had probably saved him from banishment back to his own plane of existence. But Druzil's dedication was to the chaos curse, of which Kierkan Rufo was now the embodiment, and though Rufo would never see it, keeping this woman alive was a dangerous, dangerous thing.

Danica was off the bed by then, hopping for the door on her one good leg.

"You cannot hurt me!" Druzil rasped at her, and he came in a flurry, wings beating and tail snapping.

Danica kept her balance perfectly on her one good leg, and her hands worked to her call, spinning blocking circles in the air before her.

Druzil's tail snapped repeatedly, was parried several times, and then was caught again.

The imp growled and waggled his fingers in the air. Greenish bolts of energy erupted from their tips and shot out, stinging Danica.

"You cannot hurt me," Druzil taunted.

The imp could not keep up with the speed of Danica's next move. She jerked hard on the tail, spinning him about, then caught his wings, one in each hand, while still holding fast to the tail. Jerking and twisting, Danica tied the three ends, wing, wing, and tail, into a tight knot behind Druzil's back, and hurled the startled imp face first into the nearest wall.

"Probably knot," she agreed.

Druzil rolled about on the floor, muttering curses, not appreciating the pun, as Danica turned back for the door.

Kierkan Rufo stood before her, seeming amused at her handling of the imp. In the far corner, Histra knelt on her hands and knees, skin hanging loose to the floor, eyes downward, thoroughly beaten.

"Wonderful," Rufo congratulated, and he turned his gaze on Danica.

And Danica punched him again in the face.

Rufo turned back to her deliberately, expecting and accepting the next punch, and the third, and fourth, and the continuing barrage. Finally the vampire had enough, and with an unearthly roar that sent shivers along Danica's spine, he swept his hand across in front of him, knocking Danica off balance momentarily, and caught her by an arm.

Danica knew how to easily defeat such a tenuous hold, except that no grip she had ever witnessed was as strong as the vampire's! She was caught and feared that her elbow would shatter under the strain.

She got her free hand up to block as Rufo's wide-arcing slap raced in, but his strength blew through the defense and snapped Danica's head viciously to the side. Dazed, Danica offered no resistance as Rufo hurled her back onto the bed, and then he was atop her, his strong fingers about her throat. Danica grabbed Rufo's forearm and twisted, but again to no avail.

Then Danica simply stopped struggling, sublimated her strong survival instinct and did nothing to remove Rufo's hand from her neck, did nothing to restore the flow of air into her lungs. At that moment, Danica hoped the vampire would kill her, thought death preferable to any other option.

Then there was only blackness.

* * * * *

The trail was a winding way, sometimes looping back on itself through passable areas between towering pillars of stone. At times the view was panoramic and majestic; at others, the three companions felt almost as if they were walking along tight underground corridors.

As fate would have it, Cadderly did not see the plume of black smoke rising from the southern wing of the Edificant Library, his view blocked by the last tall mountain before the place. If he had seen the smoke, the young priest would have sought the song of his god, his magic, and walked with the wind the rest of the way to the library. For, while Cadderly was pressing anyway, anxious to aid in the battle he thought Dorigen faced, he did not listen for Deneir's song, did not want to strain his energies, which had been so sorely taxed in his battle with Aballister and Castle Trinity.

Pikel and Ivan hopped along the trail behind Cadderly, oblivious to any problems at all—except that Ivan was weary of this whole journey and badly wanted to be home again in his familiar kitchen. Pikel still delighted in wearing Cadderly's wide-brimmed blue hat, thinking it brought out the rich green in his dyed and braided hair and beard.

Ivan just thought he looked stupid.

They moved in silence for a time, and at one point, Cadderly paused, thinking he heard a song. He cocked an ear to the wind; it sounded like Brother Chaunti-

cleer's midday offering. Cadderly looked around, gaug-
ing the distance still to go, and realized there was no
way, even if the winds were perfect, that he could possibly hear Chaunticleer's song; the library was at least
five miles away.

As he moved to keep up with the bouncing dwarves,
Cadderly realized that the music he heard was not in his
ears, but in his mind.

Chaunticleer was singing—it was definitely Chaunticleer's voice—and Cadderly was hearing it the way he
heard the song of Deneir.

What could that mean?

It didn't occur to Cadderly that Chaunticleer's sweet
song might be a ward against some terrible evil. He reasoned that his own mind was tuned purely to Deneir,
and that Chaunticleer's offering, too, was in perfect harmony with the god.

To Cadderly, the song was a good thing. It didn't
remain constant in his thoughts, but came often enough
for the young priest to know that Brother Chaunticleer
was going on and on, far longer than usual. Still, the
young priest put no ominous connotations on that,
simply figured that the man must be feeling extremely
pious this day—or perhaps Chaunticleer wasn't really
singing and Cadderly was just hearing the reverbera-
tions of that perfect offering.

"Are ye thinking of setting another camp?" the increas-
ingly surly, yellow-bearded Ivan asked some time later,
drawing Cadderly from the music and its unfathomable
implications.

Cadderly looked at the rocky trail ahead and tried to
remember exactly where he was.

"Five miles left to walk, at least," he replied, "through
difficult terrain."

Ivan snorted. The Snowflakes, by his estimation, were not so difficult, not even with winter still holding fast with its last fingers. Ivan was from a place far to the north, wild Vaasa and the rugged Galena Mountains, where goblinoids were thicker than pebbles and the winter wind off the Great Glacier could freeze a man solid in minutes.

The dwarf took one last disgusted glance at Pikel, who chuckled in response, then stomped past Cadderly and took up the lead. "Tonight," Ivan explained. "We'll be walking through the front doors before the stars come clear!"

Cadderly sighed and watched Ivan take a fast-paced lead. Pikel was still chuckling when he came hopping past.

"Give me that," Cadderly snapped, seeing the source of Ivan's ire. He plucked the hat from Pikel's head, brushed it off, and tapped it atop his own crown. Then he pulled from his pack the cooking pot, the impromptu helmet the green-bearded dwarf had fashioned for himself, and plopped it over Pikel's head.

Pikel's chuckle turned into a sorrowful "Oooo."

* * * * *

Some miles from the three, to the west and north, a scrambling noise in the boughs above brought Shayleigh from her reverie. Angled in the hollow of a thick branch near the trunk of a wide elm, the elf, to an unknowing observer, would have appeared in an awkward and dangerous predicament. But a slight twist brought agile Shayleigh completely about, her back flat on the branch and her longbow somehow clear of the tangle, out and ready above her.

The elf's violet eyes narrowed as she considered the busy canopy, searching for the source of the noise. She wasn't too worried—the sun was still high above the western horizon—but she knew the sounds of the natural movements of all the area's animals, and recognized that whatever had come so noisily into the boughs of this tree had done so in wild flight.

A leaf danced suddenly, not so far above her. Back bent her bow.

Then the foliage parted, and Shayleigh eased the string back to rest, and smiled to see a familiar white squirrel staring down at her.

Percival came down in a frenzied rush, and Shayleigh's smile faded into an expression of confusion. Why would Percival, whom she'd met long ago, be so far from the library? she wondered. And what had so obviously upset the creature?

Unlike Cadderly and the dwarves, Shayleigh had seen the pillar of smoke, and, at that time, had thought to turn back and investigate. She figured it was only a ceremonial fire, though, perhaps a communal burial cairn for those priests who had died over the winter months and were now being put to their rest. So she had determined that it was not her business, that her business was, after all, to return to Shilmista with full speed, where King Elbereth, no doubt, greatly anticipated her information.

She had taken her reverie early, with the sun still high, thinking to travel through the night.

Now, seeing Percival here, hopping about and chattering frantically, Shayleigh regretted that choice to continue. She should have gone straight to the library, straight to Danica, her friend, who might have needed her help . . . and still might.

Shayleigh swung under the branch, her feet touching

lightly on the next lowest. She bent her legs and fell backward, hooking the branch with her knees, and swung down so that she caught the lowest branch in one hand. She kept with the flow of her momentum to spin lightly down to the ground. Percival, following, was hard-pressed to keep up.

Shayleigh held her arm out and made a ticking noise, and Percival leaped from the lowest branch to her, accepting the ride as the elf maiden ran full speed back to the east, back to her friend.

Twilight

I feared I had killed you."

It was Rufo's voice, from far away, but rushing closer.

Danica opened her eyes. She was on the bed, in the same room as before, but her wrists and ankles now were securely bound to the bed's four strong posts. A throbbing, burning pain in her wounded left leg did not relent, and the monk feared the binding would cut through her skin and sever the already tattered ankle.

Worse still, there was Rufo, leaning over her, his white face softened with concern.

"My dear Danica," he whispered. He came closer, trying to soften his angular features, trying to be gentle.

Danica did not spit in his face; she was beyond any

more symbolic, if ineffective, protests.

Rufo, though, recognized her disgust. "Do you not believe I can love?" he asked quietly, and a twitch on one cheek told Danica he was fighting hard to hold his calm.

Again Danica offered no response.

"I have loved you since you first came to the library," Rufo went on dramatically. "I have watched you from afar, delighting in the simple grace of your every movement."

Danica steeled her cold gaze and did not blink.

"But I am not a pretty man," Rufo went on. "Never have I been, and so it was Cadderly"—a bit of venom bubbled over at the mention of that name—"and not I who caught your fairest eye."

The self-deprecation was pitiful, but Danica held little sympathy for Rufo. "A pretty man?" she questioned. "You still cannot comprehend how small a thing that is."

Rufo backed off, perplexed.

Danica just shook her head. "You would love Histra still if she was a pretty thing," she said. "But you have never been able to see beyond the skin. You have never cared for what was in someone's heart and soul because your own are empty."

"Take care with your words," Rufo said.

"They hurt because they are true."

"No!"

"Yes!" Danica lifted her head as high as the bindings would allow, her glower forcing Rufo to retreat further. "It is not Cadderly's smile I love, but the source of that smile, the warmth of his heart and the truth of his soul. Wretched Rufo, I pity you," she decided then. "I pity that you never fathomed the difference between love and ego."

"You are wrong!" the vampire retorted.

Danica didn't blink, but she did slip back to the mattress as Rufo closed over her. She scrunched her head down on her shoulders and even whimpered a bit as he continued his advance, thinking he meant to take her against her will. For all her training and all her strength, Danica was unable to accept that possibility.

The monk, though, had touched a weakness in the vampire's heart. "You are wrong," Rufo said again, quietly. "I do love." As if to accentuate his point, Rufo brushed his hand softly down Danica's cheek, under her chin, and along her neck. Danica recoiled as much as possible, but the bindings were strong and she was weak from loss of blood.

"I do love," he said again. "Rest, my sweet. I will return when you are stronger, and I will show you pleasure, love."

Danica breathed a sincere sigh of relief as Rufo backed away, gave a final look, and swept from the room. That sigh was temporary, she knew. She tested her bindings again and, finding no luck, lifted her head to consider her wounds.

She couldn't even feel the cord holding her injured leg, only the general pain. She saw that the ankle and calf were bloated, and the exposed skin, where it was not caked with dried blood, was badly discolored. Danica felt the infection within her, adding to the weakness from the loss of blood, and she knew she could not get free of her bindings this time. Even if she could, her broken body would not give her the strength to get out of the library.

Danica rested, fell back into a sense of hopelessness greater than anything she had ever known. She saw between the boards over the room's one small, west-facing window that the sun had already crested on this new

day, to begin its journey to the horizon. Danica knew
Rufo would return with the night.

And she would have no defense.

*   *   *   *   *

The Edificant Library came into sight late in the afternoon, a square, squat structure peeping through the
more rounded and natural lines of the surrounding terrain.

That first, distant glimpse told Cadderly something
was very wrong with the place. His instincts, or maybe
the subtle warnings from Chaunticleer's song, screamed
at him, but he didn't understand the connotations. He
thought now that it was his own feelings for the library
that had given him such a start.

The building was soon out of sight, blocked by high
rocks as the group rounded another bend. Ivan and
Pikel, after whispering together, rushed past Cadderly
and set a tremendous pace, explaining that they planned
to prepare a delicious supper this very night.

The sun had not yet dipped below the skyline when
they came back in sight of the library, the companions
cutting in at the side of the grove that lined the structure's long front walkway. All three skidded to an abrupt
stop, Pikel's ensuing "Oooo" pretty much summing
things up for them all.

Wisps of gray smoke still filtered from several windows on the southern wing; the smell of burned wood
hung thick in the air.

"Oooo," Pikel said again.

Those inner pleas, Chaunticleer's continuing call to
Deneir, erupted in Cadderly's mind, shouting for him to
flee, but he ran to the doors of the place that had been

his home. He should have paused there, should have taken note of the hole in the wood, the hole Danica had kicked when Rufo had cornered her.

Cadderly grabbed at the handles and tugged hard, to no avail. He turned back to Ivan and Pikel, his face screwed up curiously. "They're locked," he said, and it was the first time Cadderly had ever known the doors to the Edificant Library to be locked.

Ivan's tremendous axe came sweeping off his shoulder; Pikel lowered his club into battering ram position and began scraping the ground with one foot, like a bull about to charge.

Both relaxed and straightened unexpectedly when they saw the doors open behind Cadderly.

"Ye're sure about that?" Ivan asked the young priest.

Cadderly turned and eyed the opening skeptically. "Swollen from the heat of the fire," he decided, and with Ivan and Pikel beside him, the young priest entered the library.

All the silent cries that he should flee flew from Cadderly the moment he crossed the threshold. He took this as a good sign, a confirmation that he had overreacted, but, in truth, Cadderly had crossed into Rufo's place, where Deneir could no longer warn him.

The foyer was not badly damaged, though the scent of soot was nearly overwhelming. To the left sat the small chapel, obviously where the fire had been most intense. The place's heavy door was apparently closed, though the friends could not see it, for a thick tapestry had been draped over it.

Cadderly eyed that tapestry for a long while. It showed elves, dark elves. Cadderly knew how valuable that tapestry was, among the finest artwork in all the library. It had belonged to Pertelope; Ivan had used its depictions to fashion the small hand-crossbow that Cadderly now wore on his belt.

What was it doing here? the young priest wondered. Who would think to use such a precious piece of irreplaceable art as a blockade against soot?

"Seems like the fire was contained," Ivan offered. Of course it had been contained, both dwarves and Cadderly realized when they took a moment to think about it. The library was more stone than wood, and there really was very little to burn in the place.

What, then, had caused so intense a fire?

Ivan started right, Pikel bobbing after, for the kitchen, but Cadderly caught him by the arm and swung him and his ducking brother about.

"I want to check the main chapel," the young priest stated, his voice detached. Ivan and Pikel looked to each other, shrugged, then turned curious gazes at Cadderly, who stood still for a long while, his eyes closed.

He couldn't hear the song of Deneir, he realized. And he could no longer hear Chaunticleer's singing, though the priest was likely closer now than when they were in the mountains. It seemed as if Deneir had flown from this place.

"What are ye thinking?" the always impatient Ivan asked.

Cadderly opened his gray eyes and looked at the dwarf.

"Well?" Ivan prompted. "What are ye thinking?"

"This place has been desecrated," Cadderly replied, and it wasn't until he had spoken the words that he understood what he was saying.

"Been burned," Ivan corrected, looking to the tapestry, not understanding what Cadderly was talking about.

"Desecrated!" Cadderly yelled, the word echoing off the stone walls and filtering up the stairway. The significance of the word, and the weight with which Cadderly had shouted it sent shivers coursing through both brothers.

"What are ye talking about?" Ivan asked quietly.

Cadderly just shook his head vigorously and spun off, making all speed for the main chapel, the holiest place in this holy place. He expected he would find priests there, brothers of both host orders, praying to their respective gods, fighting to bring Deneir and Oghma back to this library.

The chapel was empty.

Thick soot covered the intricate designs on the massive, arching pillars closest to the doors, but little else seemed out of place. The altar across the way seemed intact, all the items, the bells, the single chalice, and the twin scepters atop it exactly where they belonged.

Their footsteps resounding, the three huddled close together and made their way toward the front.

Ivan saw the body first, and pulled up to a quick stop, holding out a strong arm that bent Cadderly over at the waist and forced him to hold as well.

Pikel continued forward a step, came around when he realized that the others were not following, and used their stunned expressions to guide his own eyes.

"Oooo," the green-bearded dwarf muttered.

"Banner," Cadderly explained, recognizing the burned corpse, though its skin hung in flaps away from the bone, and its face was half skull and half blackened skin.

The eyes rotated in their sockets, settling on Cadderly, and a grotesque smile erupted, the remaining flaps of the body's lips going wide.

"Cadderly!" Banner cried excitedly, and he catapulted to a standing position, bones rattling, arms bouncing wildly, and head bobbing about.

"Oh, Cadderly, how good of you to return!"

Ivan and Pikel gasped in unison and fell back. They
had fought undead monsters before, alongside Cadderly
in the catacombs of this very building. Now they looked
to the young priest for support, for this was his place, his
chapel. Cadderly, stunned, overwhelmed, fell back, too,
and grabbed his hat and, more particularly, the holy
symbol set in its front.

"I knew—I simply knew!—that you'd come back," the
grotesque Banner rambled on. He clapped his hands,
and one of his fingers, held by a mere thread of liga-
ment, fell from the others and dangled in midair several
inches from his hand.

"I keep doing that!" the exasperated thing wailed, and
he began reeling in his dropped digit as though it were
some empty fishhook.

Cadderly wanted to talk to Banner, to ask some questions, to get some answers. But where to begin? This
was too crazy, too out of place. This was the Edificant
Library, the sanctuary of Deneir and Oghma! This was a
place of prayer and reverence, and yet, standing here
before Cadderly was a creature that mocked that reverence, that made all the prayers sound like pretty words
strung together for no particular purpose. For Banner
had been a priest, a well-respected and high-ranking
priest of Cadderly's own god! Where was Deneir now?
Cadderly had to wonder. How had Deneir allowed this
grim fate to befall one so loyal?

"Not to worry," Banner assured the three, as if they
were concerned about his finger. "Not to worry. I've
become quite good at putting the pieces back together
since the fire, actually."

"Tell me about the fire," Cadderly interjected, seizing
that one important event and holding on to it like a litany
against insanity.

Banner looked at him weirdly, the bulging eyeballs rolling this way and that. "It was hot," he replied.

"What started it?" Cadderly pressed.

"How would sleeping Banner know that?" the undead thing answered bruskly. "I have heard that the wizard . . . "

Banner paused and smiled widely, and began waggling his finger in the air before him, as though Cadderly had asked a question that was out of bounds. That waggling finger, like the one before it, dropped free, this one falling all the way to the floor.

"Oh, where did it go?" Banner cried in desperation, and he whipped himself to a crouched position and began hopping about the pews.

"Are ye wanting to talk to this one?" Ivan asked, and the dwarf's tone made it obvious which answer he preferred.

Cadderly thought for a moment. Banner had stopped short of an answer—and the hint he had offered did not settle well with Cadderly! But why had the wretched thing stopped? the young priest wondered. What had compelled Banner to hold back? Cadderly did not know exactly what Banner was. He was more than an unthinking zombie, Cadderly knew, though the young priest wasn't well versed in the various versions of undeath. Zombies, and others of the lowest form of animated undeath, didn't converse, were simply unthinking instruments of their masters, so Banner apparently ranked somewhere above them. Cadderly had once battled a mummy, but Banner didn't seem to fit that mold either. He seemed benign, almost, too foolish to be a threat.

Yet, something, some impulse, had held Banner from answering.

Cadderly eyed the scrambling creature directly, presented his holy symbol, and in commanding tones said,

"Banner! Spirit of Banner. I ask you again and, by the power of Deneir, demand an answer. Who started the fire?"

The undead thing stopped his frantic movements, froze perfectly still and stared at Cadderly, or, more particularly, at Cadderly's holy symbol.

Banner seemed to wince several times. "By the power of who?" he asked innocently, and then it was Cadderly who winced. What had happened to this place to push his god, so very far, away?

Cadderly lowered his arm, lowered the symbol of Deneir, knowing then that he would gain no useful information.

"Are ye wanting to keep talking to this thing?" Ivan asked.

"No," Cadderly said simply, and before the word had fully fallen from his lips, Ivan's axe went into a tremendous overhead arc, slicing down and taking Banner's left arm from his shoulder.

The undead thing looked curiously at that lost arm, as if wondering how he was supposed to reattach it. "Oh, I'll have to fix that," his almost lipless mouth said matter-of-factly.

Even more devastating was Pikel's attack, the tree-trunk club slamming hard atop Banner's exposed skull, dropping the undead thing into a crumpled, broken pile of flesh and bones.

Both eyes popped from their sockets and rolled about on long, thin strands. "Now that hurt," Banner said, and all three companions jumped at the unexpected response. They realized then, to their horror, that the eyeballs were not rolling randomly, but seemed to be inspecting the damage!

"So much to do!" Banner whined.

The three slowly backed away, Pikel last, whimpering a bit and shaking his head in denial. Five feet from the broken monster, they found the courage to turn away, and started off, legs pumping to gain them full speed.

"Oh, Rufo will make me fix it alone!" Banner cried.

Cadderly skidded to a stop; Ivan crashed into him, and Pikel crashed into Ivan.

"Rufo?" Cadderly asked, turning back.

"Rufo?" Ivan echoed.

"Oo oi!" Pikel agreed.

"You remember Rufo, of course," said a calm and familiar voice from behind them.

Slowly and in unison the three turned back toward the exit of the chapel to see Kierkan Rufo standing at his usual angle, not quite perpendicular to the floor.

Cadderly noticed immediately that the brand he had given Rufo had been marred, clawed away.

"You do not belong in this place!" the young priest roared, finding his courage, reminding himself that this was his home, Deneir's home.

Rufo's laughter mocked him.

Cadderly moved inevitably closer, drawing the dwarves in his wake. "What are you?" he demanded, understanding that something was terribly amiss, that something stronger than Kierkan Rufo now faced him.

Rufo smiled widely, opened his mouth in a feral hiss, proudly showing his fangs.

Cadderly nearly swooned, then caught himself. He yanked his holy symbol free of the wide-brimmed hat, and plopped the hat awkwardly on his head in the same movement. "By the name of Deneir, I banish—" he began.

"Not here!" Rufo roared back, his eyes flashing like red dots of fire. "Not here."

"Uh-oh," muttered Pikel.

"He's not a vampire, is he?" Ivan asked, and, like everything Ivan seemed to ask in here, it was obvious what answer he wanted—needed—to hear.

"If you could only understand the meaning of that word," Rufo answered. "Vampire? I am *Tuanta Quiro Miancay*, the Most Fatal Horror! I am the embodiment of the mixture, and in here, I rule!"

Cadderly's mind whirled along the terrible possibilities. He knew that name, *Tuanta Quiro Miancay*. He, above anyone else, understood the power of the chaos curse, for he had been the one to defeat it, the one who had put it in the bowl, immersed in holy water.

But he had not destroyed it; Rufo was proof of that. The chaos curse had returned, in a new and apparently more deadly form. Cadderly felt a warmth along his leg, emanating from his pocket. It took him only a moment to remember that he had a pin in there, an amulet that Druzil had placed on Rufo in Shilmista. The amulet was tuned to the imp, so that its possessor and Druzil could be easily joined telepathically. It was warm now, and Cadderly feared what that might mean.

"Your god is gone from this place, Cadderly," Rufo chided, and Cadderly could not deny the truth of that statement. "Your order is no more, and so many have come over willingly to my side."

Cadderly wanted to argue that, wanted to not believe it. He knew of the cancer that had crept into the order of Deneir, and of Oghma, even before this newest incarnation of the chaos curse. He thought of his last encounter with Dean Thobicus. Even as he had left the Edificant Library in the early winter, Cadderly knew that he would have to return and battle the ways that had become so ingrained on this place, ways contrary to the brother gods.

Now there was Rufo, and the fall of the library seemed

to make perfect sense.

The pause now, the proverbial calm before the storm, could not last long, not with two volatile and scared dwarves at Cadderly's side. Ivan shattered that calm, roared and charged forward, and hit Rufo full force with a sidelong swipe of his great axe.

The vampire lurched and flew half a dozen feet to the side, but came up straight and seemed unhurt—indeed, was even laughing!

Pikel lowered both his head and his club and charged, but Rufo casually slapped him aside, launching him end over end to crash right through two wooden pews.

Ivan charged again, and Rufo spun to the side, snapped his hand out in the air. Some force emanated from that hand, some mighty energy that slammed Ivan and sent him flying off as wildly as if he had run into the edge of a tornado. The dwarf grunted, his breath blasted from his lungs, and flew off. He hit the edge of an arch with a sharp, sickening retort, rocketed head over heels to the floor, and skidded and bounced along, leaving a trail of blood behind him.

Cadderly feared that the blow had killed Ivan. He wanted to rush to his friend's side, to call upon Deneir's healing gifts and take away Ivan's pain. Not yet, he realized. He could not go to Ivan yet. He kept his holy symbol high in the air, presented with all his faith, as he steadily approached the vampire. He was chanting, praying, demanding that Deneir hear his call and come back to this place.

Rufo winced, and seemed pained by the presented symbol, but did not back down.

"You do not belong here," Cadderly said through gritted teeth, and the symbol, flaring with a silvery flame, was barely a foot from the vampire's snarling visage.

Rufo reached out and clenched his hand over the eye above candle, closed his fist upon it. There came a hiss, and wafts of smoke rose, and Rufo was obviously pained. But the vampire held on stubbornly, proving that this was his place and not Deneir's, that Cadderly's holy magic was no good, not in here.

Gradually straightening, the vampire widened a smile, his free hand, in a clawing position, rising up to his ear, ready to strike, ready to lash out for stunned Cadderly's throat.

Pikel hit the vampire from the side, and, though his club did no real damage, the jolt saved Cadderly, pushing him and Rufo far apart.

Rufo and Pikel engaged in a wrestling and slugging match, but the vampire was too strong, and Pikel was soon hurled away. Rufo turned immediately on Cadderly, the prized prey of this group, who had staggered back many feet.

A tremendous, inhuman leap brought Rufo flying up to block Cadderly's way. Perched atop a pew, the vampire raised his arms wide and leaned forward, meaning to fall over Cadderly.

Up came Cadderly's holy symbol, and this time, the quick-thinking young priest enhanced the presentation. He pulled out his light tube, popped off the end cap, and put the beam right behind the forward-thrusting symbol.

Rufo recoiled, struck and pained by the sudden glare. He spun away, his robes flying defensively as a dark barrier against the burning beam, and wailed an ungodly, unearthly wail that resounded off every wall in the library, that fell upon the ears and tugged at the heartstrings of the many minions the evil vampire had fashioned.

The building itself seemed to rise in answer to that call, responding wails and moans coming into the chapel from every direction.

Rufo melted away, transforming suddenly into a bat, and fluttered about the wide hall. Another bat came in hard through the open door, and then something bigger than a bat, but with batlike wings.

Cadderly recognized Druzil, and the imp's presence answered many questions indeed.

They heard the shuffling of stiff-legged zombies in the hall outside; they heard those of the dark rising to Rufo's side.

They had to get out—Cadderly knew they had to flee this place. Pikel, obviously thinking along the same lines, staggered to the young priest's side and together they turned for Ivan, neither of them knowing how they were supposed to carry the battered dwarf out of there.

But Ivan wasn't down. Somehow, he was standing and seemed to have shaken off the terrific hit.

The three joined and ran for the door, Rufo's laughter echoing in their ears every step. They cascaded down the hall and plowed into a jumble of zombies congregating in the foyer.

Ivan and Pikel cut through the throng like the prow of a ship through water, scattering bodies and limbs in every direction. Ivan's axe cleaved monsters in half or took limbs with every tremendous swipe, and the dwarf lowered his head and gored like a charging elk, ripping wide holes in zombie chests. Pikel flanked his brother, knocking zombies aside with his club, and Cadderly came right behind them, ready to strike, and yet, with the dwarves so efficient, the young priest had nothing to strike at!

For all their progress, though, Rufo was right behind, and a horrible, scarred vampire—Histra!—was beside him, along with that wretched imp.

Bolts of energy launched from Druzil's fingertips, scorching Cadderly's back. Rufo's mocking laughter and Histra's hungry hissing licked at the young priest's sensibilities.

"Where will you run?" Rufo cried.

Ivan's axe cut a zombie in half at the waist and the way to the open door (open to the twilight) was clear before them.

The doors swung closed with a bang that sounded like a nail in Cadderly's coffin.

"Where will you run?" Rufo cried again, and another barrage of Druzil's energy stung the running priest so badly that he nearly tumbled.

Cadderly thought to run past those doors, knowing that Rufo had closed them, that the vampire had placed a spell on them that would keep them closed.

Ivan and Pikel were never that subtle, or that quick-thinking, especially on those few occasions when they were truly terrified. They cried out together, lowered their heads together, and hit the doors together, and no enchantment Rufo or anyone else could have placed on the doors would have held the portal against that charge.

The two dwarves rolled outside amidst flying splinters. Cadderly, running full out behind them, tried to jump clear of the tangle, but hooked his foot on Pikel's chin and went flying headlong to the ground.

Even that evasive, if unintentional, maneuver did not save the young priest from yet another of Druzil's volley's. Pain raced along Cadderly's razed spine. Ivan and Pikel each hooked him under one arm and ran along, dragging him with them. Ivan kept the presence of mind to scoop up the young priest's dropped light tube and holy symbol.

The slow zombies ambled out in pursuit, but the vampires did not, for the night had not fallen in full. Twenty paces down the path, Cadderly and the dwarves were running free.

But for how long? all three wondered. The sun was out of sight; the library was lost.

Nightfall

Shayleigh squatted atop the roof of the low structure behind the Edificant Library, eyeing the large, square building with mounting suspicion. She could tell that the fire had been fairly concentrated, as she would expect in a structure made mostly of stone, but it wasn't so much the fire that now worried the elf maiden. Two things struck her as more than a little odd. The first was the simple lack of activity around the library. Winter was on the wane and the trails were open, yet Shayleigh saw no priests milling about the place, stretching their weary limbs in the warming sunshine.

Even more curious, Shayleigh could not understand why all the windows were boarded over, especially after the fire—to her thinking, the library should have been thrown open wide to allow the smoke to filter out and fresh air to blow in. As it was, the Edificant Library was far from an airy place, but with the windows blocked, at least the ones on this side of the structure, the smoky air inside must be nearly overwhelming.

Percival, hopping along the branches of the nearest tree, did not provide much comfort. The squirrel was still obviously agitated—so wild, in fact, that Shayleigh feared he might have contracted some disease. He ran down right near her—she thought for a moment he was going to crash against her arm.

"What is it?" she said softly, trying to calm the squirrel as he hopped a circular dance on the branch.

Percival hopped down to the mausoleum roof, did that spinning dance again, chattering loudly, as if in protest, then leaped high, back to the low branch and sat facing the mausoleum squarely, still chattering.

Shayleigh ran a delicate hand through her golden hair, not beginning to understand what all of this was about.

Percival repeated the action, and this time, the squirrel's dance atop the low structure's roof was one of frenzy. He went flying back to the branch, again sitting facing the mausoleum directly, again sputtering protests.

Shayleigh realized that the squirrel was watching the low building, not watching her or the library.

"In here?" she asked, pointing straight down to the mausoleum roof. "Is something in here?"

Percival did a somersault on the branch, and his shriek sent shivers along the elf's spine.

Shayleigh stood up straight and stared down at the twig-covered slate roof. She knew enough about the customs of the humans to understand that this was a burial house, but that fact alone should not bother a squirrel, even one such as Percival, who seemed to have more understanding than a squirrel should.

"Something is in there, Percival?" she asked again. "Something bad?"

Again the white squirrel went into its frantic dance, chattering wildly.

Shayleigh crept to the front edge of the mausoleum and peeked over. There was one window, dusty and dirty, and the door was closed—but the elf maiden's keen vision showed her how clean the edges of that doorjamb were, showed that the door had been opened recently.

Shayleigh looked all around at the small field and the library's back grounds. With no one in sight, she gripped the edge of the mausoleum and gracefully rolled over, putting her feet near the ground, and hopped down.

Percival was on the roof then, near her and making more noise than the elf wanted to hear.

"Do be quiet!" Shayleigh scolded, her voice a harsh whisper. Percival sat very still and silent, his little nose twitching.

Shayleigh could see nothing moving beyond the dirty window. She fell into a deep trance and forced her eyes into the night vision of elves, where they could view things in the infrared spectrum, seeing heat and not reflected light.

From this perspective, too, the place seemed empty.

Shayleigh took little comfort in that as she let her eyes slip back into the normal spectrum of light and moved for the door. This was a crypt, after all, and any monsters inside might well be undead. Dead creatures were cold; they gave off no body heat.

Shayleigh winced at the creak of the old door as it rolled on its rusty hinges. Dim twilight filtered into the

place, barely illuminating it. Shayleigh and her kin in
Shilmista lived more under the stars than the sun,
though, and she didn't need much light. She kept her
eyes focused in the normal spectrum and silently entered,
leaving Percival, who was chattering again despite her
scolding, on the lip of the roof above the open door.

The mausoleum seemed empty, but the hairs on the
nape of Shayleigh's neck told her otherwise. She slipped
her longbow off her shoulder, as much to have something to prod about with as to have a weapon in hand,
and moved in farther. She looked back to the door with
nearly every step and noticed Percival perched nervously on the outside sill of the window, staring in with
bulging eyes. The sight of the concerned animal almost
made her laugh despite her trepidations.

She passed the first of the stone slabs, noticed then
that there was more than a little blood—fairly fresh, it
seemed—on the floor, along with a tattered burial
shroud. The elf maiden shook her head at the continuing riddle. She slipped past the second slab, and looked
at the far wall, the wall to the left of the door, lined by
marked stones that she knew were grave markers.

Something—something out of place—about the far
stone, the stone in the corner near the back wall of the
mausoleum, caught her attention.

Shayleigh eyed it curiously for a moment, trying to
discern what it was.

It was hanging crooked just a bit. Shayleigh nodded
and slid a cautious step closer.

The stone flew off the wall, and the elf maiden leaped
back. Out came a fat corpse, a bloated and rotting thing,
to fall in a heap at the base of the wall. Shayleigh had
barely registered the gruesome scene when another
form leaped out of the open crypt, springing with incred-

ible agility to stand atop the slab nearest the wall, barely a dozen feet from the startled elf.

Dean Thobicus!

Shayleigh recognized him despite the fact that half his skin had somehow melted away, and the remaining pieces were blistered and torn. She recognized the dean, and understood that he had become something terrible, something powerful.

The elf maiden continued to backpedal, thinking to cross the last slab between her and the door, use the final pillar as a block behind her, then turn and bolt. The day was long, but she knew that the light, any light, would be her ally against this one.

Thobicus crouched, animal-like, on the slab; Shayleigh, her muscles tense, expected him to spring at her. He just stared without blinking, without breathing, and she could not figure out the source of that stare. Was it hunger or fear? Was he a malicious monster or a pitiful thing?

She came beside the last slab, felt the pillar behind her shoulder. Her foot slid back and subtly turned.

The elf exploded into motion, darting behind the pillar, but the move had been anticipated and the heavy door swung closed with a tremendous crash.

Shayleigh skidded to a stop, saw Percival doing frantic somersaults on the windowsill. She felt the coldness of the dead man's approach at her back and knew then the truth, the foul demeanor of this undead monster. She spun about and went into a defensive crouch, backpedaling as Thobicus slowly stalked in.

"The door will not open," the vampire explained, and Shayleigh didn't doubt the claim. "There is no escape."

Shayleigh's violet eyes darted back and forth, searching the room. But the building was solid, with only a single window (leaded glass, which she could never get through in time) and the single door.

The vampire opened his mouth wide, proudly displaying his fangs. "Now I will have a queen," Thobicus said, "as Rufo has Danica."

The last statement hit Shayleigh hard, both for the proclamation of wretched Kierkan Rufo's return and the fact that he apparently had Danica in his clutches.

She looked to the door, and to Percival in the window, searching, searching, but she could not deny the truth of Thobicus's next statement.

"There is no escape."

* * * * *

By the time they stopped running, the library was barely visible, back along the winding trail and beyond many sheltering trees. Cadderly stood bent at the waist, gasping for breath, and not just for sheer physical exertion. What had happened to his library? his thoughts screamed at him. What had happened to the order that had guided him through all the years of his life?

Pikel, bleeding from several wounds, hopped about the small clearing frantically, several times even rebounding off the boulders lining the place on the south (which did not help his injuries), and sputtering, "Oo oi!" over and over. Ivan just stood solemnly, staring back at the one visible top corner of the library, shaking his shaggy head.

Cadderly couldn't think straight, and Pikel's frenzy wasn't helping him any. On more than one occasion, the young priest's concentration narrowed on the problem at hand, seeking a solution, but then Cadderly would be brushed by Pikel, or loudly interrupted by an emphatic "Oo oi!"

Cadderly stood straight and eyed the green-bearded dwarf directly, and was about to scold Pikel, when he heard clearly the song of Deneir. It swept him away like he was a twig that had fallen into a swift stream. It didn't ask if he wanted to go along; it just took him in the current, gaining speed, gaining momentum, and all the young priest could do was hold on.

After a few moments, Cadderly found some control of his spiraling thoughts and he willingly steered himself to the middle of the stream, to the strongest notes of the song. He hadn't heard the melody this clearly since Castle Trinity, since he had destroyed his own father, Aballister, by sundering the ground beneath the evil wizard's feet. It sounded sweet, so very sweet, and relieved Cadderly of the grief for the library and his fears for the future. He was purely with Deneir now, basking in the most perfect music.

Corridors began to open wide to him, tributaries of the main river. Cadderly thought of the *Tome of Universal Harmony*, the most holy book of Deneir, the book inscribed with the very words of this song, though they were translated things. In the song, there were only notes, pure, perfect, but these notes corresponded exactly to the written text, the human translation of Deneir's music. Cadderly knew this—Pertelope had known this—but they were the only two. Even Dean Thobicus, head of the order, had no idea of the way this music played. Thobicus could recite the words of the song, but the notes were far beyond his comprehension.

To Cadderly, it was as simple as turning pages, as following the flow of the river, and he went down one of those offered tributaries now, to the sphere of healing, and pulled spells of mending from the waters.

Minutes later, Pikel was calmed, his bleeding stopped,

and Cadderly's few wounds were no more. The young priest turned to Ivan, who, by all appearances, had been hit the hardest in the brief encounter with the vampire, but to Cadderly's surprise, he found the yellow-bearded dwarf standing quietly, seeming unharmed.

Ivan returned Cadderly's dumbfounded stare, not understanding its source. "We got to hide," the dwarf reasoned.

Cadderly shook himself from his stupor; the song faded from his thoughts, but he kept faith that he could recall it if the need arose. "The open is better," the young priest reasoned. "In the light, away from the shadows."

"The light won't last!" Ivan sternly reminded him. The dwarf poked a finger to the west, where even the distant and tall mountains loomed dark now, their rim glistening in the very last rays of the day.

Without a word, or even a grunt, of explanation, Pikel rushed off quickly into the brush. Ivan and Cadderly watched him go, then turned to each other and shrugged.

"We shall find a place to hide the night," Cadderly remarked. "I'll seek the answers we need with Deneir. His blessing will protect . . . " Cadderly stopped abruptly and looked back to the library, his gray eyes wide with horror. The note of fear sounded again in his thoughts. Perhaps it was Deneir-inspired; perhaps it was just a logical conclusion by Cadderly, a moment when he considered everything in a light more clear. As mysterious as Pikel, the young priest ran back to the west, back toward the library.

"Hey!" Ivan roared as he took up the chase. Pikel came out of the bushes, then, smiling broadly and carrying his dripping waterskin.

"Huh?" he asked, seeing the others running fast back for the library. The dwarf gave a little whistle and rambled off in pursuit.

Cadderly cut to the side, a tight corner around some brambles. Ivan went right through the tangle and rammed the young priest sidelong out the other side.

"What?" the dwarf demanded. "Ye just said we'd be finding a place to hide! I'm not for going back in . . . "

Cadderly scrambled to his feet, his legs pumping before he ever got his balance, propelling him away from the grumbling dwarf. Ivan took up the chase again and paced him, and Pikel, taking similar, if painful short-cuts, was soon bobbing along on Cadderly's other side.

"What?" Ivan demanded again, trying to catch hold and stop the stubborn priest. They were at the edge of the library's entry walk then, between the lines of silent and well-groomed trees, in sight of the battered doors, closed again and apparently barricaded from behind.

"What?" Ivan growled wildly.

"She's in there!" Cadderly offered. Taking longer strides, the young priest moved ahead of the dwarves on the flat and open ground.

"Ye can't go in!" Ivan bellowed, not really understanding what Cadderly was talking about. "Night's falling full! Night's his time, the time of vampires!"

"Oo oi!" Pikel heartily agreed.

Cadderly's answer blew away any logic that Ivan could muster against going back into the library, against facing Rufo, whether or not the night had fallen.

"Danica is in there!"

Their legs were shorter, but their love for Danica was no less, and as Cadderly straightened and slowed, trying to figure out how to get through the barrier, trying to discern if the portal had been dangerously warded or trapped, Ivan and Pikel flew past him, heads down, call-ing out a united "Oooo!"

Rufo had bolstered the doors with both enchantments and heavy furniture and had placed half a dozen zombies behind the barrier, with orders to stand very still and simply hold the doors closed.

He shouldn't have bothered. By the time Ivan and Pikel had played out their momentum, they were face-down in the foyer, with splintered wood and furniture and zombies raining down all about them.

Cadderly came in on the heels of the dwarves, his holy symbol held out strong and chanting the melodies of Deneirian music. He felt his power diminish as soon as he crossed the threshold into the desecrated place, but had enough of his momentum with him, and enough sheer anger and determination, to complete his call to his god.

The six zombies rose stubbornly and advanced on the dwarves and Cadderly. Then they froze in place, expressionless, and a golden light limned them all, head to toe. The edge where that light met either ragged clothing or skin blurred, and the glow intensified.

A moment later, the zombies were piles of dust on the floor.

Back by the entrance, Cadderly slumped against the jamb and nearly swooned, amazed at the effort it had taken him to bring Deneir into this place—amazed yet again that the Edificant Library, his library, his home, had become a place so foreign and uninviting.

* * * * *

She did not scream when Rufo leaned over her, because she did not think that anyone could hear. Neither did she struggle, for her bindings were too tight, her weakness too complete.

"Danica," she heard Rufo say softly, and the sound of her own name disgusted her, coming from that one.

The monk fell deeper into herself, tried to fall away from her corporeal body, for she knew what was to come. And for all that Danica had endured in her short life, the loss of her parents, the years of brutal and unforgiving training, the battles on the trail, she did not think she could survive this.

Rufo leaned closer; she smelled the stench of his breath. Instinctively, she opened her eyes and saw his fangs. She struggled hard against the unyielding bonds. She closed her eyes tightly, trying to deny the reality of this hellish scene, trying to will it away.

Danica felt the sting as Kierkan Rufo's fangs punctured her neck.

The vampire groaned in ecstacy, and Danica was filled with disgust. All she wanted was to get away, to flee her own battered body. She thought she would die, and she wanted to die.

To die.

The idea hung in her swirling thoughts, a flicker of salvation, the one route of escape from this horrid monster and the state of undeath that he desired for her.

Danica felt the sickness in her leg, felt the pain through all her beaten body, and she let go her defenses, accepted that sickness and pain, basked in it, called to it.

To die . . .

* * * * *

Kierkan Rufo knew true ecstacy for the first time in his life, a greater pleasure than even imbibing the chaos curse, when he felt the pulse of Danica's blood coming to his taste. Danica! This was far better than any vampiric meal he had tasted thus far. Danica! Rufo had desired her, craved her, since the moment he had first seen her, and now she would be his!

So lost was the vampire in the realization of his own fantasy, that it took Rufo a long moment to understand that the woman's blood was no longer pumping, that any sweetness he extracted from the wound on Danica's neck had to be taken forcefully. He kicked back to a kneeling position, staring down, perplexed, at this woman who would be his queen.

Danica lay perfectly still. Her breast did not rise and fall with the rhythms of breath; the dots of blood on her neck did not increase from the continuing flow of blood. Rufo could see that he had hit her artery perfectly. With other victims, the blood spurted wildly from such wounds.

But not now. Just little red dots. No force; no pulse.

"Danica?" the vampire asked, fighting hard to keep his voice steady. He knew, though. Beyond any rational doubts, the vampire knew, for Danica's face was too serene, too pale. And she was too, too perfectly still.

Rufo had wanted to bring Danica from life into undeath, into his realm to be his queen. She was tied and weak and could not escape, or so he thought.

Rufo's body trembled as he realized what had happened, what Danica had done. He fell back farther from her, to the bottom of the huge four-poster bed, brushed an arm across his bloody face, dark eyes wide with horror, and wider still with outrage. Danica had found an escape; Danica had found the one way out of Rufo's designs and desires.

Danica had died.

Pikel's Punch

f all the things they had ever heard—the cries of wild animals in a mountain night, the screams of the dying on a field in Shilmista, the roar of a dragon deceived—none of them, not Cadderly or even hardy Ivan and Pikel, had felt their bones so melted as by the unearthly shriek of Kierkan Rufo, of the vampire who had lost his most precious of treasures.

Cadderly, when his wits returned, instinctively believed they should follow that sound, that it would lead to Rufo, and he, in turn, would lead to Danica. The young priest had a difficult time telling his dwarven companions that, though, and had a difficult time in his own mind in rationalizing any decision that would put him closer to the one who had loosed that wail! He

looked behind him, out the door, and into the empty
night. One step back, he knew, and the song of his god
would sound more clearly in his thoughts. One step
back . . . but Danica was ahead.

"Deneir is not with me," Cadderly whispered, to himself and not the others, "not close."

"Where are we off to?" Ivan prompted impatiently, his
gnarly, hairy brow showing droplets of sweat, more
from nerves than exhaustion.

"Up," Cadderly answered. "It came from the second
floor, the private quarters."

They crossed the foyer and several smaller chambers,
past the kitchen where Ivan and Pikel had worked as
cooks for many years. They met no enemies, but the
library was awakening around them. They knew that,
could feel the sensation, a sudden chill in air that was
not moving.

"Cadderly." The voice, the lewd, feminine voice, froze
the three in their tracks, barely a dozen steps up the
winding stair that led to the second floor. Cadderly, at
the head of the line, his light tube in hand, turned about
slowly, putting the beam over the low heads of Ivan and
Pikel to shine directly on the scarred face of Histra.

The vampiress, baring her fangs, curled and hissed at
the intruding light.

Pikel squeaked and launched himself, and his swinging club, smack into her, sending both of them tumbling
down the stairs.

Cadderly swung about instinctively, facing up the
stairs again, and threw up a defensive arm just in time to
catch the charge of a ragged zombie. Back stumbled the
priest, and Ivan, not really turning enough to comprehend what was happening up front, ducked and braced.

Over the low and immovable dwarf went Cadderly and

the zombie, rolling in a clinch to join Pikel and Histra in the hallway below.

Pikel did a series of short hops, trying to flank the crouching vampiress. He waggled his club threateningly, then came forward in a rush, angling the club out and turning a complete spin, once and then again. He swirled out of the ineffective routine, and, dizzy, stumbled a single step.

"Eh?" the confused dwarf asked, for Histra was not in front of him, not where she had been.

Her fist connected on his shoulder, and Pikel spun again. Fortunately for the dwarf, he rotated the other way this time, and somehow the counterspin took all the dizziness from him, so that when he stopped (and luck again was with him), he found himself facing the advancing vampiress squarely.

"Hee hee hee," Pikel snickered, and he came forth in a tremendous burst, stepping somewhat to the side of his foe. Histra veered quickly to keep square, but Pikel, solid on his big dwarven feet, shifted one foot ahead of the other and threw himself at her in a purely straightforward attack. Hardened muscles corded and snapped, and the dwarf's tree-trunk club sneaked past Histra's upraised arm to smack her squarely in the face. She flew back as though launched from a crossbow, to slam the wall, but before Pikel could utter another "hee hee hee," he realized he had not, in any way, hurt her.

Pikel looked down at his club, then to the confident vampiress, then back to the club again, as though the weapon had deceived him.

"Uh-oh," the green-bearded dwarf muttered an instant before Histra's powerful slap sent him spinning. He did a perfect two-and-a-half somersault, ending up standing on his head against the wall.

Cadderly had better success against the zombie. He came up much faster than the awkward thing, and his finger was already set in the loop of the cord to his spindle-disks, two small disks joined by a short metal rod. He sent the adamantine disks spinning down to the end of their cord and recalled them to his hand, once and then again to tighten the string. As the zombie finally pulled itself to its feet, Cadderly snapped them out viciously at the thing's face.

The young priest winced at the sound of crunching bone. The zombie staggered backward several steps, but, compelled by commands it had not the intelligence to question, it came right back in, arms stupidly out wide.

The spindle-disks slammed home again, right under the chin, and when the thing began its next advance, its head lolled weirdly, with all of the supporting neck bones shattered.

It didn't rise again after the third hit, but as it fell to the floor, a tumbling dwarven missile, Pikel Boulder-shoulder, went right over it, leaving the ground between Cadderly and Histra wide open.

Cadderly heard Ivan up on the stairs, engaged with some enemy. He glanced that way momentarily, then looked back to find that Histra had closed the ground, standing just a couple of feet before him, smiling that terrible, fanged smile.

Cadderly hit her solidly in the chest with the spindle-disks as she brazenly walked in, but the weapon only knocked her back a step, and she smiled again, even more widely, showing that it had not hurt her.

"Dear Cadderly," she purred. "You have no defense against me." Cadderly, like Pikel before him, looked down to the disks as if he had been deceived.

"Would you not prefer the fate I offer you?" Histra said teasingly. She seemed such a grotesque caricature to Cadderly, a mocking insult to the alluring, sensual woman she had once been. As a priestess of Sune, the Goddess of Love, Histra had primped and perfumed, had kept her curvy body in perfect physical condition, and had kept a light in her eyes that promised the purest of pleasure to any man she deemed worthy.

But now the skin of her face sagged, as did her cleavage, showing between the tatters of what had once been a beautiful crimson gown. And no perfume could overcome the burned stench that surrounded the maimed vampiress. Even worse, by Cadderly's estimation, was the look in her eyes, once a promise of pleasure, now the diabolical fires of unholiness, of evil incarnate.

"I offer you life," the ugly vampiress purred. "A better deal, for Rufo will offer only death."

Cadderly bolstered himself in the face of that awful image, and in the mere mention of Kierkan Rufo, using both to reinforce his faith, using both as a symbol, a clear reminder, of the fall to temptation. Up came his holy symbol, the light tube behind it, and never had the young priest presented the light of Deneir with so much of his heart in it.

Rufo had resisted Cadderly's symbol earlier, but Histra was not the master here, was still far from the full powers of vampirism. She stopped her advance immediately and began trembling.

"By the power of Deneir!" Cadderly cried, advancing a step, holding the symbol high and angling it down so that its flaring weight drove Histra to her knees.

"Well, we ain't going out that way!" A bruised and bloody Ivan cried as he half ran, half tumbled out of the stairway.

Cadderly growled and pushed the light lower, and Histra groveled and whimpered. Then the young priest
looked to the stairs, to the host of zombies that were shuffling down behind Ivan. He looked across the hall, to
Pikel, who was thankfully up again and running in circles
—no, dancing, Cadderly realized. For some reason that
Cadderly could not understand, Pikel was dancing around
his club, gesturing with his stubby hands, his mouth moving more than Cadderly had ever seen it move.

Ivan took up the fight again at the entrance to the
stairs, his mighty, wickedly sharp axe taking limbs off
reaching, stubborn zombies with every swing. "There's
a hunnerd o' the damned things!" the dwarf bellowed.

Something faster and more sinister than the zombies
stepped through their ranks to stand before the dwarf.
Ivan's axe met it head-on, and right in the chest, but as
the blade connected, the vampire, not flinching, caught
it by the handle and pushed it harmlessly aside.

"Hunnerd and one," the dwarf corrected dryly.

Cadderly growled and forced the symbol of his god
right down on Histra's forehead, acrid smoke belching
from the wound. The vampiress tried to reach up and
fight off the attack, but there was no strength in her
trembling arms.

"I deny you, and I damn you!" Cadderly growled,
pressing with all his strength. Again, Histra was caught
by the fact that she had not yet mastered her new state
of undeath, that she could not quickly and easily trans-
form into a bat or some other creature of the night, or
melt into vapors and flow away.

"Hold him back!" Cadderly, knowing he had Histra
defenseless, cried to Ivan. He started to call to Pikel, but
just grunted, seeing that the dwarf was still weirdly
dancing, worried that the dwarf's sensibilities had been

knocked clear of his green-bearded head.

Ivan growled and launched a furious attack on the vampire, hitting the thing several times. But the monster, and its horde of zombies behind it, inevitably advanced. If it had been a loyal thing, a true comrade, the vampire would have rushed past the dwarf to save Histra, but as one of Rufo's two remaining vampiric minions, Baccio of Carradoon looked upon the powerful young priest and his flaring holy symbol and knew fear. Besides, Baccio realized, the demise of Histra would only strengthen his position as Rufo's second.

And so the vampire allowed this frantic and ineffective dwarf to hold him at bay.

Soon Cadderly was engulfed with black smoke. He kept up his call to Deneir, kept pressing the eye-above-candle on Histra's forehead, though he could no longer even see her through the acrid cloud. Finally, the vampiress collapsed, and Cadderly heard the thump as Histra fell hard to the floor. As the smoke wafted away, Cadderly saw that it was finished. He could only imagine—and he shuddered when he did!—the reward that awaited Histra. He thought of black, huddled shadows pouncing on her damned soul, dragging her down to hellish eternity. Still, the vampiress seemed much more peaceful in real death than she had a moment before. Her eyes reverted to their natural color, and she seemed almost at rest. Perhaps even great sins could be forgiven.

Cadderly had no more time to think about Histra. A single glance over his shoulder told him that he and his friends were being beaten back once more, that they could not, despite their fears for Danica and their determination to rescue the monk, defeat the library, Rufo's library, in the dark of night.

Baccio, too, had seen enough. With a single swipe of his hand, he sent Ivan flying away, skidding across the floor right beside Pikel. Pikel picked up his club with one hand and his battered brother with the other.

Cadderly cried out and faced the vampire squarely, presenting his symbol as he had against Histra. Baccio, an older and wiser man, and one who had more willingly gone into Rufo's service, flinched, but did not back down.

Cadderly thrust his arm forward, and Baccio winced again. Cadderly called out to Deneir and advanced a step, and Baccio found that he had to fall back. It lasted only a second, and Cadderly knew he had the upper hand, knew that if he pressed on with all his faith, he could destroy this one as he had destroyed Histra.

Baccio knew it, too, but the vampire smiled wickedly, unexpectedly, and mentally commanded his legion of zombies to swarm about him, to block him from the light of Cadderly's faith.

The first of those unthinking monsters was limned with light, as were the zombies Cadderly had met and defeated when first he and the dwarves had come back into the library. That one dissolved to dust, as did the next, but there were simply too many of the things.

Another shriek, a most terrifying wail, resounded off the walls, echoed down the stairway.

"The master is coming," Baccio mused from the back of the horde.

"To the door!" Ivan cried, and Cadderly, though his heart ached to think of Danica in this ungodly place, knew the dwarf was correct.

They rambled down the hall, easily outdistancing the slow-moving zombies. Pikel spun around the first door, slammed it closed behind them, and threw its latch.

"We will take another way up," Cadderly remarked, and he began scouring his memories, searching for the fastest route to the back stairs.

Baccio's hand smashed through the door, and the vampire's fingers casually began searching for the latch.

The three friends were running again, through the small rooms, past the kitchen, closing every door behind them. They came into the foyer, the dwarves angling for the open door, and Cadderly tried to push them straight across, toward the south wing and main chapel, where there was a balcony that led up to the second floor.

"Not out!" the young priest insisted.

"Not in!" Ivan promptly countered.

Kierkan Rufo was before them suddenly, halfway between the door to the open night and the door to the hall that would take them to the main chapel.

"Not anywhere," Ivan, skidding to a stop, remarked.

Up came Cadderly's holy symbol, the light tube shining behind it, casting its image on Rufo's face.

The vampire, trembling with rage at Danica's death, didn't shy away in the least, but began a steady approach that promised nothing short of a terrible death to the young priest.

Cadderly invoked Deneir's name a dozen futile times. They had to get out over the threshold, he realized, out of the place that Rufo had come to call home.

"Get to the door," he whispered to his companions, and he boldly stepped out in front of them. He was Cadderly, he reminded himself, chosen priest of Deneir, who had faced a dragon alone, who had sent his mind into the realm of chaos and had returned, who had destroyed the evil artifact, the Ghearufu, and who had overcome the terrible legacy of his heritage.

Somehow none of that measured up now, not against Rufo and the fall this vampire represented, not against the ultimate perversion of life itself.

Somehow, somewhere, Cadderly found the strength to move out from the dwarves, to face Rufo squarely and protect his friends.

So did Ivan. The brave dwarf realized that Cadderly alone might be able to face off against Rufo and win. But not in here, Ivan knew. Cadderly could beat Rufo only if the young priest could get out of this desecrated place. The yellow-bearded dwarf gave a whoop, charged past Cadderly, and skidded up before the vampire (who never took his flaming eyes off the young priest, his mortal enemy). Without fear, without hesitation, Ivan whooped again and slammed Rufo with a wicked overhead chop.

Rufo brushed the axe away and seemed to notice Ivan for the first time.

"I'm getting real tired o' this," Ivan grumbled at his ineffective axe.

The only luck poor Ivan had was that Rufo's mighty punch launched him in the general direction of the open door.

Cadderly came in hard and fast.

"You cannot hurt me!" Rufo growled, but the young priest had figured something out. He presented his symbol as best he could, holding both it and his light tube in one hand, but the real weapon was in his other hand. His finger was still fast in the loop of the spindle-disks, but they bounced along low to the floor at his side, for Cadderly now understood that they would have no real effect on a vampire. As he rushed, he had taken his second weapon off his belt, his ram's-head walking stick, which had been enchanted by a wizard friend in Carradoon.

Rufo unwittingly accepted the blow, and the enchanted weapon tore the skin from half of his face.

Cadderly's arm pumped again for a second strike, but Rufo caught his wrist and bent it over backward, forcing the young priest to his knees. Cadderly straightened his arm holding the holy symbol, used it to intercept Rufo's closing, leering face.

They held the pose for what seemed like eternity, and Cadderly knew he could not win, knew that in here even his supreme faith could not defeat Rufo.

He felt a splash against his cheek. Cadderly thought it blood, but realized in an instant that it was clean, cool water. Rufo backed off unexpectedly, and Cadderly looked up to see that a line of burned skin had creased the vampire's other cheek.

A second stream drove Rufo back, forced him to relinquish his grip on Cadderly's arm. The surprised young priest grew even more confused as Pikel stalked by, his waterskin tucked under one arm, every press sending a line of water at the vampire.

Rufo slapped at the water with smoking fingers and kept backing until his shoulders were against the foyer wall.

Pikel stalked in, his face as determined as Cadderly had ever seen it, but Rufo, too, straightened and stiffened his resolve, the moment of surprise past.

Pikel hit him again with the spray, but the snarling vampire accepted it. "I will tear out your heart!" he threatened, and came a step from the wall.

Pikel exploded into motion, turning a complete spin that dropped him to one knee and sent his club knifing across low to catch Rufo on the side of the leg. Surprisingly, there came the resounding crack of snapping bone, and the vampire's leg buckled. Down went Rufo heavily, and squealing Pikel was up and over him, club raised for a second strike.

"We got him!" unsteady Ivan bellowed from the door. Even as his brother cried out in victory, Pikel's club banged hard off the stone floor, rushed right through the mist that Rufo had become.

"Hey!" roared Ivan.

"Oooo!" agreed an angry and deceived Pikel.

"That's not fightin' fair!" Ivan spouted, and the yell seemed to take the last of his energy. He took a step toward his brother, stopped and regarded both Pikel and Cadderly curiously for an instant, then fell down flat on his face.

Cadderly glanced all around, trying to discern their next move—back in or out into the night?—while Pikel went for his brother. The young priest understood that Rufo was not defeated, knew that the other vampire and the host of zombies were not far away. Cadderly's eyes narrowed as he carefully scanned the foyer, remembering that Druzil, wretched and dangerous Druzil, was probably watching them even now. Cadderly had not forgotten the painful bite of the imp's magic, and even more so, of the imp's poisonous sting. That venom had dropped Pikel once, long ago, and while Cadderly had spells of healing to counter the poison, he suspected he would not be able to access them in here.

The night had fallen, and they were ill-prepared.

But Danica was in here! Cadderly could not forget that, not for an instant. He wanted to go after her—now! To search every room in this massive structure until he found her and could hold her once more. What had awful Rufo done to her? his fears screamed at him. Spurred by that inner alarm, the young priest almost ran back toward the kitchen, back toward the zombie host and the lesser vampire.

Cadderly heard a calming voice, Pertelope's voice, in his head, reminding him of who he was, of what responsibilities his position entailed.

Reminding him to trust in Deneir, and in Danica.

It was a harder thing for the young priest than even entering this unholy place had been, but Cadderly moved to Pikel and helped support unconscious Ivan, and the three made their way back out into the open air, back out into the night.

Seventeen

One Night Free

They scrambled down the library's long front walk, between the rows of tall trees, and Cadderly, despite his urgency, could not help but think of how often he had viewed these trees as a sign that he was home. Cadderly's world had changed so dramatically in the last few years, but none of the previous turmoil, not even the deaths of Avery and Pertelope or the revelation that evil Aballister was, in truth, his father, could have prepared the young man for this ultimate change.

Cadderly and Pikel had to carry Ivan, the dwarf's head lolling back and forth, his bushy yellow hair scratching the exposed areas of Cadderly's skin. The young priest could hardly believe how much weight was packed into Ivan's muscular frame. Stooped low as he was to keep Ivan fairly level between himself and Pikel, Cadderly quickly began to tire. "We need to find a hollow," he reasoned.

The green-bearded dwarf bobbed his head in agreement.

"Yes, do," came a reply from above. Cadderly and Pikel skidded to a stop and looked up in unison, the distraction costing them their hold on poor Ivan. The unconscious dwarf pitched forward to hit the ground face first.

Rufo squatted on a branch a dozen feet above the companions. With an animal-like snarl—and it seemed so very fitting coming from him!—he leaped out, stepping lightly on the path behind the two. They spun about, crouching low, to face the vampire.

"I am already fast on the mend," Rufo chided, and Cadderly could see that the monster spoke truthfully. The wound Cadderly's walking stick had opened on Rufo's cheek was already closed, and the scar from Pikel's water had turned from an angry red to white.

The howl of a wolf cut the night air.

"Do you hear them?" Rufo said casually, and Cadderly found the vampire's confidence more than a bit unnerving. They had hit Rufo with every weapon they could muster, and yet, here he was, facing them again and apparently unafraid.

Another howl echoed through the night air.

"They are my minions, the creatures of the night," the vampire gloated. "They howl because they know I am about."

"How?" Cadderly asked bluntly. "How are you about? What have you done, Kierkan Rufo?"

"I have found the truth!" Rufo retorted angrily.

"You have fallen into a lie," the young priest was quick to correct.

The vampire began to tremble; Rufo's eyes flared an angry red, and it seemed as if he would rush forth and throttle his nemesis.

"Uh-oh," muttered Pikel, expecting the charge and knowing that neither he nor Cadderly could stop it.

Rufo calmed suddenly, even smiled. "What of this might you understand?" he asked Cadderly. "You who have spent your days in worthless prayers to a god that keeps you small and insignificant. What of this might you understand? You who cannot dare to look beyond the limitations Deneir offers you."

"Do not speak his name," Cadderly warned.

Rufo laughed at him. He laughed at Deneir, and Cadderly knew it, knew that everything Kierkan Rufo had become mocked Deneir and all the goodly gods, mocked the value of, the very concept of, morality. And in Cadderly's thinking, that, in turn, mocked the very purpose of life.

The young priest, gray eyes steeled against this instrument of perversion, began a slow chant, demanding that the song of Deneir come into his head. Fire, Cadderly knew. He needed a spell of fire to hurt this one, to burn wounds that would not regenerate. How he wished Dorigen's onyx ring still held its dweomer!

Cadderly dismissed that wasted, unproductive thought and focused on his call to Deneir. He needed fire to cleanse the perversion, fire given to him, channeled through him, by his god. Cadderly's head began that familiar ache, but Cadderly did not relent, sent his thoughts sailing into the main flow of the melody's stream.

"I have her," he heard cocky Rufo say, and Cadderly's heart fluttered at that moment, and his concentration, for all his sense of purpose, wavered.

Pikel gave a squeal and rushed out in front of Cadderly, waterskin tucked under his arm. He howled and pressed, and the skin responded with a flatulent burst. Pikel looked down at the empty thing, the last drops of water dripping from its end. Then the dwarf looked to Rufo, looked into the monster's angry scowl.

"Uh-oh," Pikel whimpered, and he was diving aside before Rufo's backhand even connected. He rolled through several tight somersaults, until he collided with a tree, then hopped up, dropped his club to the ground again, and began that same curious dance he had taken up in the corridor of the library.

Cadderly did not turn aside, did not, would not, retreat from Rufo this time. The reference to Danica had disrupted his concentration, had pushed him from the flow of Deneir's song, and he had no time to fall back into it. He had his faith, though. Above everything else, young Cadderly had his convictions and would not show fear in the face of the vampire. He planted his feet firmly and presented his holy symbol, crying with all the strength he could muster, "Get you back!"

Rufo staggered to a stop and nearly retreated a step before he found, within the evil swirls of the chaos curse, the strength to resist. There was no smile on the vampire's face, though, and where his expression had once shown confidence, now there was only determination.

Cadderly advanced a step, so did Rufo, and they stood facing each other, barely three feet apart.

"Deneir," Cadderly said clearly. How the young priest wanted to fall back into the song of his god, to find a spell of fire, or a most holy word that would send waves of agonizing discord through the vampire's skinny frame! He could not, though, not with Rufo so close and so very strong. This had become a contest of will, a test of faith, and Cadderly had to hold on to the ground he had found, had to present his symbol with all his heart, and all his focus, squarely behind it.

The very air seemed to spark between them, positive and negative energy doing battle. Both men trembled with the strain.

In the distance, a wolf howled.

Every second seemed an eternity; Cadderly thought he would burst from the pressure. He could feel Rufo's evil, a tangible thing, washing over him, denying his faith. He could feel the strength of *Tuanta Quiro Miancay*, a diabolical brew he had battled before, a curse that had almost defeated him and all the library. Now it was personified, stronger still, but Cadderly was older and wiser.

Rufo tried to advance, but his feet would not come to the call of his desires. Cadderly concentrated on merely holding his ground. He didn't hope that Pikel would come rushing in, as before. He didn't hope for anything. His focus was pure. He would hold Rufo here until the dawn if necessary!

Bolts of green energy slammed into the young priest's ribs. He gasped and recoiled, and by the time he straightened and regained the edge of concentration, Kierkan Rufo was upon him, clutching his wrist, holding Cadderly's arm high to keep the symbol of Deneir out of his face.

"Allies have their places," Rufo chided.

Cadderly managed to glance to the side, to see Pikel hopping about and swinging his club desperately, chasing a teasing Druzil around the lowest branches of the nearest trees.

Rufo pressed forward, and Cadderly struggled helplessly. Ivan groaned on the ground behind him—Cadderly was surprised that the dwarf was even close to consciousness. Ivan would be of no help, though, not this time.

"I have her," Rufo said again, confident of his victory, and despite the rage that welled within Cadderly, he was caught in such a disadvantageous position that he could do nothing against the vampire's terrifying strength. Rufo was bending him backward; he thought his backbone would snap.

The vampire jerked suddenly, then again, and Rufo straightened, easing the pressure on Cadderly's spine. Rufo jerked again and groaned, his features twisted in pain.

As the fourth sting hit him, Rufo hurled Cadderly backward to the ground and wheeled about, and Cadderly saw four long arrows sticking from his shoulder blades. A fifth bolt whistled in, slamming Rufo's chest, staggering him, his red-glowing eyes wide with surprise.

Shayleigh continued a steady walking advance, calmly putting another arrow to her bowstring and sending it unerringly into the vampire. From the side, Pikel, tired of the fruitless chase, came bobbing out of the trees, club held high as he bore down on Rufo. The dwarf skidded between Cadderly and the vampire, and readied the club.

Rufo spun about suddenly, his hand thrusting in the air, sending forth a wave of energy that froze Pikel momentarily.

"Come find your lover, Cadderly," the vampire spat, taking no heed of yet another arrow that dove into his side. "I will be waiting."

Rufo's form blurred, a green mist coming up about him, engulfing him. Pikel came from his trance, shaking his head vigorously, his generous lips flapping noisily,

and wound up to swing, but stopped abruptly as Shayleigh's next arrow passed right through the insubstantial vampire and thudded hard into the club.

"Oo," muttered the dwarf, considering the bolt.

"Is he going to keep doing that?" roared Ivan, and
both Cadderly and Pikel swung about, surprised by the
outburst.

Cadderly, back to his knees, stared hard at the tough
dwarf—tough indeed, for Ivan's wounds, injuries the
young priest had thought nearly fatal, did not seem so
bad now!

Ivan noticed the stare and returned it with a wink,
holding up his left hand to display a ring, a ring that Vander had given him at their parting. Cadderly knew the
item, an instrument of healing that could even bring its
wearer back from the grave, and everything then made
sense to him.

Everything concerning Ivan, at least. The young
priest rose to his feet and looked back the other way, to
Shayleigh. What was she doing here, and how much
might she know of Danica's fate?

"I have just returned," Shayleigh greeted as she
neared the three, as though Cadderly's impending
stream of questions were obvious to her. "I left Danica
and Dorigen yesterday, in a pass high from this place,
and would be halfway to Shilmista."

"Except?" Cadderly prompted.

"I saw the smoke," Shayleigh explained. "And your
friend, Percival, came to me. I knew then that there was
trouble at the library, but . . . "

Cadderly's face gave her pause, the young priest leaning forward, eyes wide, mouth open in anticipation.

"But I know not of Danica's fate," Shayleigh finished,
and Cadderly slumped back on his heels. Rufo had told

him Danica's fate, and he found that now, with Shayleigh's confirmation that Danica and Dorigen had reached the library, he could not deny the vampire's claim. Also, knowing the fate of the library, and the apparent probability that Danica and Dorigen had walked into its midst, Cadderly believed he now understood the source of the fire in the small chapel. Starting a conventional fire that would so consume a room in the stone library would not be easy, for there was little fuel to feed the flames. A wizard's fireball, though (and Dorigen was quite adept at those), would have sufficed.

"More than fire has attacked the library," Cadderly replied grimly to the elf. "Rufo has become something sinister."

"A vampire," Shayleigh said.

Cadderly nodded. "And there are others."

"One less," Shayleigh replied, to which the three friends looked at her curiously. "I found Dean Thobicus behind the library," the elf explained, "in the burial vault. He, too, was undead, but he was wounded by sunlight, I believe, and not so strong."

"And ye beat him?" Ivan asked, the dwarf neither sounding nor looking very hurt at all anymore.

Shayleigh nodded. She stepped near Pikel and pulled hard on the arrow embedded in the dwarf's tree-trunk club. It came out with a pop, and Shayleigh held its tip up for the others to see. Its sharp point glistened a bright gray in the moonlight.

"Silver-tipped," Shayleigh explained. "The purest of metals, and one that the undead cannot ignore. I have few left, I fear," she explained, indicating her nearly empty quiver. "We encountered some trolls . . . "

"So we saw," said Ivan.

"I recovered some of those, and all the ones I used

against Dean Thobicus," Shayleigh said. "But Kierkan Rufo just took a few with him, and I fear that my supply of arrowheads grows small." To emphasize her point, she reached down to a belt pouch and jiggled it.

"Me axe wouldn't hurt the things," Ivan huffed.

"Adamantine?" Shayleigh asked, nodding her head expectantly.

"That and iron," Ivan explained.

"Neither would my spindle-disks hurt Rufo," Cadderly added. "But my walking stick"—he held the fabulous ram's-headed baton up before him—"is enchanted, in addition to being silver. It struck Rufo a terrible blow."

Ivan's head bobbed in agreement, then both he and Cadderly looked curiously at each other. Together they slowly turned their heads to regard Pikel, who sheepishly slipped his club behind his back.

"Just a club," Ivan remarked, sliding over to his brother and pulling the huge weapon out from behind Pikel. "I seen him take it from the trunk of a dead tree meself!"

"Just a club," Cadderly agreed. "Yet it hurt Rufo."

Pikel leaned over and whispered something into Ivan's ear, and the yellow-bearded Bouldershoulder brightened with understanding.

"He says it's not a club," Ivan explained to Cadderly. "Me brother calls it a . . . " Ivan turned a questioning glance back at Pikel, who hopped back to his toes and whispered again into Ivan's ear.

"Calls it a Sha-lah-lah," Ivan explained happily.

Cadderly and Shayleigh echoed the curious word together, and then Cadderly figured it out. "A shillelagh," he said, and for a moment it made perfect sense, a shillelagh being a magical cudgel often used by druids. Such a weapon would certainly harm a vampire. A moment later, of course, it made no sense at all—where in the world did Pikel get a druid's enchanted cudgel?

"And the water?" Cadderly asked Pikel.

The proud dwarf jumped up on his tiptoes to put his lips to Ivan's ear.

Ivan's look soured as he, too, began to figure it all out, began to digest the impossibility of it all. "Druid water," he said dryly, his voice even-toned.

"Doo-dad!" Pikel squealed.

Again came the curious stares, all three wondering what in the world was happening with Pikel. Shayleigh and Ivan had seen Pikel tame a snake in Castle Trinity, but that, unlike the club and water, could be explained in other ways. But these events . . . What explanation might there be except that Pikel had found some measure of druidic magic?

With everything going on, though, this wasn't the time to press the issue, or to question their apparent good luck. Cadderly, Shayleigh, and even Ivan silently realized that if they told Pikel firmly enough that dwarves could not become druids, he might just believe them. That would do nothing except give them fewer weapons to use against Rufo.

"Then we do indeed have the means to strike Rufo," Cadderly stated firmly, ending the debate. "We have to get back into the library."

Pikel's smile went away, and Ivan was shaking his head before Cadderly ever finished the proclamation.

"On the morrow," Shayleigh put in. "If Danica and Dorigen are there, and we do not know that they are, there is nothing we can do for them this night. Trust in them. Rufo is strongest in the hours of dark."

A wolf's howl cut the night, answered by another, then a third and a fourth.

"And the vampire is mustering his forces," Shayleigh went on. "Let us be far from this place. In the night, movement is our only ally."

Cadderly looked back toward the library. Despite what Shayleigh had said, he did know, in his heart, that Danica was in there. Dorigen was in there, too, though the young priest had a terrible feeling that the wizard had met her end. Shayleigh's words about Rufo were true enough, though. This was Rufo's hour, and his allies would soon be all about them. Cadderly could not defeat Rufo, not at night, not inside the library.

He agreed and followed the elf maiden's lead as she led them off into the woods, Pikel pausing long enough to refill his skin with the clear water of a nearby stream.

Eighteen

Every Weapon

The howls erupted from every corner of shadow, from every bit of Rufo's night. Cadderly had known there were wolves in the Snowflakes, many wolves—everyone knew that—but none of the four friends suspected there were so very many so close!

Shayleigh kept the group on the move, shifting at unexpected angles through the mountain night, knifing between high lines of stone, along the very rim of deep gorges. The elf could see in the dark, and so could the dwarves, and Cadderly had his light tube, its beam kept very narrow, half concealed under his gray traveling cloak so as not to attract too much attention.

As the wolves inevitably closed in, their howls sounding like one long, mournful keen, the young priest was

229

forced to cap the light and put the tube away. He stumbled along as best he could in a night that had grown
darker still, with Pikel supporting him on one side, Ivan
on the other, and Shayleigh trying hard not to get too far
ahead.

At one point, it seemed as if they had been cut off,
with a group of wolves howling farther along the same
path they were traveling. Shayleigh looked back to the
other three, her violet eyes shining clearly, even to Cadderly's poor night vision, and her expression revealing
that she was fast running out of answers.

"Looks like we're fighting again," Ivan grumbled, and
it was the first time Cadderly had ever seen the sturdy
dwarf so obviously upset with that prospect.

Unexpectedly, the wolf pack up ahead ran on its way,
across the trail and not down it at the companions. The
wolves howled excitedly into the night, as if they had
found some new quarry to pursue.

Shayleigh asked no questions about their good for-
tune. She spurred her friends ahead at full speed and
came to a grove of fruit trees. Shayleigh would have preferred evergreens, where dark needles might offer
some cover, but the pursuing pack was not far behind
and these trees were easy to climb, even for short-
limbed dwarves. Up the four went, as high as the
branches would allow, Shayleigh finding a secure nook
and stringing her bow immediately.

The dark shapes of the large wolves came into the
clear area to the side of the grove, their fur bristling silver and black in the meager light. One came to the tree
right below Cadderly and Pikel, sniffing the air, then
loosing yet another terrifying howl.

It was answered by all its dozen companions at the
grove, and then by a larger group, the group that had

been ahead of the four companions, somewhere off to the east. The cries to the east continued, heightened, and though this group had the four treed, they could not ignore the thrill of the chase. Off the pack ran, but Shayleigh and the others did not come down, the elf explaining that this might be the best defensible spot they would find for miles.

The howling continued for many minutes, frantic, as if the wolves were indeed on a fresh trail. Cadderly's heart fluttered at every cry—might it be Danica the beasts were chasing?

Then the howls lessened and became mixed with resonating snarls, and it seemed to the companions that whatever the wolves had been chasing was trapped.

"We must go help," Cadderly announced, but none of the others seemed ready to leap to the ground behind him. He looked at them, particularly at sturdy Ivan, as if he had been deceived.

"Three dozen wolves," the yellow-bearded dwarf remarked, "maybe more. All we'll be doing is giving them more to eat!"

Cadderly didn't flinch as he picked his way down to the next lowest branch.

Ivan huffed and shuffled in his own roost, moving close enough to slap Pikel and get him, too, moving. Agile Shayleigh was already on the ground, waiting for them.

Cadderly smiled secretly, glad to confirm once more that he was blessed by brave and righteous friends. The young priest's grin went away, though, and all four of the companions froze (except for Pikel, who was knocked from his perch and fell hard to the ground), when a tremendous explosion rocked the very ground under their feet and a ball of fire rose into the air in the east, accompanied by the cries of many wolves.

"Dorigen?" both Cadderly and Shayleigh asked together, but neither of them moved, not knowing what they should do.

Pikel groaned and regained his footing, shaking the twigs out of his green beard. Above, high in the tree, a small form skittered along, verily flying from branch to branch.

Ivan, in the highest perch, let out a shout and turned about, lifting his axe, but Shayleigh's call stopped him in time.

"Percival," the elf maiden explained. "It is only Percival."

Cadderly scrambled as high as he could go, meeting his squirrel friend. Percival chattered excitedly, hopping in circles on the branch, and Cadderly understood that the squirrel had been more than a casual observer in all of this, when, a moment later, he heard the frantic cries of a man, and the howls of the remaining wolves in pursuit.

Shayleigh and Pikel went back up into the tree, and all four, and the squirrel as well, fell silent, watching to the east. Shayleigh caught the movement first, and up came her bow, an arrow streaking off unerringly to take down a wolf that was nipping at the fleeing man's heels.

The man, startled and not believing he had any allies in this dark place, cried out as the bolt flew past. Cadderly recognized the voice.

"Belago," the young priest muttered.

Ivan dropped down branch by branch until he was at the lowest limb, Pikel joining him there. Both looked to the running man, figuring the angle of approach, and they shifted side by side to put themselves in line. Pikel braced Ivan's feet as the dwarf rolled under the branch, hooking his knees, his arms hanging down.

On came Belago, blindly, more wolves nipping at his heels. Another arrow sliced past him, the elf's aim perfect, but the frightened man seemed to not even register that fact. He seemed oblivious to everything except his belief that he was alone and helpless in a dark night and was about to be eaten by wolves.

He ran under the tree, only because that course was straightest, for he knew he had no time to climb.

Then he was caught, and he screamed as he went up suddenly, hoisted by powerful dwarven hands. Not knowing Ivan for an ally, he squirmed and lashed out, connecting on the dwarf's face with several solid hits. Ivan just shook his head and muttered curses against "stupid people."

Belago wasn't beginning to break free, but his squirming was preventing Ivan from getting him high out of harm's way. Finally the dwarf heaved Belago as high as he could and butted the man right in the face. Belago went limp in his arms, and Ivan, with Pikel's help, tugged him up to the branch.

Shayleigh's bow sang out several times, keeping the pack at bay as the dwarves straightened themselves out and hauled dazed Belago up a couple of branches.

"By the gods!" Vicero Belago whispered repeatedly, tears flowing freely when he at last came out of his stupor and recognized his saviors. "By the gods! And Cadderly! Dear Cadderly!" he wailed, standing on the branch to be closer to the young priest. "You have returned too late, I fear!"

Cadderly slipped over on the branch and stepped down to Belago's level, trying to calm the man. "Was Dorigen with you?" Cadderly asked at length, thinking still of the telltale explosion.

Belago didn't seem to recognize the name.

"Danica?" the young priest asked frantically. "What of Danica?"

"She was with you," the wiry alchemist replied, seeming sincerely confused.

"Danica came back to the library," Cadderly answered sharply.

"I have been out of the library for several days," Belago replied, and he quickly told his tale. As it turned out, the four friends knew more about the place than he; all the poor alchemist knew was that he had been put out, and that very dark things, it seemed, had subsequently occurred in the library. Belago had not gone to Carradoon, as Dean Thobicus had instructed. He figured to wait for Cadderly's return, or at least for the warmer weather. He had friends on the mountain and had taken refuge in a small shack with a hunter he knew, a man named Minshk, east of the library.

"Dark things were about," the alchemist remarked, referring to that time in the hunter's lodge. "Minshk and I knew that, and we were going to go to Carradoon tomorrow." He looked to the east, his eyes sad, and mournfully repeated, "Tomorrow.

"But the wolves came," the alchemist continued, his voice barely a whisper. "And something else. I got away, but Minshk . . . " Belago slumped on the branch and went quiet, and the four friends turned their attention back to the pack surrounding the grove. The wolves couldn't get to them, but those continuing howls would likely bring in something, or someone, that could.

"We should be getting outta here," Ivan offered.

For the first time, Vicero Belago's expression brightened. He reached under his heavy cloak and produced a flask, handing it toward Cadderly.

Pikel, meanwhile, had his own idea. He snapped his

stubby fingers and grabbed the heavy axe from his brother's back.

Cadderly, concerned with Belago's offering, paid little heed to the dwarves' ensuing argument.

"*Oil of Impact*," the alchemist said excitedly. "I was going to make you another bandolier of explosive darts, but I hadn't the time before Thobicus . . . " He paused, overwhelmed by the painful memory. Then his face brightened again and he pushed the flask out toward Cadderly.

"I had another flask," he explained. "Maybe you saw the blast. I was hoping to do another one, right before Ivan caught me, but I hadn't the time."

Cadderly then understood the fireball that had risen in the east, and he gingerly—so very gingerly!—accepted the gift from the alchemist.

"Hey!" Ivan cried, drawing everyone's attention. Pikel had won this round of their argument, shoving Ivan over so hard that he had to hang on to the branch by his fingertips to prevent himself from falling to the gathered wolf pack. Before the yellow-bearded dwarf could right himself or further protest, Pikel brought the axe down hard on the trunk of the tree, causing a small split. As soon as Ivan regained his balance, Pikel handed the axe back, and Ivan snatched it away, eyeing his brother curiously.

Not as curiously as Cadderly was watching. He, above all the others, even Ivan, understood what Pikel had become, what the dwarf's love of trees and flowers had given him, and the gravity of Pikel's action, the fact that the would-be druid had just brought a weapon against a living tree, did not escape the young priest. Cadderly shifted past Ivan, who was more than willing to slide away from his unpredictable brother, and came to

Pikel's side, to find the green-bearded dwarf muttering—no, chanting—under his breath, a small knife in hand.

Before Cadderly could ask, for the young priest did not want to interrupt, Pikel slashed his own hand with the knife.

Cadderly grabbed the dwarf's wrist and forced Pikel to look at him directly. Pikel smiled and nodded, pointed to Cadderly, to the wound, and to the wound he had inflicted on the tree.

Cadderly came to understand as a single drop of Pikel's blood fell from his hand to land on the rough bark beside the small cut in the tree. The blood instantly rushed for the crack in the trunk and disappeared.

Pikel was chanting again, and so was Cadderly, trying to find, in Deneir's song, some energy that he could add to the dwarf's attempt.

More blood flowed from Pikel's wound, every drop finding its way unerringly to the tree's crack. A warmth rose up from that crack, the smell of springtime with it.

Cadderly found a stream of thought, of holy notes that fit the scene, and he followed it with all his heart, not knowing what would happen, not knowing what Pikel had begun.

He closed his eyes and sang on, ignoring the continuing snarls and howls of the wolves, ignoring the astonished gasps of his friends.

Cadderly opened his eyes again when the branch heaved under him, as though it had come to life. The tree had blossomed in full, large apples showing on every branch. Ivan had one in hand already, and had taken a huge bite.

The dwarf's look soured, though, and not for the taste. "Ye think I might be fattening meself up to make a better wolf meal?" he asked in all seriousness, and he pelted the apple onto the nose of the nearest wolf.

Pikel squealed with delight; Cadderly could hardly believe what he and Pikel had done. What *had* they done? the young priest wondered, for he hardly saw the gain of prematurely flowering the tree. The apples provided missiles they could throw at the wolves, but certainly nothing that would drive the pack away.

The tree heaved again, and then again, and then, to the amazement of everyone on the branch, except, of course, Pikel, it came alive, not alive as a plant, but as a sentient, moving thing!

Branches rolled up and snapped down, loosing showers of apples with tremendous force, pummeling the wolf pack. Even worse for the wolves, the lowest branches reached down to club them, crunching their legs under them or sending them spinning away. Belago nearly tumbled, fell right over his branch and held on desperately with wrapped arms. Ivan did fall, bouncing from branch to branch all the way to the ground. He came up at once, axe ready, expecting a dozen wolves to leap at his throat.

Shayleigh was beside him in an instant, but the dwarf needed no protection. The wolves were too busy dodging and running. A moment later, Pikel and Cadderly, and finally Belago (who came down only because he fell), were at Ivan's side. Some of the closest wolves made halfhearted attacks at the group, but the four friends were well armed and well trained, and with most of the pack scattering, they easily drove the stragglers away.

It was soon over, several wolves lying dead on the ground, the others gone from sight. The tree was just a tree again.

"Your magic bought us some time and some space," Shayleigh congratulated Cadderly. The young priest nodded, but then looked to Pikel, the green-bearded "doo-dad" smiling ear to ear. Cadderly didn't know how much of this animation had been his doing, and how much Pikel's, but now wasn't the time to explore the mystery.

"If they come back, use the flask," Belago offered, moving to Cadderly's side.

Cadderly considered the wiry man for a moment and realized that Belago was unarmed. He handed back the flask. "You use it," he explained, "but only if we absolutely need it. We've got a darker road still to travel, my friend, and I suspect we shall need every weapon we can muster."

Belago bobbed his head in agreement, though he did not know, could not know, the depth of the darkness of which Cadderly spoke.

As it turned out, they did not need Belago's flask that night, or anything else. Shayleigh put them on the move immediately, back to the west, to a grove of thick pines, and there they spent the rest of the dark hours, the five friends, and Percival, too, keeping a watchful eye from the highest boughs.

Cadderly could only assume they had hurt Rufo badly, for the vampire did not find them. That was a good thing, on the surface, but the young priest could not get it out of his mind that if Kierkan Rufo was not with him, the vampire might be with Danica.

Cadderly did not fall asleep until the night was almost at its end, until exhaustion overwhelmed him.

Nineteen

Lost Soul

Percival's chattering heralded the new dawn and brought poor Cadderly from a fitful sleep filled with nightmares. He remembered little of those horrid dreams when he opened his eyes to the glistening light of a bright new day, for they were surely the stuff of a dark night.

The young priest did know, however, that he had dreamt of Danica, and he was unnerved at that thought. For while he was out here, in the morning light, his dear Danica was in there, in the library, in Rufo's evil hands.

The library.

Cadderly could hardly stand to think about the place. It had been his home for most of his young life, but now that time seemed so very long ago. If all the windows and doors of the Edificant Library were thrown wide now, the structure would remain a place of shadows, a place of nightmares.

Cadderly was shaken from his private thoughts by the sound of Ivan's rough voice, the dwarf taking command while sitting on a thick tangle of branches below the young priest.

"We got the weapons," Ivan was saying. "Belago there's got his bottle."

"Boom," Pikel remarked, throwing his hands up high. The force of the sudden movement nearly sent Ivan tumbling from the branch.

Ivan caught himself and started to nod, then stopped and slapped Pikel on the back of the head. "Me brother's got his club," the dwarf went on.

"Sha-lah-lah!" Pikel whooped in delight, interrupting again in an equally expressive manner. This time Ivan didn't react fast enough, and by the time he realized what had happened, he was sitting on the ground, picking clumps of sod out of his teeth.

"Uh-oh," Pikel moaned, figuring that last move would cost him another slap, as his brother began the steady climb back up to his branch.

He was right, and he accepted the punishment with a shrug. Ivan turned back to Shayleigh.

"Sha-lah-lah," Pikel said again, quietly this time, and without the expressive movement.

"Yeah," Ivan agreed, too exasperated to argue further. "And ye got yer silver arrows," he said to Shayleigh, though he was still eyeing his impetuous brother, expecting still another remark.

"My sword will prove effective as well," Shayleigh explained, holding up her fine, slender elven blade, its silver inlays gleaming bright in the morning light.

Ivan continued to scrutinize Pikel, who by this point

had taken to whistling a cheery spring morning tune.

"Even better," the yellow-bearded dwarf said to Shayleigh. "And I got me axe, though it's not for hurting them vampire things. But it'll take a stiff-legged zombie in half!"

"Cadderly has his walking stick," Shayleigh offered, noticing the young priest stirring, looking for an easy route down to their level. "And more weapons than that, I would assume."

Cadderly nodded and fell heavily onto the branch tangle, sending it dipping. "I am ready for Rufo," he said groggily when the branch stopped bouncing.

"Ye should've slept more," Ivan grumbled at him.

Cadderly nodded in agreement, not wanting to get into an argument now, but in his heart he was glad he had not slept much. He would be wide awake when the trouble started, pumped full of adrenaline. His only enemy now was despair, and if he had dreamt longer of his missing love . . .

Cadderly shook his head, shook away the counter-productive thought.

"How far are we from the library?" he asked, looking to the west, where he thought the library should be.

Shayleigh motioned for him to look the other way. "Three miles," she explained, "to the east."

Cadderly didn't argue. The run through the trails had been confusing at best, especially to one not blessed with elven night vision. Shayleigh knew where they were.

"Then let us be on our way," the young priest offered. "Before we lose any more daylight." He started down from the branch, but had to pause for Belago. The alchemist winked Cadderly's way and opened his weather-worn cloak, producing the volatile flask.

"Boom!" Pikel shouted from the branch above.

Ivan growled, Pikel quickly jumped to the next lowest branch, and Ivan's ensuing slap hit nothing but air, causing the dwarf to overbalance and tumble from his perch. He managed to grab Pikel's green hair during his descent, taking his brother with him.

They hit the ground together, side by side, Ivan's deer-antlered helm and Pikel's cooking pot flying away. Up they bounced to face each other squarely.

Cadderly looked to Shayleigh, who was trying to subdue a laugh and merely shook her head in disbelief.

"At least you didn't have to walk all the way back with them," the young priest offered. Belago let him pass, and Cadderly hopped down to break up the fight. In a way, the young priest was glad for the distraction. With the dangerous task and the grim possibilities staring them in the face, they could all use a bit of mirth. But Cadderly did not appreciate the dwarves' antics, and he let both the brothers know it in no uncertain terms when he finally pried them apart.

"His fault," Ivan huffed, but Cadderly, and Cadderly's accusing finger, was in his face, warning him to say no more.

"Oooo," Pikel muttered. When Belago came down a moment later, the dwarf leaned over and whispered "Boom," into his ear.

Cadderly and Ivan spun about, but Pikel was only whistling again, that cheery, innocent morning tune.

Shayleigh led them quickly, surely, and without hesitation along the myriad forks and turns in the confusing trails. The sun had barely begun its climb in the eastern sky when the Edificant Library, dark and cold, came into view, its square walls seeming to deny the warmth of the day.

They moved along the path five abreast, Ivan and Pikel

The Chaos Curse 243

on one end, Shayleigh and Cadderly anchoring the other, and poor, trembling Belago in the middle. It was only as they made the final approach, the broken doors in sight, that Cadderly took any real notice of their newest companion, the wiry man who was not a fighter. The young priest stopped the march with an upraised hand.

"You have no business going in there," he said to Belago. "Go instead to Carradoon. Warn the townsfolk of Kierkan Rufo and his creatures of the night."

Vicero Belago looked up at the young priest as though Cadderly had just slapped him across the face. "I'm not much for fighting," he admitted. "And I'm not thrilled at the prospect of seeing Kierkan Rufo, vampire or not! But Lady Danica is in there—you said it yourself."

Cadderly looked to Shayleigh, who nodded solemnly. "Determination is the only true weapon against one of Rufo's ilk," the elf put in.

Cadderly dropped a hand on Belago's shoulder, and could feel that the alchemist had drawn strength from his own words. As they resumed the march and neared the doors, though, the man trembled visibly once more.

This time it was Ivan who stopped them. "We should have our path marked out afore we go in," the dwarf reasoned.

Cadderly looked skeptical.

"We have no idea where Danica might be," Shayleigh said, "or where we might find Rufo and his most powerful allies."

"If we go wrong, we'll fight everything in the place afore we ever find Danica," Ivan argued, but then, as if he suddenly realized what he had just said, especially the part about fighting everything in the place, the fiery dwarf shrugged as if it no longer mattered and turned back to the door.

Cadderly took out his light tube and popped open its back compartment. He slid out the enchanted disk; even in the bright sunlight its glow was powerful. Then he took off his hat and set the glowing disk behind his mounted holy symbol.

The young priest looked back to the doors and sighed. At least now they would not be walking in dark places. Still, Cadderly wasn't thrilled with the prospect of wandering through the massive structure, with so many enemies to face, and with a limited amount of time. How many rooms could they search in one day? Certainly not half the number in the Edificant Library.

"We'll begin in the lower levels," Cadderly said. "The kitchen, the main chapel, even the wine cellar. Rufo probably took Danica and Dorigen to a place of darkness."

"You are assuming he has them," Shayleigh remarked, her tone reminding Cadderly that both the monk and the wizard were resourceful and cunning. "Let us keep in our thoughts that Danica might not even be in there."

Cadderly knew better. In his heart, he knew without doubt that Danica was in the library and in trouble. He started to answer the elf's doubts, but Percival answered for him, the squirrel doing a sudden, wild dance across the branches just above their heads.

"Hey, ye little rat!" Ivan bellowed, shielding his head with his burly arm.

Pikel seemed equally excited, but unlike his brother, the green-bearded dwarf wasn't protesting in the least. He pointed a stubby finger at the white squirrel and hopped up and down.

"What is it?" Cadderly and Shayleigh asked together.

Percival ran along the branch and, with a great leap, caught the edge of the library's roof, dancing along the gutter, turning a somersault and chattering excitedly.

Cadderly looked to Pikel. "Percival has found them," he stated more than asked.

"Oo oi!" the perceptive (at least where nature was concerned) dwarf agreed.

Cadderly turned back to his rodent friend. "Danica?" he asked.

Percival leaped high in the air, turning completely about.

Ivan roared in protest. "The rat found them?" he bellowed incredulously.

Pikel slapped him on the back of the head.

"We have nothing better," Shayleigh reminded the volatile Ivan, trying to stay yet another fight between the brothers.

Cadderly wasn't even listening. He had been with Percival for three years and knew the squirrel was not a stupid thing. Far from it. Cadderly did not doubt Percival understood they were looking for Danica.

He followed Percival, and his friends followed him, around to the south wing of the library. Much of the wing showed damage from the fire, but the wall and windows near the back of the building did not. Percival moved gracefully along the gutters, then picked his way carefully down the rough and cracked stone. With a final leap, he landed on the sill of a small second-floor window.

Cadderly was nodding before the squirrel ever stopped.

"Danica's in there?" Ivan asked doubtfully.

"The private room of Dean Thobicus," Cadderly explained, and it all made sense to him. If Rufo had Danica, a woman he had long desired, he would likely show her the most comfortable and lavish room in the library, and none was better suited than the dean's private chamber.

With Cadderly's confidence came a moment of sheer

dread. If his logic was on track, and Percival was right, then Rufo did indeed have Danica!

"What's the quickest route through the building to that room?" Ivan asked, deciding not to continue his useless arguing.

"The quickest route is straight up," Cadderly remarked, drawing all their eyes skyward. Ivan grumbled for a bit, trying to figure some way to get them all up there. Finally he just shook his head, and when he looked back to the young priest to denounce the plan, the dwarf jumped in surprise. In place of his regular arms and legs, Cadderly now had the limbs of a squirrel, a white-furred squirrel!

Shayleigh, not so surprised, gave Cadderly the end of a fine cord, and up he went, easily scaling the wall to sit on the narrow ledge beside Percival.

The window was only a few inches wide, barely a squared crack in the wall. Cadderly peered in, the light from the disk on his hat casting a glow into the room. He couldn't see much of the chamber, though, for the window was more than a foot deep. He did see the bottom edge of the bed, though, and on it, under a satiny sheet, the outline of a woman's legs.

"Danica," he whispered harshly, straining to get a better angle.

"What do ye see?" Ivan called from below.

It was Danica. Cadderly knew it was Danica. He shifted back, willed his arms and legs to return to normal, and fell into the song of Deneir. He was too close now; he would not be stopped by simple stone.

"What do ye see?" Ivan demanded again, but Cadderly, lost in the song, the magic of his god, did not register the call.

He focused on the stone surrounding the window, saw

it for what it was, saw its very essence. Calling to his god, he pulled his waterskin around from his back and squirted it in strategic locations, then placed his hands on the suddenly malleable stone and began to shape the material.

The window's thick glass fell out, past entranced Cadderly's working hands, and nearly clobbered Ivan as he stood, hands on hips, on the ground below.

"Hey!" the dwarf yelled, and Cadderly, even in the throes of the song, heard him. He considered his handiwork and remembered his friends, and worked a spur in the stone, that he could loop Shayleigh's cord securely about it.

Then it was done, and the window was wide, and Cadderly crawled into the room. Deneir went away from him when he entered the unholy place; he would have recognized that fact clearly if he had concentrated. Even the glow of the lighted disk, fixed on the front of his wide-brimmed hat, seemed to dim.

This, too, Cadderly did not notice. His eyes, and his thoughts, were squarely on the bed, on the figure of Danica, lying too still and too serene.

Shayleigh practically ran up the rope, rushing into the room beside Cadderly. Ivan, and then Pikel, powerful dwarven arms pumping, came up fast behind, with Pikel pausing long enough at the sill to haul poor Belago up the fifteen feet to the window.

Cadderly stood beside the bed, staring down, not finding the strength to reach out and touch Danica.

She would be cold to his touch. He knew that. He knew she was dead.

Shayleigh couldn't bear the suspense anymore; she could not bear to see Cadderly in such awful torment. She bent low over the bed and put her sensitive ear to

Danica's pursed lips. A moment later, she rose, staring straight at Cadderly and slowly shaking her head. Her hand moved as well, shifting Danica's tunic to reveal the puckered wounds on the monk's neck, the twin punctures of a vampire's bite.

"Oooo," Ivan and Pikel moaned together. Vicero Belago sniffled and fought back tears.

That tangible confirmation that Danica was gone, that Rufo had taken her, sent a ball of grief spiraling through Cadderly, a spiked ball that pained the young priest in every corner of his soul, that tore at his heart and all his sensibilities. Danica dead! His love taken from him!

This Cadderly could not tolerate. By all the power of Deneir, by all the edicts of callous fate, Cadderly could not allow this to be.

He commanded the song of Deneir into his thoughts, forced its flow past the dullness of the evil veil that permeated this place. His head throbbed for the effort, but he did not relent. Not with Danica, his love, lying so pale before him.

Cadderly's thoughts careened into the flow, pushed open closed doors and rushed to the highest levels of power. He was gone from his friends, then, not physically, for his body stood very still beside the bed, but spiritually, his soul rushing free of its mortal coil into the realm of spirits, the realm of the dead.

So it was that Cadderly did not hear Shayleigh's shriek, and did not react as the strong hand shot out from under the bed to clasp the elf's ankle.

* * * * *

Cadderly could see the events in the room, but they were distant from him, somehow disconnected. Through a thick veil of smoky gray he saw his own body standing very still, saw that Shayleigh, for some reason, had apparently gone down to the floor and was being pulled under the bed.

Cadderly sensed the danger back in the room, sensed that his elven companion was in trouble. He should go to her, he knew, go to the aid of his friends. He hesitated, though, and stayed clear of his corporeal form. Shayleigh was among powerful allies—Ivan and Pikel were moving, he could see, probably rushing to her side. Cadderly had to trust in them now, for he knew that if he left this realm, he would not soon find the strength to return, not in the desecrated library. He was looking for a spirit, and spirits were fleeting things. If he hoped to get Danica back, he had to find her quickly, before she took her place in the netherworld.

But where was she? Cadderly had gone into the spirit world on several occasions, had gone after Avery Schell when he had found the headmaster lying dead, his chest torn wide, on a table in the Dragon's Codpiece tavern in Carradoon. Cadderly had gone into the spirit world after the souls of men he had killed, assassins who had been pulled down by shadowy things before the young priest could call out to them. He had gone into the spirit world after Vander, and had held back the malignant assassin Ghost while Vander found his way back to life through the enchantment of his regenerative ring.

The ring!

Cadderly saw it glowing clearly on Ivan's gnarled finger, the only distinctive thing in the room. He could use it, he believed, as a gate to get Danica back to the realm of the living. If he could somehow get Ivan to put the ring on Danica's finger, he might be able to find an easier way to usher her spirit back to her corporeal form.

But where was she? Where was his love? He called out to Danica, let the images in the room fade from his thoughts and sent his mind out in every direction. Danica's spirit should be here; she could not have been dead for long. She should be here, or at least there should be some trail of her passing that Cadderly could follow. He would pull her from the arms of a god if need be!

There was no trail. There was no spirit. No Danica.

Cadderly weakened with the realization that she was lost to him. Suddenly there seemed no purpose in his life, no reason to even bother returning to his body. Let Deneir take him now, he thought, and be done with his torment.

He saw a flicker of clarity in the dull plane he had left behind, a movement within the room. Then he saw the vampire, as clearly as he had seen Ivan's ring, coming out from under the bed.

Baccio ripped at a dull form—Shayleigh, Cadderly knew—and leaped up to his feet. He was undead, existing on both planes, as tangible to Cadderly in the spirit world as he obviously was to Ivan and the others in the material room. Yet the vampire took no note of Cadderly. Baccio's thoughts were squarely on the battle at hand, on the battle against Cadderly's friends!

Cadderly's focus became pure anger. His spirit shifted behind Baccio, his will narrowing like a spike.

* * * * *

Shayleigh was out of the fight before it ever really began. She hit the floor hard beside the bed and slid under, the vampire's strong hands slamming her shoulder as she tried to reach for her short sword.

The silver-tipped arrows had bounced free of Shayleigh's quiver with the impact, and that alone saved the wounded elf. Sheer luck brought her free hand atop one of those bolts and, without hesitation, Shayleigh whipped the thing around, sticking its silvery point deep into Baccio's eye.

The vampire went into a frenzy, battering Shayleigh, bouncing the bed up and down on its supports. Pikel lay flat on the floor by then, using his club like a billiard stick, poking it straight into Baccio's face to keep the vampire busy while Ivan yanked Shayleigh out into the clear.

Baccio came out, too, wailing and thrashing, most of his strikes landing squarely on poor Shayleigh. Pikel hit him good a couple of times, but the vampire was strong, and he accepted the blows and returned them tenfold.

Belago shrieked and cowered; Ivan rushed in with a vicious swipe, but his axe was useless against the vampire. Baccio had them on the defensive, had them dead.

The vampire lurched suddenly as if something had hit him from behind, and indeed, he had been struck, by Cadderly's spirit. He staggered forward, his trembling arms reaching behind him for some unseen wound.

What a beautiful target that presented eager Pikel. The green-bearded dwarf spat in his hands and rubbed them for a tighter grip on his shillelagh, then spun two complete circuits, building momentum, before bringing the tree-trunk club to bear against Baccio's face.

The broken monster flew away, crashing into the far wall. Still, Baccio reached around to his back, reached for the spike, the manifestation of Cadderly's will, which the young priest had driven into his back.

Cadderly's corporeal form shuddered then as the priest came back to the Material Plane. He moved deliberately, mercilessly. He reached for his hat, then changed his mind and went instead for a fold in his traveling cloak, a pocket he had sewn into the cloak during his weeks in the cave on the northern side of the Snow-flakes, producing a thin, dark wand. Cadderly shook his head as he considered the instrument—over the weeks of idleness and during the excitement of the last day, he had nearly forgotten about this wand. Advancing on Bac-cio, the wand's tip leading the way, the young priest said calmly, "*Mas illu.*"

A myriad of bright colors exploded from the wand, every color of the spectrum.

"Ouch!" Pikel wailed, blinded by the explosion, as were all of Cadderly's friends. Cadderly, too, saw spots behind his eyelids, but he did not relent. "*Mas illu,*" he said again, and the wand complied, spewing forth another colorful burst of light.

To the friends, the bursts were optically painful but otherwise benign, but to the vampire, they were pure agony. Baccio tried to recoil from the explosions, tried to curl into a little ball and hide, to no avail. The shower of lights clung to him, attacked his undead form with the fury of hot sparks. To a living creature, the spark shower could only blind; to an undead monster, the shower could burn.

"*Mas illu,*" Cadderly said a third time, and by the time the last burst ended, Baccio sat limply against the wall, staring at Cadderly with pure hatred and pure impo-tence. Cadderly put away the wand and pulled the holy symbol down from his head. He walked up to stand before the wounded vampire and calmly, methodically, placed the glowing symbol on Baccio's broken face.

The vampire's trembling hand came up and clasped Cadderly's wrist, but the young priest didn't waver. He held firm his symbol and intoned a prayer to Deneir as he struck repeatedly with his ram's-headed walking stick, thoroughly destroying the monster.

Cadderly turned about to see his four friends staring at him incredulously, amazed by the sheer, unbridled fury of the display.

Pikel moaned, and the end of his club dropped limply to the floor.

Shayleigh grimaced against the pain as she regarded Cadderly. Her right shoulder was badly torn, and the wheezing in her voice told Cadderly that Baccio's beating had probably broken a few ribs and collapsed one of her lungs. He went to her immediately, without saying a word, and sought the distant song of Deneir.

The melody's flow was not strong this time; Cadderly could not seek the higher levels of clerical power. The day was young, but he was already tired, he realized, so he accepted the weakness and found his way instead to minor spells of healing, pressing his hands gently but firmly against Shayleigh's ribs and then her shoulder.

Cadderly came back to full consciousness to find the elf resting more easily, the magic already knitting the wounds.

"You did not find Danica," Shayleigh reasoned, her voice determined but trembling from her pain and weakness. It was obvious to them all that she needed rest and could not go on.

Cadderly shook his head, confirming the elf's fears. He looked plaintively to the bed, to the serene form of his lost love. "She is not undead, though," he offered, more to bolster himself than the others.

"She escaped," Shayleigh agreed.

"Danica should not be in this place," Cadderly said. He looked determinedly to each of his friends. "We must take her from here."

"The mausoleum is clear," Shayleigh offered.

Cadderly shook his head. "Farther," he said. "We will take her to Carradoon. There, away from the darkness of Kierkan Rufo, I can better tend your wounds, and can put Danica to rest."

His voice broke as he finished the thought.

"No!" Ivan said unexpectedly, drawing Cadderly's attention.

"We're not for leaving!" the dwarf argued. "Not now, not while the sun's in the sky. Rufo got her, and he'll get another if we walk away. Yerself can go if ye need to, but me and me brother are staying."

"Oo oi!"

"We'll pay that one back for Danica, don't ye doubt!" Ivan finished.

Pay that one back. The sentiment bounced about Cadderly's thoughts for a while, gaining momentum and imparting strength. Pay that one back! Indeed, Cadderly would pay Rufo back. He found his heart in the thought of revenge.

"Take Danica to the mausoleum," he said to Belago and Shayleigh. "If the dwarves and I do not come to you by the time the sun has begun its descent, set out far from this place, to Shilmista or Carradoon, and do not return."

Shayleigh, as angered by the loss of Danica as any of them, wanted to argue, but as she started to reply, sharp pain racked her side. Cadderly had done all he could for her wounds; she needed rest.

"I will go with Belago to the mausoleum," she reluctantly agreed, accepting that she would only hinder her friends in her weakened state. She grabbed Cadderly's arm as he started to move away from her and locked his gray eyes with her violet orbs. "Find Rufo and destroy

him," she said. "I'll not leave the mausoleum unless it is
to come back into the library to your side."

Cadderly knew there was no way he would convince
the valiant elf otherwise. Danica had been like a sister to
Shayleigh, and the elf would never walk away from the
one who had killed her sister. Understanding that sentiment, that he, too, would never walk away from this
place unless Rufo was destroyed, Cadderly accepted her
pledge with a knowing nod.

Twenty

Anguish

Ivan and Pikel quickly rigged the rope so that Danica's body could be lowered gently. Both the tough dwarves had tears in their eyes as they worked; Ivan reverently removed his deer-antler helm, and Pikel did likewise with his cooking pot.

When the rope was ready, Cadderly could hardly bring himself to move Danica into position. His anger could not hold against that wave of grief, the feeling of finality as he tenderly looped the elven cord under Danica's stiffened arms. He thought of going again into the spirit world to search for her, and would have gone, except that Shayleigh, as if reading his thoughts, was beside him, her hand on his shoulder.

When the young priest looked at the battered elf, her whole body quaking as she tried to hold her balance, he understood he could not expend the energy to go off again into the spirit world after Danica, that the consequences might be too high. He looked to Shayleigh and nodded, and she backed away, seeming satisfied.

It was decided that Belago should go down first, to cushion Danica's descent. The alchemist, seeming more determined than any of them had ever witnessed, took up the rope in both hands and hopped up onto the windowsill. He paused, though, then motioned for Ivan to come near.

"Ye got to do it," the dwarf said, coming close. "We need ye . . . " Ivan stopped in midsentence, realizing Belago's intentions, as the alchemist extended his arm.

"Take it," Belago offered, pushing the flask of explosive oil to Ivan. "You will need every weapon."

As soon as the dwarf had the flask in hand, Belago, without hesitation, slipped over the sill and descended quickly to the ground. Danica's body went next, and then Shayleigh, the injured elf needing nearly as much support as had Danica.

Cadderly watched forlornly from the window as the group slipped away toward the back of the library and the mausoleum. Belago had Danica's form over one shoulder, and though the load was extreme for the alchemist, he still had to pace himself so that the wounded Shayleigh could keep up.

When Cadderly turned away from the window, back to the room, he found Ivan and Pikel, helms tucked under their arms, heads bowed and cheeks streaked with tears. Ivan looked up first, his sorrow transformed into rage. "I gotta fix me axe," the dwarf said through gritted teeth.

Cadderly looked at the weapon skeptically—it seemed fine to him.

"Gotta put some silver in the damned thing!" Ivan roared.

"We haven't the time," Cadderly replied.

"I got a forge near the kitchen," Ivan retorted, and Cadderly nodded, for he had often seen the setup, which doubled as a stove.

Cadderly looked out the window. The morning light was full, sending long shadows to the west. "We have just one day," Cadderly explained. "We must finish our business before nightfall. If Rufo recognizes that we have been inside the library, as he surely will when he realizes that Baccio is destroyed, he will come after us with all his forces. I would rather face the vampire now, though only my walking stick and Pikel's club—"

"Sha-lah-lah!" the dwarf said determinedly, popping the cooking pot on top of his green hair.

Cadderly nodded, even managed a slight smile. "We must be done with Rufo this day," he said again.

"But ye'll have to kill him quick," Ivan protested, presenting his axe once more. "Kill him to death. Quick, or he'll just go into that green mist and melt away from us. I got a forge . . . " Ivan stopped in midramble and turned a wicked look toward Pikel. "A forge," he said again, slyly.

"Huh?" came Pikel's predictable reply.

"Makes the fire hot," Ivan explained.

"You will need a fire very hot to singe Rufo," Cadderly interjected, thinking he was following the dwarf's reasoning. "Magical flames that no forge could match."

"Yeah, and if we hurt him, he'll just go into a cloud," Ivan said, aiming the remark at Pikel.

Pikel considered the information, tried to connect the forge to Rufo. His face brightened suddenly, his grin ear to ear as he returned his brother's hopeful stare.

"Hee hee hee," both dwarves said together.

Cadderly didn't understand, and wasn't sure he wanted to understand. The Bouldershoulder brothers seemed secure in their secret plans, so the young priest let it go at that. He led them along the corridors of the second floor, the library quiet and brooding about them. They tore the covers from every window they crossed, but even with that, the squat stone structure was a gloomy place.

Cadderly took out his wand once more. Every time he noticed a particularly gloomy area, he pointed the wand at it and uttered the command "*Domin illu*" and, with a flash, the area became as bright as an open field under a midday sun.

"If we cannot find Rufo this day," the young priest explained, "let him come out to find his darkness stolen!"

Ivan and Pikel exchanged knowing looks. Rufo could likely counter the young priest's spells of light—Rufo had been a cleric, after all, and clerics understood such magic. Cadderly wasn't brightening the library for any practical reasons, then, but merely to challenge the vampire. The young priest was throwing down a gauntlet, doing everything he could to slap Rufo across the face. Neither Ivan nor Pikel was thrilled at facing the powerful vampire again, but as they followed their companion through the library, his anger unrelenting, the image of beaten Baccio still clear in their thoughts, they came to the conclusion that they would rather have Rufo as an enemy than Cadderly.

The three came down to the first floor, having met no resistance. Not a single zombie, vampire, or any other monster, undead or otherwise, had risen against them. Not a single answer had been offered to Cadderly's open challenge. If he had stopped to think about it, Cadderly would have realized that was a good thing, a sign that perhaps Rufo was not yet aware that they had come into his domain. But the young man was consumed with thoughts of Danica, his lost love, and he wanted something, some ally of Rufo's, or especially Rufo himself, to block his path. He wanted to strike with all his might against the darkness that had taken his love.

They came into the hallway that led to the foyer. Cadderly promptly started that way, for the main doors and the southern wing beyond them, where the fire had been. There lay the Edificant Library's main chapel, the place Rufo would have to work the hardest to desecrate. Perhaps the young priest might find sanctuary there, a base from which he and the dwarves could strike in different directions. Perhaps in that area Cadderly would find clues that would lead him to the one who had taken Danica from him.

His steps were bold and swift, but Ivan and Pikel caught him by the arms, and no amount of determination would have propelled the young priest against that strong hold.

"We got to go to the kitchen," Ivan explained.

"You have no time for silver-edging your axe," Cadderly replied sharply.

"Forget me axe," Ivan agreed. "Me and me brother still got to go to the kitchen."

Cadderly winced, not thrilled with anything that would slow the hunt. He knew he would not change Ivan's mind, though, so he nodded. "Be quick," he said to them. "I will meet you in the foyer, or in the burned-out chapel near it."

Ivan and Pikel leaned to the side to exchange concerned looks behind Cadderly's back. Neither were excited about the prospect of splitting the already small group, but Ivan was determined to go to his forge, and he knew that Cadderly would not be held back.

"Just the foyer," the dwarf said sternly. "Ye go sticking yer nose about, and ye're likely to put it somewhere it shouldn't be!"

Cadderly nodded and pulled free of the dwarves, immediately resuming his swift pace.

"Just the foyer!" Ivan shouted after him, and Cadderly didn't respond.

"Let's be quick," Ivan said to his brother as they both looked at the young priest's back. "He won't be stopping in the foyer."

"Uh-huh," Pikel agreed, and the two skittered off for the kitchen and the forge.

Cadderly was not afraid in the least. Anger consumed him, and the only other emotion nipping at its edges, fraying the wall of outrage, was grief. He cared not that Ivan and Pikel were separated from him, that he was alone. He hoped Kierkan Rufo and all his dark minions would rise to stand before him, that he might deal with them once and for all, that he might damn their undead corpses to dust, to blow on the wind.

He got to the foyer without incident and didn't even think of pausing there to wait for his companions. On he pressed, to the burned-out chapel, the room where the fire had apparently started, to search for clues. He tore down the tapestry blocking the way and kicked the charred door open.

The smoke hung heavy in the place, as did the stench of burned flesh, with nowhere to go in the library's stagnant, dead air. Cadderly knew immediately, just from that smell, that at least one person had perished here. Horribly. Thick soot lined the walls, part of the ceiling had collapsed, and only one of the many beautiful tapestries remained even partially intact on the wall, though it was so blackened as to be unidentifiable. Cadderly stared at the black cloth long and hard, trying to remember the image that had once been there, trying to remember the library when it had basked in the light of Deneir.

So deep was he in concentration that he did not see the charred corpse rise behind him and steadily approach.

He heard a crackle of dried skin, felt a touch on his shoulder, and leaped into the air, spinning so forcefully that he overbalanced and nearly fell to the floor. His eyes were wide, anger stolen by horror as he looked at the shrunken, blackened remains of a human being, a small figure of cracked skin, charred bone, and white teeth—those teeth were the worst of the terrible image!

Cadderly fumbled his walking stick and wand, finally presenting the wand before him. This creature was not a vampire, he realized, probably not nearly as strong as a vampire. He remembered his ring, its enchantment expired, and understood that the same could happen with the wand. Suddenly Cadderly felt foolish for his tirade in the upper level, for his waste of the wand's energy in stealing shadows. He tucked the wand under his arm and grabbed his hat instead. His free hand reached alternately for his walking stick and his spindle-disks, not sure of which would be the most effective, not sure if only enchanted weapons would bite into the flesh of this animated monster, whatever it might be.

Finally, Cadderly calmed and presented his hat, and his holy symbol, more forcefully. "I am the agent of Deneir!" he said loudly, with full conviction. "Come to purge the home of my god. You have no place here!"

The blackened thing continued its approach, reaching for Cadderly.

"Be gone!" Cadderly commanded.

The monster didn't hesitate, didn't slow in the least. Cadderly lifted his walking stick to strike, and reached back with his other hand, dropping the hat, to grab the wand. He growled at his failure to turn the thing away, wondering if the library was too far from Deneir now for him to invoke the god's name.

The answer was something altogether different, something Cadderly could not anticipate.

"Cadderly," the blackened corpse rasped, and though the voice was barely audible, the movement of air a strained thing from lungs that would not draw breath, Cadderly recognized the way his name had been spoken.

Dorigen!

"Cadderly," the dead wizard said again, and the young priest, too stunned, did not resist as she moved closer and brought her charred hand up to stroke his face.

The stench nearly overwhelmed him, but he stubbornly held his ground. His instincts told him to lash out with the walking stick, but he held firm his resolve, kept his nerve, and lowered the weapon to his side. If Dorigen was still a thinking creature, and apparently she was, then she must not have given in to Rufo, must not have gone over to the other side against Cadderly.

"I knew you would come," dead Dorigen said. "Now you must battle Kierkan Rufo and destroy him. I fought him here."

"You destroyed yourself with a fireball," Cadderly reasoned.

"It was the only way I could allow Danica to escape," Dorigen replied, and Cadderly did not doubt the claim.

The look that came over the young priest's face at the mention of Danica told Dorigen much.

"Danica did not escape," she whispered.

"Lie down, Dorigen," the young priest replied softly,

as tenderly as he could. "You are dead. You have earned your rest."

The corpse's face crackled as Dorigen bent her tortured features into a grotesque smile. "Rufo would not permit me such rest," she explained. "He has held me here, as a present to you, no doubt."

"Do you know where he is?"

Dorigen shrugged, the movement causing flecks of skin to fall from her withered shoulders.

Cadderly stared long and hard at the gruesome thing Dorigen had become. And yet, despite her appearance, she was not gruesome, he realized, not in her heart. Dorigen had made her choices, and, to Cadderly's thinking, she had redeemed herself. He could have held her there, questioned her intensely about Kierkan Rufo and perhaps even garnered some valuable information. But that would not have been fair, he realized, not to Dorigen, who had earned her rest.

The young priest bent and retrieved his hat, then lifted his holy symbol and placed it atop the corpse's forehead. Dorigen neither retreated from it, nor was pained by it. It seemed to Cadderly as if the lighted emblem brought her peace and that, too, confirmed his hopes that she had found salvation. Cadderly lifted his voice in prayer. Dorigen relaxed; she would have closed her eyes, but she had no eyelids. She stared at the young priest, at the man who had shown her mercy, had given her a chance to redeem herself. She stared at the man who would free her from the torments of Kierkan Rufo.

"I love you," Dorigen said quietly, so as not to interrupt the prayer. "I had hoped to participate in the wedding, your wedding with Danica, as it should have been."

Cadderly choked up, but forced himself to finish. The light seemed to spread out from his holy symbol, limning the corpse, pulling at Dorigen's spirit.

As it should have been! Cadderly could not help but think. And Dorigen would indeed have been at the wedding, probably standing with Shayleigh behind Danica, while Ivan and Pikel, and King Elbereth of Shilmista stood behind Cadderly.

As it should have been! And Avery Schell and Pertelope should not be dead, should be there with Cadderly to witness his joining.

Cadderly kept his rage sublimated. He did not want that to be the last image poor Dorigen saw of him. "Farewell," he said softly to the corpse. "Go to your deserved rest."

Dorigen nodded, ever so slightly, and the blackened form crumpled at Cadderly's feet.

Cadderly considered it for a moment, was glad that Dorigen was free of Rufo. A moment later, he screamed, as loudly as he had ever screamed, the primal roar torn from his heart by the agony of the realization. "As it should have been!" he yelled. "Damn you, Kierkan Rufo! Damn you, Druzil, and your chaos curse!"

The young priest started for the chapel exit, nearly fell over in his haste. "And damn you, Aballister," he whispered, cursing his own father, the man who had abandoned him, and who had betrayed everything that was good in life, everything that gave life joy and meaning.

Ivan and Pikel thundered into the chapel, weapons held high. They skidded to a bumbling stop, falling over each other, when they saw that Cadderly was not in danger.

"What in the Nine Hells are ye yelling about?" Ivan demanded.

"Dorigen," Cadderly explained, looking to the charred corpse.

"Oo," Pikel moaned.

Cadderly continued to push for the exit, but then he noticed the large, boxlike item strapped to Ivan's back and paused, his face screwed up with curiosity.

Ivan noticed the look and beamed happily. "Don't ye worry!" the dwarf assured Cadderly. "We'll get him this time!"

Despite all the pain, all the despair, the memories of Danica, and the thoughts of what should have been, Cadderly could not prevent a small, incredulous chuckle from escaping his lips.

Pikel hopped over and put his arm across his brother's shoulders, and together they nodded confidently.

It was impossible, Cadderly realized, but these were the Bouldershoulders, after all. Impossible, but Cadderly could not deny that it just might work.

"Me brother and me been thinking," Ivan began. "Them vampires don't much like the sunlight, and there's places here that never get any, windows or no windows."

Cadderly followed the reasoning perfectly—it scared him a little to think he could follow Ivan and Pikel's logic so easily!—and the notion led him to exactly the same conclusion as the dwarves had already reached.

"The wine cellar," Cadderly and Ivan said together.

"Hee hee hee," added a hopeful Pikel.

Cadderly led the charge through the kitchen and to the wooden door. It was closed and locked, barred from the inside, and that confirmed the companions' suspicions.

Ivan started to lift his heavy axe, but Cadderly beat him to it, bringing up his spindle-disks in a short, tight spin, then heaving them with all his strength at the barrier. The solid adamantite smashed through the door's wood and slammed the metal bar on the other side so forcefully that it bent and dislodged.

The door creaked open, showing the dark descent.

Cadderly did not hesitate. "I am coming for you, Rufo!" he cried, taking his first step down.

"Why don't ye just warn him!" Ivan grumbled, but Cadderly did not care.

"It does not matter," he said, and down he went.

Twenty-One

Bagged

The three had barely stepped off the rickety stairs when Rufo's zombies closed in on them. Dozens of dead priests—men who had held to their faith, Cadderly knew, and had not given in to Rufo's tempting calling—filtered around the wine racks, bothered not at all by the light shining from the young priest's wide-brimmed hat.

"Where we going?" Ivan asked, hopping out in front of the others, obviously intent on leading. A zombie reached for him, and his great axe promptly removed the thing's arm from its torso. That hardly stopped the mindless zombie, but Ivan's next chop, a downward strike on the collar bone, angled to go across the monster's chest, surely did.

Pikel immediately dropped his club to the floor and began that curious dance again.

"Where we going?" Ivan asked again, more urgently, the battle rage welling inside him.

Cadderly continued to ponder the question. Where indeed? The wine cellar was large, filled with dozens of tall racks and numerous nooks. Great shadows splayed across the floor, angled away from Cadderly and the lone source of light, making the room even more mysterious and foreboding.

Both Ivan and Pikel were into it by then, hacking and banging, Ivan ducking his head to thrash his antlers into one zombie's midsection, Pikel occasionally giving a squirt of his waterskin to keep the monstrous horde at bay.

"Close your eyes!" Cadderly cried, and the dwarves did not have to ask why. A moment later, a spark shower cut through the zombie ranks, dropping several of the monsters in their tracks. Cadderly could have wiped them all out, but he realized the dwarves were in control here and that he should use the valuable wand with restraint.

The dwarves could cut through the throng, but where should they go? Cadderly considered the cellar's layout. Using one of the lesser functions of the wand, he put a minor globe of light between the racks to his right, for he knew that at the end of those racks loomed a deep alcove. The light illuminated the cubby fully, and it was empty.

"To the back!" Cadderly called to his companions. "Straight across the cellar to the back wall." It was only a guess, for though Cadderly was confident that Rufo would have sought the underground chambers (and the appearance of so many zombies added credence to this), where exactly he might find the vampire in this odd-shaped and uneven chamber was beyond him. He took up the rear as the dwarves plowed through the throng, cutting a wake so that Cadderly wasn't too engaged in fending off the zombies. The young priest's eyes darted back and forth, looking side to side as they crossed the racks, hoping to catch a glimpse of Rufo. Cadderly scolded himself for not keeping his light tube intact then, for the light on his hat was dispersed and could not seek the deepest crannies.

He pulled down both the lighted disk and the holy symbol, that he might better direct the illumination. Something fluttered across the shadows at the other end of the long racks, moving too quickly to be a zombie. His attention fixed on that spot, the young priest didn't notice the monster reaching for his back.

The blow nearly knocked Cadderly from his feet. He stumbled forward several steps and swung about, sensing the pursuit, his walking stick flailing across. It came up short of the mark, though, and the zombie waded in behind. Purely on instinct, Cadderly thrust out his holy symbol and cursed the thing.

The zombie stopped, held fast by the priest's magical strength. Yellow light limned its form, began to consume the edges of the zombie's material being.

Cadderly felt a wave of satisfaction in the knowledge that Deneir was with him. He pressed his attack, clenching his hand tight about the emblem of his station. The eye-above-candle flared to greater intensity; the glowing flames licking the zombie leaped and danced.

But the zombie remained, tapping the dark power of its master—its nearby master, Cadderly realized—for battle. Dark lines creased the fiery glow, breaking it apart.

Cadderly growled and stepped closer, invoking the name of Deneir, singing the melodies of the god's song. Finally, his holy symbol made contact with the zombie, and the thing burst apart, falling into a mess of macabre chunks and puffing dust.

Cadderly fell back, drained. How powerful had Rufo become that the vampire's lesser minions could resist his holy powers so strenuously? And how far had the library gone from Deneir when Cadderly's call to the god could barely destroy such a minor creature?

"Get the durned thing off! Get the durned thing off!" Ivan yelled, drawing Cadderly's attention. The dwarf's goring horns had done their work too well, it seemed, for Ivan had a zombie stuck atop his head. It lay flat out and flailing away with its arms and legs. Pikel hopped frantically beside his brother, trying to line up a hit that would dislodge the zombie without taking Ivan's head off.

Ivan chopped the legs from another zombie that waded too near, then took a hit in the face from the one above. The dwarf tried a halfhearted swing high with his axe, but the striking angle was wrong. He went into a spin instead, the momentum forcing the zombie flat out.

Pikel braced himself and took up his heavy club. Around came the zombie's head, whipping past. Pikel was ready the next time, and he timed his strike perfectly.

The zombie was still impaled—Ivan had to carry it around for a while—but it was no longer fighting.

"Took ye long enough," was all the thanks Ivan offered his brother. A short burst launched them side by side into the next rank of zombies, which broke apart into bits in the face of dwarven fury.

Cadderly rushed to keep pace. A zombie intercepted, and it pained the young priest greatly to view his newest foe, for the dead young man had, in life, been a friend. A clubbing arm came across, and Cadderly parried. He dodged a second strike, fighting defensively, then consciously reminded himself that this was not his friend, that this animation was merely an unthinking toy of Kierkan Rufo. Still, it was not easy for Cadderly to strike out, and he winced as his walking stick obliterated his former friend's face.

The young priest pressed on to catch the dwarves. He recalled that he had seen something, something dark and quick, in the shadows.

Out it came from the side, from the wine racks. Pikel squealed and turned to meet the charge, but got bowled over and tumbled away with the monster. They rolled past Ivan, who was quick enough to chop the newest adversary's leg.

When the axe didn't bite in, both Ivan and Cadderly knew the nature of this foe.

"*Mas illu*!" the young priest cried, and the vampire howled as sparks fell over it.

"That one's yer own!" Ivan cried to his brother, and he rubbed the temporary blindness out of his eyes and went back to his zombie chopping. He paused and dipped his head, grabbing at the dead weight entangled there, and a host of monsters closed in, arms clubbing.

Cadderly started for Pikel, but saw that Ivan, with his encumbering load, was in more trouble. He rushed to join Ivan, smacked away those zombies he could reach, then took hold of the corpse and finally pulled it free of the dwarf's antlers.

Cadderly overbalanced as it fell loose, then found he was sailing backward even faster as a zombie punched him in the chest. He hit the stone floor hard, felt the breath blasted from his lungs, and his precious wand flew free of his grasp. By the time he regained his sensibilities, a zombie had its strong hands clasped firmly about his throat.

* * * * *

The vampire was agile, but none could roll better than a round-shouldered dwarf. Pikel enjoyed the ride, throwing his weight into every turn with enthusiastic abandon. Finally the living ball slammed a wine rack, and the old structure buckled, showering Pikel and the vampire with splintered wood and shards of breaking bottles.

Pikel took the worst of that, the breaking rack doing no more damage to the vampire that Ivan's axe had done. Pikel, cut in a dozen places, one eye closed by a sliver, found himself in tight quarters suddenly, the vampire against him, holding him tight in its impossibly strong arms, its sharp fangs digging at his throat.

"Oooo!" the dwarf growled, and he tried to pull free, tried to wriggle one arm out, that he might hit his adversary.

It was no use; the vampire was too strong.

* * * * *

Cadderly thought to invoke Deneir's name, thought to present his holy symbol, thought to grab his walking stick and slam the zombie on the side of the head. He thought all of it and more at once, his mind whirling as the monster, its bloated face devoid of emotion, held the needed breath from his lungs.

Suddenly that bloated face rushed at Cadderly, slammed him hard, drawing blood from his lips. At first he thought the zombie had launched a new attack, then, as the thing steadily lifted from him, its grasp on his neck relaxed, the young priest understood.

"Durned things keep getting stuck," Ivan grumbled, hoisting his axe higher and bringing the impaled zombie with it. He brought the blade close and tried to pry the zombie loose.

"Behind you!" Cadderly called.

Too late. Another of the monsters pounded Ivan hard on the shoulder.

Ivan looked at Cadderly and shook his head. "Will ye wait a minute?" he screamed into the zombie's face, and the monster promptly punched him again, raising a welt on his cheek.

Ivan's heavy boot stomped on the zombie's foot. The dwarf launched himself forward with all his weight, the sudden movement dislodging the last zombie from his axe. The two foes staggered backward, but the zombie somehow held its footing.

Ivan's hand whipped around, bringing the handle of the axe behind the zombie's shoulder, then back in front of its face. The dwarf's other hand went in a similar movement, grabbing the other end of the handle, just below the axe's huge head. With his hands behind the zombie's back and the handle crossing in front of it, tight across its shoulders and throat, Ivan had the thing off balance. It continued to club at the dwarf's back, but it was in too tight to be effective.

"I telled ye to wait," Ivan explained casually, and the muscles on his powerful arms corded and bulged as he pressed backward and down, folding the monster in half the wrong way.

Cadderly didn't see the powerful move. He was up and moving again. He searched for his wand, but saw no sign of it in the tangle and the darkness. He started for

Pikel, but ran into a wall of zombies. Taking a circular route that moved him deeper into the cellar, Cadderly's attention was grabbed by something off to the side: three coffins, two open and one closed.

The young priest saw something else there, a blackness, a manifestation of evil. Huddled, shadowy images danced atop that closed coffin. Cadderly recognized the aura sight for what it was. As he had come to decipher the song of Deneir, the general weal of people he encountered was often revealed to him by shadowy images emanating from them. Normally Cadderly had to concentrate to see such things, had to call upon his god, but here the source of evil was too great for the shadows to be concealed.

Cadderly knew Pikel needed him, but he knew, too, that he had found Kierkan Rufo.

* * * * *

Pikel didn't like the feeling at all. The dwarf was a creature of natural order, who prized nature above all, and this foul, perverted thing was violating him, sinking its filthy fangs into the personal temple that was nature's gift to the dwarf.

He screamed and thrashed, to no avail. He felt his blood being drawn out, but could do nothing to stop it.

Pikel tried another tactic. Instead of pressing out with his arms, he tightened them to his sides, hoping the vampire would loosen its grip.

The monster's eyes widened in shock, and it began to tremble violently. Pikel understood when he felt the water, the "doo-dad" water being forced from his waterskin, soaking the front of his baldric and breeches.

The vampire broke the hold and leaped back, crashing into the part of the wine rack that had not collapsed, sending bottles flying. Smoke wafted from its chest, and Pikel saw that his squirting waterskin had drilled a neat hole there, right into the vampire's heart.

On came the raging dwarf, pounding with his club, crushing the perversion into the floor. He turned, sensing that zombies were converging from behind, but the undead wall parted as Ivan burrowed through to his brother's side once more.

* * * * *

Cadderly's remaining light source dimmed as he approached the coffins, his eyes set firmly on the dancing shadows, on the box that held Kierkan Rufo. He felt a warmth in his pocket then, which confused him for just a moment.

Cadderly stopped suddenly and lashed out to the side with his walking stick, smashing several bottles. A shriek and a flap of wings told him he had guessed right.

"I see you, Druzil," the young priest muttered. "Never will I lose sight of you!"

The imp became visible, crouched on the lip of one of the opened boxes.

"You desecrated the library!" Cadderly accused.

Druzil hissed at him. "There is no place here for you, foolish priest. Your god has left!"

In answer, Cadderly thrust forth his holy symbol and, for a moment, the light flared, stinging Druzil's sensitive eyes. These two had battled before, on several occasions, and each time Cadderly had proven stronger.

So it would be again, the young priest determined, but this time, Druzil, that most malicious imp, would not escape his wrath. Cadderly pulled forth the amulet, the link between him and the imp, and sent a telepathic wave at Druzil, calling loudly the name of Deneir. The image manifested itself in both combatants' thoughts as a sparking ball of light, floating toward Druzil from Cadderly.

Druzil retorted with the discordant names of every denizen of the lower planes he could think of, forming a ball of blackness that floated out to engulf the light of Cadderly's god.

The two wills battled halfway between the combatants. First Druzil's blackness dominated, but sparks of light gradually began to flash through.

Suddenly the black cloud shattered and the sparking ball rolled over the imp.

Druzil shrieked in agony; his mind was nearly torn asunder, and he fled, half-crazed, looking for a corner, a place of shadows, a place far from the terrible, bared power of Cadderly.

Cadderly thought to pursue, to be rid of troublesome Druzil once and for all, but then the lid of the coffin flew away and a deeper darkness wafted out. Kierkan Rufo sat up and stared at Cadderly.

This was the way it had to be, they both knew.

Behind Cadderly, Ivan and Pikel continued to rain carnage on the unthinking minions, but neither the young priest nor Rufo noticed. Cadderly's focus was straight ahead, straight on the monster who had destroyed the library, who had taken Danica from him.

"You killed her," Cadderly said evenly, fighting hard to keep the tremor out of his voice.

"She killed herself," Rufo countered, needing no explanation as to whom Cadderly was speaking of.

"You killed her!"

"No!" Rufo countered. "You killed her! You, Cadderly, fool priest, and your ideas of love!"

Cadderly fell back on his heels, trying to sort through Rufo's cryptic words. Danica had died of her own accord? She had given up her life to escape Rufo, because she could not love Rufo, and could not accept his offers?

A tear gathered in Cadderly's gray eye. Bittersweet, it was, a mixture of pain at the loss and pride in Danica's strength.

Rufo came easily out of the coffin. He seemed to glide toward Cadderly, making not a sound.

But the room was far from quiet. Even Ivan was disgusted at the crunching sounds the zombies made when he hacked them, or when Pikel swatted them across the room. Fewer and fewer targets presented themselves.

Cadderly didn't hear it; Rufo didn't hear it. Cadderly presented his holy symbol, and the vampire promptly clamped his hand atop it. Their struggle found its apex in that small emblem, Rufo's darkness against Cadderly's light, the focus of the young priest's faith, the focus of the perversion's outrage. Acrid smoke sifted out between Rufo's bony fingers, but whether it was the vampire's flesh or Cadderly's symbol that was melting, neither could tell.

They held fast for seconds that became minutes, both trembling, neither having the strength to lift his other arm. It would end here, Cadderly believed, with these two conduits, himself for Deneir and Rufo for the chaos curse.

As the moments continued to slip by, as Cadderly forced himself to higher levels of power, remembering Danica and all that had been stolen from him, and as Rufo matched him every time, Cadderly began to understand the truth.

This was Rufo's place. For all his rage and all his power, the young priest could not hold out against the vampire, not here.

Cadderly grimaced, refusing to accept what he knew was reality. He pressed on, and Rufo matched him. His head ached to the point where he thought it would explode, but he would not let go of the song of Deneir.

Despair, black discord, found its way into the notes of that melody. Chaos. Cadderly saw red fumes in the crystalline, flowing river. The notes began to break apart.

Ivan hit Rufo hard from the side, with both his axe and his thrashing helmet. Neither weapon truly injured the vampire, but the distraction cost Rufo his moment of conquest, gave Cadderly the opportunity to break the clinch he could not win.

With a feral snarl, Rufo slapped the dwarf away, sent Ivan spinning head over heels into the nearest rack, to crash amid broken glass and splintered wood.

Cadderly's walking stick flashed across, tearing the vampire's upper arm.

Pikel came in next, pressing hard on his waterskin, forcing the last drops to spray forth.

Rufo cared nothing for the puny attack, and Pikel learned the hard way, to his dismay, that his enchantment had expired on the club. He hit the vampire full force, but Rufo didn't flinch.

"Ooooooo," Pikel wailed, following his brother's aerial course into the jumble.

Ivan's eyes were wide as he held one unbroken bottle, staring at it nervously.

Cadderly hit the vampire again, solidly in the chest, and Rufo grimaced in pain.

"I have you," the vampire promised, not backing down, and Cadderly could not disagree. The young priest went into a fury then, slapping wildly with his enchanted weapon.

Rufo matched him, and the vampire's strong fists soon gained him the advantage. In this desecrated place, in this chamber of darkness, Rufo was simply too strong.

Cadderly somehow managed to break the battle and retreat a step, but confident Rufo waded in right behind.

"Cadderly!" Ivan yelled, and both Cadderly and Rufo glanced to the side to see a curious missile heading for the vampire.

Rufo instinctively threw his arm up to block, but seemed unconcerned. Cadderly, recognizing the missile for what it was, timed his strike perfectly, hitting the flask at the same instant it bounced against Rufo's arm.

"The *Oil of Impact* exploded with tremendous force, hurling Rufo against the far wall, throwing Cadderly backward to the floor.

The young priest sat up at once and considered the splintered handle of his ruined walking stick. Then he considered Kierkan Rufo.

The vampire leaned heavily against the back wall, his arm hanging loose by a single strip of skin, his eyes wide with shock and pain.

Cadderly came up with a growl, turned the remaining piece of his weapon in his hand to hold it like a stake.

"I will find you!" Rufo promised. "I will heal and I will find you!" A ghostly green light limned the vampire's form.

Cadderly cried out and charged, but slammed hard into the wall as Rufo dissolved into a cloud of vapors.

"No, ye don't!" Ivan bellowed, rising from the pile and pulling the boxlike item from his back.

"Oo oi!" Pikel agreed, rushing beside his brother, taking one of the offered handles. They skidded into the green vapor and pulled fiercely on the handles of the bellows they had stripped from their forge.

In his gaseous state, Rufo could not resist that suction, and the mist disappeared into the bellows.

"Ooooooo!" Pikel squealed and popped his fat thumb over the opening.

"Get him outside!" frantic Ivan roared, and the dwarves ran off for the stairs, yelling "Oooooooo!" in unison.

Cadderly charged hard to keep up, holding his light ahead to show them the way. He spotted his lost wand, but had not the time to go for it.

The Highest Test

He's coming back!" Ivan yelled, and the bellows bulged weirdly as Rufo's corporeal form began to take shape once more, as the vapors began to solidify.

"Ooooooo!" Pikel wailed, careening down the halls, the foyer in sight.

Cadderly skidded in first, throwing all his weight against the barricade that had been put in place to block the opening. He didn't move the material much, but he lessened its integrity, and when Ivan and Pikel hit, everything, Cadderly included, flew away. The young priest shook his head, both at the amazing power of rambling dwarves and to take the dizziness away, then he took up his wand, and followed closely.

Out into the sunlight scrambled the dwarves. Pikel's

finger was no longer over the pointy opening of the bellows, but it didn't matter, for Rufo was no longer gaseous. Leather bulged and tore as a clawing hand ripped through the side of the bellows.

The dwarves ran on, dragging their load, getting Rufo as far from the gloomy library, his source of power, as possible. They cut under the shadows of the trees, out into an open, sunny field.

Rufo tore free and dug a firm hold on the turf. Both dwarves pitched headlong to the ground and came up sitting, each holding a broken handle.

With some effort, the vampire stood straight, cursing the sun, shielding his eyes from the blazing light. Cadderly stood before Kierkan Rufo, holy symbol presented with all his heart. The young priest, out from under the desecrated structure, felt his god strongly again. Rufo, too, felt Deneir keenly, Cadderly's words echoing painfully in his mind.

Rufo started for the library, but Cadderly danced around to intercept, his blazing holy symbol blocking the way.

"You cannot escape," the young priest said firmly. "You have made your choice, and you have chosen wrong!"

"What do you know?" the vampire scoffed. Rufo stood tall, defying the sun, defying Cadderly and his god. He felt the tumultuous swirl of the chaos curse within him, of *Tuanta Quiro Miancay*, that Most Fatal Horror. It was a concoction of the Abyss, of the very lowest planes.

Even in the sunlight, even battered as he had been in the fight, his arm hanging grotesquely at his side, Rufo stood strong. Cadderly could see that, could feel it.

"I deny you," the personification of *Tuanta Quiro Miancay* said evenly. The words filtered through Cad-

284 R. A. Salvatore

derly's thoughts, throwing up barriers, damming the river of his god's song. Rufo had spoken to Deneir, Cadderly realized, not to him. Rufo had made the claim that his choice had not been wrong, that his power was real and tangible—and he had made that claim against Deneir, against a god!

"They hold us back, Cadderly," the vampire went on, his calm tones showing strength and defiance. "They keep their secrets to themselves, cover them with pretty flowers and sunshine, petty dressings to keep us satisfied and behind which they might hide the truth."

Looking at the vampire now, standing tall and straighter than Kierkan Rufo had ever stood in life, Cadderly almost believed that Rufo had found truth. It seemed, too, as if a protective shell had formed about Rufo, a dark lining to battle the burning sunlight. How strong this one had become! The vampire continued, and Cadderly closed his eyes, the arm holding his holy symbol inevitably dropping low. The young priest didn't distinguish any of the words, just felt the hum, the alluring vibrations, deep in his soul.

"Well?" came a blunt and gruff question. Cadderly opened his eyes to see Ivan and Pikel, sitting side by side in the grass, still holding the broken handles and considering the face-off.

Well, indeed, the young priest thought. He looked squarely into his adversary's dark eyes.

"I deny Deneir," Rufo said calmly.

"You choose wrongly," Cadderly replied.

Rufo starting to hiss a response, but Cadderly froze the words in the vampire's throat, lifting again the symbol, the opened eye above a lighted candle. The sunlight brought new sparkles to the emblem, heightened its glory and strength.

In the face of that revealing glare, Rufo's dark shell melted away, and suddenly the vampire seemed not so powerful, rather a pitiful thing, a fallen man, a man who had chosen the wrong course and had spiraled down to the depths of despair.

Rufo hissed and clawed at the air. He reached for the holy symbol, meaning to engulf it as he had done inside, but this time the flesh on his skinny hand erupted into flames and curled away, leaving only whitened bone. Rufo howled in agony. He turned for the library, but Cadderly paced him, keeping that flaring symbol right in his face. And Cadderly began to sing the melodies of his god, a tune Kierkan Rufo could not withstand. Inside the library Rufo had gained the advantage, but out here, in the daylight, Deneir's song played strong in Cadderly, and the young priest opened himself up as a pure conduit for the truth of his god.

Rufo could not withstand the light of that truth.

"Oo," Pikel and Ivan muttered together, as Rufo fell back to the earth. Cadderly pressed low, singing with all his heart. Rufo rolled over and clawed at the ground to get away, like a desperate animal, but Cadderly was there in front of him, corralling him, forcing him to see the truth.

Horrible, wailing sounds escaped the vampire's throat. Somehow, Rufo managed to struggle back to his feet, to stare at the shining holy symbol in one last desperate act of defiance.

His eyes whitened, then fell back into his skull, and through the black openings wafted the red mist of the chaos curse. Rufo opened his mouth to scream, and from there, too, came the red mist, forced from his body into the open air, where it would diminish and cause no more pain.

When Rufo collapsed to the ground, he was no more than a hollow, smoking husk, an empty coil, and a lost soul.

Cadderly, too, nearly collapsed, from the effort and from the weight of the grim reality that now descended on him. He looked over his shoulder at the squat library. He considered all the losses he had witnessed, the losses to the order, the loss of his friends, of Dorigen. The loss of Danica.

Ivan and Pikel were beside him immediately, knowing he would need their support.

"She did right in choosing death," Ivan remarked, understanding that the tears rimming Cadderly's gray eyes were for Danica most of all. "Better that than fallin' in with this one," the square-shouldered dwarf added, motioning to the empty husk.

" . . . in choosing death," Cadderly echoed, those words striking a strange chord within him. She had killed herself, Rufo had said. Danica had willingly chosen death.

But why hadn't Rufo animated her? Cadderly wondered. As the vampire had animated so many of the others? And why, when he had gone into the netherworld, had Cadderly not been able to find Danica's spirit, or any trace of its passing?

"Oh, my dear Deneir," the young priest whispered, and, without a word of explanation, Cadderly ran off toward the northwestern corner of the library.

The dwarves looked to each other and shrugged, then chased off after him.

Cadderly scrambled wildly, crashed through roots and bushes, clawing his way around to the back of the building. The dwarves, better at trailblazing than the taller man, nearly caught up to him, but when Cadderly got into the open field between the library and the mausoleum, he left the brothers in his dust.

He hit the mausoleum door at full speed, never considering that Shayleigh and Belago might have found a way to lock or brace it. In it swung, and in spilled Cadderly, skidding hard to the floor, scraping his elbows.

He hardly cared about the minor wounds, for when he looked to the left, to the stone slab where the two had placed Danica, he saw the "corpse" under the shroud rising to a sitting position. He saw also that Shayleigh, with a terrified Belago beside her, was perched on the bottom of the slab, her short sword poised to plunge into Danica's heart.

"No!" Cadderly cried. "No!"

Shayleigh glanced at him, and she wondered in that instant if Cadderly, too, had been taken by the darkness, if he had come to save his lover in undeath.

"She's alive!" the young priest cried, clawing to propel himself toward the slab. Ivan and Pikel rambled in then, wide-eyed and still not understanding.

"She's alive!" Cadderly repeated, and Shayleigh relaxed a bit as he arrived at the slab and pulled the shroud from fair Danica and wrapped his love in the tightest embrace they had ever shared.

Danica, back with the living again, returned it tenfold, and the day was brighter indeed!

"What of Rufo?" the elf asked the dwarves.

"Hee hee hee," Pikel replied, and both he and Ivan ran their fingers across their throats.

The four left Cadderly and Danica then, waited outside in the light that seemed brighter and warmer and more alive than any spring previous. Cadderly and Danica came out a few minutes later, the young priest supporting the injured woman. Already Cadderly had called for spells of healing to help the monk, particularly her ruined ankle, but the wound was sore and infected, and even with Cadderly's aid, it would take some time before it could support Danica's weight.

"I don't get it," Ivan stated, for all of them.

"Physical suspension," Cadderly answered for Danica. "A state of death that is not death. It is the highest mark in the teachings of Grandmaster Penpahg D'Ahn."

"You can kill yerself and come back?" Ivan balked.

Danica shook her head, smiling like she thought she would never smile again. "In suspension, one does not die," she explained. "I slowed my heart and my breathing, slowed the flow of blood through my veins, to where all who regarded my body thought I was dead."

"Thus you escaped the hunger of Kierkan Rufo," Shayleigh reasoned.

"And escaped my attention as well," Cadderly added. "That is why I could not find her when I entered the spirit realm." He looked at Danica and gave a wistful smile. "I was looking in the wrong place."

"I nearly killed you," Shayleigh said, stunned by the proclamation, her hand going to the hilt of her belted sword.

"Bah!" Ivan snorted. "It wouldn't be the first time!"

They all laughed then, these friends who had survived, forgetting for a moment the loss of the library, the loss of Dorigen, and the loss of their own innocence. And loudest among them was Pikel's "Hee hee hee."

* * * * *

Cadderly led them back into the library the next day, seeking any lesser vampires left in dark holes, and putting to rest any zombies they encountered. When they came outside late that afternoon, the friends were certain the first two floors were clean of enemies. The next morning, Cadderly started his friends to work removing the most precious artifacts of the library, the irreplaceable artwork and ancient manuscripts. Danica was thrilled to find that all of Penpahg D'Ahn's notes had survived.

Even more thrilled was the monk, and all the others, when they found a single sanctuary within the darkness, a single spot of light that had somehow held out against the encroachment of Kierkan Rufo. Brother Chaunticleer had used his melodies as a ward against the evil, and his room had not been desecrated. Half-starved, his hair whitened from the terror he had endured, he fell into Cadderly's arms with sobs of joy and knelt upon the ground in prayer for more than an hour when the friends escorted him out.

Later that same day, a host of four score soldiers arrived from Carradoon, having received word of the attack on the merchant caravan. Cadderly quickly put this group to work (except for a band of emissaries he sent back to the town with news of what had occurred and warnings to beware any strange happenings), and soon the library was emptied of its valuables.

Their encampment was on the lawn to the east of the library, at the back end of the field, closer to the wild trails than the gaping doors. This was too close, Cadderly informed them, so they broke down their tents, gathered up supplies, and moved down onto the trails.

"What is this all about?" Danica asked the young priest as the soldiers set up the new camp. A week had passed since the fall of Kierkan Rufo, a week in which the young priest had gathered his strength, had listened to the words of Deneir.

"The building is spoiled," Cadderly replied. "Never again will Deneir or Oghma enter it."

"You mean to abandon it?" Danica asked.

"I mean to destroy it," Cadderly replied grimly.

Danica started to ask what Cadderly was talking about, but he walked past her, back toward the field, before she could figure out where to begin. The monk paused a while before following. She remembered the scene outside Castle Trinity, Aballister's bastion of wickedness, after the wizard's fall. Cadderly had meant to destroy that dark fortress as well, but had changed his mind, or had learned that he had not the strength for such a task. What, then, was he thinking now?

Gathering black clouds atop the cliff to the north of the Edificant Library alerted all in the camp that something dramatic was going on. The soldiers wanted to secure their tents, pack their supplies tightly, fearing the storm, but Ivan, Pikel, Shayleigh, and Belago understood that this fury was well guided, and Brother Chaunticleer understood it perhaps best of all.

The group found Danica standing several feet behind Cadderly on the lawn before the squat stone structure. Silently, not wanting to disturb these obviously important happenings, they gathered about her. None but Chaunticleer dared approach the young priest. He regarded Cadderly and offered a knowing, confident smile to the others. And, though he was not a part of what was happening with Cadderly, he began to sing.

Cadderly stood tall, arms upraised to the heavens. He, too, was singing, at the top of his lungs, but his voice could hardly be heard above the roar of the wind and thunder from the black clouds, now swarming over the top of the cliff, edging their way toward the desecrated building.

A searing blast of lightning hit the library's roof. A second followed, then the wind tore in, launching shingles, then joists, to the south, across the mountainside.

More lightning started several small fires. The clouds came low, seemed to hover and gather strength, then a tremendous gust of wind lifted the edge of the roof and ripped it away.

Cadderly cried out with all his strength. He was a direct conduit for the power of Deneir. Through the young priest the god sent his fury, more lightning, more wind. The roof was gone.

A solitary figure—it seemed as if one of the gargoyles lining the gutters had come to life—perched on the edge of that roof, shouting curses at Cadderly, invoking its own gods, denizens of the evil lower planes.

But here Cadderly was the stronger, Deneir the strongest by far.

A searing bolt of lightning hit the roof right beside Druzil, igniting a tremendous fire and throwing the imp far away.

"Bene tellemara," Druzil rasped, clawing his way toward the flames, realizing then that his time on this plane was at its end. He would leave now or be destroyed. He made it to the flames, blasts striking all about him, and uttered an incantation. Then he threw a bag of powder, which he had concocted in the library's deserted alchemy shop, into the fire.

The flames lifted and danced, blue then white-hot, and Druzil, after shouting one more curse Cadderly's way, stepped in and was gone.

The storm's fury intensified, bolt after bolt slamming the stone walls, diminishing their integrity. A darkness, funnel-shaped, reached down from the clouds. The finger of a god, it seemed, reaching down for the desecrated building.

Cadderly cried out, as if in pain, but Danica and the

others resisted the urge to run to him, feared the consequences of disturbing what he had begun.

The storm crashed down in full, and the earth itself rolled to life, great waves of ground heaving at the library's foundation. The northern wall buckled first, fell inward, and, with it gone, both the front and back collapsed. Still the lightning blasted away; still the tornado grabbed at pieces of rubble and lifted them into the air, heaving them, like so much waste, far across the mountainside.

It went on unabated for many minutes, and the soldiers feared the very mountains would fall. Cadderly's friends knew better, though. They saw in their comrade a resolve and a glory beyond anything they had ever witnessed; they knew Cadderly was with Deneir fully, and that Cadderly's god would not harm him or them.

Then it was over, suddenly. The clouds broke apart so that shafts of sunlight shone down. One fell over Cadderly, outlining his form in silvery hues so that he seemed much more than a man, much more than a priest.

Danica approached him cautiously, Shayleigh and the dwarves right behind her. "Cadderly?" she whispered.

If he heard her, he did not show it.

"Cadderly?" she asked more loudly. She gave him a shake. Still there was no response. Danica thought she understood. She could appreciate the emotions that must be running through her lover, for he had just destroyed the only home he had ever known.

"Oo," Pikel and Ivan, and even Shayleigh, muttered in unison.

But their sympathy was misplaced, for Cadderly felt no remorse. He remained with his god and was seeing now a new vision, the vision that had haunted his dreams for many years. Without a word of explanation, he moved toward the scarred, rubble-strewn area, his friends in tow. Danica continued to call to him, to shake him, but he could not hear.

The vision was all-encompassing. The young priest remembered the extradimensional mansion that Aballister had created in Castle Trinity, remembered how he had marveled at how similar were the properties of magically created material.

A specific spot on the ground, a place flat and smooth and devoid of rubble, beckoned to him. That single spot on the ground became the only clear thing Cadderly could see outside of his mind's eye. He went to it, feeling the power of Deneir keenly, knowing what he must do. He began to sing again, and the notes were much different than those he had used to bring down the Edificant Library, These were sweet and cumulative, a building song with a crescendo that seemed very far away. He sang for minutes that became a half hour, then an hour. The soldiers thought him insane, and Brother Chaunticleer merely shook his head, having no insight as to what his fellow Deneirian might be doing. Danica didn't know how to react, didn't know whether to try to stop Cadderly or just to stand back. In the end, she decided to trust her love, and she waited as the hour became two.

Long shadows filtered from the west, and Cadderly continued. Even Ivan and Pikel began to wonder if the storm and the earthquake had broken the man, had reduced him to a babbling idiot.

Danica held her faith, though. She would wait for Cadderly to finish—whatever he was doing—through all the next day if need be, even beyond that. She, all of them, owed the young priest at least that.

As it turned out, Danica did not have to wait through the night. With the western horizon pink with the last moments of the setting sun, Cadderly's voice lifted suddenly.

Brother Chaunticleer and many of the others ran near him, thinking that something grand was in store.

They were not disappointed. There came a sharp hissing sound, a crackle as if the sky itself were being torn asunder.

Then it appeared, on the ground before Cadderly, rising like a tree growing out of control. It was a tower, a decorated pillar of stone, an aerial buttress. It continued to grow, its tip rising into the air before Cadderly and the astonished onlookers.

Cadderly stopped his singing and fell back, exhausted, to be caught by his friends. The crowd murmured dozens of questions, most prominent among them, "What have you done?"

Danica asked that very question of Cadderly when she looked closely at his face, at the flecks of silver suddenly showing in his tousled brown hair, at the crow's-feet, the wrinkles that had not been there before, running out about his eyes.

She looked back to the buttress, a tiny portion of the cathedral of which Cadderly had oft spoken, and then back to her love, who had obviously aged with the effort. Danica grew worried, and still more with the serene look that had come over the tired and suddenly not-so-young priest.

Epilogue

Shayleigh had gone to Shilmista, and had come back in high summer to view the progress on Cadderly's new cathedral. She had expected a virtual army would be hard at work on the place, and was amazed at how few people were actually about, just Cadderly and Danica, Vicero Belago and Brother Chaunticleer, the Bouldershoulders, and a handful of sturdy men from Carradoon.

Progress had been made, though, and Shayleigh realized she should have expected no less. This was a construction of magic, not of physical toil, and it seemed as if Cadderly needed little help. Many areas were clear now of rubble, a tribute to the dwarves and the men from Carradoon, and three of the aerial buttresses were set in a line along the northern edge of what would be

295

the new library. Twenty feet from them, to the south, Cadderly had begun construction on the wall, a delicate-looking structure.

Shayleigh gasped when she saw what the priest was now working on, a huge, arching window of multicolored glass and black iron that would fit into the wall in clear sight of the spaced buttresses. Cadderly paid attention to every detail as he worked over the rough design, flaring the tips of iron symmetrically, forming patterns with varying colors of the pieces of glass.

The elf was a creature of the forests, of the myriad beauties that nature offered and that men could not replicate, but Shayleigh found her heart lifted now, felt her spirit soaring as her imagination pictured this finished cathedral. There were too many fine details, too many intricate designs, for her to even appreciate them. It was like a wide-spreading elm, she thought, and Cadderly was painstakingly placing every individual leaf and twig.

Shayleigh found Danica along the eastern edge of the library's grounds, intently looking over a pile of parchments. Brother Chaunticleer was close by, singing to his god, calling up spells of preservation and protection as he watched over the piles of artwork and priceless manuscripts that had been brought out of the old library. Belago was close by him, inspecting the piles and singing, too. Apparently the wiry alchemist had at last found his way to a specific religion. And who could blame him? Shayleigh thought, and she smiled as she considered the man. Given the wondrous sights Belago had witnessed, most marvelous among them the construction continuing every day right in front of him, how could he not find his way to Deneir?

Danica's face brightened when she saw that her friend had returned. They exchanged warm greetings and hugs, and perceptive Shayleigh knew at once that Danica's smile hid much that was not so bright.

"He does that all day," the monk offered, pointedly looking to Brother Chaunticleer, though Shayleigh understood she was referring to Cadderly.

Shayleigh, trying to subtly change the subject, looked to the parchments on the ground before Danica.

"Lists," she explained. "Lists of men and women who will accompany me to Nightglow and the dragon's treasure. I have already sent emissaries to Shilmista."

"I passed them on the trails," Shayleigh remarked. "They probably have met with King Elbereth already, though I suspect they will tell my king nothing he does not already know."

"They will invite Shilmista to join the expedition," Danica said.

"That was expected," Shayleigh replied with a calm smile. "We understand and appreciate the friendship you and Cadderly have begun."

Danica nodded and, despite her resolve, could not help but look at her lover at the mention of his name. Cadderly was still full of energy—brimming with energy —as he worked on his vision, but he no longer appeared as a man in his early twenties. Despite the toil, his body had thickened somewhat; his muscles were broader and still strong, but not quite as sharp and hardened as they had once been.

"The construction takes a toll," Shayleigh remarked.

"The creation," Danica corrected. She sighed deeply, commanding the elf's full attention. "It was a choice," Danica began, "a choice between Deneir, this course, this purpose that Cadderly has found in his life, and . . . "

"And Danica," Shayleigh interjected softly, placing a sympathetic hand on the sitting monk's shoulder.

"And Danica," the monk admitted. "A choice between Deneir's calling and the life that Cadderly, as a man, truly desired."

Shayleigh looked hard at the monk and knew that Danica truly believed her words. The generous young woman understood that Cadderly had chosen a higher love, a love that no mortal could ever match. There was no jealousy in Danica's tone, but there was indeed a sadness, a profound pain.

The two sat in silence, watching Cadderly and the dwarves. Ivan and Pikel had marked off another area, and were apparently discussing the next logical step to support the structure's already-standing towers.

"He will complete the cathedral," Danica said.

"A new Edificant Library."

"No," the monk replied, shaking her head and lifting her almond-shaped eyes to regard Shayleigh. "Cadderly never liked that name, never thought it fitting for a house of the god of literature and art and the god of knowledge. 'The Spirit Soaring' will be the name he gives this cathedral."

"How long?" Shayleigh asked.

"Cadderly and the dwarves have drawn up the plans," Danica answered, her voice trailing to a whisper. "Five years."

"Five years," Shayleigh echoed quietly, and yet, Danica had pointedly mentioned that Cadderly would live to see the completion. Only five years! "The creation takes from him," Shayleigh remarked. "It is as if he gives his own being for the cathedral's materials."

Exactly, Danica thought, but she had not the strength to answer. Cadderly had discussed it all with her, had told her this was his purpose in life. This cathedral, the Spirit Soaring, would stand for millennia, a tribute to the god he served. He had told her what the price would be, and together they had cried for the life they would not share. Soon after, Danica had bitten hard on her bottom lip and bravely added to Cadderly's point, telling him that the Spirit Soaring would be a tribute, too, to Cadderly, to the priest who had sacrificed so much.

Cadderly would hear nothing of it. The cathedral was for only the gods, and the fact that he was allowed to construct it was a gift, not a sacrifice.

"He hopes to live long enough to offer one service in the new cathedral," Danica whispered.

Shayleigh rubbed her hand over Danica's shoulder, then, stricken mute, she walked away, to speak with Brother Chauntleer and Vicero Belago. She could hardly believe the young priest's sacrifice. Humans lived a short enough time, but for one to give back perhaps three-fourths of that span was inconceivable to the long-living elf.

Danica watched Shayleigh for just a few steps, then her eyes inevitably turned back to Cadderly, back to the man she loved, and loved all the more for his determination in following the course his god had shown him. And yet, she found she hated Cadderly, too, hated that she had ever met the man and had given him her heart. When he was gone, and she was still young, how could she love another?

No, she decided, shaking her head against the pervasive pain. Better to have met and known Cadderly. Better to have loved him. That thought sent Danica's hand gently rubbing over her abdomen. She was hoping to conceive, hoping to give Cadderly another legacy, a living, breathing legacy.

Danica's smile, as she continued to watch the man, was bittersweet. She wondered if her eyes would ever again be free of tears.

FANTASY ADVENTURE

SIEGE OF DARKNESS

An Excerpt

by R. A. Salvatore

PROLOGUE

By all appearances, she was too fair a creature to be walking through the swirling sludge of this smoky layer of the Abyss. Too beautiful, her features were sculpted fine and delicate, her shining ebony skin giving her the appearance of animated artwork. She was an obsidian sculpture come to life.

The monstrous things around her, crawling slugs and bat-winged denizens, monitored her every move, watched her carefully, cautiously. Even the largest and strongest of them, gigantic fiends that could sack a fair-sized city,

302

kept a safe distance, for appearances could be deceiving. While this fine-featured female seemed delicate, even frail by the standards of the gruesome monsters of the Abyss, she could easily destroy any one, any ten, any fifty, of the fiends now watching her.

They knew it, too, and her passage was unhindered. She was Lloth, the Spider Queen, goddess of the drow, the dark elves. She was chaos incarnate, an instrument of destruction, a monster beneath a delicate facade.

Lloth calmly strolled into a region of tall, thick mushrooms clustered on small islands amid the grimy swirl. She walked from island to island without concern, stepping so lightly about the slurping sludge that not even the bottoms of her delicate black slippers were soiled. She found many of this level's strongest inhabitants, even true tanar'ri fiends, sleeping amid those mushroom groves, and roused them rudely. Inevitably, the irritable creatures came awake snarling and promising eternal torture, and just as inevitably, they were much relieved when Lloth demanded of them only a single answer to a single question.

"Where is he?" she asked each time, and, though none of the monsters knew of the great fiend's exact location, their answers led Lloth on, guided her until at last she found the beast she was looking for, a huge bipedal tanar'ri with a canine maw, the horns of a bull, and tremendous, leathery wings folded behind its huge body. Looking quite bored, it sat in a chair it had carved from one of the mushrooms, its grotesque head resting on the upraised palm of one hand. Dirty, curved claws scratched rhythmically against its pallid cheek. In its other hand the beast held a many-tongued whip and, every so often, snapped it about, lashing at the side of the mushroom chair, where crouched the unfortunate lesser creature it had selected for torture during this point of eternity.

The smaller denizen yelped and whined pitifully, and that drew another stinging crack of the merciless fiend's whip.

The seated beast grunted suddenly, head coming up alert, red eyes peering intently into the smoky veil swirling all about the mushroom throne. Something was about, it knew, something powerful.

Lloth walked into view, not slowing in the least as she regarded this monster, the greatest of this area.

A guttural growl escaped the tanar'ri's lips, lips that curled into an evil smile, then turned down into a frown as it considered the pretty morsel walking into its lair. At first, the fiend thought Lloth a gift, a lost, wandering dark elf far from the Material Plane and her home. It didn't take the fiend long to recognize the truth of this one, though.

It sat up straight in its chair. Then, with incredible speed and fluidity for one its size, it brought itself to its full height—twelve feet—and towered over the intruder.

"Sit, Errtu," Lloth bade it, waving her hand impatiently. "I have not come to destroy you."

A second growl issued from the proud tanar'ri, but Errtu made no move for Lloth, understanding that she could easily do what she had just claimed she had not come here to do. Just to salvage a bit of his pride, Errtu remained standing.

"Sit!" Lloth said suddenly, fiercely, and Errtu, before he registered the movement, found himself back on the mushroom throne. Frustrated, he took up his whip and battered the sniveling beast that groveled at his side.

"Why are you here, drow?" Errtu grumbled, his deep voice breaking into higher, crackling whines, like fingernails on slate.

"You have heard the rumblings of the pantheon?" Lloth asked.

Errtu considered the question for a long moment. Of course he had heard that the gods of the Realms were quarreling, stepping over each other in intrigue-laden power grabs and using intelligent lesser creatures as pawns in their private games. In the Abyss, this meant that the denizens, even greater tanar'ri such as Errtu, were often caught up in unwanted political intrigue.

Which was exactly what Errtu figured, and feared, was happening here.

"A time of great strife is approaching," Lloth explained. "A time when the gods will pay for their foolishness."

Errtu chuckled, a grating, terrible sound. Lloth's red-glowing gaze fell over him scornfully.

"Why would such an event displease you, Lady of Chaos?" the fiend asked.

"This trouble will be beyond me," Lloth explained, deadly serious, "beyond us all. I will enjoy watching the fools of the pantheon jostled about, stripped of their false pride, some perhaps even slain, but any worshipped being who is not cautious will find herself caught in the trouble."

"Lloth was never known for caution," Errtu put in dryly.

"Lloth was never a fool," the Spider Queen quickly replied.

Errtu nodded but sat quietly for a moment on his mushroom throne, digesting it all. "What has this to do with me?" he asked finally, for tanar'ri were not worshipped, and, thus, Errtu did not draw his powers from the prayers of any faithful.

"Menzoberranzan," Lloth replied, naming the fabled city of drow, the largest base of her worshippers in all the Realms.

Errtu cocked his grotesque head.

"The city is in chaos already," Lloth explained.

"As you would have it," Errtu put in, and he snickered. "As you have arranged it."

Lloth didn't refute that. "But there is danger," the beautiful drow went on. "If I am caught in the troubles of the pantheon, the prayers of my priestesses will go unanswered."

"Am I expected to answer them?" Errtu asked incredulously.

"The faithful will need protection."

"I cannot go to Menzoberranzan!" Errtu roared suddenly, his outrage, the outrage of years of banishment, spilling over. Menzoberranzan was a city of Faerun's Underdark, the great labyrinth beneath the world's surface. But, though it was separated from the region of sunlight by miles of thick rock, it was still a place of the Material Plane. Years ago, Errtu had been on that plane, at the call of a minor wizard, and had stayed there in search of Crenshinibon, the Crystal Shard, a mighty artifact, relic of a past and greater age of sorcery. The great tanar'ri had been so close to the relic! He had entered the tower it had created in its image, and had worked with its possessor, a pitiful human who would have died soon enough, leaving the fiend to his coveted treasure. But then Errtu had met a dark elf, a renegade from Lloth's own flock, from Menzoberranzan, the city she now apparently wanted him to protect!

Drizzt Do'Urden had defeated Errtu and, to a tanar'ri, a defeat on the Material Plane meant a hundred years of banishment in the Abyss.

Now Errtu trembled visibly with rage, and Lloth took a step backward, preparing herself in case the beast attacked before she could explain her offer. "You cannot

go," she agreed, "but your minions can. I will see that a
gate is kept open, if all the priestesses of my domain
must tend it continually."

Errtu's thunderous roar drowned out the words.

Lloth understood the source of that agony; a fiend's
greatest pleasure was to walk loose on the Material
Plane, to challenge the weak souls and weaker bodies of
the various races. Lloth understood, but she did not sympathize. Evil Lloth never sympathized with any creature.

"I cannot deny you!" Errtu admitted, and his great,
bulbous, bloodshot eyes narrowed wickedly.

His statement was true enough. Lloth could enlist his
aid simply by offering him his very existence in return.
The Spider Queen was smarter than that, however. If
she enslaved Errtu and was, indeed, as she expected,
caught up in the coming storm, Errtu might escape her
capture or, worse, find a way to strike back at her. Lloth
was malicious and merciless in the extreme, but she
was, above all else, intelligent. She had in her possession
honey for this fly.

"This is no threat," she said honestly to the fiend.
"This is an offer."

Errtu did not interrupt, still, the bored and outraged
fiend trembled on the edge of catastrophe.

"I have a gift, Errtu," she purred, "a gift that will allow
you to end the banishment Drizzt Do'Urden has placed
on you."

The tanar'ri did not seem convinced. "No gift," he
rumbled. "No magic can break the terms of banishment.
Only he who banished me can end the indenture."

Lloth nodded her agreement; not even a goddess had
the power to go against that rule. "But that is exactly the
point!" the Spider Queen exclaimed. "This gift will make
Drizzt Do'Urden want you back on his plane of exis-

tence, back within his reach."

Errtu did not seem convinced.

In response, Lloth lifted one arm and clamped her fist tightly, and a signal, a burst of multicolored sparks and a rocking blast of thunder, shook the swirling sludge and momentarily stole the perpetual gray of the dismal level.

Forlorn and beaten, head down—for it did not take one such as Lloth very long to sunder the pride—he walked from the fog. Errtu did not know him, but understood the significance of this gift.

Lloth clamped her fist tight again, another explosive signal sounded, and her captive fell back into the veil of smoke.

Errtu eyed the Spider Queen suspiciously. The tanar'ri was more than a little interested, of course, but he realized that most everyone who had ever trusted the diabolical Lloth had paid greatly for their foolishness. Still, this bait was too great for Errtu to resist. His canine maw turned up into a grotesque, wicked smile.

"Look upon Menzoberranzan," Lloth said, and she waved her arm before the thick stalk of a nearby mushroom. The plant's fibers became glassy, reflecting the smoke, and, a moment later, Lloth and the fiend saw the city of drow. "Your role in this will be small, I assure you," Lloth said, "but vital. Do not fail me, great Errtu!"

It was as much a threat as a plea, the fiend knew.

"The gift?" he asked.

"When things are put aright."

Again a suspicious look crossed Errtu's huge face.

"Drizzt Do'Urden is a pittance," Lloth said. "Daermon N'a'shezbaernon, his family, is no more, so he means nothing to me. Still, it would please me to watch great and evil Errtu pay back the renegade for all the inconveniences he has caused."

Errtu was not stupid, far from it. What Lloth was saying made perfect sense, yet he could not ignore the fact that it was Lloth, the Spider Queen, the Lady of Chaos, who was making these tempting offers.

Neither could he ignore the fact that her gift promised him relief from the interminable boredom. He could beat a thousand minor fiends a day, every day, torture them and send them crawling pitifully into the muck. But if he did that for a million days, it would not equal the pleasure of a single hour on the Material Plane, walking among the weak, tormenting those who did not deserve his vengeance.

The great tanar'ri agreed.

PART 1

Rumbles of Discord

I *watched the preparations unfolding at Mithril Hall, preparations for war. Although we, especially Catti-brie, had dealt House Baenre a stinging defeat back in Menzoberranzan, none of us doubted that the dark elves might come our way once more. Above all else, Matron Baenre was likely angry, and having spent my youth in Menzoberranzan, I knew it was not a good thing to make an enemy of the First Matron Mother.*

Still, I liked what I was seeing here in the dwarven stronghold. Most of all, I enjoyed the spectacle of Bruenor

Battlehammer.

Bruenor! My dearest friend, the dwarf I had fought beside since my days in Icewind Dale—days that seemed long ago indeed! I had feared Bruenor's spirit broken when Wulfgar fell, that the fire that had guided this most stubborn dwarf past seemingly insurmountable obstacles in his quest to reclaim his lost homeland had been forever doused. Not so, I learned in those days of preparation. Bruenor's scars were deeper now—his left eye was lost, and a bluish line ran diagonally across his face, from forehead to jawbone—but the flames of spirit had been rekindled, burning bright behind his good eye.

Bruenor directed the preparations, from agreeing to the fortification designs being constructed in the lowest tunnels to sending out emissaries to the neighboring settlements in search of allies. He asked for no help in the decision-making, and needed none, for this was Bruenor, Eighth King of Mithril Hall, veteran of adventures, a dwarf who had earned his title.

Now his grief was gone; he was king again, to the joy of his friends and subjects. "Let the damned drow come!" Bruenor shouted often, and always he nodded in my direction if I was about, as if to remind me that he meant no insult.

In truth, that determined war cry from Bruenor Battlehammer was among the sweetest things I had ever heard.

What was it, I wondered, that had brought the grieving dwarf from his despair? And it wasn't just Bruenor; all about me I saw an excitement, in the dwarves, in Cattibrie, even in Regis, the halfling known more for preparing for lunch and nap than for war. I felt it, too. That tingling anticipation, that camaraderie that had me and all the others patting each other on the back, offering praises for the simplest of additions to the common defense, and raising our voices together in cheer whenever good news was announced.

What was it? It was more than shared fear, more than giving thanks for what we had while realizing that it might soon be stolen away. I didn't understand it then, in that time of frenzy, in that euphoria of frantic preparations. Now, looking back, it is an easy thing to recognize.

It was hope.

To any intelligent being, there is no emotion more important than hope. Individually or collectively, we must hope that the future will be better than the past, that our offspring, and theirs after them, will be a bit closer to an ideal society, whatever our perception of that might be. Certainly a warrior barbarian's hope for the future might differ from the ideal fostered in the imagination of a peaceful farmer. And a dwarf would not strive to live in a world that resembled an elf's ideal! But the hope itself is not so different. It is at those times when we feel we contribute to that end that we feel true elation, as it was in Mithril Hall when we believed the battle with Menzoberranzan would soon come. When we believed we would defeat the dark elves and end, once and for all, the threat from the Underdark city.

Hope is the key. The future will be better than the past, or the present. Without this belief, there is only the self-indulgent, empty striving of the present, as in drow society, or simple despair, the time of life wasted in waiting for death.

Bruenor had found a cause—we all had—and never have I been more alive than in those days of preparation in Mithril Hall.

— Drizzt Do'Urden

CHAPTER 1

Diplomacy

Her thick auburn hair bouncing below her shoulders, Catti-brie worked furiously to keep the drow's whirling scimitars at bay. She was a solidly built woman, a hundred and thirty pounds of muscles finely toned from living her life with Bruenor's dwarven clan. Catti-brie was no stranger to the forge or the sledge.

Or the sword, and this new blade, its white-metal pommel sculpted in the likeness of a unicorn's head, was by far the most balanced weapon she had ever swung. Still, Catti-brie was hard-pressed, indeed, overmatched, by

her opponent this day. Few in the Realms could match
blades with Drizzt Do'Urden, the drow ranger.

He was no larger than Catti-brie, a few pounds heavier
perhaps, with his tight-muscled frame. His white hair
hung as long as Catti-brie's mane and was equally thick,
and his ebony skin glistened with streaks of sweat, a tes-
tament to the young woman's prowess.

Drizzt's two scimitars crossed in front of him (one of
them glowing a fierce blue even through the protective
padding that covered it), then went back out wide, invit-
ing Catti-brie to thrust straight between.

She knew better than to make the attempt. Drizzt was
too quick, and could strike her blade near its tip with
one scimitar, while the other alternately parried low, batting the opposite way near the hilt. With a single step
diagonally to the side, following his closer-parrying
blade, Drizzt would have her beaten.

Catti-brie stepped back instead, and presented her sword
in front of her. Her deep blue eyes peeked out around the
blade, which had been thickened with heavy material, and
she locked stares with the drow's lavender orbs.

"An opportunity missed?" Drizzt teased.

"A trap avoided," Catti-brie was quick to reply.

Drizzt came ahead in a rush, his blades crossing,
going wide, and cutting across, one high and one low.
Catti-brie dropped her left foot behind her and fell into a
crouch, turning her sword to parry the low-rushing
blade, dipping her head to avoid the high.

She needn't have bothered, for the cross came too soon,
before Drizzt's feet had caught up to the move, and both
his scimitars swished through the air, short of the mark.

Catti-brie didn't miss the opening, and darted ahead,
sword thrusting straight.

Back snapped Drizzt's blades, impossibly fast, slamming the sword on both its sides. But Drizzt's feet weren't positioned correctly for him to follow the move, to go diagonally ahead and take advantage of Catti-brie's turned sword.

The young woman went ahead and to the side instead, sliding her weapon free of the clinch and executing the real attack, the slash at Drizzt's hip.

Drizzt's backhand caught her short, drove her sword harmlessly high.

They broke apart again, eyeing each other, Catti-brie wearing a sly smile. In all their months of training, she had never come so close to scoring a hit on the agile and skilled drow.

Drizzt's expression stole her glory, though, and the drow dipped the tips of his scimitars toward the floor, shaking his head in frustration.

"The bracers?" Catti-brie asked, referring to the magical wristbands, wide pieces of black material lined with gleaming mithril rings. Drizzt had taken them from Dantrag Baenre, the deposed weapon master of Menzoberranzan's first house, after defeating Dantrag in mortal combat. Rumors said those marvelous bracers allowed Dantrag's hands to move incredibly fast, giving him the advantage in combat.

Upon battling the lightning-quick Baenre, Drizzt had come to believe those rumors, and after wearing the bracers in sparring for the last few weeks, he had confirmed their abilities. But Drizzt wasn't convinced that the bracers were a good thing. In the fight with Dantrag, he had turned Dantrag's supposed advantage against the drow, for the weapon master's hands moved too quickly for Dantrag to alter any started move, too quickly for Dantrag to improvise if his opponent made an unexpected turn. Now, in these sparring exercises, Drizzt was learning that the bracers held another disadvantage.

His feet couldn't keep up with his hands.

"Ye'll learn them," Catti-brie assured.

Drizzt wasn't so certain. "Fighting is an art of balance and movement," he explained.

"And faster ye are!" Catti-brie replied.

Drizzt shook his head. "Faster are my hands," he said. "A warrior does not win with his hands. He wins with his feet, by positioning himself to best strike the openings in his opponent's defenses."

"The feet'll catch up," Catti-brie replied. "Dantrag was the best Menzoberranzan had to offer, and ye said yerself that the bracers were the reason."

Drizzt couldn't disagree that the bracers greatly aided Dantrag, but he wondered how much they would benefit one of his skill, or one of his father's skill. It could be, Drizzt realized, that the bracers would aid a lesser fighter, one who needed to depend on the sheer speed of his weapons. But the complete fighter, the master who had found harmony between all his muscles, would be put off balance. Or perhaps the bracers would aid someone wielding a heavier weapon, a mighty warhammer, such as Aegis-fang. Drizzt's scimitars, slender blades of no more than two pounds of metal, perfectly balanced by both workmanship and enchantment, weaved effortlessly, and even without the bracers, his hands were quicker than his feet.

"Come on then," Catti-brie scolded, waving her sword in front of her, her wide blue eyes narrowing intently, her shapely hips swiveling as she fell into a low balance.

She sensed her chance, Drizzt realized. She knew he was fighting at a disadvantage and finally sensed her chance to pay back one of the many stinging hits he had given her in their sparring.

Drizzt took a deep breath and lifted the blades. He owed it to Catti-brie to oblige, but he meant to make her earn it!

He came forward slowly, playing defensively. Her sword shot out, and he hit it twice before it ever got close, on its left side with his right hand, and on its left side again, bringing his left hand right over the presented blade and batting it with a downward parry.

Catti-brie fell with the momentum of the double block, spinning a complete circle, rotating away from her adversary. When she came around, predictably, Drizzt was in close, scimitars weaving.

Still the patient drow measured his attack, did not come too fast and strong. His blades crossed and went out wide, teasing the young woman.

Catti-brie growled and threw her sword straight out again, determined to find that elusive hole. And in came the scimitars, striking in rapid succession, again both hitting the left side of Catti-brie's sword. As before, Catti-brie spun to the right, but this time Drizzt came in hard.

Down went the young woman in a low crouch, her rear grazing the floor, and she skittered back. Both Drizzt's blades swooshed the air above her, and before her, for again his cuts came before his feet could rightly respond and position him.

Drizzt was amazed to find that Catti-brie was no longer in front of him.

He called the move the "Ghost Step," and had taught it to Catti-brie only a week earlier. The trick was to use the opponent's weapon and swinging arms as an optical shield, to move within the vision-blocked area so perfectly and quickly that your opponent would not know you had come forward and to the side, that you had, in fact, stepped behind his leading hip.

Reflexively, the drow snapped his leading scimitar straight back, blade pointed low, for Catti-brie had gone past in a crouch. He beat the sword to the mark, too quickly, and the momentum of his scimitar sent it sailing futilely in front of the coming attack.

Drizzt winced as the unicorn-handled sword slapped hard against his hip.

For Catti-brie, the moment was one of pure delight. She knew, of course, that the bracers were hindering Drizzt, causing him to make mistakes of balance—mistakes that Drizzt Do'Urden hadn't made since his earliest days of fighting—but even with the uncomfortable bracers, the drow was a powerful adversary, and could likely defeat most swordsmen.

How delicious it was, then, when Catti-brie found her new sword slicing in unhindered!

Her joy was stolen momentarily by an urge to sink the blade deeper, a sudden, inexplicable anger focused directly on Drizzt.

"Touch!" Drizzt called, the signal that he had been hit, and when Catti-brie straightened and sorted out the scene, she found the drow standing a few feet away, rubbing his sore hip.

"Sorry," she apologized, realizing she had struck far too hard.

"Not to worry," Drizzt replied slyly. "Surely your one hit does not equal the combined pains my scimitars have caused you." The dark elf's lips curled up into a mischievous smile. "Or the pains I will surely inflict on you in return!"

"Me thinking's that I'm catching ye, Drizzt Do'Urden," Catti-brie answered calmly, confidently. "Ye'll get yer hits, but ye'll take yer hits as well!"

They both laughed at that, and Catti-brie moved to the

side of the room and began to remove her practice gear.

Drizzt slid the padding from one of his scimitars and considered those last words. Catti-brie was indeed improving, he agreed. She had a warrior's heart, tempered by a poet's philosophy, a deadly combination indeed. Catti-brie, like Drizzt, would rather talk her way out of a battle than wage it, but when the avenues of diplomacy were exhausted, when the fight became a matter of survival, then the young woman would fight with conscience clear and passion heated. All her heart and all her skill would come to bear, and in Catti-brie, both of those ingredients were considerable.

And she was barely into her twenties! In Menzoberranzan, had she been a drow, she would be in Arach-Tinilith now, the school of Lloth, her strong morals being assaulted daily by the lies of the Spider Queen's priestesses. Drizzt shook that thought away; he didn't even want to think of Catti-brie in that awful place. Suppose she had gone to the drow school of fighters, Melee-Magthere, instead, he mused. How would she fare against the likes of young drow?

Well, Drizzt decided, Catti-brie would be near the top of her class, certainly among the top ten or fifteen percent, and her passion and dedication would get her there. How much could she improve under his tutelage? Drizzt wondered, and his expression soured as he considered the limitations of Catti-brie's heritage. He was in his sixties, barely more than a child by drow standards, for they could live to see seven centuries, but when Catti-brie reached his tender age, she would be old, too old to fight well.

That notion pained Drizzt greatly. Unless the blade of an enemy or the claws of a monster shortened his life, he would watch Catti-brie grow old, would watch her pass from this life.

Drizzt looked at her now as she removed the padded baldric and unclasped the metal collar guard. Under the padding above the waist, she wore only a simple shirt of light material. It was wet with perspiration now and clung to her.

She was a warrior, Drizzt agreed, but she was also a beautiful young woman, shapely and strong, with the spirit of a foal first learning to run and a heart filled with passion.

The sound of distant furnaces, the sudden, increased ringing of hammer on steel, should have alerted Drizzt that the room's door had opened, but it simply didn't register in the distracted drow's consciousness.

"Hey!" came a roar from the side of the chamber, and Drizzt turned to see Bruenor storm into the room. He half expected the dwarf, Catti-brie's adoptive, overprotective father, to demand what in the Nine Hells Drizzt was looking at, and Drizzt's sigh was one of pure relief when Bruenor, his fiery red beard foamed with spittle, instead took up a tirade about Settlestone, the barbarian settlement south of Mithril Hall.

Still, the drow figured he was blushing (and hoped that his ebon-hued skin would hide it) as he shook his head, ran his fingers through his thick hair to brush it back from his face, and likewise began to remove the practice gear.

Drizzt looked up at beautiful Catti-brie. He didn't want to picture her growing old, though he knew she would do it with more grace than most.

Catti-brie walked over, shaking her thick hair to get the droplets out. "Berkthgar is being difficult?" she asked, referring to Berkthgar the Bold, Settlestone's new chieftain.

Bruenor snorted. "Berkthgar can't be anything but difficult!"

"He's a proud one," Catti-brie replied to her father, "and afraid."

"Bah!" Bruenor retorted. "What's he got to be afraid of? Got a couple hunnerd strong men around him and not an enemy in sight."

"He is afraid he will not stand well against the shadow of his predecessor," Drizzt explained, and Catti-brie nodded.

Bruenor stopped in midbluster and considered the drow's words. Berkthgar was living in Wulfgar's shadow, in the shadow of the greatest hero the barbarian tribes of faraway Icewind Dale had ever known. The man who had killed Dracos Icingdeath, the white dragon; the man who, at the tender age of twenty, had united the fierce tribes and shown them a better way of living.

Bruenor didn't believe any human could shine through the spectacle of Wulfgar's shadow, and his resigned nod showed that he agreed with, and ultimately accepted, the truth of the reasoning. A great sadness edged his expression and rimmed his steel-gray eyes, as well, for Bruenor could not think of Wulfgar, the human who had been a son to him, without that sadness.

"On what point is he being difficult?" Drizzt asked, trying to push past the trying moment.

"On the whole damned alliance," Bruenor huffed.

Drizzt and Catti-brie exchanged curious expressions. It made no sense, of course. The barbarians of Settlestone and the dwarves of Mithril Hall already were allies, working hand in hand, with Bruenor's people mining the precious mithril and shaping it into valuable artifacts, and the barbarians doing the bargaining with merchants from nearby towns, such as Nesme on the

Trollmoors, or Silverymoon to the east. The two peoples, Bruenor's and Wulfgar's, had fought together to clear Mithril Hall of evil gray dwarves, and the barbarians had come down from their homes in faraway Icewind Dale, resolved to stay, only because of this solid friendship and alliance with Bruenor's clan. It made no sense that Berkthgar was being difficult, not with the prospect of a drow attack hanging over their heads.

"He wants the hammer," Bruenor explained, recognizing Drizzt and Catti-brie's doubts.

That explained everything. The hammer was Wulfgar's hammer, mighty Aegis-fang, which Bruenor himself had forged as a gift for Wulfgar during the years the young man had been indentured to the red-bearded dwarf. During those years, Bruenor, Drizzt, and Catti-brie had taught the fierce young barbarian a better way.

Of course Berkthgar would want Aegis-fang, Drizzt realized. The warhammer had become more than a weapon, had become a symbol to the hardy men and women of Settlestone. Aegis-fang symbolized the memory of Wulfgar, and if Berkthgar could convince Bruenor to let him wield it, his stature among his people would increase tenfold.

It was perfectly logical, but Drizzt knew Berkthgar would never, ever convince Bruenor to give him the hammer.

The dwarf was looking at Catti-brie then, and Drizzt, in regarding her as well, wondered if she was thinking that giving the hammer to the new barbarian leader might be a good thing. How many emotions must be swirling in the young woman's thoughts! Drizzt knew. She and Wulfgar were to have been wed; she and Wulfgar had grown into adulthood together and had learned many of life's lessons side by side. Could Catti-brie now get beyond that, beyond her own grief, and follow a logical course to seal the alliance?

"No," she said finally, resolutely. "The hammer he cannot have."

Drizzt nodded his agreement, and was glad that Catti-brie would not let go of her memories of Wulfgar, of her love for the man. He, too, had loved Wulfgar, as a brother, and he could not picture anyone else, neither Berkthgar nor the god Tempus himself, carrying Aegis-fang.

"Never thought to give it to him," Bruenor agreed. He wagged an angry fist in the air, the muscles of his arm straining with the obvious tension. "But if that half-son of a reindeer asks again, I'll give him something else, don't ye doubt!"

Drizzt saw a serious problem brewing. Berkthgar wanted the hammer, that was understandable, even expected, but the young, ambitious barbarian leader apparently did not appreciate the depth of his request. This situation could get much worse than a strain on necessary allies, Drizzt knew. This could lead to open fighting between the peoples, for Drizzt did not doubt Bruenor's claim for a moment. If Berkthgar came to demand the hammer as ransom for what he should give unconditionally, he'd be lucky to get back into the sunshine with his limbs attached.

"Me and Drizzt'll go to Settlestone," Catti-brie offered. "We'll get Berkthgar's word and give him nothing in return."

"The boy's a fool!" Bruenor huffed.

"But his people are not foolish," Catti-brie added. "He's wanting the hammer to make himself more the leader. We'll teach him that asking for something he cannot have will make him less the leader."

Strong, and passionate, and so wise, Drizzt mused,

watching the young woman. She would indeed accomplish what she had claimed. He and Catti-brie would go to Settlestone and return with everything Catti-brie had just promised her father.

The drow blew a long, low sigh as Bruenor and Catti-brie moved off, the young woman going to retrieve her belongings from the side of the room. He watched the renewed hop in Bruenor's step, the life returned to the fiery dwarf. How many years would King Bruenor Battlehammer rule? Drizzt wondered. A hundred? Two hundred?

Unless the blade of an enemy or the claws of a monster shortened his life, the dwarf, too, would watch Catti-brie grow old and pass away.

It was an image that Drizzt, watching the light step of this spirited young foal, could not bear to entertain.

* * * * *

Khazid'hea, or Cutter, rested patiently on Catti-brie's hip, its moment of anger past. The sentient sword was pleased by the young woman's progress as a fighter. She was able, no doubt, but still Khazid'hea wanted more, wanted to be wielded by the very finest warrior.

Right now, that warrior seemed to be Drizzt Do'Urden.

The sword had gone after Drizzt when the drow renegade had killed its former wielder, Dantrag Baenre. Khazid'hea had altered its pommel, as it usually did, from the sculpted head of a fiend (which had lured Dantrag) to one of a unicorn, knowing that was the symbol of Drizzt Do'Urden's goddess. Still, the drow ranger had bade Catti-brie take the sword, for he favored the scimitar.

Favored the scimitar!

How Khazid'hea wished that it might alter its blade as it could the pommel! If the weapon could curve its blade, shorten and thicken it . . .

But Khazid'hea could not, and Drizzt would not wield a sword. The woman was good, though, and getting better. She was human, and would not likely live long enough to attain as great a proficiency as Drizzt, but if the sword could compel her to slay the drow . . .

There were many ways to become the best.

* * * * *

Matron Baenre, withered and too old to be alive, even for a drow, stood in the great chapel of Menzoberranzan's first house, her house, watching the slow progress as her slave workers tried to extract the fallen stalactite from the roof of the dome-shaped structure. The place would soon be repaired, she knew. The rubble on the floor had already been cleared away, and the bloodstains of the dozen drow killed in the tragedy had long ago been scoured clean.

But the pain of that moment, of Matron Baenre's supreme embarrassment in front of every important matron mother of Menzoberranzan, in the very moment of the first matron mother's pinnacle of power, lingered. The spearlike stalactite had cut into the roof, but it might as well have torn Matron Baenre's own heart. She had forged an alliance between the warlike houses of the drow city, a joining solidified by the promise of new glory when the drow army conquered Mithril Hall.

New glory for the Spider Queen. New glory for Matron Baenre.

Shattered by the point of a stalactite, by the escape of that renegade Drizzt Do'Urden. To Drizzt she had lost her eldest son, Dantrag, perhaps the finest weapon master in Menzoberranzan. To Drizzt she had lost her daughter, wicked Vendes. And, most painful of all to the old wretch, she had lost to Drizzt and his friends the alliance, the promise of greater glory. For when the matron mothers, the rulers of Menzoberranzan and priestesses all, had watched the stalactite pierce the roof of this chapel, this most sacred place of Lloth, at the time of High Ritual, their confidence that the goddess had sanctioned both this alliance and the coming war had crumbled. They had left House Baenre in a rush, back to their own houses, where they sealed their gates and tried to discern the will of Lloth.

Matron Baenre's status had suffered greatly.

Even with all that had happened, though, the first matron mother was confident she could restore the alliance. On a cord about her neck she kept a ring carved from the tooth of an ancient dwarven king, one Gandalug Battlehammer, patron of Clan Battlehammer, founder of Mithril Hall. Matron Baenre owned Gandalug's spirit and could exact answers from it about the ways of the dwarven mines. Despite Drizzt's escape, the dark elves could go to Mithril Hall, could punish Drizzt and his friends.

She could restore the alliance, but for some reason that Matron Baenre did not understand, Lloth, the Spider Queen herself, held her in check. The yochlol, the handmaidens of Lloth, had come to Baenre and warned her to forego the alliance and instead focus her attention on her family, to secure her house defenses. It was a demand no priestess of the Spider Queen would dare disobey.

She heard the harsh clicking of hard boots on the floor behind her and the jingle of ample jewelry, and she didn't have to turn about to know that Jarlaxle, the mercenary, had entered.

"You have done as I asked?" she questioned, still looking at the continuing work on the domed ceiling.

"Greetings to you as well, First Matron Mother," the always sarcastic male replied. That turned Baenre to face him, and she scowled, as she and so many other of Menzoberranzan's ruling females scowled when they looked at the mercenary.

He was swaggering—there was no other word to describe him. The dark elves of Menzoberranzan, particularly the lowly males, normally donned quiet, practical clothes, dark-hued robes adorned with spiders or webs, or plain black jerkins beneath supple chain mail armor. And, almost always, both male and female drow wore camouflaging *piwafwis*, dark cloaks that could hide them from the probing eyes of their many enemies.

Not so with Jarlaxle. His head was shaven and always capped by an outrageous wide-brimmed hat featuring the gigantic plume of a diatryma bird. In lieu of a cloak or robe, he wore a shimmering cape that flickered through every color of the spectrum, both in light and under the scrutiny of heat-sensing eyes looking in the infrared range. His sleeveless vest was cut high to show the tight muscles of his stomach, and he carried an assortment of rings and necklaces, bracelets, even anklets, that chimed gratingly—but only when the mercenary wanted them to. Like his boots, which had sounded so clearly on the hard chapel floor, the jewelry could be silenced completely.

Matron Baenre noted that the mercenary's customary eye patch was over his left eye this day, but what, if anything, that signified, she could not tell.

For who knew what magic was in that patch, or in

those jewels and those boots, or in the two wands he wore tucked under his belt, and the fine sword he kept beside them? Half those items, even one of the wands, Matron Baenre believed, were likely fakes, with little or no magical properties other than, perhaps, the ability to fall silent. Half of everything Jarlaxle did was a bluff, but half of it was devious and ultimately deadly.

That was why the swaggering mercenary was so dangerous.

That was why Matron Baenre hated Jarlaxle so, and why she needed him so. He was the leader of Bregan D'aerthe, a network of spies, thieves, and killers, mostly rogue males made houseless when their families had been wiped out in one of the many interhouse wars. As mysterious as their dangerous leader, Bregan D'aerthe's members were not known, but they were indeed very powerful—as powerful as most of the city's established houses—and very effective.

"What have you learned?" Matron Baenre asked bluntly.

"It would take me centuries to spew it all," the cocky rogue replied.

Baenre's red-glowing eyes narrowed, and Jarlaxle realized she was not in the mood for his flippancy. She was scared, he knew, and, considering the catastrophe at the high ritual, rightly so.

"I find no conspiracy," the mercenary honestly admitted.

Matron Baenre's eyes widened, and she swayed back on her heels, surprised by the straightforward answer. She had enacted spells that would allow her to detect any outright lies the mercenary spoke, of course. And of course, Jarlaxle would know that. Those spells never seemed to bother the crafty mercenary leader, who